BRAiN WEB

Douglas E. Richards

Paragon Press

PART 1
Outed

"Sons of Islam everywhere, the jihad is a duty—to establish the rule of Allah on earth and to liberate your countries and yourselves from America's domination and its Zionist allies. It is your battle—either victory or martyrdom."

—Ahmed Yassin, founder of Hamas

1

Abdul Hakim zipped up a gray jumpsuit to fully cover his elegant black tuxedo, protecting it from being marred by moist clay or dirt when he—inevitably—brushed up against the cramped tunnel walls. Clay or dirt residue on his tuxedo would give the world an obvious clue to his methods, which he wanted to avoid. Far better for all to believe that the appearance of his team was almost supernatural. His methods would ultimately be discovered, but the longer this could be postponed the better.

Hakim surveyed the eight men who surrounded him, each wearing a tux as well, as they also zipped up jumpsuits identical to his own for their journey through the tunnel. These were his brothers. He could not love them more, or be more proud of what they had accomplished together. And most importantly, what they would soon accomplish. A feat so daring, so flawless, and so perfectly executed that it would carve a deep psychological scar into the psyche of the West. Perhaps one even greater than that delivered by the brave heroes who had crashed jumbo jets into skyscrapers on September eleventh.

A tear came to Hakim's eye as he considered the glory of what was to come. He blinked it away and gathered himself.

"Very soon," he said to his brothers in Arabic, his voice echoing faintly off the steel walls of the nearly empty shell of a warehouse, "our existence on this earth will come to an end. But life is fleeting. And by dying in the name of Allah, for a great cause, we earn our just reward in Heaven."

Hakim's eyes burned with a zealous intensity and he struck a pose of determined, heroic nobility. "And not only will we live forever in Heaven, but our names and our legend will live forever on *Earth*. Our names, and what we are about to achieve, will be woven into the very fabric of the glorious history of our people's ascendance. The events of these next many hours will never be forgotten. We will deliver a devastating hammer strike to the genitals of the infidel. One that will forever horrify the West, and bring great joy and pride to all true children of Islam."

He paused, catching the eye of each man in turn and nodding slowly. "Allahu Akbar," he whispered passionately with a mixture of pride, purpose, and ecstasy, and together the eight men responded in kind. "God is great," they echoed, and several pairs of eyes were moist at the enormity of what they were doing.

Their emotion didn't reflect fear of death, Hakim noted, his chest swelling even further with pride, but their eagerness to fulfill their noble purpose, to die as well as any man had ever died.

A poem ran through his mind, unbidden, recounting the courage of ancient warriors, hopelessly outnumbered, fighting to the death to protect the city of Rome.

Then said the brave Horatius,
The Captain of the Gate,
"To every man upon this earth,
Death cometh soon or late.
And how can a man die better
Than facing fearful odds.
For the ashes of his fathers,
And the temples of his Gods."

How could a man die better, indeed, thought Hakim. The verse didn't rhyme in Arabic, but this didn't detract in the slightest from the immense power of these words.

With their jumpsuits now in place, each of Hakim's comrades returned their lethal KH2002 assault rifles to their original positions, slung across their chests, to add to the hand-guns strapped to their sides. The Iranian designed KH2002 could spew death at a rate of eight hundred armor-piercing rounds per minute, each traveling three times the speed of sound.

Each man had packed designer leather duffel bags, filled with gas canisters, gas masks, night vision equipment, dozens of spare clips, and any and all other items they might possibly need. The bags were also large enough to conceal their assault rifles when necessary.

The operation had been planned to perfection, every possibility covered, every contingency accounted for.

Hakim took one last look around the empty warehouse that they had called home for many long months, and sighed. It, too, would not live out the next few days. It had been purchased almost a year earlier with generous funds supplied by an emir in Qatar, and was just over seven blocks away from their destination, the Cosmopolitan Theater.

Despite this proximity, tunneling through the seemingly impenetrable Los Angeles clay, even with power equipment, had been a slow and demanding task. Especially given the need to work only at night and to carefully relocate the earth they had removed, all the while being more cautious than field mice living among hawks.

But it had been well worth it. They had finished all but the last of the tunnel months earlier, ending it five feet below a closet located in the corner of a private office. A backstage office designated for use by the director of whatever production was taking place in the theater during its run.

The last five feet of progress had been the slowest and most carefully done. Cutting through the theater's thick concrete foundation and then through the closet floor, and constructing an undetectable trap door, had taken several additional weeks. But their care had paid off, and they had not been detected.

They had then had almost six weeks of after-hours access to the theater. Six weeks to prepare it for their needs. Six weeks to conduct drill after drill after drill, until they were more familiar with every last square inch of the Cosmopolitan than they were with their own bedrooms. Their confidence grew every night, as did their eagerness and anticipation, all convinced that their audacious plan would lead to a truly stunning outcome.

Two of the eight men now with Hakim would remain in the warehouse, securing it. When the operation reached its glorious conclusion, Hakim's two-man rear guard would martyr themselves, destroying both the warehouse and the tunnel in such a way that no evidence would be left behind. The plan was truly a work of art.

The Cosmopolitan Theater had just been completed thirteen months earlier, and unlike the theater it had usurped, it was state of the art. Terror proof.

Which was perfect for their needs.

The Cosmopolitan had as few entrances as fire safety would allow, so there were fewer doors for security to watch and protect. And when the theater was in high-security mode, there were so many cameras watching all possible outside approaches for so many blocks around it, a gnat couldn't have snuck up on it without being detected while still in its larval stage.

The walls of the theater were reinforced and could protect the inside against massive assaults. And if any incursion *was* attempted, the doors could all be simultaneously sealed as tight as vaults, wirelessly, with the proper electronic code given by someone with the proper authorization.

The stage, along with a shallow area just behind it for those waiting in the wings to go on, could be completely isolated from the rest of the structure, the spacious and extensive backstage, with the three doors between these two sections automatically closing after they were used.

It was the most secure theater ever built.

And yet, with enough planning, enough time, and enough money, digital architectural drawings of the theater could be obtained. And electronic frequencies and door codes could be bought. Not only bought, but reset, so that the original keepers of the codes could no longer control them.

But even with codes, the Cosmopolitan was virtually unbreachable from the outside. They had studied it carefully and knew this was true.

After all, this was the very thing they were counting on.

2

General Justin Girdler clung upside down to an inverted wall. After hanging like a bat for ten seconds, his feet and hands splayed and pressing hard against four small, oddly spaced holds, he took a deep breath, intensified his focus even further so that his entire universe consisted of a shallow, three-inch-long fingerhold four feet away, and lunged. He hit the hold and fought to stabilize himself, but failed, tearing a layer of skin from two fingertips as he did so and crashing awkwardly into the thick mat a story below him.

He was about to make another attempt at the bouldering problem when his phone spat out a tune, one that indicated the call was of the highest possible priority.

"Goddammit," he mumbled in frustration. He was finally close to conquering a climb he had been working on for hours, but perhaps it wasn't meant to be. Sunday or no Sunday, an emergency was an emergency.

He reached for his phone, resting peacefully on the mat beside his small nylon chalk bag. He had no idea what to expect, but having the caller turn out to be Robert Snyder, the Secretary of Homeland Security, wouldn't have been high on his list of guesses.

Snyder wasted no time. "General, we have a credible and imminent terror threat. And I need your help. Urgently."

Girdler's eyes narrowed. Until six months ago, he had been a colonel, in charge of the Black Ops division of PsyOps. But he had been promoted and was now in charge of *all* Black Operations, making him one of the most powerful men in the world, with far more authority even than many of those who outranked him. But this still didn't explain Snyder's call.

"I'm listening," said Girdler simply.

"I need you to interrogate a man we picked up yesterday. Immediately."

Silent alarms went off in Girdler's head. Could the Secretary of Homeland Security know that Nick Hall was alive?

"Why me?" said the general cagily. "You have access to better interrogators than I do."

There was a sigh at the other end of the line. "I don't know about that, General. Rumor has it that you've had some pretty miraculous successes recently. None of my sources have any idea what methods you're using. But they tell me the intel you've generated has been dead accurate—and comprehensive. So what's your secret?"

Girdler blew out a long breath. He hadn't realized he was building a reputation. He had taken steps to see this didn't happen, but these steps had clearly failed. Only a handful of people in the world knew he had been instrumental in averting a disaster of epic proportions in the Nick Hall case, which had been the principle reason for his promotion. And only one other member of the military or government, his second-in-command, Mike Campbell, who had been promoted to colonel and had assumed Girdler's old duties as head of PsyOps, had any idea that Hall was still alive.

But the men and women who rose to positions of prominence in the military—excluding the occasional backstabbing psychopath who had climbed the ladder over the corpses of more talented colleagues—tended to be very smart, and would put two and two together very soon. If he wasn't careful, it wouldn't be long before they would conclude that Nick Hall was less dead than advertised.

Girdler considered refusing the request. But only for an instant. Given the urgency of the situation, he couldn't possibly refuse. And he wouldn't be able to disguise his magical success when Hall instantly sucked the prisoner dry of all relevant information, which would raise even more questions.

"My secret?" repeated Girdler with mock innocence, glancing around to make sure no one was in eavesdropping range. The gym was nearly empty, except for a fellow climber in the next room suspended from a rope three stories above the thick mats. "Turns out I'm just naturally charming and persuasive."

"Why do I get the feeling you're using methods hatched in those Black Ops labs of yours?" said the Secretary of Homeland Security. "Or perhaps hatched by the aliens some people think you have stashed in Area 51," he added with an amused tone.

Then, serious once more, as though realizing the situation was far too urgent for banter, Snyder added, "Look, we don't have the luxury of time. I don't want your secrets. Just your results."

"Where is your prisoner?"

"In the air. In anticipation that you'd agree to take a crack at him, I scrambled a jet to fly him your direction. He'll be wheels-down at Nellis in twenty minutes. I've sent all the background intel to your computer."

Girdler nodded. "I'll read it, but give me the thirty-thousand-foot overview."

"Confidence is high that something major will go down before midnight. In the US mainland. We've intercepted extensive chatter for weeks, and it's been building. But yesterday, the chatter dropped off a cliff. A classic pattern. An ugly stormfront brewing, followed by a breath-holding, cautious calm just before the actual storm. We've managed to acquire other intel and it all points in the same direction."

Snyder paused. "We fed everything to Nessie," he added, referring to the NSA's Expert System in Fort Meade, the most sophisticated supercomputer, running the most sophisticated software, in all of history. "She added this to some threads she was already tracking. She's estimated the chances of a major strike today at over seventy percent."

"Do we know who's behind it?" asked Girdler.

"We think so. We aren't certain, but all signs point to Islamic Jihad. Nessie agrees."

Girdler nodded, not surprised. This was an old terror organization that had metastasized over the past few years, rapidly becoming the most dangerous organization of its kind in the world, and the most determined to strike additional blows in America, making use of the ever-growing vein of American-born jihadists.

"And the target?"

"On that, we're completely clueless," said Snyder in frustration. "But we think it involves the first attempted use of a new explosive they've developed. Similar to standard plastics, but even more shapeable. Can be modified to have the properties of other materials. So it can be built right into a wooden chair, to give one example, and even sound like wood if you were to rap on it."

"But the electronic bloodhounds can still detect it, right?" said Girdler with a sick feeling in the pit of his stomach.

"Not yet," replied the secretary gravely, confirming Girdler's worst fears. "We haven't been able to obtain a sample. Without one, we don't have a scent signature we can use to program the bloodhounds."

Girdler closed his eyes and shook his head. This was far grimmer than he had thought. Even nukes were detectable.

There had been an ongoing arms race between terrorists and anti-terrorist organizations for some time now. The terrorists tried to find better and better ways to conceal explosives, and the anti-terrorist forces tried to find better and better ways to detect them. This arms race had taken a sharp turn in favor of the good guys a few years earlier when an electronic bloodhound device had been perfected. This device was able to out-sniff the most highly trained dog, and, unlike a canine, could be easily issued to every member of a security detail.

But an explosive that could be baked into everyday items and was undetectable was Homeland Security's worst nightmare. This could be used to cause untold damage, and untold terror, until they could get a handle on it.

"How soon until we get a sample?" asked Girdler.

"Not soon enough. They know it's vital to keep it out of our hands, so we think they plan to only make it when they need it. We'll need to stop an attack that involves the use of this explosive before they can detonate it."

Girdler decided it was time to change gears. He could read the precise details of the intel later. "Tell me about the prisoner," he said.

"Jibril Awad. An American. But one who received most of his schooling overseas, in Iran. We've known he was a member of Islamic Jihad for some time, and we've been monitoring him. For reasons I don't have time to go into, we're convinced he knows something of the coming attack. We picked him up this morning, but our interrogations have gotten nowhere, and given his responses, we're certain we won't get what we need in time. I wouldn't be calling you if I wasn't desperate."

General Girdler was certain of that. "I understand. I assume you'll let everyone know I have full operational control from here on out?"

"Yes."

"Okay, but before you hand over the reins, order a chopper to meet Awad on the runway when he lands at Nellis. Have four of your best commandos fly this asshole to a small structure in the California desert, about twenty miles from Palm Springs. It's as isolated as you could ever want, but there is a small helipad on site. I'll send you the coordinates."

"Why do I have the feeling that I wouldn't be able to find this structure on a list of known military installations?"

Girdler ignored him. "Just stay frosty," he advised, knowing Hall would have answers within minutes of Awad landing in California. "In case I get lucky."

3

Nick Hall checked his fake beard, adjusted the rimless gunmetal glasses that he didn't need, and entered the interrogation room that had been built just for him, twelve miles from the facility he and Megan Emerson had been working at for six months.

He studied the clean-cut olive-skinned man strapped to a steel chair bolted to the floor.

The man, Jibril Awad, was an American citizen, but despised America and its culture. He had joined Islamic Jihad three years earlier and had rapidly risen through the ranks, due to his ruthlessness, passion for the movement, and a native's ability to speak unaccented English and blend into American culture seamlessly.

Awad wore a triumphant sneer that belied his helpless position.

Hall nodded at the four lean, hardened men who had brought Awad to the facility with such great urgency. He reached into their minds and confirmed they hadn't recognized him behind his beard and glasses, and then pushed deeper to get a sense of their backgrounds.

Images rushed into Hall's head as though he were watching the trailer of a big-budget Hollywood commando movie. But these scenes of highly classified operations weren't generated by teams of special effects experts. What flashed across his mind's eye was very real. Images of these men and their comrades rappelling down ropes suspended from helicopters, parachuting into the dead of night. Images of assaults on heavily fortified buildings, of explosions that were temporarily blinding, and of machine gun fire. Of friends and enemies alike, missing the better part of their faces or heads.

Hall couldn't help but shudder. "That will be all for now, gentlemen," he managed to croak out. "Please wait outside until further notice."

The men did as ordered, but all were wondering what the fuck was going on, and all assumed this was a secret torture facility—a secret they had sworn to keep. And while they bristled at having to take orders from someone they assumed was a sadistic civilian, they had been instructed to do so by both the Secretary of Homeland Security and the head of Black Ops, so they managed to keep their resentment to themselves.

As usual, however, their inner thoughts, on full display for Hall to read, told a very different story.

Hall waited for them to leave and faced his prisoner, who coughed up thick sputum and spat it toward Hall's face in one smooth motion. Hall read the intent and dodged the disgusting missile easily. He had thought this was something that only happened in overly dramatic movies, but perhaps there was more realism to this move than he had thought. It was the only act of absolute defiance open to someone affixed into immobility in this way.

"Are you receiving this?" thought Nick Hall, and the electronic implants buried in four precise locations in his brain picked up these unspoken words, converted them into digital audio information that sounded remarkably close to his own voice, and transmitted them via the Web to a distant cell phone. His four implants represented the smallest, most sophisticated computers known to man, rivaling the best supercomputers available just years earlier.

General Girdler, at his office in Fort Bragg, North Carolina, heard the words coming from what he thought of as a cell phone inside of Hall's head, and responded in the affirmative, a response that was transmitted back through the Internet to Hall's implants, which were tied into both his auditory and visual cortices.

In a hidden room behind him, Megan Emerson responded as well, but not through a phone. Instead, she responded directly into his mind, the telepathic connection between them perfect, as always.

"Do your thing, Nick," she thought at him supportively.

While he could read the vast majority of minds in a range of six to ten miles, Megan was a very rare exception, for reasons that still remained unclear. But although he couldn't read her thoughts, they *were* able to communicate telepathically, up to a distance of about five miles.

Hall had been trained as a marine biologist, and a year earlier had been onboard the Scripps Institute of Oceanography's seagoing vessel, the *Explorer*, when it disappeared. Not a single body was ever found and the *Explorer* was presumed to have sunk.

But this was not the case. Instead, Hall and twenty-six other scientists and crew, were kidnapped and imprisoned in a warehouse in Fresno, California. There, over a period of many months, they had been used as unwilling guinea pigs by Kelvin Gray, the CEO of a company called Theia Labs, to perfect a technology that Nick Hall now possessed. Each of their brains had been the subject of numerous surgeries and experiments.

The scientific progress Gray was able to achieve in this way was as spectacular as it was merciless. A subject would be chosen and repeatedly violated over many days and weeks until he or she finally died from the trauma.

After which the ruthless, but brilliant, Kelvin Gray would dispose of the body, digest what he had learned, and start anew on the next prisoner. He had zealously turned the brain tissue of innocents into Swiss cheese in his quest to determine the precise placement of four advanced electronic implants, and to perfect a lexicon that mapped electrical brain activity to individual words.

His goal was to perfect a system that would allow an implant recipient to surf the Web with his or her thoughts alone. Since the implants would also be tied into the auditory and visual cortices, Web content delivered by the implants directly into the brain would appear to be seen and heard normally, through eyes and ears.

Alex Altschuler, who was now the CEO of Theia Labs, headquartered in Fresno, had been head of research at the time. He had been blissfully unaware that his boss had become a mass murderer, churning through innocent people like they were so many lab rats.

But he *should* have known. It was the only possible explanation for the perfect data he was being fed. *Miraculous* data—to which

Altschuler had applied his unparalleled genius to develop complex algorithms and perfect the technology.

It had long been known that individual thoughts could be ferreted out and used to control video games, artificial limbs, and the like, but Theia's achievement was as big a leap over these rudimentary capabilities as a supercomputer was over an abacus. Gray's shortcut of savagely using humans as lab animals had accelerated progress by at least a decade, and probably more.

Twenty-six subjects had paid for this progress with their lives.

Nick Hall was the twenty-seventh. The lottery winner.

Not only did the experiments finally result in implant placement, and software, that allowed Hall to surf the Web with his thoughts, but as Gray had repositioned Hall's implants numerous times in search of the eureka coordinates, the resulting neuronal stimulation, damage, and re-wiring had resulted in an unexpected and truly re-markable side effect.

Nick Hall became able to read minds. Perfectly.

Not only surface thoughts, but all memory and experience. He could access and mine the brain of a stranger as though it were his own. Nothing could be kept secret from him.

But while mind reading enabled Hall to survive and escape, it was a curse he wouldn't wish on his worst enemy. He could suppress most of the incoming input, but he couldn't entirely shut it off. Whenever he was in the presence of others, he had a constant buzz of their thoughts swimming in his head. And although he could transform much of it into a white noise, which was still maddening, being near a large crowd could be debilitating.

Worse, the most powerful or emotionally charged thoughts were most likely to break through the noise. Which often meant those that were hateful, vitriolic, graphic, or sexual. He thought he was well aware of the enormous diversity and endless perversions of human sexual preference and fantasy, but he hadn't known the *half* of it. There were any number of disturbing sexual images and desires he had read from others that would haunt him the rest of his life.

And *Homo sapiens* learned to lie at a young age for good reason. The thoughts of most people, if totally exposed, were judgmental and often cruel.

Hall had barely managed to stay alive and elude mercenaries hired by Kelvin Gray. While doing so, he had crossed paths with Justin Girdler, who learned of his ESP. When the story of the *Scripps Explorer* and the Hitlarian way the implants had been perfected had made international headlines, Nick Hall became perhaps the most recognizable figure in the world.

But while the public knew of his Web-surfing capabilities, his mind-reading ability was only rumored. Girdler became convinced that knowledge of this ability would ignite an international ESP arms race, since no government could chance that other countries would learn how to unlock this game-changing capability. And he also believed, as did Hall, that if ESP were ever perfected, the human race would self-destruct in months, if not days.

If mind reading became widespread, what would protect secrets? Identities? Passwords?

Theft and cheating would be rampant. Children would learn what their parents really thought of their third grade art projects. Spouses would learn of infidelities, both thoughts and actions. Of perversions. Bosses would learn what employees really thought of them. And so on. Society would break down almost instantly.

With Hall alive, governments and powerful private players were sure to pull out all the stops to capture him to learn what made him tick. So Girdler decided he had to discredit rumors of Hall's ESP, and remove him from the grid. So he had faked Hall's death. Megan Emerson's as well, although this hadn't really been necessary, since he had already made sure no one knew that she was connected to Hall in any way.

Girdler had then set up a secret facility in Palm Springs where they could study Hall's mind-reading ability, and try to learn the secret of Megan's immunity. If they could discover a way to nullify Hall's ability, civilization could protect itself if it ever came into widespread use.

Only Girdler, Mike Campbell, Alex Altschuler, and Heather Zambrana, Altschuler's fiancée, knew that Hall and Megan were still alive.

Although Hall's first and foremost priority was finding a defense against his own abilities, he had also agreed to conduct interrogations in certain emergency cases. And the man immobilized in the steel chair before him, Jibril Awad, was just such a case. Not that reading critical information from a prisoner's mind like it was a glossy graphic novel could really be called an interrogation.

Awad had no plans to spit again, but his mind was consumed with hatred. And with triumph. "Torture me all you want," he barked. "But you won't get shit!" A malicious smirk came over his face. "Not that it matters. You and the entire world will have your answers soon. Very, very soon."

Hall sifted through Awad's thoughts as if they were his own. The prisoner, while fluent in Arabic, had grown up in the States and still thought in English. Which made Hall's life easier, but wasn't a requirement. Alex Altschuler had solved this issue the first time Hall had run into a language barrier.

Hall's implants continuously monitored his every thought, ignoring any that weren't direct commands to the system. But the implants could also pick up the reflected thoughts he read from others. So Altschuler had programmed the technology to instantly translate any foreign languages encountered into English at Hall's mental command, allowing him to navigate within any mind, regardless of language.

Awad's thoughts turned to the new explosive Islamic Jihad had developed, and if a mind could drool, his would have. He ran through a myriad of possibilities for the use of this new weapon, which he had obviously spent considerable time imagining, and his thrill at the mass destruction and panic it would bring about was so powerful and pure it seemed almost sexual.

The imminent use of this explosive was a test cruise. A spectacular test cruise, to be sure, but only phase one. When the world was reeling from this event, Islamic Jihad would use this weapon in dozens of simultaneous terror acts, each perhaps less glamorous and psychologically debilitating than the first, but with even higher body counts.

"What you're about to witness is only the beginning!" said Awad with a sneer. "You'd better grab your ankles tight and apply some Vaseline. Because you and the rest of the West are about to be totally *fucked in the ass!*"

4

Hall made no response to the prisoner's taunts and his face remained impassive, which he could read annoyed the crap out of the deranged, sadistic asshole before him. *Good.*

Hall thrust deeper into Awad's thoughts, although this was hardly necessary. The man didn't have complete operational knowledge of the coming terror attack, but what he did know was at the very top of his mind. He was fantasizing about it. Replaying it in his head. Relishing it.

The more layers Hall peeled back, the more horrified he became. His face whitened and he began to feel lightheaded.

It was a terror scheme that could only have been hatched by Satan in the bowels of Hell.

It would commence in mere minutes, but could well last several days. While the aftermath of terror attacks in the past had been long, the attacks themselves had been quick. But this would be different. This was an act of terror that could not be prevented, and one that would command the world's undivided attention for a period of time that would seem an eternity.

And it was too late to stop it.

Any efforts in this regard would blow up in their faces—literally. The operation had been set up like a sophisticated timer on a bomb, one that would immediately jump to zero if any tampering was detected.

Awad didn't have enough operational details for Hall to know if anything could even be done to lessen the full impact of the attack. The only thing Hall knew for certain was that if a way did exist, he was the only person alive with any chance to find it.

He rushed through the door, leaving Awad behind to wonder what kind of interrogator left the room without asking a single question, or uttering a single word.

"Megan!" he shouted telepathically as he was leaving. *"Major emergency. No time to explain now. Meet me outside."*

Hall all but ran over to the ranking member of the commando group that had just left the interrogation room. "Captain Briarwood," he said, not caring if the man wondered how he knew his name, "we need to take the helo to LA. Immediately!"

As he spoke Megan joined him. Without waiting for a response from Briarwood, the two civilians climbed into the helicopter that was parked on a slab of concrete beside the small interrogation room.

Briarwood glanced at his second-in-command and raised his eyebrows. This order was totally unexpected, as was the presence of the petite young woman now making herself at home in the helo.

"No time to check with others, Captain!" barked Hall, reading his mind. "You were instructed to follow my orders. And this is very much an order. Let's move!"

The captain's eyes narrowed for just a moment before he nodded. "Yes sir," he said, and less than a minute later the helicopter lifted from the ground. As it did so, Hall began to regret taking Megan along for this ride. It was selfish. While he didn't think she'd be in any danger, why take any chances?

Megan Emerson was absolutely critical to his work, and to his sanity. And this would have been true even if they hadn't fallen in love.

The moment they were airborne, Hall put this out of his mind. Too late to second-guess himself now. Instead, using his implants and telepathy, he described the imminent terrorist strike to the general and Megan as quickly and efficiently as he could, and let Girdler know he was even now en route to LA to attempt to minimize the damage.

"Minimize?" said Girdler. "Are you saying we can't stop it?"

"No. If we try, we make things worse. They get a single whiff of us and they blow it early."

Hall paused, forcing himself to ignore the thunder of the chopper blades whipping through the air and the potent thoughts of the men next to him. "The four commandos who delivered Awad are with me. But scramble two other four-man teams to LA, just in case. And if I do discover a way to disrupt their plans, I'll need you for support and to get clearances."

"Roger that," said Girdler.

Hall had become so facile at using his internal Internet connection that he had called up the distance to LA from the Web, and the nearest heliport to their destination, without being consciously aware that he had. The information hovered in crystal clarity, displayed in vivid color in the corner of his visual field. The Internet had become an extension of himself, like a trillion-page encyclopedia that could be accessed as easily as his own memory.

"I'll contact you when I've reached ground zero and managed to get more intel," finished Hall, ending the connection with Girdler.

"*Nick, just remember, you're a marine biologist,*" cautioned Megan telepathically beside him. "*Not a commando. You're one of a kind. So let the trained professionals take the risks,*" she added, trying to keep even the slightest hint of panic from entering her telepathic thoughts, but failing to fully hide her fears.

Hall frowned. They both knew that he was the only hope of averting a disaster of spectacular proportions. "*Don't worry, Megan,*" he broadcast back at her, trying his best to lighten the mood. "*You know how hard I am to kill.*"

"*I know,*" replied Megan. "*But a curtain of bullets or a massive bomb isn't going to spare your life because you can read minds.*"

Hall nodded, but said nothing. Because she was right. His abilities, as extraordinary as they were, still didn't make him bulletproof.

5

Abdul Hakim led his men through the tunnel silently. When they reached its end, he removed a tablet computer and flexible video scope from his bag. He forced the tiny camera at the tip of the thin snake through a hidden hole in the trap-door and then slowly worked it under the closet door.

Hakim glanced down at the images the camera was sending to his tablet. As he had expected, the office was uninhabited.

The seven jihadists emerged from the closet single-file with practiced quiet and quickly removed their gray jumpsuits. Hakim shoved the garments into a small nylon bag, dropped them back down into the tunnel, and replaced the trap-door.

They had entered the theater each night for some time now, using this same method. As for the rest of their mission, while this would be their first time, they had rehearsed and rehearsed until they could do the complex choreography of the attack in their sleep.

Hakim snaked the camera under the outer door of the private office. He extended it less than an inch and turned it up to get a panoramic view while his team packed away their assault rifles into long leather duffels. Seeing nothing troubling, Hakim opened the door a crack to get a firsthand look at the lands beyond.

The coast was entirely clear. They could not have chosen any better.

Television monitors were everywhere, displaying the events on the stage in brilliant, ultra-high-definition 3-D clarity. Monitors that could display content in three dimensions, without the requirement of special glasses, had been perfected only a few years previously, but had already become as common as the domestic cockroach.

Hakim checked the digital readout on his tablet. Three minutes and fourteen seconds until the next commercial. Three minutes and *thirteen* seconds. *Twelve. Eleven . . .*

At exactly three minutes, Hakim gave the signal, and his team exited the office and fanned out in a prearranged pattern. While they moved with purpose, they each put on a relaxed smile and walked without urgency. If they were spotted, no one would think twice about seeing yet another tuxedoed unknown.

Yes, carrying a duffel this large was unusual, but it wasn't a military rucksack, which Hakim's men would have preferred, but rather a designer bag that had cost thousands. And who would possibly be suspicious since the theater was terror-proof in any case?

Hakim checked the monitors. When the two presenters slated next exited the backstage to wait in the wings, Hakim gave the final signal. The timing was coming along *perfectly*. Almost exactly a minute until they would cut to a series of commercials.

In three teams of two, Hakim's men opened assigned doors to the trio of post-award interview rooms. Each was packed with journalists, stars, celebrity interviewers, and others. The celebrities were laser focused on building their brand by conveying just the right mixture of charm, wit, and humility. And those who weren't stars were busy fawning over those who were.

In fact, every single person in each room was *so* preoccupied that Hakim's men wouldn't have gotten a second look had they activated a spinning, blaring ambulance siren. Too many eyes were star-struck, and thus blinded. There was too much glamour in the room. Too much excitement.

And things were about to get even more exciting.

In a practiced motion, each of Hakim's two-man teams reached into their bags and pulled the pins on gas canisters, rolling them as gently as they could to all corners of their assigned rooms before reclosing the doors in front of them. The gas was an extremely potent knockout agent, colorless and odorless, and anyone who breathed even a small amount would find the light of their consciousness extinguished within seconds.

The glamorous crowds within the rooms, preening like peacocks in their perfectly tailored formal attire, dropped like termites in a tented house, in near simultaneous perfection. Just outside, the terrorists affixed gas masks to their faces, waited another fifteen seconds for good measure, and then entered, delighted to find exactly what they had expected inside.

One member of each pair raced through the room and put a single silenced bullet into the foreheads of each man or woman on the floor, since the gas was fast acting but not lethal, while his partner captured these actions on video.

While this was happening, Hakim was doing his part, taking out the three celebrities waiting in the wings with a short burst of directed gas, more lethal than the type used by his brothers, since even a silenced gun this close to the stage could have attracted attention.

Hakim noted with pride that his men had been able to destroy sixty-eight Western pigs—celebrities, hangers-on, members of the press, and so on—within minutes of their emergence from the tunnel. And the three celebrities he had taken out brought the tally to seventy-one.

And the fun was only just beginning.

Hakim's men slipped silently through one of the three backstage doors and joined him on the wings of the main stage, barely glancing at the three bodies lying haphazardly on the floor, the gas now fully dispersed.

The terrorist leader stood near a marble table, on top of which sat eight identical statues, each depicting a knight standing on a reel of film, clutching a crusader's sword. After taking one last glance around the area, Hakim gave a signal to his right-hand man, Sherif Ismail, who sent the stolen electronic codes and authorization handshakes to seal every door, including those between the theater and its backstage.

Hakim eyed one of the ubiquitous monitors, which continued to tile nearly every wall, helping to ensure their timing was precise. A commercial for a luxury car had just begun. He checked his watch and then nodded. "Showtime," he whispered in Arabic.

He adjusted his classic black tuxedo so he looked as good as possible and began walking purposefully, but casually, toward the podium. Few in the teeming audience would know who was supposed to be traversing the stage at this time to present the Oscar for Best Original Screenplay.

And *none* would know that these presenters, Dorothy Chance and Kim Harris, stars of a new sitcom, were both now dead backstage, as was the Oscar host, an aging Hugh Jackman. Hakim had taken great satisfaction in killing Jackman, one of the most universally beloved stars in Hollywood, demonstrating that the famous Wolverine was not so immortal, after all.

The director of this year's Oscars, J. Sebastian Cole, and his television minions would know something was amiss, as would several others throughout the auditorium, but Hakim was counting on his elegant attire to keep everyone in their seats, with no reason to panic. And for all anyone knew, his arrival instead of the host and two sitcom stars was simply part of a surprise practical joke, inserted at the last minute.

After all, ever since Ellen DeGeneres had had pizza delivered to the previous Oscar venue, the Dolby Theater, a number of years earlier, *anything* was possible.

6

The helicopter Hall was in landed just beyond his mind-reading range of the Cosmopolitan, and he, Megan, and the four men with them were rushed into a waiting van before the chopper blades had even come to a halt. Two additional commando teams were already in place near the theater, but out of sight, and the van raced to join them.

Hall remained silent, streaming the televised 3-D Academy Awards presentation directly into his visual cortex. Best Production Design had just been announced, and the giddy winner, Amy McRaney, a plump woman in a sequined green gown, was droning on a bit long, prompting the gentle beginnings of the designated hurry-it-up music, signaling for her to finish. The moment she did, the full orchestra sprang to life and played the broadcast off to the first of a string of commercials.

While Jibril Awad hadn't had perfect operational knowledge of the attack, he did know it was timed to take place in the last part of the production, when the more coveted awards were to be given, ensuring a concurrent spike in global viewership.

The software in Hall's implants reacted to his mental command and instantly pulled up a chronological listing of the Oscars to be given out, displaying it just to the left of the television feed.

The final eight awards, the heavy hitters, were next. Best original score and original song. Best adapted screenplay. Best original screenplay. Best actor and actress. Best director. And then, finally, to close out the night, best film of the year.

The attack would happen in minutes. But Islamic Jihad had spotters, inside and outside of the theater, who would turn the Cosmopolitan to magma if they had even a hint that it was being evacuated. Or at the slightest sign of anti-terror preparations. Which is why the two commando teams already present were staying well out of sight, and why Hall wouldn't let the men who were accompanying him now leave the van when they arrived.

This team of ruthless, barbaric jihadists was a freight train tearing around a bend. But as much as Hall ached to scream a warning to the innocent people standing on the tracks, he could not. All he could do was watch it happen, defying his every instinct.

It was absolutely *maddening*.

Hall's jaw clamped shut, forcing his teeth to grind against one another, and he willed the van to go faster.

7

Abdul Hakim knew he had to bring the audience fairly gently to their new reality, or risk spooking the herd, which would result in him having to blow the place much earlier than he would want.

The trick wasn't just to create terror, but to prolong it. To turn this auditorium into a living, writhing hell, that would rip flesh away from raw nerves around the world and expose these nerves to an unimaginably slow and steady torture, hour after endless hour.

But if he incited panic, if the pathetic, spoiled Hollywood royalty bolted for the exits, locked though they were, or rushed the stage, he'd have to mow many of them down. And this would only serve to intensify their hysteria, forcing him to kill them all immediately. It would still be an epic attack that would never be forgotten, but only a tenth as excruciating as a fully successful attack would have been. A mistake to be avoided at all costs.

Hakim reached the podium at the end of an enormous stage that could only be described as glorious. He had walked out onto this stage before during drills, but never when it was fully prepared for the Academy Awards.

Everything was so much larger than life. Everything glowed, glittered, and dazzled the senses. The venue pulsated with a powerful sheen and vitality, bursting with untold megawatts of light from the two-story *Academy Awards* sign behind him and other oversized props. Everything was gold and silver and crystal. Two thirty-foot reproductions of the famous Oscar statues stood guard on either side of a stage so polished it seemed almost radioactive, and golden rows of stairs ran along its entire length.

Hakim gazed out at an ocean of human decadence, row after endless row. While the stage was magnificent, the auditorium was even more so, surpassing even the Dolby Theater that had long housed this narcissistic ceremony. The domed auditorium ceiling was five stories high, with regal pillars of box seats on either side. It had a seating capacity of just over four thousand, almost eight hundred greater than the Dolby, and it was currently packed with a sea of elites in designer gowns and tuxes.

The first ten or twenty long rows were filled predominantly with scrubbed, massaged, and manicured Hollywood royalty, whose jobs often depended on being fit, looking great, and exuding elegance and superiority like a skunk exuded stink. Additional rows were also filled with the privileged, but far more of these were overweight or unattractive: the media, writers, FX and other tech specialists, families, and additional behind-the-scenes experts.

Twenty-six musicians were situated in an oval trench carved below the back of the stage, which could be crossed by a wide bridge. While orchestra pits were traditionally in front, the Oscars' organizers had long since decided they didn't want to wedge musicians between the audience and the stage.

Before the Cosmopolitan had been constructed, in 2013, the organizers had even gone so far as to have the orchestra located a mile from the theater. There the musicians watched the proceedings on monitors so the live, if somewhat dislocated, orchestra music could be piped through fiber optic cables to the two hundred and one individually powered Dolby loudspeakers inside the Dolby Theater.

The Cosmopolitan Theater had taken a different approach. The orchestra pit was under the back half of the stage, in an acoustically pure room. When the entire stage wasn't needed, the pit was open to the air. When this valuable real estate was needed for a major production number, however, the stage floor could be extended so that it slid over the pit, sealing the orchestra into a soundproof cocoon in a matter of seconds, after which the music would be piped the short distance to the loudspeakers.

Hakim took a deep breath and began. "Hello," he said gently, unthreateningly, into the microphone, as if trying to entice a shy squirrel to take a nut from his hand. "For those of you expecting a different presenter right now," he continued in nearly perfect English with a gracious, Hollywood smile, "I want you to know we've arranged for a surprise this year. But you won't consider this a *good* surprise," he added, his tone still pleasant. "But here is the key: if everyone remains calm, remains seated, everyone will get through this."

There was a low rumble from the crowd and hundreds of glances were exchanged throughout the theater, as everyone tried to gauge the reaction of others to the incongruity of these words. If this was a practical joke, the audience wasn't sure it was funny.

Fixed cameras were scattered throughout the auditorium, stage, and even orchestra pit, with the director and his team in a separate facility nearby, surrounded by endless feeds and electronics. Four men were also in the aisles with handheld network cameras, racing around like track athletes to get the best close-ups of stars in their seats.

"To director Sebastian Cole, and those of you filming and broadcasting these proceedings," continued Hakim, "I'll need you to continue to do so. All of our lives depend on it."

He paused to let this sink in, but only for a second. "Our lives also depend on everyone remaining calm, quiet, and in your seats," he added evenly into the microphone, and his voice boomed from two hundred and forty speakers, an unnecessary overkill designed to one-up the Dolby Theater and its own excessive sound system.

So far, so good, thought Hakim. The crowd was squirming, troubled, and confused. But they had not panicked.

Now that they were somewhat braced and forewarned, he waved a hand, and his six colleagues, all in black tuxes like his own, rushed onto the stage from the wings, their KH2002 machine guns held out in front of them and pointed toward the ocean of humanity seated in the auditorium.

Most in the audience blanched, and some looked as if they were about to vomit, but there were a few vapid faces who Hakim could have sworn were waiting for this to be revealed as a tasteless practical joke. Waiting for the seven terrorists to break into a dance number, sort of a terrorist version of *Springtime For Hitler*.

Hakim's demeanor visibly darkened, a charming Satan suddenly sprouting horns. "We are Islamic Jihad!" he hissed. "And we now *own* this theater. And all of you!"

The crowd chatter grew to a roar and numerous people rose.

"Sit down and shut up!" shouted Hakim, and the speakers delivered his roar as though God himself had issued this demand.

At Hakim's nod, Sherif Ismail shot a burst from his assault rifle into the ceiling. As plaster rained down the reality of the situation became clear, and the entire auditorium was cowed into silence, rapidly retaking their seats as ordered.

Another of Hakim's men sent a digital command through his phone, and the floor of the stage zipped along hidden tracks and trapped dozens of musicians inside their soundproof pit.

"This theater has been completely sealed," continued Hakim, his voice no longer either pleasant or heated, but rather icy cold, measured, and in command. "All exits have been locked down, including the two in the orchestra pit behind me. There is no way out unless we *let* you out."

After they had chewed on this for a moment he continued. "In addition, we've mined this entire structure. Powerful explosives are part of the walls, floor, and ceiling. Enough to turn this theater into a fireball that will light up the entire city, killing every one of you." He raised his eyebrows. "And every one of us."

Hakim paused, and then, with a dramatic flourish added, "But *we* are fully prepared to die. Can you say the same? If not, or if you don't want to be responsible for four thousand deaths, you will remain calm and silent.

"Here are the rules: all who are here, and those watching on TV, need to listen very carefully. We have full control of all security cameras. So we can see all approaches. Second, there are members of Islamic Jihad monitoring all major television stations around the world. So don't even think about cutting the feed. The world will not be allowed to look away. If the television coverage ever stops, we will blow this theater."

Hakim's eyes burned with an almost demonic passion as he continued. "If anyone from the outside makes the slightest attempt to enter, we will blow this theater. If power is cut off, we will blow this theater. If I feel too strong of a breeze, we will blow this theater." He leaned forward intently and glared into the stationary camera that had zoomed in on his face. "Are you listening, President Cochran? The evil that you and your murderous military have visited upon the children of Islam has come home to roost. And all of your men and jets and bombs are powerless to stop us."

A malicious smirk appeared on Hakim's face. "As an example of our resolve, you should know that seventy-one infidels backstage are already lying in pools of their own blood."

As he spoke, the technical specialist on his team began transmitting the video footage of the slaughter they had orchestrated backstage to a small screen he had removed from his bag, which was facing the audience. Behind the stage, three evenly spaced twenty-foot-tall monitors displayed the network television feed, so those sitting in the back could see more clearly the fine detail of the proceedings.

Hakim glanced behind him at one of the two-story screens and was infuriated to see a massive image of his face rather than the video footage of their massacre backstage. "Sebastian Cole, zoom in on our screen!" he demanded of the unseen director. "Now! Or I'll spray the front row."

In seconds, what was being displayed on the tiny screen could now be seen on the towering ones behind him, and on television screens around the world. In high-definition 3-D clarity. The images of helpless, unconscious innocents—celebrities and unknowns alike—being shot in the head caused absolute pandemonium. Members of the audience screamed, or gasped, or whispered in horror. Chatter grew to a roar and numerous attendees rose once again from their seats.

Hakim had been fully prepared for this reaction. He pumped several non-silenced rounds into the ceiling, right next to the microphone. The shots were ear crushing when transmitted through the powerful speakers, and their thunder filled the entire theater, causing such severe vibrations that they momentarily turned the Cosmopolitan into the epicenter of a small earthquake.

"Quiet!" shouted Hakim as an additional hail of plaster rained down onto the proceedings, and the entire auditorium complied at once. An unnatural, tomblike silence engulfed the room.

Hakim faced the main camera with a grim expression, aware that he was now being watched by hundreds of millions of people in over one hundred and fifty countries around the world. Other than the World Cup of soccer, no single event on the planet was seen live by more people, making this the perfect terror target. Hakim practically drooled from the prospect of milking this for all it was worth.

"Now I'm aware that some watching this, live or on television, might think I'm bluffing about this theater being wired," he said. He removed a remote electronic device from his pocket and began entering digits. "Sebastian Cole," he demanded of the show's director, "show the feed from the orchestra pit."

When Hakim saw a 3-D view of the members of the orchestra on the screen behind him, he entered the last digit.

Dozens of tiny explosions rocked the pit, all directed inward. Although the structure itself was not breached, the explosives had been placed so carefully, and had been so well modulated in power, it was as if each musician had individual mini-bombs attached to their belts, which had blown them to shreds in an instant. Blood spray and body parts flew through the small enclosed space and slammed into the walls and ceiling, as though the members of the orchestra were cats that had been placed in a working microwave oven. Several in the large crowd vomited.

Hakim was pleased to note that despite the horror they felt at what they had just witnessed, they remained silent and in their seats, his previous demonstrations having finally sunk in.

"I trust you don't think I'm bluffing now," said Hakim icily, and his associates, who were still fanned out behind him, continued to point their machine guns at the crowd. "Fortunately, Islamic Jihad does not require any musical accompaniment."

The terrorist leader leaned in menacingly. "One last thing. And I'm speaking to you, President Cochran. Even if your special ops people could somehow mount an attack that we couldn't see coming—which is impossible—and even if they took all of us out simultaneously before we blew this theater, this would gain you *nothing*. We have three of our people in the audience. Dressed like the rest. Indistinguishable from the rest. And each has the means to detonate the explosives in this theater as well."

Hakim gazed at the audience, and every member wore a horrified expression that hadn't changed since he had shown the footage of the carnage backstage. "For those of you in the auditorium," he continued, "all I care about is that you remain silent and in your seats. If you have to urinate, you will have to soil yourself, because you aren't getting a bathroom pass."

He threw out his hands in a magnanimous gesture. "But feel free to use your phones. Not to make calls, because if you don't maintain absolute silence, you will be killed. But to text. E-mail. Tweet. Instagram. Blog. Send selfies to your Facebook pages. Whatever you want. Contact your Department of Homeland Security. I don't care. You—and they—are *powerless*."

As Hakim had expected, many hundreds in the crowd immediately pulled cell phones from their pockets, already silenced for the occasion. Whether this was to reach out to friends, fans, and loved ones, as he had indicated, or just to get a distraction from the horror of their predicament, he didn't know, and didn't care.

"One of my men has just sent a message to your President Cochran, detailing a list of our demands. Starting with freeing all Islamic prisoners you have long tortured and wrongfully detained. But after this, the demands are not so simple. But I have every confidence President Cochran will ultimately give us what we want. If he does, the vast majority of you will get out of this alive."

He smiled cruelly. "But several of you almost certainly will not. But this is as it should be. For you were chosen for a reason. Because all of you in this room are symbols of the decay of the West. You are pampered and spoiled and empty. You exemplify a lifestyle that is an abomination to Allah. You are perfect examples of everything that is wrong with your culture. It's decadence. Its superficiality. It's excesses. It's godlessness. And its hypocrisy."

His eyes narrowed and his lip curled up in disgust. "How much money have you spent tonight on hair and stylists? How many millions, total, on decadent gowns? How many tens of millions on jewelry? You waste vast wealth preening. While millions starve, you congratulate yourselves on the smut you belch out to numb your people to their empty lives. You use your voices, not to encourage virtue. Not to encourage a life that would be pleasing to Allah. But to do the *opposite*.

"While the world burns, you become ever more obsessed with the plight of your homosexuals. Despite the fact that those who engage in sodomy *already* thrive in your culture, when they would be stoned to death in mine. Your women are whores who not only don't cover their faces, but who parade around nearly naked. And instead of being where they belong, at home raising children and caring for their husbands, they are attending schools—schools that do nothing but perpetuate the sickness of your culture."

Hakim paused for effect.

"And you degrade yourselves with endless pornography," he continued. "Something that has become as common in the West as air."

Hakim forced himself to pause once again. He had rehearsed this speech many times, and he suspected he was delivering it a little too quickly. He needed to give the worldwide television audience time to digest his words.

"Your Kim Kardashian rose to fame after her appearance on a sex tape. Yet you have turned her, and her ilk, into royalty. Your reality television is depraved, morally corrupt, and despicable, and yet its popularity grows like a cancer. You worship the false gods of hedonism and technology, obsessed with your televisions and video games and cell phones and selfies. Your culture is a blight on this planet, one that makes Sodom and Gomorrah look like cities of the virtuous."

Hakim clenched his fist and held it out before him, so the cameras couldn't miss it. "So you are being held up as an example. A warning.

To show the world what Islamic Jihad is fighting for—and fighting against. You have raped our countries. Savaged our way of life. And called us murderers."

He sighed, almost as though he was sorry for what the behavior of the West was forcing him to do. "So, until your president meets every one of our demands, starting one hour from now, we will execute one of your Hollywood stars every fifteen minutes. Around the clock."

There was a chorus of gasps from the crowd and panicked chatter that rose to a low roar. Hakim shouted into the microphone once more, threatening to kill a dozen people immediately if order was not restored, and this had the desired effect.

"We're prepared to stay here as long as it takes," continued Hakim once the theater was quiet again. "Days. Weeks. We have enough food for ourselves, so we won't weaken. But your president has one hour. After this, for every fifteen minutes that passes without him doing the right thing, one of you will die. Almost a hundred of you for each day your president hesitates. And we will continue this until our demands are met." He held out his hands helplessly. "Or until everyone in this auditorium is dead. Whichever comes first."

Abdul Hakim stared into the camera with a predatory gleam. "Your move, Mr. President."

8

President Timothy Cochran checked a digital clock on the wall and forced himself to stay calm. The terrorist they had identified as Abdul Hakim had just issued his ultimatum five minutes earlier, giving them a little over an hour before the first celebrity was to be executed inside the Cosmopolitan Theater. Given the number of people this group had already murdered in ice-cold blood, there could be little doubt that this man would make good on his threats.

The president mopped sweat from his face with a paper towel and waited for the air-conditioning to chill the room further as he had ordered. Less than an hour ago he had been on the White House tennis court, his backhand in rare form, one of the only presidents in recent memory who wasn't a golfer.

He had managed to take a three-minute shower and change into casual slacks and a button-down shirt while the Situation Room was being readied, and while members of his National Security Council were either racing to the White House or finding secure locations from which to join the meeting via video. But even after the shower, his body refused to stop sweating.

Robert Snyder, Secretary of Homeland Security, had insisted he call this emergency meeting, based on intel gathered by General Justin Girdler, predicting the imminent attack on the Oscars. He had also been adamant that any move they made to prevent the attack would blow up in their faces. President Cochran was both impressed and sickened that the attack had commenced just as Girdler's intel had predicted.

His top advisors had already confirmed what he knew in his gut: any military operation they tried would fail. Islamic Jihad held all the cards. It was too difficult to breach the theater, and too easy for them to trigger the explosives.

Three additional members of his National Security Council arrived around the table, two via video and one live, and Cochran decided he needed to start the proceedings. He gazed down the endless polished table that was the central fixture in the White House Situation Room, a five-thousand square foot conference room and intelligence management center in the basement of the West Wing.

Although initially created in 1961 by John F. Kennedy, the Situation Room had undergone repeated renovations to keep up with technology, and its communications capabilities were sophisticated enough to allow the president to exercise his full command-and-control authority with US forces around the world from within its confines.

The Vice President, Secretary of State, Secretary of the Treasury, and the Assistant to the President for National Security Affairs had not arrived, in person or virtually. Even so, Cochran had waited too long already, and the people who were truly key were all in attendance: his Chief of Staff, the Director of National Intelligence, the Chairman of the Joint Chiefs of Staff, the Secretary of Defense, and the Secretary of Homeland Security, along with dozens of underlings, intelligence analysts and others, many of whom the president didn't recognize.

And, of course, General Justin Girdler, the man who had uncovered the key piece of intel and had pulled the alarm, who was joining them by video broadcast. Girdler's and Snyder's briefings to the president had been recorded and sent to all other members of the Council so they could be brought up to speed while making their way to the meeting.

Cube-shaped monitors had telescoped up from recessed compartments in the table, in front of empty seats, to serve as virtual stand-ins for any key participant unable to be there physically. While three-dimensional viewing had become exceptionally lifelike, this was not true if you were viewing the monitor from a severe angle or from behind, so the cubes displayed a participant on each of its four walls, ensuring they could be seen from any angle.

"I assume you've all read the terrorists' list of demands," said the president without preamble, a statement rather than a question. "What would it take to comply with them?"

"With all due respect, Mr. President," said the cube across from him and to his right, displaying the hardened face of Admiral John Janikowski, Chairman of the Joint Chiefs of Staff. "You aren't seriously considering caving in to their demands? We have a strict policy of never negotiating with terrorists."

"I know that!" snapped Cochran irritably. "I simply want to get a holistic sense of what we're dealing with. I want to discuss any and all options, even those we assume we won't, or *can't*, pursue. Thinking outside the box is our only hope. If we even *have* a hope," he added miserably. "Now anyone want to jump in and answer my question? You know, before Islamic Jihad starts executing more innocent civilians."

"They've listed fourteen demands," said Snyder. "But most are window dressing. The three at the heart of it are as follows. One, transfer fifty billion dollars to the accounts of Islamic Jihad. This isn't easy or painless," he added as an aside, "but it's the most doable of their core demands. Two," he continued, "release all Islamic prisoners we're holding around the world. To say this would be thorny is a monumental understatement. Especially for those who are being incarcerated in partnership with other countries, whose governments aren't going to be keen on cooperating when it comes to letting these men go. And three, pull every last member of our military and covert ops out of every last Muslim country and terrorist theater."

Snyder shook his head. "The last two aren't even possible in the time frame we're looking at."

"Why not?" said the president.

"Because freeing all prisoners, or rounding up all of our forces and withdrawing, are quite involved processes. They can only be rushed so much. No matter how many people and resources we throw at them. You know the old adage: nine women can't make a baby in a month. Well, neither can nine *hundred*. No matter what is at stake."

The president rubbed his chin in thought. "Given the level of sophistication of the attack, they must know we can't cave to their demands, even if we wanted to. So either they have no intention of letting their captives live, no matter what," he concluded, "or they're taking an extreme initial position, in expectation of a negotiation."

Cochran turned toward the image of Girdler, who appeared to hover in front of the cube-face directly across from the president. "What is *your* analysis, General? We need to understand their endgame. You brought us the key intel and you headed PsyOps for many years. So how do you assess this attack and our options?"

"So far the attack is flawless," responded Girdler. "And our options go from incomprehensibly dismal to even worse. I'll run through the analysis momentarily," he added. "But first, I'd like to recommend that we set up a blockade, an eight-square-block or so perimeter around the theater. We can't risk someone, or some group, trying to be heroic and spooking these men into setting off their powder keg. And if they do blow the theater, we can't be sure of the blast zone, so it's wise to clear the area anyway."

"I agree with the general," said Synder, and looking around the room it was clear that most thought this was so painfully obvious that, despite the commotion and the fact that Hakim's ultimatum had been issued only ten minutes earlier, this should have already been ordered.

"Lou," said the president to his National Security Advisor, who was the best wordsmith in the room, "write a message to Hakim for me to review. As soon as possible. First, let him know we'll be setting up a perimeter. We don't want our efforts to ensure no one spooks them to, ah . . . *spook* them."

Cochran paused in thought. "Then, tell them we're considering their demands. But that we need more time. If they promise a twenty-four-hour stay before any further killing, I'll go on television and tell the world we're in discussion with them and considering their demands. I'll react publicly to their threat. Humiliate myself. Make them look strong and us weak. But only if they give us twenty-four hours." He turned to Admiral Janikowski. "Meanwhile, John, set the wheels in motion so our people can begin clearing a perimeter around the theater the moment Hakim has received the message."

The admiral nodded at one of his staff members who rushed off screen to begin issuing frantic orders.

The president returned his stare to Girdler while he waited for his National Security Advisor to finish composing his requested message. "Please continue with your analysis, General."

"You know the file on this group. Ruthless and barbaric. Attracting only the most sadistic fundamentalists. Will happily behead men and women at their slightest whim. So their end-game is very clear: they intend to martyr themselves and take down the Cosmopolitan and over four thousand people. No matter what else happens. I'm absolutely positive. It's as simple, and as complicated, as that."

"*Absolutely* positive, General?" challenged Cochran. "How can you have that level of certainty?"

Girdler sighed. "You've heard Secretary Snyder's report," he replied. "They've spent weeks or months concealing a revolutionary new plastic explosive within the Cosmopolitan. Even if they were able to remove it all before leaving, which is unlikely, the scent of it would linger long enough for an electronic bloodhound to get a fix on it. Believe me, they plan to wreak as much hell as they can with this explosive until we learn to detect it. So they *have* to blow the theater. No matter what happens."

There were grim nods all around the table as Girdler's logic hit home.

"From a PsyOps perspective," continued the general, "this is an extraordinarily well-planned and effective terror effort. Better than even my best people might have hatched. The physical, psychological, and political impact will be *incalculable*. They've boxed us in brilliantly. They've captured a group of people known and loved around the world. Stars of movies shown in every country. These actors, and the characters they portray, are often a more integral and important part of people's lives than are their own *relatives*. They've already killed Wolverine. Who's next. Star-Lord? James T. Kirk? Katniss Everdeen? Aunt May's head on a stick, for Christ's sake?"

The already grim expressions worn by everyone in attendance became even grimmer.

"So they kill beloved stars one by one while they force the entire world to look on," continued Girdler. "It's the reality show from hell. And every time they kill they remind the world that we—*you*, Mr. President—could have prevented it by simply conceding to their *reasonable* demands. And every murder shows us to be impotent. So we're either heartless bastards who won't negotiate, or we're helpless and weak. Either way, we lose considerable prestige around the globe."

Girdler paused for several long seconds to see if anyone would challenge this analysis, and then continued. "Meanwhile, they're letting every audience member use their phones however they want. A *masterstroke*. Not only do we witness their suffering on ultra-high-definition, 3-D television, which is more vivid, and will make the murders more graphic, than if we were there in person, but we're also treated to endless tweets from the victims. Messages to loved ones. Facebook posts. And these celebrities have many millions of followers. We get outpourings of love, terror, misery, and hopelessness. We get correspondence with spouses and family, dripping with primal emotions. Love. Fear. Loss. Heartbreaking, terrible stuff that will go viral like never before. Ellen DeGeneres tweeted a selfie of some stars from the awards a number of years back, and it was the most re-tweeted message in history. How many retweets do you think the messages streaming out of there now are going to get?"

Girdler cleared his throat while everyone attending the meeting stared at him in spellbound horror. "So basically, we're fucked!" he finished, not shying away from this coarse but accurate depiction of their situation. "If we do nothing, or attempt to negotiate, the world watches a slow-motion slaughter. One that will go on and on and on until we do something to try to stop it. When we do, our attack will fail, further diminishing us, and they blow the entire theater. At that point, since our actions triggered the final outcome, it will appear to many that we have the blood of thousands on our hands."

Several members of the Council visibly shuddered. The temperature in the room, already chilly, seemed to drop another ten degrees.

"If everything the general says is true," said Admiral Janikowski, breaking the long silence, "and I believe it is, I think we have to consider launching an immediate strike on the theater. Even knowing it's bound to fail."

"So send in a team to *purposely* trigger the explosion?" said the president in disbelief.

"It's going to happen anyway," replied the admiral, "no matter what we do. On a scale of one to ten, with ten being an unmitigated disaster, triggering the deaths of thousands of innocents is a ten. But letting these monsters spend days prolonging this with the eyes of the world upon them, days pulling legs off of spiders, only to kill everyone in the end anyway, would rate a *hundred*. It would be playing into their hands, without altering the end result."

The president surveyed expressions around the room and didn't like what he saw. The admiral's logic was unassailable. This could well be something they would be forced to do.

The president considered. If one became certain a person would be tortured to death, without any hope of a reprieve, would killing them quickly be the humane thing to do?

Probably so, he had to acknowledge.

"The ethics of going this route are troubling enough," said Cochran finally. "But how do we, in good conscience, turn an assault team into a kamikaze squad? Knowing their purpose is to act as a detonator? Who would agree to such a mission if they knew?"

"That probably won't be necessary," said Snyder. "We have two plainclothes marshals inside the theater. For an event of this importance, this is standard practice. The public is only aware that there are marshals hidden on certain high-risk jumbo jets. But we plant them at other events as well."

"Why wasn't I told of this immediately?" demanded the president.

"Frankly, because it doesn't change a thing," replied the Secretary of Homeland Security. "You heard Hakim. They've planted three ringers of their own. Even if our marshals were able to take out all seven terrorists before they could trigger the explosives, which is very unlikely, they have no way of knowing who the three plants are."

He paused. "But the marshals' presence does change how we go about provoking an early end to this. We'll order them to try to take out Hakim and the others. They'll have no chance. But tragically, these men are already destined to die, no matter what. At least we can give them the dignity of going down fighting. "

"I agree with the secretary," said Girdler quickly, before anyone else could jump in. "But I must insist that we don't force the terrorist's hand for at least thirty more minutes."

The president looked at him quizzically. "We won't," he replied. "We'll wait until just before the first scheduled execution. We're not about to make a decision of this magnitude until we've exhausted all other possibilities." The president's eyes narrowed. "But who are you to *insist*?" he demanded. "And what's the magic of thirty minutes?"

"I have a man exploring the situation now," replied the general, ignoring the commander in chief's first question. "It's likely we have no way out. But despite what's been said here, there just might be a slim chance, after all. But my agent won't know for certain until he's in proximity of the Cosmopolitan."

Eyebrows shot up all around.

"What kind of a chance?" said the president.

"Too small for me to waste any more of this group's time," he replied. "But I promise, if the impossible happens, and he's able to come up with something, you'll be the first to know."

9

As the van neared the Cosmopolitan Theater, Nick Hall was assaulted by an avalanche of terrified thoughts that hit him like a nuclear shock wave, and he was certain his head would burst. He wanted to scream in agony, but too many agonized thoughts were already screaming into his brain. Being in proximity to dense groups of people was always a dizzying, maddening shock to his system that could send him reeling, which is why Girdler had isolated him in the desert.

But this time the tight knot of humanity numbered in the thousands, and each individual within this group was broadcasting thoughts at mind-searing decibel levels: visceral, emotional, panicked thoughts that blasted at his head and psyche like a jackhammer.

Hall balled his hands into fists and squeezed his eyes shut, fighting to surface from under a tidal wave of everyone-shrieking-at-once thoughts that never stopped coming. As he neared a point at which he felt himself losing consciousness, perhaps his mind's way of protecting itself from madness, he marshaled all of his will and experience to push the maelstrom of thoughts down, to shunt them away to a still-deafening, but survivable, white noise.

He had known he would need to fight through this and had asked Megan to be stoic while he did so, not wanting an additional distraction. He had ordered the soldiers to remain silent until he told them otherwise, but unlike Megan they had no idea what was happening to him. He read they feared he had gone into an epileptic seizure, and he somehow managed to throw up a forestalling hand just as they were about to attend to him.

After several more minutes of the most intense effort he had ever put forth, he managed to get enough of a grip that he was able to fully gather his senses once again. Taking a deep mental breath, and knowing he couldn't delay, he plunged back into the semi-contained sea of noise, desperately trying to locate at least one of the terrorists.

He got *nowhere*. The intense thicket of thoughts was too overwhelming. He couldn't sort through them all in time. It was *impossible*. He had become expert at isolating minds and searching for needle-in-a-haystack thoughts. But not for thoughts hidden within a shrieking, panicked haystack such as this.

And then an idea materialized, breaking through the crippling pandemonium of inner voices. *He knew how to find the needle.* It was obvious. He just needed to zoom in on anyone who was thinking in Arabic, which would narrow the field considerably.

Nick Hall plunged in once again, this time with a specific goal, and found what he was after. He worked to isolate this first mind, and keep it isolated, locking in the mental coordinates before trying to isolate the next. Within five minutes he had found all seven terrorists.

Now that he had isolated minds to focus on, the white noise wasn't quite as maddening. He activated Altschuler's translation program and went to work. His fishing expedition was more difficult than it would have been had these men thought in English, but the software in his implants still allowed him to make the progress he needed.

The plan was pure evil, on an even grander scale than he had previously appreciated. They would begin the massacre with a single bullet to the head of their victims, but this would rapidly escalate to beheadings and worse. They would continue to kill stars in ever more inventive and barbaric ways, hoping they could get key concessions along the way, potential icing on their cake. And they would never relent, until the US had no choice but to storm the castle, with disastrous results.

But there just might be a way for him to stop it . . .

Hall contacted Justin Girdler on his internal cell phone.

"What've you got, Nick?" said Girdler, answering this communication in seconds. "I'm muting a meeting of the National Security Council to take this, so be efficient."

"Their demands are a sham," Hall thought at his implants, forcefully enough for Megan to pick up telepathically. "They plan to kill everyone, and themselves, no matter what. They'll milk this for all it's worth, for as long as they can, eventually forcing us to mount an attack, so the world will blame us when it finally blows."

"I knew that already," said Girdler impatiently. "Any chance to prevent this?"

"Yes," replied Hall, steadying himself as the speeding van he and Megan were in hit a jarring pothole in the road. "It's dangerous, and there are no guarantees, but it is possible."

As Hall began quickly outlining the key intel he had gleaned from the terrorists and the broad brushstrokes of his plan, a part of him expected protests from Megan. But while he could read the anguish on her face, she didn't issue a single telepathic interruption or complaint.

He had underestimated her. She was an amazing woman, and she would see this was something he had to do, despite the risks.

They had been forced together and had fallen in love, and their time with each other the past six months had only intensified these feelings. Megan was a petite five foot five, in her late twenties to his early thirties, with short hair, as black as his own, and a flawless complexion. And while she was cute, she wasn't nearly as stunning as many of the women Hall had dated, including the woman he had planned to marry when they had met.

But Megan Emerson was so much more fun to be around than any other woman he had ever known. So much more down-to-earth. She had rescued him. Not just from assassins who were trying to kill him, but from a marriage that would have been unhappy and that would have, inevitably, failed early.

He had been a shallow jackass, and she had demonstrated what a true connection could be like, above and beyond a physical relationship.

Life without her had become unthinkable. And he knew she felt the same way. But she would also know he was the only hope to save thousands of lives. So no matter how big a risk he planned to take, failing to make the attempt would be even *more* unthinkable.

When Hall finished the rough outline of his plan, there was a brief pause as Girdler mentally examined it from every angle.

"It might work," said the general finally. "With one thorny wrinkle. You'll have to lead a team of highly seasoned special forces commandos. Men who will need to follow your every order without question or hesitation. No matter how strange. No way they risk their own lives, and others, by blindly following a civilian with zero combat experience. Not without very good reason."

"Good point," said Hall in frustration. This was something he had failed to consider. "So you're suggesting I'd have to tell them about my psionic abilities."

"Not just tell them. Demonstrate. Convince them beyond any shadow of a doubt. It's the only way they'll follow you. And the president will have to be convinced, as well, or he'll never sanction the attack under your command."

Hall blew out a long breath. "We can't let these people die just to protect my identity."

"Every shred of decency I possess agrees with you," said Girdler. "But we've discussed this. This terrorist act will kill thousands. But if your abilities becomes widely known, eventually leading to the discovery of the secret to perfect mind reading, worldwide civilization will self-destruct. Or, at minimum, retreat back into the stone age. Many millions will almost certainly die."

Hall responded without hesitation. "You know that I believe this is true. But it doesn't matter. Maybe the key to cracking ESP will never be found. I don't know. But I can't let these people die on the *chance* that outing myself will lead to an even greater catastrophe. *Possibly. In the future.* It doesn't work that way. This may be a horrible decision that the world will come to regret. But we have to take that chance."

"I agree," said Girdler, and this immediate capitulation surprised Hall, who had expected additional arguments from the man, or at least hesitation. "But I needed to be certain you had thought this through."

The general took a deep breath. "Okay then. Here goes nothing. I'm going to rejoin the president's meeting. Stay tuned, Nick." He paused. "I can't tell you how sorry I am that it's come to this."

"Me too," replied Hall. "Me too."

10

"What about issuing an ultimatum of our own?" said Aaron Anderson, the Secretary of Defense, as Girdler rejoined the meeting. "Threaten these fuckers back, for a change. Tell them if they evacuate the theater now, we'll let them go. But if they kill anyone else, we won't rest until every last member of Islamic Jihad has been hunted down and killed. That we'll put the full might of the United States of America into crushing every last one of these cockroaches."

"Might make *us* feel better," responded Janikowski, "but it wouldn't work. They'd actually love for us to react this way. So they could stand up to our threat and prove their resolve. Show that they're prepared to martyr their entire movement if they have to. And they know our limitations with respect to carrying out such a threat. We spent years trying to eliminate the leadership of al-Qaeda. And while we had great success, we certainly didn't get them all. And our efforts didn't improve our position in the slightest. The group just metastasized to any number of spin-off groups that were worse than the original."

"I agree," said the president. "We can't get them to back down. And given this attack, I'm sure they know we'll be going after them relentlessly anyway."

Cochran paused for just a moment, obviously intending to continue, when Girdler jumped in. "Mr. President, I just received the report I've been waiting for, from my agent in the field. It's promising, and suggests there is a way to end this without further loss of life on our side."

Cochran looked at the 3-D image across from him as though the general had lost his mind. "I find this impossible to believe," he said bluntly. "You said yourself the construction of this booby trap is flawless."

"It is. But there is a vital piece of intelligence you don't know," explained Girdler. "That you *need* to know. I don't have time to beat around the bush, so I'll just come out with it. Nick Hall—the famous Nick Hall with the implants—is alive and well. And he's been working with me since his supposed death six months ago."

There were gasps and mouths hanging open all around. The repercussions of thought-controlled Web surfing had continued to reverberate around the world like nothing else that had come before. Congress was even now deliberating on the proper safeguards and oversight of the implant technology. And this technology, and Nick Hall's involvement, was the biggest story of the past hundred years.

"Who else knows about this?" demanded the president, recovering his mental equilibrium.

"No one else, sir," replied Girdler.

"You've been keeping Hall's existence secret? What, using him as your own personal asset? Without any buy-in from your superiors?"

Girdler nodded. "Yes, sir," he said simply.

"You know that pulling something like this is a court-martialable offense?" said the president in dismay. He shook his head. "But that is a discussion for another time." He paused to gather his thoughts. "So how does Nick Hall's existence help us? Surfing the Web, with thoughts or otherwise, doesn't kill terrorists, or disarm bombs."

"You're familiar with the rumors that Hall could read minds as well, correct?"

"You're saying these are true?" said the president.

"Yes. Within a range of about six miles. Nick was the one who learned the attack on the Cosmopolitan was imminent. And obviously, he's the field agent I've been speaking of. Which is why it was critical he relocate to just outside the theater. That's what I've been waiting for."

"So he could read the minds of the terrorists inside?" said the president.

"Exactly," replied Girdler, who then quickly briefed the gathering on what Hall had learned, and his proposed plan of action.

"For this to work," said the Director of National Intelligence when Girdler was finished, "Hall's ESP would have to be perfect. More than perfect."

"It is," said Girdler.

"We have no other options," said the president. "I get that. But before I put this mysterious, back-from-the-dead Hall in command of an assault team, I need a personal demonstration."

Girdler shook his head. "Can't be done quickly enough," he said. "You're well out of his range. If you weren't, he could convince you in seconds. But trust me, the *last* thing you'd ever want is to be anywhere *near* him. He can read your every thought, every memory—every *secret*," he said pointedly. "Your taste in porn. What you say to yourself when no one is listening. He can find every last skeleton you've ever hidden in a matter of seconds. I have absolute respect, admiration, and affection for this man. But I won't get within ten miles of him."

The president considered. "So I have to authorize this based on your word alone? The word of a man who admits to violating the chain of command, and keeping information vital to the national interest from his superiors? Is that what you're telling me?"

"No. Don't take my word for it. Order the strike. We have three teams of four on site now. Tell them to only follow Nick Hall if they're absolutely convinced of his abilities. They'll all report exactly what I'm telling you. Because a man who can effortlessly read your every thought can demonstrate this in seconds."

The president rubbed his chin in thought. "Okay," he said decisively after only a brief pause. "I'm formally ordering this operation to go forward, with the conditions just discussed. Let's set some speed records, people. I need Hall to convince the team of his abilities and for them to be ready to breach in ten minutes. Or less. I'll place a brief call to them while they're en route."

"To give them the final order personally?" said Girdler.

President Timothy Cochran shook his head grimly, the weight of the world on his shoulders. "No," he replied softly. "To wish them all Godspeed."

11

Captain Floyd Briarwood had been trained to react on the fly. To assimilate new information, no matter how emotionally charged, without missing a beat. To expect the unexpected.

But nothing in all of human experience could have possibly prepared him for *this*.

The past few hours had begun strangely, and had so rapidly spun out of control into the realm of *Alice in Wonderland*, he couldn't help but think he would awaken at any moment. If only he was reacting to something more mundane, like seeing a UFO, or a bunch of pigs flying, he almost could have believed it.

This had begun when he and three other members of his twelve-man A-team had been scrambled for an urgent babysitting mission. Tasked with flying a prisoner into the middle of the desert to be interrogated by someone they had assumed was a torture specialist.

Strange duty, but not beyond the realm of imagination.

When this specialist had emerged from the interrogation room after less than a minute, and had ordered them to fly to LA, this was a bit more surprising, and odder still.

But this was still only the appetizer. They had no idea they were about to be hit with a machine-gun barrage of bizarre and surreal. Learning of the attack on the Oscars. Getting briefed for one of the most consequential missions ever attempted while being whisked to a warehouse about a mile away from the Cosmopolitan Theater, where two other four-man teams had already prepared weapons and other gear they would need.

And then learning that the famous Nick Hall was alive and well. And not only able to surf the Web with his thoughts, but to read minds as well. His demonstration to the team was as rapid as it was dazzling, showing he could not only instantly recite any number they thought of, but tell them what girl they liked in fifth grade, the name of their pet hamster, or where they had hidden the spare key.

And now this. The briefest of calls piped into each of their earpieces from President Timothy Cochran *himself*. Holy shit! It was ten lifetimes of improbability crammed into a few short hours.

And it was only just beginning.

They were all piled into—of all things—a mini church bus, several blocks away from the warehouse, and continued gearing up for their mission while Nick Hall gave them an overview of how he expected the op to go down. The petite young woman Hall had brought along, whom he introduced as Megan, sat quietly as far out of the way as she could manage, but looked as if she might vomit at any moment. Hall had asked them not to reveal that Megan had been with him under any circumstances, and they had agreed.

When Hall had finished the overview, he added, "You men are far more capable in an assault situation than I am. I know that. Under normal conditions, I would never think of issuing orders." He forced a smile. "And I know you would never think of *taking* them. But I've proven what I can do. An ability that represents our only chance. So I need you to trust me a thousand percent and do *exactly* what I tell you to do. Without hesitation or question. If I tell you to quack like a duck, I need to hear quacking *immediately*. Don't pause to wonder why. Maybe I've read that one of the terrorists has a lifelong fear of ducks. Maybe I'm creating a diversion. Is everyone with me on this?"

"Yes, sir," rang out Briarwood and eleven others in chorus.

Briarwood knew that this speech was unnecessary. He and his comrades didn't need a diagram to understand the tactical advantage Hall's ability gave them. Hall had made them believers, and they knew there was only one way of getting out of this alive. One way to save thousands.

Nick Hall's way.

Although, at the moment, the mind reader in question was wincing in pain, as though being jabbed with an ice pick from the inside of his head, unable to completely hide the immense hell that proximity to the highly charged thoughts of thousands was forcing him to endure.

"Okay. Let's do this," said Hall, managing to push back the pain once again, "and live to deny we had any knowledge of the operation," he added with a thin smile.

He pulled a black ski mask over his head, and all twelve men followed suit. It was vital that they all remain anonymous.

Hall surveyed the group he was now commanding. With the knit mask covering his face, and still in civilian clothing, he looked more like a ski instructor than a commando. "Captain Briarwood, Lieutenant Austin, you're with me," he said.

Briarwood joined Austin, and they both followed Nick Hall from the bus. And so did the woman Hall had brought. When they reached the pavement she hugged Hall and then backed away, tears now streaming down her face. While neither said a word, there was something about their body language that made Briarwood think they were communicating even so.

While Hall's expression was impossible to read behind the tightly-knitted mask, Briarwood didn't need to be a mind reader to see the love and concern pouring out of this Megan, along with her tears. She gave Hall one last look and then quickly retreated back into the bus.

Hall shook his head to clear it and turned away from the vehicle and the other ten commandos. He had already explained that he wanted to secure the warehouse with a small team before bringing in the rest. Apparently, there were two terrorists inside the warehouse who were not only watching the Academy Awards, but also monitoring all approaches to the warehouse through closed-circuit cameras. So the smaller Hall's assault force, the better.

Hall would read the terrorists' minds and know when they were looking away from the monitors so the three of them could advance.

"Stay tight on my heels," said the voice of Nick Hall, although he had never actually spoken these words. He had explained that he could use the remarkable technology in his skull like a cell phone, one that could turn his thoughts into words they could hear in their earpieces. This allowed Hall to issue clear and complex orders without making a sound, another clear advantage.

Hall led them behind a small building adjacent to the light-blue corrugated steel warehouse that was their target, a two-story rectangular structure that was as boring and unaesthetic as it was functional.

"When I say move, follow me to a position behind that dumpster," he instructed, pointing to the large steel container, painted green, about half the distance to their goal, where they could not be seen by any cameras.

Precious minutes ticked by, during which Briarwood tensed every muscle in his body.

"Go!" commanded Hall, taking off in a sprint toward the hulking green surveillance haven fifteen yards away. Briarwood and Austin followed instantly, being careful not to overtake the mind-reading civilian. The dumpster stank like rotting fish, but this was the least of their concerns.

Briarwood wondered what Hall had seen in the terrorists' minds. Were they now chatting with each other? In the toilet? Only Hall knew for certain, but they had obviously taken their eyes off the monitors for the necessary few seconds.

After another delay, followed by another well-timed sprint, the three men found themselves flush against the warehouse wall, unobserved. The steel felt smooth to the touch, and the entrance door was thick and locked tight, well beyond their ability to gain entry without alerting the men inside, who would then signal Hakim to blow the theater, just before they blew themselves up in the warehouse.

The only way they were going to get in was if the door was opened from the *inside*. Which is where Hall came in. Without him, they would never have known about the warehouse and tunnel in the first place, and would have had no chance at success, even had they known.

"Okay, gentlemen," said Hall non-vocally into their earpieces. "Here's the plan. I'm going to send an e-mail message to Basir, the terrorist closest to the outer door. I'll pretend it's from Abdul Hakim. I've fished out the proper authentication codes needed before and after the message, so Basir will be absolutely convinced the message is legitimate."

Briarwood shook his head. Authentication codes? These animals didn't miss a trick. It was alarming how smart and sophisticated they were becoming.

In Arabic, right? mouthed Austin frantically beside him, after getting Hall's attention.

"Yes, Lieutenant," replied Hall into both of their earpieces, his lips never moving. "But thanks for making sure I don't do something catastrophically stupid. I've already sent the completed message to Secretary Snyder's best Arabic expert to ensure it's phrased perfectly. And the tech wizards will make it appear to have been sent from Hakim's tablet. The contents are as follows:

"Basir, one of our brothers who has infiltrated the infidels . . ." Hall stopped. "Just so you know, I've read Hakim's mind, and this is really how he would phrase this," he reassured them. "One of our brothers who has infiltrated the infidels," he repeated, "believes the US military may be staging a possible attack near your location. On Acorn Drive. If your monitors show no one outside, get to Acorn and tell me what you see. Quickly. Respond only when you're ready to report."

Nice, thought Briarwood. This Hall was one crafty bastard.

"Captain Briarwood," added Hall. "I need you to wait behind this door. I've read in your mind that you have the most experience with a knife, and that even a silenced bullet would make too much noise. You'll need to put this Basir down before he can make the slightest sound. Like you did during Operation Asylum in Tikrit."

Briarwood's eyes widened. In Tikrit, he had waited outside a door like this for five hours, and had still remained alert enough that when the man he was waiting to ambush finally emerged, he had dispatched him so quietly a dog couldn't have heard. Briarwood realized Hall hadn't chosen him by accident. His past was not only an open book to this man, but an open book that was instantly searchable.

Only seconds after Hall's faked message from Hakim had been sent, Briarwood could hear locks being disengaged inside. Basir was a good soldier and was responding to Hakim's order immediately.

Briarwood removed his seven-inch Ka-Bar combat knife from its sheath and balanced it in his hand, gripping it firmly but lightly. The Ka-Bar had been used by the Marines during World War II, and eight decades later was still widely popular.

Briarwood held his breath as Basir emerged. The terrorist stared straight ahead, convinced that the coast was entirely clear since he and his partner had not seen anyone in the monitors for some time.

Briarwood threw his left arm around Basir's head from behind, clamping his hand over the terrorist's mouth and yanking his head back, exposing his carotid artery. In perfect synchronicity of movement, he drew the knife across Basir's throat, and then twisted the terrorist, and the gusher of blood emerging from the man's neck, away from himself and to the ground, placing Basir's limp body there as gently as he would a newborn baby.

One down, one to go.

Hall wore a sick, horrified expression, but it melted away immediately as he barked additional orders into their earpieces. He didn't have the luxury of being squeamish. "Enter quietly and take up firing positions facing the office at the back of the warehouse. Full automatic."

Briarwood and Austin didn't hesitate, pushing open the door and following Hall's instructions. The civilian was right on their heels as they entered. "He's in the far right corner of the office. Spray it at chest height now!"

Both men shot multiple bursts from their assault rifles into the right side of the office, twenty feet away, until Hall screamed into their earpieces that the second terrorist was down. Not surprising, since a fly couldn't have survived the barrage they had just unleashed. Sawdust and debris hovered in a cloud near the office wall, which had been pulverized.

Hall wasted no time waiting to regain his hearing or congratulating himself. "Warehouse is secure!" he broadcast to the ten other members of their assault force, waiting impatiently in the small church bus for the word to move out. "Join us as fast as possible! They've chosen their first victim, Scarlett Johansson, and they'll be bringing her up on stage soon. Let's move like we've got a purpose!"

12

Nick Hall had kept his six-foot frame in excellent shape, something of which he had always been quite proud, but he was a sloth compared to the elite troops he was commanding now, even when they were burdened down with heavy gear, ready for every contingency.

Given he could enter the minds of the men he commanded and see from their eyes, he could direct the team without necessarily having to be right next to them, so he sent all twelve men ahead of him through the tunnel. They could traverse the cramped seven blocks much faster than he could, especially while he continued to be battered by a sea of visceral thoughts and was monitoring a feed of the Oscars playing in the corner of his visual field. He could only juggle so many things at once, and watching a television feed, mining minds for information, and determining an optimal strategy would overload any man, no matter how gifted, leaving little room to focus on rapid movement.

And every second counted now. It was going to be close. *Too* close.

Scarlett Johansson had just been brought to the stage and was on her knees, the bottom of her long, gold, off-the-shoulder gown bunched up on the stage behind her. Hakim held a gun to her head and taunted her, a large predatory cat playing with its meal before the kill.

While not as stoic as many of the characters she had played, Johansson didn't give the terrorists the satisfaction of pleading for her life or reacting to the taunts, but a steady stream of tears were running down her distinctive face, matched by many hundreds of teary-eyed, horrified faces in the audience. Little could possibly be more incongruous than the sight of a terrorist in a tuxedo preparing to execute a star in a designer gown, who was known by billions, on the grandest stage in the world.

Hall had read the initial list of victims from Hakim's mind, and like everything else about the operation, it was brilliantly conceived. If the siege went on long enough, they would eventually get to male stars, but the first group were all female, to provoke the most emotional reaction possible from those witnessing these atrocities.

Hakim had searched the Web for lists of the most beloved female stars; for worldwide popularity. Scarlett Johansson would be followed by Sandra Bullock, Jennifer Anniston, Zoe Saldana, Jennifer Garner, Amy Adams, Angelina Jolie, and Ann Hathaway, an all-star cast of victims whose brutal murders would leave the world utterly devastated.

Hall saw in his mind's eye that his team was emerging from the tunnel and into the director's office backstage. He sent them directions to the three doors between the back and front stage, and sent the technology specialist on the team, Engineering Sergeant Mike Doherty, the codes and frequencies required to re-open the sealed doors remotely, which he had read from Hakim.

The team was waiting at these doors, four men behind each, when Hall finally emerged from the tunnel minutes later. He composed a brief message as he closed the trap door behind him. *Marshal Chavez,* he texted through his implants, *please confirm you're getting this communication and have been properly briefed by your superiors.*

Ronaldo Chavez was the marshal closest to the ringer Islamic Jihad had planted in the auditorium. Hakim had lied when he claimed there were three ringers, but even so, without Hall, even one unknown plant would have served as an absolute deterrent to a counterattack.

Message received, came the immediate texted reply from Chavez. *I've been told you have special abilities and to follow your every command, no matter how unusual.*

Good. Word has it that you're a great shot. How great?

Expert level, sir, came the quick texted response.

Almost before it had fully registered on Hall that he wasn't certain what this meant, his implants had taken the cue, had searched the web, and had delivered the requisite information, which floated before him. Expert was the army's highest level of achievement, ahead of Marksman and even Sharpshooter.

Perfect, texted Hall. *I want you to bring up a mental picture of the man you'll be targeting. Don't ask why, just do it,* he finished, wanting to be sure Chavez had the right man in his sites. He could have entered the marshal's mind and searched through it to get this information, but he was taxed to his limits already.

Chavez did as Hall asked, and sure enough, he was targeting the sleeper.

How certain are you that you can take him out? asked Hall.

Positive, texted Chavez. *The shot isn't difficult, but it is obstructed.*

Obstructed how?

By a tall bald guy sitting one row behind the target.

Shit! thought Hall, finally joining his team, still waiting at the three doors between the backstage and the wings of the main stage for further instructions. He should have known a shot would be obstructed. Even standing, a shooter couldn't get enough of a downward angle to clear a guest seated just behind the target.

This complicated the situation even further. Hall was being forced to play three-dimensional chess while someone was jackhammering his brain, and he knew he was on his last legs.

He took a deep breath and willed himself to focus for just a little longer. He could collapse afterward.

Stare at the bald guy until I tell you to stop, he instructed, knowing this would help him locate the man in the crowd.

Hall borrowed the feed from Chavez's eyes, getting a good enough sense of the bald man's appearance and location that he could search nearby minds, looking for someone whose self-image was a match. He found who he was looking for in seconds, Jay Coleman, and read the man's cell phone number from his mind.

Hall continued to check the television feed in the corner of his visual field, un-muting periodically. Hakim was still holding the gun to Scarlet Johansson's head, but his demeanor had changed, as though he was done playing with his food.

The terrorist made a show of looking at a digital countdown on the screen, which he had ordered the director to place there, and shook his head in mock regret. "Your President Cochran can still save you," he said, words heard by an audience that had now grown to over a billion people worldwide. "But he is down to his last three minutes. I wish I could hold out hope, but he is too selfish. Too arrogant. He and your government have committed endless crimes against the Muslim people, they have—"

Hall muted his internal television feed once more and took several additional deep breaths. It was now or never. This innocent actress was almost out of time.

Jay Coleman, he texted to the bald man as fast as he could think the words. *I'm with the US military.* Not entirely true, but in this case, not entirely false either. *Your ATM code is 568923. Your mother's maiden name is Benford. I hope this is enough to convince you of my legitimacy. Your life depends on you following my instructions.*

Hall didn't need to see the return text to know he had gotten the attention of Coleman. He read from Coleman's mind that he was prepared to consider his instructions, but this all depended on what they *were*.

Hall made sure that all of the terrorists were facing either Johansson or the audience and ordered Engineering Sergeant Doherty to trigger the release of the door locks, and for all twelve men to quietly file through them and wait in the wings for a full assault, on his command. They knew how to assign targets between themselves, so Hall left this part up to the professionals. He followed about ten yards behind them, juggling minds and feeds like a circus performer.

The digital clock on the screen now indicated the alluring star had only thirty-two seconds to live. But the very countdown Hakim was using to maximize the drama was ideal for Hall's needs, helping him set perfect timing.

He texted Coleman. *When the clock gets to eight seconds, duck down low. Instantly. Your life will depend on this. But it's critical you wait until the exact moment the countdown reaches eight.*

Hall didn't waste time reading Coleman's mind to see if he would comply. He either would or wouldn't. But they were out of time.

Marshal Chavez. Take out the target when the countdown reaches seven. The bald guy should be ducking on eight. If not, shoot right

*through him, because if you fail to bring down the terrorist, we all
die.*

Understood.

The clock continued counting down. Twenty. Nineteen. Eighteen . . .

Hall sent a message to his strike team. "You'll be hearing rapid-fire gunshots coming from the audience in just a few seconds," he broadcast through their ear-pieces. "This should occur when the digital clock on the monitor reaches seven."

Fifteen. Fourteen . . .

"This will be one of the marshals taking out the terrorist ringer. The instant you hear gunfire you're go for a full assault. I repeat, breach immediately at the sound of gunfire."

Eleven. Ten. Nine . . .

Eight!

Jay Coleman jackknifed his head below his knees.

Seven!

Ronaldo Chavez sent three bullets in quick succession screaming through what would have been Coleman's neck and into the brain of the man seated in front of him. The terrorist ringer lurched from the impact and was dead before his mind even registered the sound of the shots.

Hakim was moments away from putting a bullet into Johansson's head, as promised, but he and his six comrades jumped at the sound of gunfire. Before they could react, the twelve-man commando team flowed onto the stage behind them with the military equivalent of balletic grace, their weapons set on semi-automatic.

The seven terrorists never had a chance, mowed down like weeds before they could even think of triggering a detonation, each torn into dozens of pieces by the hellish firepower ripping into them.

Johansson screamed and rolled to the stage, her scream drowned out by the sound of automatic weapons. Her arm was grazed during the assault and she was bleeding, but considering the situation the strike had been absolutely surgical. The team had performed brilliantly, taking out Hakim and his comrades with no loss of innocent life, including Johansson's.

One of the commandos drew the sobbing, shrieking actress into his arms to comfort her as the audience erupted into pandemonium. Some launched themselves from their seats. Many others shut their eyes tight, sure that the ringers in the audience would trigger an explosion that would rip them to their constituent atoms, and braced for oblivion.

Nick Hall stumbled to the main podium while his team checked to be absolutely certain each terrorist was dead.

"Sit down!" screamed Hall at the top of his lungs into the microphone, words that rocked the theater as they thundered from the speakers. His exhausted, besieged brain was screaming for relief, but he needed to hold on for a few seconds longer.

"It's over. You're all safe. No ringers. No explosion coming. Remain calm and we'll clear the theater row by row."

Everyone looked at each other in dismay. Could it be? Most had resigned themselves to a certain death. Who was this man? This savior?

The hubbub began to subside as the crowd retook their seats with stunned looks, still not fully able to believe this was real.

"I repeat," said Hall, "this is over. Teams of police and other authorities are on their way to help ensure an orderly exit. Remain calm, and we'll have the doors unlocked momentarily."

And with that, Nick Hall slid to the floor, and his mind finally succumbed to a merciful unconsciousness.

PART 2
Politics

"Politics, noun: [Poly 'many' + tics 'blood-sucking parasites']"

—Larry Hardiman

"We hang the petty thieves. The master thieves we appoint to public office."

—Aesop

"Any American who is prepared to run for president should automatically, by definition, be disqualified from ever doing so."

—Gore Vidal

13

The Tina Berger Solution
Host: Tina Berger
CNN

TINA BERGER: Tonight, we continue with our marathon coverage of the barbaric terrorist act that took the lives of ninety-seven innocent people four days ago, including an entire orchestra and the beloved star of stage and screen, Hugh Jackman. A terror act that we all know could have been far, far worse.

We're back with our guests, Captain Tom Doubleday, a SEAL instructor for the past decade at the Naval Special Warfare Center in Coronado, California, and General Cole Poole, past director of the Defense Intelligence Agency.

Now, we've all seen the footage of the successful counter-terrorist attack at the Cosmopolitan Theater, most of us many times, but let's take another look before we speak with our guests.

[Pauses for video of the attack, shown from several camera angles, concluding when a masked, unarmed man at the microphone tells everyone to remain calm, collapses to the stage, and several minutes later is carried backstage by several commandos]

For this segment, I'd like to ask my esteemed guests to shed some light on the mystery man at the microphone during the attack. Here is what we know. We know that twelve heroic soldiers, who have been dubbed the Oscar Angels, saved thousands of lives. And we'll address a rumor momentarily that their actions probably saved hundreds of thousands more. We know that a thirteenth man, the man who addressed the audience before collapsing, was also involved, but was not armed and was dressed in casual clothing. And we know that the military will not make any of these men available for the media, or release their identities.

(frowning and shaking her head) Which is very much a shame, because a grateful nation and world are eager to shower them with the accolades and honors they deserve.

(turning to her guests) So what about this Mystery Microphone Man? Let's call him Triple M for short. Do we know anything? Can we guess anything? His ski mask not only hid his face, but distorted his voice, so we have very little to go on.

But who was Triple M? What role did he play? Why did he collapse?

Let me first turn to you, Captain Doubleday. What is your best guess?

CAPTAIN DOUBLEDAY: (shrugging uncomfortably) I only wish I *had* a guess. But I have to admit, I don't have the slightest idea. The twelve men who actually carried out the op, these brave heroes, were obviously special forces. Four of them were Navy SEALs, and eight of them Green Berets.

TINA BERGER: How do you know that?

CAPTAIN DOUBLEDAY: From the way they operated during the assault. How they moved. How they held their weapons. Their firing patterns. It's subtle, but if you know what to look for, each group of special forces has minor variations in their training. Signature styles.

TINA BERGER: And Triple M?

CAPTAIN DOUBLEDAY: That's just it. He had no business being any part of this. It's the strangest thing I've ever seen. He had no weapons and no gear. He held back while the others secured the theater.

TINA BERGER: General?

GENERAL POOLE: I agree with the captain. His presence makes no sense.

TINA BERGER: (still facing the general) Okay, shifting gears for a moment, do you have any insight into how the terrorist plant in the audience, who was put down when the attack began, was identified?

GENERAL POOLE: No. Those who know aren't saying. What I can tell you is that I'm all but certain the man who put him down was a marshal, seeded into the audience as a precaution. He probably had a partner or two elsewhere in the crowd, and all would be armed.

But how the terrorist sleeper was identified is just one of the many mysteries of this operation. The terrorist leader, Abdul Hakim, had said there were *three* sleepers in the crowd. So how were our forces so certain there was really only one? How did we learn of the warehouse and tunnel used by the terrorists? It's clear we weren't aware of these when the attack began. And even more exceptional, how did we manage to use these tunnels when the terrorists had booby trapped the warehouse and had left a rear-guard? How did we learn the new door codes the terrorists had programmed in?

I honestly have no idea. But I can say without hesitation that it was the most brilliant piece of intelligence work I've ever witnessed. The operation was flawless.

TINA BERGER: There are also reports that the man seated directly behind the fallen terrorist in the audience, Jay Coleman, was texted instructions to duck just before the shots were fired.

GENERAL POOLE: Yes. Remarkable stuff. Hats off to the people behind the scenes. I was inside the belly of the beast for a long time, and thought I knew all of our capabilities. But they must have grown since I left. Thank God, because this was beyond impressive. Miraculous wouldn't be too strong a word.

TINA BERGER: (nodding sagely) Miraculous indeed.

(turning to the captain) So back to Triple M, our Mystery Microphone Man. Could he have also been a special forces operative? One who just failed to suit up for some reason?

CAPTAIN DOUBLEDAY: (shaking his head in disgust) "Not a chance. He was a civilian. As green as it gets. He held back and stumbled around, a cross between a drunk and a deer in headlights. In the footage, he's staring off into space like a zombie. In the middle of a *gun battle*. Then, when it's all over, after the real heroes do the real work, he stumbles to the microphone to tell the world the attack was a success. Like a classic bureaucrat. Let others do the work and then step forward to take the credit.

TINA BERGER: I understand what you mean, Captain Doubleday, but since his identity remains hidden, he really hasn't *gotten* any credit. But regardless, he must have had *some* purpose.

CAPTAIN DOUBLEDAY: None that I could tell. Maybe he was a psychiatrist, an expert on mob psychology and crowd control. In case things got unruly, with everyone trampling each other to get to the exits. But he didn't say anything that would indicate to me he had any special knowledge. And even if he was a civilian expert, having someone like him along on an op like this is *unprecedented*.

TINA BERGER: How so?

CAPTAIN DOUBLEDAY: Lives were on the line. Those of the assault team and many thousands of others. These are the best-trained men in the world. Tough, experienced. They're well aware that the tiniest of mistakes can mean the difference between success and failure. You would never carry extra baggage in this situation. Especially not a civilian as obviously green as this man was.

TINA BERGER: Even if you were ordered to?

CAPTAIN DOUBLEDAY: Not unless the order came with an overwhelmingly compelling rationale. *Especially* in a situation like this, where you have to take out all hostiles immediately, before one of them can trigger explosives. The timing has to be perfect, and there is no room for error. You *have* to control the kill zone.

You don't take a green civilian along on an op this critical, not having any idea how he'll react under this kind of pressure. Best case, he's a distraction. Worst case, he freezes up, or panics, or makes a wrong move, or sneezes at the wrong time, and the op is blown. The stakes were much too high to let this happen. If a member of the team isn't helping you, he's *hurting* you.

TINA BERGER: So where does that put us?

CAPTAIN DOUBLEDAY: Nowhere. The only way this could happen, in my mind, is if this guy served an absolutely vital function. But we've seen the footage. He did nothing. Unless the other twelve men were all mute and couldn't work the microphone, he served no purpose at all. Believe me, Tina, if this seems strange to you, it seems even stranger to someone like me, who has spent years training men like these.

TINA BERGER: Why do you think he collapsed afterward? He didn't appear to have any injuries.

CAPTAIN DOUBLEDAY: I think he passed out from shock and terror. The attack was deadly and the aftermath wasn't pretty. Which underscores my point that he had never seen action before. He clearly had gone wobbly from the beginning.

TINA BERGER: (nodding and turning to the general) General Poole, I've heard rumors that the actions of this team saved more lives than are apparent. Can you comment on this?

GENERAL POOLE: I have no official word, so it's just speculation. But I'm quite confident in my analysis. The terrorists must have been using a new type of explosive. One that was undetectable. This was the *Academy Awards*. Homeland Security is well aware this is a very attractive soft target, even with the anti-terror safeguards in the theater. So the Cosmopolitan would have been completely scanned for explosives, using electronic bloodhound devices, at least a dozen times. Including just before the doors opened.

By capturing the theater intact, we gained access to this new explosive and can develop ways to detect it. If the theater had blown, so that we couldn't get a sample, Islamic Jihad would have continued to use it for some time to come, with devastating results. Hundreds of thousands of additional lives could well have been lost in a very short time.

TINA BERGER: (shaking her head in awe and appreciation) Even more reason to thank these brave heroes. (pausing) General, tell us more about how these electronic bloodhounds work, and how . . .

14

Alex Altschuler removed the large sunglasses he had worn to avoid being recognized and took Heather Zambrana, now his fiancée, into his arms. She gazed around the lavish master suite with her mouth hanging open, still not used to the effortless opulence that Altschuler's billions made possible. The four-deck yacht, now named *Eos*, had been purchased just days earlier, through a broker who had no idea that Altschuler would be the owner, and this was the first they had seen of it.

He could have easily afforded a yacht even more magnificent than the *Eos*, but at six million dollars it was still part of a crowd of such yachts rather than one that would truly stand alone—and thus draw attention. The yacht slept up to ten guests in five staterooms, and had a main saloon—which was the equivalent of a living room—bar, formal and informal dining areas, sundecks, and more.

But even though it was fun to see Heather dazzled by the fairytale life they could now lead, what had drawn him to her in the first place—when he was second-in-command of Theia Labs and she was a scientist there—was that wealth was very low on her list of priorities. She was on the geeky side, like him, and while attractive, was not an intimidating perfect specimen, which was also truer than he would have liked in his own case.

Heather wouldn't know how to put on airs or be materialistic if she had to. She loved science fiction and superheroes and quantum physics, and preferred comfortable clothes to designer gowns, and a total lack of adornment to using parts of her body to display the most glorious of diamonds. She would be far happier in a leaky rowboat talking passionately about the possible plot of the next Avengers movie than drinking the finest wine on the finest yacht with a group of pretentious assholes.

Still, drinking the finest wine on the finest yacht, *while* talking passionately about the next Avengers movie, wasn't a bad choice, either.

A week had gone by since the attack on the Cosmopolitan, and a long-overdue meeting of their secret six-member cabal, which had self-assembled to oversee the implant technology and ESP, had been called. Four of the six members would attend the meeting on this very yacht, with the other two videoconferencing in.

"What time is it, Alex?" asked Heather.

Altschuler's implants showed him the time without him being aware he had asked, and he told her. An off-the-charts genius, he was even more facile at using his implants than was Hall.

Nick Hall and Alex Altschuler were the only two people alive who could access the Internet with their thoughts. Although in Altschuler's case, only the six members of their group would ever know it.

When Kelvin Gray had used Nick Hall as an unwilling experimental subject, he had plowed through Hall's brain like a snowed-in driveway, looking for optimal placement of what had later come to be known as BrainWeb implants. Not only were the four implants tried in any number of locations, but different electrical levels had been used along the way as well.

Later, when Hall had escaped and had found Altschuler, an important question had been raised. Was Hall's ESP ability a one-in-a-million fluke? Was this the cumulative result of the merry path the implants had taken through his brain, unlikely to ever be replicated?

Or was his ESP entirely due to the implants' final locations and settings? Did thought-controlled Internet access bring ESP along for the ride, as an unwanted side effect? Were these two inseparable sides of the same coin?

Before the BrainWeb breakthrough was announced to the world, they had to know for sure. And Altschuler volunteered to be the test subject needed to learn the answer.

But implantation of the technology had not been authorized by the FDA. Hall's implants could be announced, because his were the doings of a psychopathic mass-murderer, so he could hardly be held accountable. But otherwise, it didn't matter if a subject volunteered, or even if the experimenter conducted self-implantation, this was against the law.

Undeterred, Altschuler had gone forward anyway, and Heather had been recruited to oversee the mostly-automated surgery. It had gone flawlessly. Their success demonstrated that thought-controlled Web access was repeatable. Perhaps even more importantly, they had verified that ESP *was not* a side effect of the placement.

But if word of Altschuler's illegal experimentation on himself leaked out, especially when the public was still horrified by Gray's activities, it was unclear just how great the ramifications would be. And since he had become the CEO of the highest-profile company, maybe in history, just after the surgery, this was something he preferred not to risk.

"So Nick and Megan aren't due here for almost an hour," Heather pointed out after learning the time. She gestured to the elegant bed, which would have looked right at home in a Medieval palace. "So what do you say, Alex?" she added salaciously, raising an eyebrow. "Do you want to christen this boat properly?"

Altschuler laughed. He couldn't believe this was now his life. Worldwide fame, unimaginable wealth, and a woman who was a perfect fit for him: a friend, lover, and brilliant colleague.

Since this was a boat no one knew he owned, and its purpose was to serve as a secret meeting location, and possibly a temporary off-the-radar home for Nick Hall and Megan Emerson, spraying a bottle of champagne across the bow and having a fancy christening ceremony wasn't possible. But even if it were, this wasn't his style anyway.

Making love to Heather Zambrana, on the other hand . . . Now *that* was the proper way to christen a boat. The proper way to christen *anything* for that matter. A couch. A table. A Jacuzzi. The floor. He couldn't help but laugh out loud at his own unspoken joke.

The *Eos* was still moored at the Huntington Beach Marina. And while it swayed in the current, its motion was so subtle one had to concentrate to feel it. "I don't know," said Altschuler wryly, "what if our passion is so great, we create a tidal wave out here? We could do a lot of damage."

Heather leaned in and kissed him. "I'm willing to take that chance," she said with a broad grin.

"Outstanding," said Altschuler. But just as he was about to jump into the bed, his face scrunched up unhappily. It wasn't as if Nick would wand the master suite with an ultraviolet light. But still . . .

"We should probably use one of the other rooms," he said, gesturing to the door. "If Nick and Megan really do need to lie low here for a while, we don't want to give them a room that's been . . . you know . . . *christened*."

Heather laughed and led him to one of the staterooms on the periphery of the boat, where they wasted no time tearing each other's clothes off and making love with wild abandon. When they finished, a warm glow engulfed them both, as changes to their brain chemistries worked magic on their psyches, rewarding them for doing their part to perpetuate the species, their limbic systems unaware that birth control had been invented.

As they dressed, a disquieting thought came to Altschuler. What if Nick Hall was less than six miles away? He imagined Hall reaching out to read his recent memory of Heather's writhing body and the heated, carnal thoughts he had had while thrusting into her. Nasty, brutish, unseemly thoughts generated by the most primitive regions of his brain.

He had come to love Nick Hall like a brother, and Hall deserved to be celebrated among the greatest heroes of all time for the brave and brilliant actions he had taken to thwart the attack on the Cosmopolitan. But even so, Altschuler was not relishing his upcoming proximity to the man. He hated himself for feeling this way, but he knew it was a sentiment shared by Heather as well.

And who could blame them? Knowing that every thought or memory they ever had was exposed was extremely unsettling. And it was also uncomfortable to know that any negative thoughts they might have about Nick—perhaps he had a bad haircut or they thought he said something stupid—could also be intercepted.

Hall had promised to do everything in his power to ignore residual thoughts he was picking up while with them. And to never dig through their memories. He understood how they were feeling.

Hall had even joked that he would surely be punished for breaking this oath, since if he ever intercepted a memory of Altschuler naked it would haunt him, and make him sick to his stomach, for the rest of his life. And this would be even *worse*, Hall had said, shuddering for effect, if he read a naked-Alex image from *Heather's* mind.

Altschuler trusted Hall would keep his word, but he also understood why the other two members of their six-person clan, Justin Girdler and Mike Campbell, only attended meetings with Hall via videoconference. They had access to eyes-only information that no one, not even Hall, was authorized to know, and they had a far rougher, ethically-challenged past than he and Heather.

The military members of their cabal never came out and said they were avoiding Hall like the plague, but it was obvious.

Hall's life had become tragic in Altschuler's view. He had become King Midas, with an ability that was truly astonishing and priceless, but one that kept him totally isolated from the rest of the human race.

Thank God for Megan Emerson. A woman Hall loved but could not read. The ultimate blessing for a man cursed in his way.

Nick, I trust you're still on your way, thought Altschuler at his implants, and these words were sent out as a text directly to Hall. *Any trouble?*

Whenever he and Hall chose to do so, their thoughts could be shuttled between implants and converted to words "heard" by the other's auditory cortex, and the voices would match their real voices. In practice it was very much like the telepathy Hall shared with Megan, except with unlimited range.

Altschuler had designed the software to make this seamless, but they never began in this mode, since it was so invasive. Their initial messages were the equivalent of sending a text to a friend, asking if now was a good time to call.

"*No trouble,*" came the response, this time one that Altschuler heard inside his head. "*Believe me, you'd be the first to know. I'm not reading any tails. We'll be there in about fifteen minutes.*"

"*Great,*" replied Altschuler. "*See you soon.*"

15

The *News of Note Hour*
Host: Blake Shaw
ABC Sunday

BLAKE: Aside from a bushman or two in Kalahari, there is probably no one left on earth who is not aware of Theia Labs' new implant technology, recently dubbed *BrainWeb*. Although not yet approved, once the BrainWeb implants are installed, they promise to deliver perfect thought-controlled Web-surfing capabilities to users.

This technology burst onto the scene from out of nowhere, twenty years earlier than the expectations of the most optimistic experts. And we all know the tragic story of the passengers and crew of the *Scripps Explorer*, who unwillingly gave their lives to gain this progress. And of Nick Hall's emergence, however briefly, onto the world stage, before he was also killed.

Ever since these events, the prospect of accessing the Web with the mind has stirred passions everywhere. Both positive *and* negative.

The Transhumanism movement, whose goal is the fundamental enhancement and transformation of humanity through the use of technology, has seen explosive growth around the world. This group, and others like it, see BrainWeb as a first step toward a better brand of humanity. A key leap forward that will fairly rapidly lead to human transcendence.

Yet others see it as an unmitigated disaster. *Worsening* the human condition rather than improving upon it.

So as Congress works through approval of a clinical trial design, and appropriate safeguards, for BrainWeb, we've decided to revisit both sides of this argument.

To help us with this, let me give a warm, *News of Note* welcome to Jacob Resnick, Director of the Institute of Global Transhumanism, and author of *Self-Directed Evolution: Why Transcendence is Just Around the Corner*. And Sandra Finkel, a fellow at Impact Analysis, a Seattle-based think-tank, and author of *Just Because We Can, Doesn't Mean We Should*.

JACOB: Thank you Blake.

SANDRA: Yes, thanks. It's a pleasure to be here.

BLAKE: Let me start with you, Sandra. These implants offer the perfect cure for blindness. For deafness. Should we turn our back on restoring sight and hearing to millions, just because we're afraid of the technology?

SANDRA: (emphatically) Absolutely not! And no one is suggesting that we do. But the restoration of sight and hearing aren't part of the topic under discussion. This is truly a miracle, which doesn't require software that can match thoughts to words, and doesn't require Web access. I couldn't be more supportive of it.

BLAKE: Thanks for this clarification. So let's move on to the main course, then. BrainWeb promises to expand our capabilities manyfold. To give us instant access to nearly unlimited information and entertainment. And everything we hear and see could potentially be streamed to the Cloud for later access. I'm sure you'd agree that human recall is poor and subject to error.

SANDRA: Absolutely. And the advantages of having an external photographic memory are obvious. When my husband and I have different recollections, it would be great to be able to check the tape, as it were, to prove to him that I'm always right (smiling wryly).

But the disadvantages are far greater. People will lose all faith in the accuracy of the memories they've accumulated *before* BrainWeb came along. They will quickly realize just how unreliable their memory really is. And baggage can hang around forever. Ill-advised words can be dredged up again and again, never forgotten. Every mistake potentially recorded for eternity.

Most important, and most often discussed, is the complete lack of privacy. This has always been a major issue in the Internet and digital camera age, but BrainWeb amplifies this problem a thousand-fold.

BLAKE: Yes, the privacy argument has been made repeatedly, and forcefully. BrainWeb technology essentially turns human eyes and ears into digital cameras, always on. Such that no social interaction can ever again be guaranteed to be private. Anything anyone says or does in view of anyone else can be secretly recorded, and can come back to haunt them. Every sexual encounter could possibly be filmed, without knowledge or consent, and even posted instantly for the world to see.

(nodding thoughtfully) Jacob, how would you respond to these concerns?

JACOB: As with any new technology, the transition will be disruptive. There is no perfect world. Some people will get hurt. It's called *creative destruction*, and it is unfortunate, but necessary. To quote the great English philosopher, Alfred North Whitehead: "It is the business of the future to be dangerous. The major advances in civilization are processes that all but wreck the societies in which they occur."

BLAKE: You're saying this will wreck society?

JACOB: Not at all. Just making the point that no major advance occurs without hiccups. But human ingenuity will find answers. Congress is trying to do this right now, well aware of the issues. Ideas are being considered, such as making sure each implant is tagged with its own unalterable address, so that anything someone deposits to the Web can be traced, if need be, unambiguously to the person who did the uploading.

And Artificial Intelligence programs can be constructed to identify when content is being uploaded from a person's auditory or visual data stream, when the danger of violation of privacy is greatest. In these cases, the AI can block any content that contains nudity, for example, sent to public sites. In addition, stern penalties can be written into the legal code for anyone who finds ways to skirt these safeguards and uses BrainWeb to violate privacy.

Cheating is another issue. But test centers in schools and elsewhere can be equipped with an Internet dampening technology, ensuring that students aren't giving each other answers through cyberspace.

SANDRA: (shaking her head) And what happens in schools when tests *aren't* being taken? What happens in life? When the Internet isn't dampened? Mr. Resnick's solutions sound good at first blush, but trust me, Blake, I could fill up a dozen hours of your program refuting these fixes, and pointing out numerous issues that they wouldn't resolve. I encourage viewers to spend just a little time thinking about the absolute death of privacy and what a devastating impact this will have on society.

But let me move on, since time is limited. Because privacy isn't even my biggest concern.

BLAKE: What is, then? Addiction?

SANDRA: Yes. But first let me come at this from the perspective of *distraction.* Blake, I know you have teenagers at home. So do I. Teens who are always plugged in, to one digital distraction or another. When was the last time you were confident that your kids actually *listened* to something you said? Heard it, focused on it, digested it?

BLAKE: (laughing) You have a point, there. If a kid has a phone in his or her hand, you have no chance to communicate. They're texting, tweeting, FaceBooking, taking selfies, playing games, you name it. The phone is the world's greatest distraction machine, I'll give you that. And I've never met a parent who wouldn't agree.

SANDRA: (smiling) If my daughter were on *fire,* I couldn't get her to listen to me explain how to put herself out. Not unless I confiscated her phone. And how many times have you thought one of your kids heard something important that you told them, only to find out later, after negative consequences ensued, that they really didn't?

BLAKE: Too many to count.

JACOB: I have kids myself, and I admit this is a problem. But despite this, the world is still spinning on its axis.

SANDRA: Yes, but BrainWeb makes this problem inconceivably worse. Now teens will be able to watch movies or YouTube in their heads. They can be reading, playing games, Googling,

Facebooking—*whatever*—without anyone knowing it. They can be staring straight at you while you speak to them, and you have no way to know if they're listening or not. Unless you check with them every ten seconds. And even if they nod yes, they probably aren't.

And this applies to *everyone*, not just teens. Even the most addicted Internet junkies among us can manage to keep their phones in their pockets when interacting socially with others. But now, with BrainWeb, they won't be able to resist attempting to multitask. Tuning out the world, thinking no one will be the wiser. Tuning out their bosses. Their spouses.

JACOB: (smiling) Which actually argues against your last concern. If people are too distracted to pay attention to others, they're too distracted to steal their privacy by streaming to the Web.

SANDRA: Well, yeah. So either your privacy is in peril, or you're being ignored. But regardless, BrainWeb will ensure we complete what we've already begun: creating an entire generation of self-absorbed zombies.

So let me turn to addiction, which is what will drive this self-obsession, this distraction. Internet Addiction is now a recognized malady and is being treated in ever-growing numbers.

The Boston Consulting Group surveyed consumers in nineteen countries in 2014, trying to gauge the importance of various habits, various addictions. They asked what people would be willing to forgo to keep their Internet access. The majority of respondents would be willing to sacrifice coffee, chocolate, and fast-food before they would sacrifice the Internet. Fair enough. But a significant percentage would give up their *cars*. Many would give up showering—for a *year*.

Most stunning of all, twenty-one percent of Americans, and *fifty-six percent* of Japanese, would abstain from sex. Sex! For a year. Just to stay online.

BLAKE: (laughing) Well, the ones giving up showering for a year probably aren't getting too much sex anyway. At least not from anyone with a sense of *smell*.

SANDRA: (showing signs of annoyance at having the momentum of her argument interrupted by a joke, but faking a smile) But think about what this survey shows, Blake. People are willing to give up *sex*. The most potent evolutionary imperative of all, a drive imbedded deep in our DNA.

In one experiment, two hundred students at the University of Maryland were asked to give up the Internet for twenty-four hours and then blog about their experiences. Their blogs detailed strong and swift feelings of anxiety. Depression. Withdrawal symptoms. In my view, the blogs of these students, reeling from disconnecting for a single day, should be required reading.

And not only is the Internet wildly addictive, it facilitates *other* addictions. Gambling. Video games. Virtual life. Porn. With BrainWeb, porn addicts can watch these movies in their mind's eye at any time—at work, while driving, in the grocery store—without anyone having a clue.

BLAKE: (smiling) Well, when it comes to *men*, at least, there might be a telltale, um . . . sign, shall we say, that they're watching porn. But I take your point.

(turning to Jacob) So how would you respond to the addiction argument?

JACOB: Addiction will be a problem. No doubt about it. But people identified hosts of problems with every major technology ever developed, and we've never let this stop progress.

I'll raise another issue that I'm sure Ms. Finkel is about to bring up: driving. I'll be the first to admit the danger of people getting behind the wheel with this technology in their heads. For many drivers, the temptation to have texts or e-mails displayed in one corner of their visual fields, or to thought-surf the web, will be too great to resist.

But even this can be overcome with the proper planning. Congress is considering mandating that cars be equipped with Internet dampening fields. Fields that would automatically activate around the driver's seat when the car senses a driver with BrainWeb implants. And consider this: the first self-driving cars are about to be approved for use. Within a decade, no one will drive their own cars anyway.

BLAKE: So you acknowledge there are major issues. But you believe that for every problem, we'll eventually find a solution.

JACOB: Exactly. People innovate. And adapt. They have been since the dawn of civilization.

A few weeks ago, I visited my brother in Denver. My four-year-old niece has had a kids touchscreen tablet since she was old enough to drool. While I was there, I handed her a kids magazine. She had no idea what to do with it. She kept swiping the cover with her finger to try to scroll through additional pages. There was a part she wanted to see bigger, so she tried to touch it and splay out her fingertips to enlarge it.

Now I could be horrified at her ignorance of magazines. I could mourn the demise of print media. But instead, I choose to celebrate how effortlessly she's adapted to the far superior digital media. People find solutions. People adapt. It's what we do.

In 1880, the US asked a group of the most accomplished experts in the world to analyze New York City, one of the fastest-growing and important cities in North America. They wanted to know what the city might be like in a hundred years.

The experts extrapolated the likely growth during this period, and the expected consequences. They then confidently proclaimed that if population growth wasn't halted, by 1980, New York City would require so many horses to stay viable, that every inch of it would be knee-deep in *manure. Knee-deep!* In *horse manure!* The result was irrefutable.

The moral here is obvious. As Yogi Berra once said: "It's tough to make predictions. Especially about the future." The experts in 1880 couldn't imagine a technology, a solution, that would completely obsolete the horse.

And that's where we are today. We can see the problems with BrainWeb easily. But there are solutions. It's just that these solutions aren't always as obvious as the problems. And paradigm-shifting technologies that are certain to come along, like the automobile, are all but impossible to predict.

BLAKE: A compelling argument. (making a face) And given that our show is based in New York, I, for one, am quite happy that the manure here is, um . . . slightly less than knee-deep.

SANDRA: (smiling) I understand Mr. Resnick's point. But just because you can find examples of problems that resolved, that doesn't mean this will always happen.

BLAKE: Also a compelling argument.

SANDRA: And Mr. Resnick's story about his niece reminds me of another point. We're adapting to the Internet, but the changes this adaptation is causing within us can be alarming. The Internet is making us superficial. Shallow. It's reducing our mental acuity, not strengthening it. Our attention spans are shrinking. We're stimulus junkies. BrainWeb will accelerate this as well.

BLAKE: Do you have any evidence for this?

SANDRA: Yes. A number of studies have shown that Internet use actually *rewires* our brains. Making addiction and shallow thought, not just a problem with our software, so to speak, but with our hardware as well.

Americans are now averaging well over twenty hours a week online, and this figure is growing every year. But the reading of books has been declining just as rapidly. We get information and entertainment in staccato bursts. Sound bites. We don't have the patience to focus and think deeply on a subject. Students struggle. The Internet generation is less and less capable of deep thought every year.

I could cite endless studies, but let me finish by quoting Nicholas Carr. His book, *The Shallows*: *What the Internet is Doing to Our Brains,* came out back in 2011.

(glancing down at her notes) "The Net delivers precisely the kind of sensory and cognitive stimuli—repetitive, intensive, interactive, addictive—that have been shown to result in strong and rapid alterations in brain circuits and functions. The Net may well be the single most powerful mind-altering technology that has ever come into general use."

(pausing and returning her stare to the camera) If it's powerfully mind-altering *now*, how mind-altering is it going to be when we actually put it *in our minds?*

And yes, with BrainWeb we could call up any information we needed, without ever having to commit anything to memory. But when we struggle to force information into our memories, this changes the structures of our brains in a *good* way, helping us to think deeply and to form creative connections. The implants are a nuclear-powered crutch. One that will neuter our intellect. To give an analogy, a technology that would do away with the need for us to use our own muscle power would definitely save effort, but it would just as definitely cause our muscles to waste away.

BLAKE: (turning toward Jacob). I know you'd like to respond to these points, Jacob, but I'm afraid we're running out of time. So could you give us a parting thought?

JACOB: (nodding) Ms. Finkel is very skilled at inciting fear. Fear of change. Fear of the unknown.

But consider this: she's painted a terrifying picture of the Internet as it exists today. I'd be running for the hills if I didn't have decades of personal experience with it. Think about how the Web has transformed every aspect of our society. And almost exclusively for the better.

I won't argue that there won't be any negative side effects of BrainWeb, or any growing pains. I won't even argue that we'll all be the same people we were before installing implants. We won't be. What we are now may even become obsolete. But, on the whole, we'll be *better. More* capable. *More* versatile. *Superior.*

SANDRA: The Net is amazing, Blake. No question about it. It's hard to imagine what we did without it. So the danger has sneaked up on us. We're lobsters loving the Jacuzzi we're in as the heat is gradually turned up. But let's throttle back and enjoy the Jacuzzi at its current setting. Let's not turn it up to boiling in one burst, learning how fatal this is only after it's too late.

And we haven't even touched on the possibility of foul play. Of hackers finding a way in. Infecting us with computer viruses. With all types of malware. And while Congress is aware of this issue, and is requiring triple redundancy firewalls and other safeguards, do we really think the bad actors of the world won't find a way in?

I'm not against technology. It's been a powerful, positive force, on the whole. But let's not take a step too far. Let's keep the Internet outside of our brains.

BLAKE: (nodding) Thanks very much to my two guests, Jacob Resnick and Sandra Finkel, for a fascinating and lively debate.

16

A message from Hall sounded in Altschuler's mind. *"We're approaching the marina now."*

Altschuler nodded to himself. The BrainWeb technology could give a powerful boost to the capabilities of the average man. But the current CEO of Theia Labs was not even close to average. As a world-class software and Internet expert, the capabilities it conferred to him were impossible for the average man to even comprehend.

He sometimes felt like a god, his senses and his reach almost limitless.

The Web consisted of billions of interconnected computers and other devices, and most of these now had cameras and other sensors attached, a living, growing organism that had fully engulfed the globe. And there were very few cells of this organism, very few of its senses, that Altschuler couldn't reach and manipulate from the command center in his skull.

Before BrainWeb he was already too fast on a computer to follow. But now that he could operate at the speed of thought, hacking any but the most secure systems had become child's play. He took control of the marina's security cameras effortlessly and monitored all feeds while his friends approached the yacht.

"No sign that you're being followed," he told his friend.

Given Hall's mind-reading capabilities, he would know this himself, but there was always the remote chance that someone following was like Megan and immune to his ability. Why take any chances?

Hall and Megan joined them on the *Eos* and there were warm embraces all around. Altschuler untied his new ship from the dock and activated the autopilot feature to take them a few miles out to sea for added privacy.

Minutes later they were all seated in the saloon, facing the 3-D virtual presences of Justin Girdler and Mike Campbell, each joining from different locations.

"I'd like to start off," said Girdler, when greetings and preliminaries were out of the way, "by catching Alex and Heather up on some recent events. Sorry we couldn't do it sooner, but it's been hectic, to say the least." He gestured toward Altschuler. "And I know you're doing the equivalent of two or three jobs right now," he added. "So your schedule has been equally hectic."

Altschuler smiled. "Plenty of time to sleep when you're dead, I guess," he said with a shrug. "But before we get started, congratulations again to you and Nick for saving the day at the Oscars. Really amazing stuff." He turned to Hall sitting beside him. "I only wish you could get the recognition you deserve."

"Recognition? Are you kidding?" Hall shook his head and a broad smile came over his face. "I'd settle for a *neutral* reaction."

"Nick is pretty much getting vilified," said Megan.

"That really sucks, Nick," said Heather. "Because you were *amazing*." She smiled. "I guess now you know how Spider-Man feels. Misunderstood."

"Yeah," he said good-naturedly. "But I can't blame the press. I've seen the footage. I did look like a useless, drugged-out accountant staring zombie-like into space while all hell was breaking loose around me." He shrugged and looked amused. "No one knows who I am anyway, so I've actually been getting a kick out of the coverage."

"You're really taking this well," said Heather.

"You know who *isn't* taking this well?" said Girdler. "The men Nick led on the raid. They know he was the only reason they succeeded, and that he did an extraordinary job of orchestrating the attack while under extreme duress. It's not sitting well with them that he's been the butt of late-night monologues. It's been all I can do to stop them from anonymously calling the talk shows to defend Nick."

"If they could even get through with all the celebrities vying for attention," said Campbell. "I get hundreds of channels, and I think half the programming lately on every one of them is a celebrity recounting his or her thoughts and emotions during the siege. They're really milking this for all it's worth."

"True," said Megan. "But I give them a pass on this one. I can't even imagine how traumatic it must have been to have been there. So I think they've earned their publicity."

Campbell was about to reply when Girdler jumped in. "We should probably get to it," he said. "Alex, given recent events, are you still scheduled to testify before Congress in a week or two?"

Altschuler nodded. As CEO of Theia Labs, he was intimately involved in all deliberations regarding the use and regulations of the new technology. "I should also add that progress at our pilot manufacturing plant has gone better than expected. The first batch of ten thousand sets of implants should be ready in the next two to three weeks."

"Why ten thousand?" asked Megan.

"That's the size of the clinical trial we'll be conducting. We wanted a relatively large sample size to really get a handle on BrainWeb's safety profile."

Megan whistled. "Wow," she said. "I had no idea you were so close to finishing that many sets." Her forehead wrinkled in confusion. "When did you build this manufacturing facility? And given how fascinated the world is by anything having to do with Theia Labs, how is it that I never heard anything about this?"

"Because we've kept it top secret," said Girdler. "I lobbied to be put in charge of security. The technology is too controversial, and the impact of someone tampering with the implants too great, to advertise the factory. Its existence and location are as secret as what's going on in Area 51, and at least as well protected. Employees either don't know what is really being made there, or have signed such iron-clad confidentiality agreements they're afraid to even tell themselves. When the implants are moved across the country, they'll be escorted like they were weapons-grade uranium."

Megan nodded, impressed. "Good to know," she said simply.

"Congratulations on the progress, Alex," said the general. "But let me get started catching you up. It's been a wild week. I know Nick's filled you in, but I wanted to give you my perspective."

"I can use as many perspectives as I can get," said Altschuler. "Nick told me that you and he met with the president's National Security Council, and then senior politicians in the president's camp, four days after the attack."

"Well, the general was there in person," said Megan with the hint of a smile. "They had Nick video in. They wouldn't let him within a hundred miles of that city if their lives depended on it."

"Nick told me," said Altschuler. "But he said he didn't need to read their minds to know it was a mixed bag. They were falling all over themselves with gratitude, but were less than entirely supportive."

Girdler frowned. "That may be an understatement."

"So how much trouble are you in, General?" asked Heather.

"That remains to be seen. But I'd say it ranges from a whole lot to a shitload. I've continued to insist that Nick and I were a gang of two. Period. Mike is under suspicion, but no power on Earth will get me to admit that he knew anything about this, and we've been very careful covering our tracks."

"I still don't feel good about leaving you hanging out to dry on this one," said Campbell.

"Why take anyone else down?" said Girdler. "This group still has important things to accomplish. Not that I'd throw you under the bus under any circumstances."

"Will you be court-martialed?" asked Heather.

"It's not clear."

"They realize you and Nick pretty much saved the world, right?" said Heather indignantly. "More or less. And you both chose to out yourselves to do it. You'd think they'd be giving you medals."

Girdler smiled wistfully. "They do appreciate the saving-the-world thing. They know that by coming clean about Nick, I enabled them to dodge the ultimate nightmare. Still, this doesn't entirely erase the fact that I perpetrated a fraud on the military and government. Worse, they saw the ah . . . *asset* I was keeping from them, the great Nick Hall, in action. That's what really has them pissed off."

"So if you were hoarding something worthless, it would be a slap on the wrist," said Megan. "But since they found out you were hoarding something of incredible value, you're screwed."

"Pretty much. The fact that I saved their asses by pulling Nick out of my hat is the only thing keeping me in my job right now. Nick and I explained at length why we made the choices we did. We spoke passionately about how widespread ESP would cause civilization to collapse. I explained that I only wanted to make sure Nick wasn't a target, and that his very existence wouldn't kick off a major ESP arms race."

"Were they receptive?" asked Altschuler.

"Some were convinced I did the right thing. Some weren't. So discussions are being had, and investigations are continuing. My fate rests on how much gratitude they feel, their assessment of the rationale for my actions, and the direction of the political winds."

"Nick says they did agree he should stay off the grid," said Altschuler, "at least for now. And continue devoting himself to finding a way to counter mind reading if it's ever widely developed."

"Yes, but for how long?" said Girdler. "Nick's arguments were passionate and forceful. No one knows the dangers of widespread mind reading like Nick does. He described in disturbing detail the kind of thoughts he reads on a daily basis. To really press home how quickly society would collapse if everyone had instant access to all the ugly and dangerous thoughts and memories we all keep hidden from each other." He sighed. "They said they got the point, but these are *politicians*. Mind reading may be *fire*, but the advantages to anyone able to play with it without getting burned are obvious. And the military intelligence types were drooling over the possibilities."

"Of course they were," said Campbell. "Nick just provided the ultimate demonstration of the value of his abilities."

"Governments like keeping secrets, right?" said Heather. "They're pissed off that *you* kept a secret, General. But if Nick is *their* secret, that should be a different matter. So maybe they'll agree to keep him off the grid for good."

"Even so," said the general, "if the powers that be know he's alive and where to find him, how off the grid would he really be? What I'm worried about is that they'll try to exploit his ESP. Have him abandon his defensive mission. They'll convince themselves he should spend all of his time producing miracles like he did at the Oscars. A position that isn't without merit."

"No matter what," said Campbell, "the secret is out. The twelve men Nick led on the raid know he's alive, and know he can read minds. The dozens of people at the National Security Council meeting, attendees and their underlings, know about him. And those in attendance at later meetings that Nick, himself, attended via video. All are sworn to secrecy, but you can bet this will leak. And when it does, any number of countries will do anything to get their hands on him."

"Which is why we're temporarily relocating Nick and Megan to your new yacht, Alex," said Girdler. "Something only this group knows about. I should have insisted they leave the desert days ago. But they've made it, and are safe, so we can count our blessings."

The general paused. "And Alex, I've seen the photo you texted of your new boat," he continued. "*Very* nice. *That* is what I call a high-end hideout. And judging from the room you're in now, the inside is even nicer than the outside. Looks like a pretty sweet, um . . . suite."

Megan patted Altschuler affectionately on the back. "It helps having rich friends. Thanks for the swanky hideout, Alex."

Altschuler turned to her and blushed. "I would have been a *dead* friend if not for you and Nick, so no thanks are necessary." He paused. "And as Nick can tell you, I couldn't be more sincere about that."

Nick held his hands out in front of him. "*I* can't tell her squat," he said innocently. "I'm staying out of your head and ignoring your thoughts. Like I promised."

"Just checking," said Altschuler with a grin. "The boat is named *Eos*, by the way," he told the gathering. "For obvious reasons."

"Obvious reasons?" said Megan, raising her eyebrows.

"You know," said Altschuler. "I'm CEO of *Theia* Labs. Probably shouldn't have chosen a name that makes a connection, but I couldn't help myself."

Megan looked blank.

"*Theia*. You know, the Greek goddess of light. And of vision."

"No kidding?" said Megan. "I never realized until now that your company had chosen such a fitting name for itself." She smiled sheepishly. "Greek gods were never my strong suit. Seems like there were more gods than people. So you'll need to help me out some more with Eos."

"Anything for you, Megan," said Altschuler cheerfully. "Theia married her brother, Hyperion, and had three children. Helios, the Sun. Selene, the Moon. And lastly, Eos, the Dawn."

"Ahh," said Megan, "*now* it makes sense. Eos was Theia's *daughter*." She paused. "Good choice for your boat's name then. A little disturbing given the brother-sister incest angle, but good." A sly smile came over her face. "So basically, Hyperion was Eos's father—*and* her Uncle."

The entire group laughed.

"Definitely narrows down the Christmas list a bit," said Hall.

After the laughs receded, Mike Campbell said, "Not to rain on the parade or anything, but we should probably get back on topic."

"I'm not sure I remember the last topic," admitted Hall.

"We were talking about you hiding out on this yacht," replied the colonel. "You know . . . *Eos*."

"But only until we can think of a better, more permanent location," clarified Girdler.

"The thing is, though," said Campbell, "we can't let the establishment suspect that your disappearance—for a second time—is the general's doing. He's in more than enough hot water already."

"I agree," said Hall. "So what did you have in mind?"

"I think you should contact President Cochran and tell him you eluded the general and are going into hiding."

"I don't get it," said Hall. "Won't the general still take heat for losing me?"

"Not much," replied Campbell. "If the president asks how you disappeared from under the general's nose, just laugh and ask him if he thinks anyone can keep a mind reader from doing anything he wants to do. After your display at the Cosmopolitan, no one can claim you aren't resourceful."

"Not to mention a bad-ass," said Megan cheerfully, giving him a quick peck on the cheek.

"Well, the talk shows have been saying that for a while now," said Hall, grinning. "They just keeping forgetting the 'bad' part of the expression. 'Ass' by itself probably isn't as complimentary."

Altschuler laughed. But part of him couldn't help but feel sorry for his friends. He was nearly certain Nick and Megan were just pretending to be in good spirits. He wondered if they would ever be able to come out of hiding. Probably not.

But at least hiding could be safer than being out in the open. As CEO of a company that was drowning in media coverage, Altschuler was as visible and high profile as it got.

And he couldn't be discounted as a target, either. From those terrified of what BrainWeb might bring, to those wishing to exploit him as the technical genius behind it.

So Girdler and Campbell had set up a security contingent around Altschuler that a president might envy. He and Heather hated the need and the invasion of privacy, but at least the security agents were consummate pros and managed to stay largely invisible. Girdler had called them off for a few hours so he and Heather could arrive at the marina undetected, but they would soon be back under the team's watchful eye.

Heather turned to the general. "Alex told me you and Nick lobbied hard to have BrainWeb approval delayed for three or four years. What changed your minds?"

The group early on had debated the merits and dangers of Brain-Web at length. While the privacy and addiction arguments were compelling, their biggest concern was the sabotage argument. If someone hacked into one's computer, it was a nightmare. But if someone hacked into one's *brain*, this was truly *unthinkable*.

And they had to admit the sobering truth: no matter how secure, no matter how many firewalls were thrown up, the rewards of crashing through into people's heads were so great, so irresistibly tempting to so many ruthless parties, that the safeguards would ultimately be breached. With disastrous consequences.

So they had leaned toward delaying the technology until quantum encryption could be developed, something scientists had been working on for decades. Quantum encryption, taking advantage of the bizarre laws of quantum physics, was absolutely unbreakable.

Alex Altschuler had recently added his prodigious intellect to the attempt, and was confident the solution was less than five years away.

But they had concluded that their arguments to delay the technology would fall on deaf ears. There was no putting this toothpaste back in the tube. Alex would just have to design the best safeguards possible and hope like hell quantum encryption was solved before the implant software was hacked.

But the general and Nick had obviously rethought this conclusion.

"What changed was the Oscars," said Girdler simply. "Now that Nick is back on the radar, we decided to argue our case, after all. Given his implants and heroic contributions, we knew they'd take him seriously. And we did have the ear of the president and the absolute highest echelon of the military and government. So we figured, what the hell."

Altschuler blew out a long breath. "I've decided to add my weight to yours," he announced, "and push to delay BrainWeb at the hearings next week." While the physical weight of the diminutive genius wasn't much, his metaphorical weight was substantial.

Heather blinked in surprise. "When did you make that decision?" she asked.

"Just now."

"Thanks, Alex," said the general. "Coming from the CEO who has the most to lose from the technology being delayed, this can't help but get their attention."

Mike Campbell nodded approvingly at Altschuler. "I agree," he said. "I'm impressed that you'd do this, Alex. And more than a little surprised."

Nick smiled. "I'm not. I've sworn off diving into Alex's mind, but I did early on, and his soul is the cleanest I've encountered. This is a very good man."

"Believe me, I'm not a saint," said Altschuler, embarrassed by the praise. "I'm just pushing for a delay, not an end to the program. And besides, even if it were killed, we'd still be going full speed ahead with applications for the blind and deaf. I'll be a billionaire many times over no matter what."

"But I don't get it," said Megan. "You're the head of Theia Labs. So why do you have to *push* for a delay. Can't you just *decide* on a delay?"

"Theia has a board of directors, and is now a public company. I'm CEO, but I'm not *king*. If the FDA and Congress let BrainWeb go forward, no chance the shareholders will agree to a substantial delay. I'm only risking advocating for this at the upcoming hearing because it's a closed-door session. But if it ever got out I did, I'd be forced to deny it. Or I'd be fired immediately."

"The general and Nick have given their pitch," said Megan. "Maybe with Alex's voice added to the chorus, we can get this delayed."

Girdler shook his head. "Doubtful," he said. "The politicians know we're all totally screwed if BrainWeb is hacked, but that won't stem the tide. They know where their bread is buttered. And BrainWeb has caught the public's fancy. Politicians won't risk votes by supporting a delay."

"So they'll let the world burn if it helps them stay in office?" said Heather.

"Are you kidding?" said Girdler. "Politicians would sell their daughters to *male prisons* to hold on to power. As far as I've been able to tell, they're the lowest form of life on the planet."

"Lower than pond scum?" asked Heather with a twinkle in her eye.

"Comparing them to pond scum is an insult to pond scum," said Girdler emphatically.

Hall laughed. "Come on, General. Quit sugar-coating your feelings. What do you really think of them?"

The stone-faced general couldn't help but smile. "The bottom line," he said, "is that you can never count on a politician doing the right thing. Even when they *know* it's the right thing. Believe me, I've interacted with far too many of them over the years."

"I wouldn't worry too much," said Altschuler, a triumphant grin spreading across his angular face. "Even if we fail to get a delay, I just bought us a lot more time to solve quantum encryption."

Everyone turned their rapt attention to Altschuler and waited for him to continue.

"I managed to convince the board to keep BrainWeb a trade secret," he said, quite pleased with himself.

"Outstanding!" said Girdler immediately. "Well done! We may just survive this technology, after all."

"Hold on," said Megan. "I'm not sure I'm following."

"Sorry," said Altschuler. "It'll help if I explain the principle reason the patent system was created. Most people don't know."

"Isn't it to protect inventors?" said Megan. "So others can't steal their inventions?"

"That's part of it. But the most important part is that it motivates inventors to provide society with blueprints of their brilliant ideas. So others can build upon the ideas to come up with additional advances. If everyone kept their inventions secret, the progress of civilization would grind to a halt."

Megan nodded slowly, but remained silent.

"So a patent is a pact between an inventor and society," continued Altschuler. "In exchange for twenty years of exclusive use of an invention, the inventor is required to disclose the invention publicly, in writing. In enough detail so that others can duplicate it. And build upon it. You can still choose to keep an invention a trade secret, of course, but if you do, you don't get protection. You basically take your chances that competitors won't learn your secret."

Megan considered this, and was able to quickly connect the dots. "I see. So if you wrote patents on BrainWeb technology, you'd be giving others insight they could use to hack it."

"Exactly," said Altschuler. "By keeping the information a trade secret, we slow them down considerably."

"But like you said," noted Megan, "you're taking your chances. What if someone reverse engineers the technology?

"First off, we're still going to patent the part of the technology that can be used to restore sight and hearing. But the BrainWeb implants and software for thought-controlled Web access are exceedingly complex, and neither can be reverse engineered. Especially the software. The algorithms and thought-to-language lexicon are hugely sophisticated, and the raw data that Kelvin Grey generated can't be repeated. I convinced the board this was the case, and that keeping all data to ourselves would enhance security considerably."

"It can't be reverse engineered, but what if your secrets leak?" said Hall. "Wouldn't that totally screw all of your shareholders?"

"Absolutely. But we've destroyed all copies of the data and algorithms except for two. Each is encrypted six ways to Sunday, and require retina and fingerprint scans to access, followed by several passwords."

"Why two?" asked Megan.

"One is for my use. The other is a backup, which each board member can access. So if something happens to me, the know-how isn't lost forever." A delighted, mischievous smile crossed Altschuler's face. "Except that the board's copy is gibberish. They just don't know it."

"Why?" said Megan.

"Well, my former boss at Theia did try to kill me. So you might say I'm not quite as . . . trusting as I used to be. In fact, the only people I truly trust are in this meeting."

"But now there isn't any backup," said Megan. "We do want the technology delayed, but we don't want to risk it being lost forever."

"I agree," said Hall. "Not that anything is going to happen to Alex," he added hastily

Altschuler considered for several seconds. "Yeah," he said finally. "I see your point."

"I have to side with Nick and Megan on this one as well," said Girdler. "I'm probably more deeply worried about the dangers of the

BrainWeb technology than any of us, but even I wouldn't want to see it lost to the world."

The general scratched his head in thought. "How about this? Why don't you give me access to a copy for safekeeping. I'm sure I'll never need to access it, but as the head of all Black Ops in the US," he added with a smile, "I'm pretty sure no one is more expert at keeping secrets than I am."

Altschuler laughed. "I can't argue with that," he said. "I'll get to work making this happen as soon as this meeting ends. Knowing that you'll be holding the data for safekeeping will certainly put any fears about losing it to rest."

"I love how you deceived your board, by the way," Mike Campbell told Altschuler in amusement. "You got them to agree to keep BrainWeb a trade secret, made them feel special by pretending to give them access, and then gave them gibberish. You know I'm running PsyOps now. We could use a man like you," he added playfully.

"I'll let you know if the CEO thing doesn't work out."

"Not to mention the billionaire thing," said Hall.

"Ah, speaking of that, Nick," said Altschuler. "You're going off the grid a second time. But this time, General Girdler can't afford to be caught funding you. So I'm going to set aside five million dollars in a checking account. I'll give you my login and password information so you can access it whenever you like. It's all yours."

Hall turned to face Altschuler and nodded appreciatively. "That's very generous, Alex. Thanks." He raised his eyebrows. "That should tide us over for a day or two," he finished with a grin.

17

Marc Fisher sipped his amber-colored Manhattan and stared out at Washington DC twenty-nine stories below him through a wall of glass, waiting impatiently for his guest. At the touch of a button the glass could turn opaque, ensuring privacy without need of curtains or shutters, but Fisher kept it transparent as often as possible, his view a reminder to himself and others of both the figurative and literal heights he had risen.

And the world hadn't seen anything yet.

On a side wall of his office hung framed photos of himself with the Chairman of the Joint Chiefs of Staff and other famous high-ranking military and intelligence members. He despised most of them, but he was all about impression management, and the fact was that he despised almost everyone.

At thirty-nine, Fisher was the youngest ever Chairman of the House Intelligence Committee, and was beginning to wield even more power behind the scenes. Until now, he had kept out of the limelight, preferring to pull strings from behind the curtain. But it wouldn't be long now before this would change. Before he would announce himself on the national stage.

If you were someone he could use, no one was more charming. If not, no one was more ruthless or intimidating. And if you were a voter, no one appeared more caring, folksy, and friendly.

Fisher paced the floor, cursing. He was not in the mood for this upcoming meeting, but it was one he knew he couldn't cancel. The congresswoman from Pennsylvania's fifth district had resigned in a scandal and there was an upcoming run-off election, and the Democrats considered this an important seat. He had worked hard for the power to control the purse-strings of certain campaigns, and since this was one of them, a meeting with Rob Engel, the campaign manager of the candidate there, Tom Sutherland, could not be ducked.

"Fuck it!" he hissed out loud.

Every second he didn't locate Nick Hall was another second the trail was growing even colder. And another second that one of his rivals might beat him to the punch.

His only solace came from the knowledge that he was among only a hundred or so people who were aware of Hall's re-emergence and his actions at the Oscars eight days earlier. Fisher was one of a very small minority who were highly-placed enough to rate knowing how the sheep in the theater were really saved.

Mind reading. Un-fucking-believable.

But also unbelievably *perfect.*

The moment Fisher learned of Nick Hall he had become *obsessed* with him. Because Hall was the key. Without him, Fisher knew he would rise very high, maybe even to the top.

But with him, he was unstoppable.

Nick Hall was the tool that would allow Fisher to go from being a relative unknown outside of Washington and the media to someone who would storm onto the national stage, from out of nowhere, to become the president when the next election rolled around. And conditions could not be more perfect. The president was a Democrat and was in his second term. His vice president had health issues that prevented him from running. So Democratic Party hopefuls were drooling all over themselves at the prospect of a wide open field.

Most politicians were dirty. Filthy. Fisher knew he was the top predator, with the most to hide, but the minds of the majority of politicians were septic tanks of secrets, scandals, and hidden bodies. Although, for most of these pussies, these hidden bodies were only metaphorical.

But if he could read the minds of those in Washington, he could learn their biggest weaknesses and vulnerabilities. The locations of their skeletons. Their campaign strategies. Their fears and their hot buttons and their pressure points.

In short, he could turn them all into his puppets.

It would be no contest. He would be Godzilla to their Bambi.

But even knowing Hall's location in the desert, the exploitation of this knowledge would take time and careful planning. First, he needed to assemble his own team of commandos. While this step would have been impossible for most, given his money and connections to the inner realms of the intelligence community, it had been surprisingly simple for him.

For decades, the business of fielding private armies had grown faster than almost any other, mushrooming during the Iraq war under George W. Bush, where these mercenary corporations had earned tens of billions of dollars. Euphemistically called *Private Military Contractors*, or *PMCs*—the most notable of which were Blackwater, DynCorp, Kroll, and Sandline International—these private armies collectively outnumbered the entire military force of the United States.

And all Fisher needed was one leader from their ranks. One man willing to form the nucleus of Fisher's own private, although very tiny, army. He needed a partner. A point person with considerable military expertise who could recruit others.

So Fisher had used his access to the country's vast intelligence databases to find the most competent, and ruthless, mercenary on file. After this it was a simple matter to describe the situation and how an alliance could benefit them both.

His new partner had worked quickly to recruit the others they would need, who would never know Fisher was involved in any way. Things were progressing even better than Fisher had expected.

And then the unthinkable had happened.

Hall had *disappeared*.

Just like that, he was gone once again. Fisher had received word of this just the day before.

Fuck!

The word was that Hall had managed this Houdini act all by himself. But Fisher didn't believe it for a second, no matter how impressive his capabilities. That fucking ape, Justin Girdler, had to have helped him. Yet another reason for Fisher to throw his weight behind ensuring Girdler was court-martialed, and to exert his considerable influence to force others to do so as well. Girdler had shown he had a hard-on for this Hall. Maybe he fancied himself Hall's guardian fucking angel.

Let's see how effective a guardian you can be when your bony ass is in military court, thought Fisher triumphantly.

Okay, so Hall had gone to ground yet again. No problem. He would find him. No matter how difficult it was, and no matter what it took. And his new mercenary partner, who had previously been drummed out of the military for being a little too . . . overzealous, could come in handy in this regard, as well.

But time was wasting!

Fisher gulped down the last of his Manhattan and slammed the cocktail glass down hard on a shelf behind his desk.

Goddammit! He needed to spend every waking second racking his brain, thinking of all possibilities. How he would find Hall, and how he would proceed once he had.

Yes, only a hundred or so people knew about Hall. For *now*. But this knowledge would spread quickly. Fisher was confident there were none more ruthless, or opportunistic, than he was, but there would be others willing to take the ultimate gamble for the ultimate prize. The hunt for Hall would turn into a gold rush, if it hadn't already, and he was determined to get there first.

But instead of holing himself up to work on his new obsession, he would be babysitting a fucking campaign manager. Fisher was still fuming about this a minute later when Engel arrived, right on time, as expected.

After cursory greetings the two wasted no time getting down to business. Fisher had Engel sit in a small chair at the foot of his imposing mahogany desk. Despite his impatience, Fisher knew that he needed to lend his political genius to be sure Tom Sutherland beat his Republican challenger, Donald Briggs. So he listened carefully as Engel ran through the highlights of his strategy.

When the man had finished, Fisher shot him a look of utter contempt. "A strategy even less impressive than I had expected," he said. "Your focus is mainly on how great Sutherland is. You're not doing enough to paint Briggs as an asshole. This isn't the fucking Miss America pageant! You're trying to win an election, not Miss Congeniality!"

"My thinking was—"

"I don't give a shit about your thinking!" interrupted Fisher. "The fifth district has a lot of women," he continued. "Most of them single. So one of your key strategic elements needs to be running Sutherland, hard, on closing the income gap."

Engel blinked rapidly. "Could you go into a little more detail as to what you had in mind?"

"Really?" said Fisher. His dark brown eyes bored into Engel's, and there was something about his unblinking stare that was unmistakably predatory. "Why had I assumed, as a campaign manager, you had actually studied *campaigning*? Since you haven't, let me make my meaning even more clear. You need to run ads pointing out that a woman only makes seventy-seven cents for every dollar a man makes. Point out that the Republican asshole, Briggs, refuses to support legislation to narrow this gap. At the end have Sutherland look earnestly into the camera and say, 'Women deserve to be paid the same as men. It's only fair.'"

"I just wanted to be certain of where you were headed with this," said Engel, fighting to keep his voice even. "Because I *have* studied campaigning. And I *do* know politics. This is an issue that's been used for well over a decade. Back in 2014, Barak Obama even raised it in his State of The Union Address. I can quote him: 'Today, women make up about half our workforce. But they still make seventy-seven cents for every dollar a man earns. That is wrong, and in 2014, it's an embarrassment.'"

"Good. Maybe you're less incompetent than I thought."

Engel's lips curled up into a snarl but he quickly returned his face to passivity. "My worry about this strategy is that even the most liberal papers gave Obama five Pinocchios on this one."

"So what? If you had a year, I could list all the falsehoods Republican presidents have used that earned *them* five Pinocchios. This is a full contact sport. And the ends justify the means."

"I know that," said Engel. "But this could backfire. This factoid was on its last legs when Obama used it. Women may make *slightly* less—maybe—but the seventy-seven cents to the dollar statistic is what men and women make, *on average*. It isn't a comparison of the two sexes in the same jobs, with the same experience. It's comparing total earnings across *all* jobs, which ends up being apples to oranges in many cases."

"Yeah, no shit," spat Fisher. "Tell me something I don't know. Men choose high-paying fields like engineering, chemistry, and mining more often than women do. Women choose lower-paying fields like education and social work more often than men do. This accounts for most of the difference. But so the fuck what? Are you in politics or the fucking priesthood? This statistic has been used so long because it always works! Truth doesn't matter! It's what people will believe that matters."

"I don't know. This has been debunked so often lately that people no longer—"

"Of course they'll still believe it!" shouted Fisher. "You're a fool. They'll believe it because they're programmed to. You construct the ad so everyone assumes you're comparing identical jobs. But even if you gave the public the absolute straight scoop—if they didn't tune you out or die of boredom—it wouldn't change a fucking thing. We've conditioned the public to believe women are only making a fraction of what men make for so long now, they'll believe the *lie* before they believe the correction. This claim has been around for so long it's created its own fucking reality. And there are cases where women really do make less for the same job."

"There are," said Engel. "But the opposite can also be true. Engineering companies desperate to attract women in the name of diversity often lure them with *higher* salaries."

"You sound like you're working for Briggs," said Fisher in disgust. "You really don't get it, do you? Most people are sheep. Stupid and uninformed. And they don't dig. They don't think for themselves. They'll trust a sincere voiceover and whatever the television tells them. But even if they dig, they have no intuition for statistics anyway. Even experts can be fooled."

His eyes continued boring into Engel's with such intensity, the man was finally forced to look away. "In the second world war," continued Fisher, "the allies conducted a study of planes returning from engagements in enemy territory. They determined the fuselages were the most exposed, because they were the most often hit. The vast majority of bullets and holes were found in the fuselages, whereas this was rarely the case when it came to the engines. So they decided to bolster the armor on the fuselages. Do you see their mistake?" asked Fisher.

Engel just blinked for several seconds and finally shook his head.

"They analyzed *returning* planes," snapped Fisher, sneering condescendingly as though Engel were a complete idiot. "Of course they found most of the bullet holes in the fuselages. When the *engines* were shot, most of the time these planes *never fucking returned*. They were shot down. Get it? The planes whose fuselages were hit, and not their engines, were the only ones making it back to be studied."

Engel's eyes widened as he saw the truth of it.

"So even experts back then, and a smart guy like you, can be fooled by simple data, simple statistics, right? So don't worry about the idiots in your fifth district. Fuck the truth squads. Fuck the five Pinocchios. For Sutherland's constituents to learn this has been debunked, they'd actually have to *read*. And care enough to check. The pay gap is visceral. It feels wrong and unfair. Voters are already predisposed to think Republicans are uncaring, country-club pricks. So how dare Briggs refuse to support legislation to narrow this pay gap?"

"You don't think it will matter that there *is* no such legislation?"

"Not a whit. You'll get called on it. But so the fuck what? The ad will be seen by everyone. The correction by almost no one."

"My feeling was that since the incumbent just resigned over a scandal, honesty would be at a premium."

"This is politics!" snapped Fisher. "Where honesty is never at a premium! You really need to find some other line of work." He shook his head in disgust. He would have liked to scold this idiot further, but he had already wasted more than enough time on him. "But we're done here. Beat the income disparity theme into voters' brains, and Sutherland will win."

"The only thing is—"

"This is not a democracy," said Fisher. "If you are interested in keeping your job, and if you don't want me to close the purse strings on you so you'll have *no* advertising, you'll do exactly as I tell you." He leaned forward with an almost primal intensity. "Now, do we understand each other?"

Engel blew out a long breath and nodded. "We do," he said miserably.

"Good," said Fisher. "Now get the fuck out of my office. I have important things to do."

18

"Is this call secure?" asked General Justin Girdler.

The face in his computer monitor, belonging to a man in his early twenties named Drew Russell, nodded. "Of course. I can't believe you could doubt me," he said in amusement.

"Never hurts to double check."

"And I've also set up a secure connection between you and Colonel Campbell, like you asked."

"You're the best, Drew."

"Tell me something I don't know," said the good-natured young man, who wore his playful cockiness like a badge of honor. But he was cocky for a good reason. He really was the best.

PsyOps had any number of remarkable computer geniuses working for them, but none were anywhere near the level of Drew Russell. Not only was he exceptionally skilled, but after Mike Campbell, he was the only other person in Girdler's sprawling organization he had become close to, and that he trusted implicitly.

Drew Russell was a software genius almost at the level of Alex Altschuler. Girdler had recruited him himself. Russell loved comic books and the Marvel Universe—who didn't these days? So Girdler had pitched BlackOps and PsyOps as being as close a real world equivalent of the SHIELD organization from the Marvel Universe as you could possibly get.

Well, absent the superheroes, aliens, gravity-defying planes, Hydra operatives rotting out the organization from within, endless scorching hot women, and a boss who wore an eye-patch, of course. Although during his efforts to recruit Russell, Girdler had offered to wear one if it would help, and call himself Fury.

In addition to appealing to Russell's patriotism, romantic streak, and geekiness, Girdler had taken the unprecedented—and illegal—step of sharing the results of ops that were at *eyes only* level of secrecy, of which only a handful of people in the world were aware.

When the military failed to prevent terrorism, destruction, and chaos on the global stage, this was known by everyone. But its many successes in stopping these events went largely unheralded. Girdler had taken a big risk, since had his sharing of these secrets been discovered, it would not have gone well for him. But he was convinced Russell was *that* important. And by sharing the brilliant successes of his organization, such as the time they had helped to design a computer virus, with Israel, that had delayed a rogue nation from completing the production of nuclear bombs, he hoped to demonstrate the importance of the work.

Eventually, his cumulative and unceasing efforts had paid off.

"I'm not sure why you're so hung up on making sure no one knows that Mike and I are talking to you," said Russell. "You *are* our commanding officer, after all. I'm pretty sure it isn't a crime for you to speak with those in your chain of command."

"This is true. But it's for your own protection, Drew. You want to appear as distant from me as possible. I'm afraid I've become toxic."

"Yeah, no kidding," said Russell, rolling his eyes. "I guess no good deed goes unpunished. I can't believe you had the audacity to pull our national pecker out of the guillotine."

"Well, we'll see how it plays out. They're still investigating. But Nick Hall has disappeared once again," he lied. Well, this was technically true if your definition of *disappearing* meant convalescing on a luxury yacht. "And this has made matters a lot worse. One of the reasons I'm calling is that it won't take long for those looking for him to guess that he can't be found using facial recognition." He paused. "Which means you're exposed."

More than six months earlier, at Girdler's orders, Russell had artfully altered the facial recognition system to prevent Hall from showing up, and hadn't asked any questions, including why this was necessary since Nick Hall was known to be dead. Given the computer maestro's intelligence, he had known full well what was going on, but Girdler had never brought him into the inner circle.

"Don't worry," said Russell. "Even if they find the software I used to do this—which is unlikely, because it's very subtle—there is no way they can trace it back to me. I clean up after myself better than anyone."

Girdler frowned. "Yeah. I was afraid of that," he said. "Let me ask you this, Drew. How many people in all of my organization could have doctored the system this perfectly, while leaving no trace behind?"

"Shit!" said Russell, as the truth dawned on him. "You mean my own greatness is doing me in?"

A smile flickered across Girdler's face. "You may be a genius with computers, but I'm not sure how long you'd last as an operative. Do you know how a teacher knows when you've helped your eleven-year-old daughter with her essay? When it's far too sophisticated for an eleven-year-old." Girdler shook his head. "Too little perfection can get you caught, true. But so can too *much*."

"*Now* you tell me," complained Russell. "Okay, I'll go back and make it less perfect, so it will look as though a lesser light, a mere mortal, had done it."

"I see that the fact I just pointed out something crucial you over-looked hasn't done anything to shake your um . . . self-confidence."

"That's part of my greatness," replied Russell with a twinkle in his eye.

"Good to know," said Girdler in amusement. "So go back and muddy the trail. But do it quickly, because it won't be long before they investigate."

The general paused. "And I have a few other very important as-signments for you. One, I need you to read the tea leaves for me, as only you can. I need any information you can learn from the various powers that be in the government and military about their investiga-tion of me in the Nick Hall matter. This will benefit you, as well, so you can make sure your part in this is never discovered. I also want to know who's pushing for a court martial, who isn't, if they'll try to stack the jury, what kind of sentence they're likely to push for if it does come to this, and so on."

Russell smiled. "No problem. I've already been on this for days."

"Why am I not surprised?" said Girdler with an approving nod. "I'm happy to hear it. So continue putting an ear to the ground, but I'd like you to devote ninety-five percent of your time to the other project I have for you. You're going to like this one. Turns out I now have the keys to BrainWeb."

Russell had no knowledge of Girdler's connection to the CEO of Theia Labs, and was absolutely stunned. "*Impossible*," he said. "Even *I* would have trouble stealing keys from Alex *Altschuler*. He may be the only person in the world who's better than me."

"So what are you saying?" said Girdler with a smile. "That for all of your greatness, there may be a reason I've gotten to the top of the organization? That I just might have tricks up my sleeve that might even baffle *you*? That even without an eye-patch, this is a feat that not even Nick Fury could match?"

"I wouldn't go *that* far," replied Russell. "Besides, Fury isn't running SHIELD anymore. Phil Coulson is in charge. But regardless, I'm definitely impressed."

"Good. Wouldn't want you to underestimate me. Now, let me explain what I want."

"I'm all ears," said Drew Russell.

* * *

Girdler ended his video call with Russell and immediately called Mike Campbell on the secure video connection Russell had established.

"I assume your sources are passing on the same whispers as mine?" said Campbell when they had completed their greetings and a few minutes of small talk.

"Probably," said Girdler. "But that depends on what you're hearing."

"I'm hearing the investigation is mostly just a delay tactic," replied the colonel. "One that will continue until those in power can decide what they want to do about this. They're not finding out much more than they already know. You faked Hall's death. You lied to your superiors. You had him working on projects that were never authorized.

And you channeled money from your department to build a facility in the desert and to fund Hall."

"That last one is really annoying," said the general. "Since I am entrusted with spending considerably more money than this on my own authority."

"Yes, but apparently not on projects that only you know about. And even if this were not the case, the fine print says that you don't have signature authority to set up a military installation, no matter how small." Campbell paused. "But regardless, my sources seem to indicate the winds have shifted toward convening a court martial. Probably within a month or so. Don't know what's turning the tide, but the push is coming from a number of directions. They'll drag out the investigation until the people pushing for this get their ducks in a row."

"Yes," mumbled the general. "This is what my sources are saying, as well. They're guessing about a seventy-five percent chance of court martial now. And it's turning more and more into a witch hunt."

Girdler knew his disdain for the political aspect of his new job was now coming back to bite him. He liked his new role as head of Black Ops, but it was so high in the pecking order that hobnobbing with key politicians on Capitol Hill was expected. And there was nothing he hated more.

He had initially considered refusing the promotion, and often wished he had. Not that he didn't love the job, aside from the odious requirements of pressing flesh in Washington. It was fascinating. Black Ops commanded a huge budget and was into some pretty wild stuff, although the purely scientific projects were his favorite.

"The fact that your commanding officer is in full support of the lynch mob, and not you, doesn't exactly help," noted Campbell.

General Nelson Sobol had been head of Black Ops, and Girdler's boss, when Girdler had run PsyOps. But Sobol had been moved up the ranks to make room for Girdler's promotion, and Girdler still reported to him.

When Girdler had first suspected Hall could read minds he had philosophical disagreements with Sobol, and Sobol had later become convinced Girdler had ignored his orders. Which was true, but Sobol had nothing other than a hunch to substantiate this.

Even so, these suspicions did nothing to endear Girdler to the man, especially when events had unfolded and Girdler was seen as a hero. Still, Sobol had been promoted because of it, to make way for Girdler and his surging popularity in the military community, so he was willing to forgive and forget.

But when Sobol recently learned that Girdler had lied to his face when he had told him Hall was dead, he had taken this very personally. He was Girdler's commanding officer, after all, so this deception was not only a slap in the face, it made him appear to be an ineffectual leader. And rubbing more salt in Sobol's wound, he hadn't been invited to the president's National Security Council meeting that had featured Girdler, nor any subsequent meetings with Girdler and Hall.

"Hard not to see his point of view on this one," said Girdler. "I did disobey his orders, and I did lie to him. And Sobol is a powerful enemy to have. But, regardless, if he was beating the drum all by himself, I'd be okay. The problem is the pressure is continuing to mount from multiple quarters."

"I have heard that President Cochran is swimming against the current on this one. He's not a bad person to have in your corner."

"Yes, Cochran has been working hard on my behalf. And I appreciate that. Unlike most everyone else, he's never forgotten Hall's heroism and what would have happened without him. But even though he wields the most power of anyone, he's likely to lose."

"You're probably right," said Campbell. "There is even a school of thought that says his support is *hurting* you."

"I wouldn't be surprised," said the general. "He's made a lot of enemies in DC. Many of whom are probably pushing for a court martial just because he's against it. To flex some muscle and to piss him off."

Campbell let out a heavy sigh. "It looks like we're on the same page then. And while we minimized the fallout from Nick disappearing again, I think this was the last straw. Talk about pissing people off. Even those who believe you aren't behind it want you to fry for negligence and incompetence."

The colonel paused. "Look, Justin, I don't want to paint too dire a picture. It looks bad, but maybe sanity will prevail after all. And even if a court martial is called, I doubt you'd be found guilty. And even if you were, I can't imagine you'd get more than a slap on the wrist."

"I wish you were right. But if they have the leverage to convene a court martial, I'll be found guilty. And at minimum, I'll lose my job and be dishonorably discharged. If things really go south, I'll have to do jail time."

"Impossible!" insisted Campbell. "No one would stand for it. What you did in the scheme of things is a misdemeanor, a speeding ticket. Worst case they sign you up for early retirement. And the good you did is practically unmatched in history. Superman saves the world, how bad are they going to punish him when they arrest him for impersonating Clark Kent?"

"I hope you're right," said Girdler. "But I have a bad feeling about this. A very bad feeling."

19

Since his meeting a week earlier with Sutherland's idiot campaign manager, Marc Fisher continued to spend every waking second trying to find the missing mind reader. Sutherland's campaign had begun to run income disparity adds and he was rapidly strengthening in the polls.

A number of newspapers and online news sites pointed out that if there was a gender-based income gap, it wasn't nearly as large as portrayed, and that there was no pending legislation to correct it if one did exist, since this kind of discrimination was *already* against the law. But, as Fisher had known, this didn't make the slightest difference.

When polled, many voters were livid about Briggs's heartlessness and misogyny. A woman was paid far less for doing the exact same job as a man. So why wouldn't Briggs support legislation that would correct this gross injustice? He must be yet another uncaring Republican asshole still living in the 1950s.

But while Sutherland was ecstatic, Fisher was miserable. Nick Hall was nowhere to be found. The mind reader was either very smart, or very lucky.

Fisher had already spent hundreds of thousands of dollars, and his hand-picked soldier-for-hire had completed recruitment of six fellow mercenaries, almost as competent and lethal as himself, to join the hunt. And Fisher had pulled strings and manipulated key assets in the intelligence community. He had bullied and charmed and cajoled, but to no avail. He didn't have as much as a single lead.

Fisher became convinced that Hall was somehow immune to cameras and facial recognition. Perhaps he had had plastic surgery, or perhaps he was using some other means. But most likely Girdler had worked some Black Ops magic to alter the computer facial recognition data on file for Hall, so he could never be identified in this way.

But no matter. Nothing worth having was easy. Regardless of how much effort it might take, Fisher was convinced his perseverance and brains would win out in the end.

He would let nothing stop him.

But then, he never did.

Marc Fisher was a psychopath, plain and simple. And not only was he well aware of this fact, he *celebrated* it. And for good reason. Psychopaths were superior.

He had known he was different from a very young age. He always seemed to know just how to get what he wanted. Other people, even his loving parents, meant *nothing* to him. They were just pawns, rubes, to be played as he saw fit.

And he had always known the precise way to manipulate people to achieve his own ends. It was his genius. He could bully or charm with equal facility, and didn't have a preference either way. He could construct elaborate webs of lies and deceit more effortlessly than other boys his age could construct buildings out of Legos.

And he soon came to realize that even when other kids knew what they wanted, and he helpfully provided a clear strategy to get it, they were often too squeamish, or too moral, or too afraid to go forward. It almost seemed like hurting others, even emotionally, hurt them in some way also. It was pathetic.

But it wasn't until he was twelve, one morning in his mother's car, when he happened to hear an expert on psychopathy on the radio, that the light bulb had gone off. He knew what he was. Why he was different. What made him so superior to others.

After this fateful morning he spent months learning about the psychopathic condition. There was a range of severity, with precious few on the Hannibal Lecter end of the spectrum. But fully one percent of the population could be classified as psychopathic, based on a number of criteria.

Psychopaths were absolutely selfish, and absolutely ruthless. They had no conscience, empathy, or remorse. They were devoid of real emotion, but could fake it to manipulate others. They were cold-blooded, fearless, and cool under pressure.

But they were also often charming and charismatic. Smooth talkers who were never embarrassed or self-conscious. Brilliant liars, manipulators, and con artists. And they were chillingly sane. They knew right from wrong: they just didn't care.

Fisher's favorite description was encapsulated in a single sentence: psychopaths are predators who see all others as prey, and who feel as much compassion for others as wolves feel for sheep.

In short, they were superior in every way. Strong where normals were weak. Decisive where normals were fearful. Unburdened by doubt, anxiety, empathy, or emotion.

Why would anyone want to be a sheep when they could be a wolf?

Psychopaths were greatly enriched among business executives, and Fisher had even read speculation that the great Steve Jobs had been a psychopath, although at the low end of the range. Fearless, charismatic, and cut-throat.

But compared to himself, Fisher knew, Jobs was as ruthless as a bunny rabbit.

Fisher took great pride from the knowledge that he was extreme, even for a psychopath. He had tortured small animals when he was young, just to see how it felt. When he was seventeen he had drugged, raped, and sodomized two girls while wearing a mask, simply to better understand what might appeal to him.

In the end, he had decided that rape was too much trouble, especially since he could seduce women with such great facility, and seduction allowed him to use them far longer, and in far more interesting ways.

When he was eighteen, he had stalked and killed a homeless man, again just to see how it felt. He had prolonged the man's agony for hours, making him beg for his life.

A useful experiment. Yielding an important result.

He learned that he didn't get off on torture and murder, but neither did it trouble him in the slightest.

Right after high school, Fisher had already decided what he would do with his life. He would aim for the ultimate heights, as befitting someone of his superiority. He would become a career politician, the profession that attracted a higher percentage of fellow psychopaths than any other. And while there were a number of pathetic men and women who had chosen politics in a sincere effort to help others, on the whole, politicians were narcissistic backstabbers. Professional liars. Totally selfish and without conscience, most couldn't care any less about others, although they could con anyone into believing they were the most compassionate people on Earth.

There was an old adage: sincerity—if you can fake that, you've got it made. And no group faked sincerity better than politicians. They were the ultimate con artists in a profession that saw all voters as marks.

A con man could ingratiate himself to others. Could be anything his mark needed him to be. Could be warm and charming and caring. A con artist could put you under such a spell, could make you love him so much, that even after he had slipped a knife between your shoulder blades, you would think that this was somehow *your* fault.

But even among the political class, the vast majority held back. They drew the line at petty forms of corruption. Graft, taking bribes, serial lying, plagiarism, stealing campaign funds, and the like.

None were prepared to get their hands as dirty as Fisher was. Fisher would do whatever it took to get to the upper ranks of power. He would let nothing stand in his way.

When he was very young, he had decided that to achieve his goals, he had to become a multi-millionaire, and he set out to do this as efficiently as possible. Wealth was easy when you weren't bound by any rules.

During summers away from school, he got a job as a pool boy in Rancho Santa Fe, California, one of the wealthiest neighborhoods in the world. When the owners were away, he would find where they kept their expensive jewelry, sometimes hiding tiny cameras pointing at their wall safes. Cameras he could later retrieve to get the combinations.

Given that this was Southern California, he had little trouble finding artists who specialized in constructing lower cost fakes of exquisite jewelry. Take them photos and dimensions and they would make perfect knock-off versions using real gold, but fake diamonds. Copies that were indistinguishable from the originals to the naked eye.

The fakes were so good that they cost a small fortune, but they were well worth it since his plans called for him to minimize the risk of being caught by swapping in the fakes for the originals. Since the owners had no idea they'd been robbed, Fisher was able to build a war chest with little fear of arrest.

Once he had enough money to get started, though, he abandoned this for even less risky thievery. Insider trading. Given Fisher had no boundaries or ethics, and in an age where cameras were practically microscopic, spying on executive computers and homes was almost routine. In the rare cases when his cameras were discovered, he would simply move on.

He made only the most leveraged trades on the information he gleaned, and by the time he was in his late twenties he had a net worth of more than twenty million dollars and was ready to run for public office.

He chose to run as a Democrat, not out of any deeply held convictions, since he had none, but simply because his district favored this party. But he was glad this was the case because he thought he could prosper more within the Democratic brand. Democrats were seen as the party who really cared. Republicans the party of wealthy assholes.

Fisher was a brilliant campaigner. There was little he enjoyed more than pretending to care about the miserable scum who would elect him. He lived to make speeches bemoaning the plight of the downtrodden while taking money from the well-heeled.

At the age of twenty-nine, Marc Fisher became the congressman for the second district of the great state of Idaho. He knew many around the country thought Idaho was filled with nothing but dumb potato farmers. But residents of this state were also seen as trustworthy. The salt of the earth. An image he cultivated with an aw-shucks demeanor and a practiced folksy way.

He climbed the party ranks rapidly, through whatever means were required. Twice over the years he was forced to kill when a person standing in his way could not be moved. But years earlier he had prepared for this possible need.

At the start of his political career he had made a study of poisons, and had learned that botulism toxin was the most deadly substance ever discovered. Just four pounds of it was enough to kill every man, woman, and child on Earth. And while it could not be produced in quantities anywhere near this great, given that less than a *billionth* of a pound was enough to kill a human being, it didn't have to be.

And it was readily available. While the raw, undiluted material was exceedingly well protected, for someone as resourceful as he was this wasn't an insurmountable obstacle.

He had loved the irony that the deadliest substance known to man had become widely available so that vain people could maintain the illusion of youth. Botulism toxin stopped communication between nerves and muscles. So when it was diluted in saline to less than one part per billion, and renamed Botox, the substance could destroy the nerves that caused wrinkles. It could help older people look younger. It was also approved for stopping eye spasms, helping alleviate migraine headaches, and for several other maladies, but its use as a cosmetic had put it on the map.

Fisher loved this toxin. Just like him, it performed its job brilliantly, with unmatched power. It was dangerous beyond all possible expectations. But stealthy. Something that could smooth out wrinkles and make people smile, or kill them ruthlessly without fail. A perfect metaphor for his own nature.

Eventually, he had managed to obtain a small vial, diluted millions-fold instead of billions-fold. At this potency, a single drop was more than enough to ensure the death of a person five times over. And he had used it, twice, many years apart. Both victims had died, inexplicably, from sudden respiratory failure, but murder had not been suspected in either case.

As he continued his meteoric ascent he managed to avoid any more killings, not because this troubled him, but simply out of expediency.

There was always the risk that a clever medical examiner would figure out the cause of death. He didn't believe they could ever trace the poisoning back to him in any case, but why take any chances?

Eventually he set his sights on the House Intelligence Committee and used techniques he had polished all of his life to gain its chair: threats, intimidation, blackmail, seduction, and charm. He became an indispensable friend and ally to key players. And in the end, he even hired a ridiculously expensive call girl to set up a rival so he could force him to remove his hat from the ring.

The Intelligence Committee was perfect. It put him in a position of power and influence and allowed him to meet the exact people he was most interested in knowing. Where the real power was.

The Intelligence Committee oversaw the CIA, NSA, Department of Defense, Department of Homeland Security, FBI, and fourteen other intelligence gathering organizations. Fisher wasted no time identifying key players in the intelligence community, both obvious and behind the scenes, and did favors for some while gathering dirt on others.

If knowledge and access were power, then Marc Fisher was a *god*.

Which is what made his current situation so maddening. Despite all of the tentacles he had deep into intelligence circles, Hall continued to elude him.

As he gazed out of his window at the human insects milling below him, racking his brain to find yet another angle of attack, his Personal Digital Assistant, which he had named Annie, sensed that he was alone, and came to life to carry out a previous instruction. "Mr. Fisher," it said from his tablet computer in a pleasant feminine voice, "the video file you've been waiting for has arrived. Please acknowledge notification."

"Acknowledged," he replied to his PDA, knowing that Annie would continue to replay the message unless he did so.

Fisher didn't expect this video to help, but he was obsessed with Hall, and determined to learn anything and everything he could about the man. He had watched the footage of Hall at the Oscars endlessly, searching for any clue that might help him.

But only recently, when he had tried to imagine Hall's journey from Palm Springs to the Cosmopolitan, did it occur to him there might be footage of the staging of the attack. When Hall was leading his team to capture the warehouse so they could use the same tunnel left behind by Islamic Jihad.

And such footage did exist. Taken by a street camera nearby. Like everything else about Hall's involvement in the attack, it had been classified and buried so deeply that it took some doing even for Fisher to resurrect it. But he had not let this deter him.

He didn't expect the footage to be worth the effort, but he wouldn't rest until he had turned over every last stone.

"Annie, notify my assistant that I don't want to be disturbed, lock all doors, and throw the video up on the television screen."

There was a brief pause. "Assistant notified. Doors locked. And your video has been sent to your television and is ready to play."

"Is there any sound, or just video?"

"Just video."

Fisher poured his now-finished Manhattan into a cocktail glass and faced the forty-inch screen hanging on one wall. "Okay. Play it now. Actual speed."

The video footage began to play out on his screen. A small church bus rolled quietly into view of the camera and stopped. A malicious grin came over Fisher's face. *A fucking church bus? Really?*

The men who had ended the siege were now commonly known as the Oscar Angels, so perhaps it was only fitting that they would prep for their attack in a church bus. *If only the public knew.*

The bus was stationary for several long minutes while Fisher continued to study his screen. Finally, Nick Hall emerged, looking just as he had on the stage of the Cosmopolitan, in a ski mask and casual clothing. Behind him, two of his team, in full combat gear, followed.

And then another.

Marc Fisher almost dropped his cocktail.

It was a girl! A girl not mentioned in any of the reports.

"Freeze footage," commanded Fisher. "Continue forward at one quarter actual."

The girl was dressed casually and was not wearing a mask. She was petite, with a pleasant face that seemed unusually expressive. He watched, spellbound, as she hugged Hall and then backed away, tears now streaming down her cheeks.

She stared into Hall's eyes like a lovesick puppy. It was absolutely sickening. After only a few seconds of this, however, she tore her eyes away from Hall and quickly retreated back into the bus. Hall tracked her as she left, and even with a mask on his body language screamed love and longing.

And weakness.

Fisher slumped into his chair in shock. She was *perfect*. He'd bet his last dollar Girdler hadn't bothered to make sure *she* was invisible to facial recognition.

But she wasn't just his ticket to finding Hall. She was his means to *control* him.

This girl was certain to provide yet another demonstration of the inherent superiority of the psychopath. Psychopaths were immune to love. But the strongest, most invulnerable heroes could be *crippled* by it.

Love was the ultimate Achilles' heel. A tried and true means to control the most powerful of men.

Superman could not be captured unless Lois Lane was used as bait. Spider-Man had Mary Jane. Thor would do anything to protect Jane Foster. Iron Man was vulnerable only when it came to Pepper Potts. The list went on and on.

Fisher had Annie rewind the video and freeze it on the image of the girl's face. He studied her as one might study a rare work of art.

"Who are you?" he mumbled to himself, almost in ecstasy. "And where have you been all my life?"

Then, with the hint of a malicious smile, he added, "And more importantly, where can I find you now?"

PART 3
Unraveling

"Adversity is like a strong wind. It tears away from us all but the things that cannot be torn, so that we see ourselves as we really are."

—Arthur Golden

20

Megan Emerson sat on a concrete bench that snaked into a long semicircle, one of several that resembled the bleachers for half of a theater-in-the-round, with palm trees and water features at the center where a stage might have been.

Bright, colorful shops of every kind flowed around and beyond these concentric semicircles of concrete like a meandering river, and Megan decided she had rarely been in a mall as tranquil and adorable as the Bella Terra Shopping Center in Huntington Beach, California.

The dining, boutiques, and retail stores were higher end than she was used to, but now that she had a five million dollar bank account, courtesy of Alex Altschuler, she could afford not to worry about such things. And she hadn't been scrimping on groceries, either.

But while this money made life easier, and despite their opulent surroundings, holing up was holing up, and even the nicest of yachts could quickly become claustrophobic.

Megan had already been clothes shopping a few times recently, for both her and Nick, since they had left Palm Springs with only the clothes on their backs. So at this point, they had everything they needed.

Still . . . maybe she would get a bikini anyway. But only if she found one truly amazing, since her real purpose in being at Bella Terra was to people watch and window shop.

And to get out of Nick Hall's hair.

Their relationship was as strong as ever, but even during the honeymoon phase there were only so many times a day a couple could make love, and so much they could talk about, before they needed some space from each other.

They had been on a boat now for two weeks. The first five to ten days had passed by quickly, but the hours were starting to drag, and

Megan knew she and Nick needed some solid time away from each other to keep things fresh. A few days earlier she had visited LA and in a few days she planned to make a day of it in San Diego.

She was beginning to feel sorry for herself, but was determined to fight this off. After all, poor Nick had it much worse than she did. He hadn't ventured out from the bowels of the *Eos* even once, not even to a sundeck. Because the upper echelon of the US government and military had learned of his existence in such spectacular fashion, they weren't about to stop looking for him anytime soon. The worst part was that he was convinced that even with a rudimentary disguise the odds he would be recognized were exceedingly small, but he couldn't justify taking *any* chance, not with the stakes as high as they were.

When they weren't making love, they continued to brainstorm experiments that they hadn't tried, new ways to get an understanding of her immunity to his ESP, but things were not going well in this regard either. They had learned a lot, but they were not much closer to their goal than when they had begun over six months before.

In many ways Megan knew her life was better than ever, and she wouldn't trade it for the world. She was in love. She had the chance to work on an extraordinary problem with a truly extraordinary man. She was friends with the head of Black Ops for the US, as spooky as that sounded, as well as the lovable geek who had become one of the most famous men alive.

Still, even a six-million-dollar yacht could get old. And living with a man who could never come out of hiding, and who would be the ultimate prize for any number of unscrupulous people and governments, was tiring. And limiting.

Megan decided she had killed enough time resting and people watching and wandered around the mall until she came to a Nordstrom's store. Although it was one of the largest in the mall, it was built to blend in with the style and architecture of the rest.

She took her time walking through the store, drinking in the impressive array of merchandise around her and the many colorful shoppers, some in simple sweats, but far more decked out in clothing as expensive as that being sold here. Just being out and about, and around others, was a godsend, a psychologically therapeutic change of pace after too many hours on the *Eos*.

She gradually made her way to the women's section and found where they displayed their bikinis, always in season in this part of the world.

"Can I help you?" said a pretty young woman.

"Just looking for now," she replied. "Thanks."

Megan checked out the colorful assortment of suits, and frowned. The trend was not her friend this year, she thought. Crochet and neoprene suits were all the rage, neither of which appealed to her in the slightest. Even worse, many of the suits had a see-through mesh connecting the bikini areas. If she was going to wear a bikini, she was going to leave her midriff bare. She wasn't sure how mesh had suddenly become so popular.

She shook her head in amusement at a suit with less fabric than a postage stamp and continued browsing.

General Girdler had assured them that their new hideout was almost ready to go, although he was busier and less accessible than ever. Also grouchier. Not that she could blame him. It looked more and more likely his actions, taken unselfishly for noble purposes, would come back to bite him. Hard.

She and Nick had discussed possible permanent residences with the general, and had settled on New Zealand. It was far away, to say the least, and English was its native language. And while neither she nor Nick had ever visited, the country had plenty of cozy, secluded areas where Nick could avoid crowds, but which were populated enough for them to have a life. If they could be discovered in a non-descript home on the outskirts of a small town in New Zealand, then their disappearance from the grid just wasn't meant to be.

Alex was financing the search for the perfect location for them Down Under, and the purchase of what would become their new home. But the real challenge was finding a way to transport them this great distance without being discovered.

Megan was nervous about the move, as anyone would be about a change this dramatic, but also eager and excited. She had a feeling she would love both the New Zealand countryside and the people, whom she expected to be warm and down-to-earth. And since her profession and passion was graphic design, she could still stoke her creative impulses, and keep herself from going mad from boredom, by bidding for jobs online. With talent, a state-of-the art computer, and access to PayPal, anyone could forge a thriving design business with total anonymity.

But while she was more in love with Nick than ever, she was also more worried about their future than she wanted to admit. Nick was still Nick—brilliant, fun, and fascinating—but he was all too often distant and unresponsive. They both knew the Internet in his head was responsible, exerting its irresistible but pernicious influence. Nick was fighting it, but the compulsion to ignore reality in favor of the endless content he could see and hear in his mind's eye could be too strong. The opportunity for both entertainment and stimulation too endless.

The longer Nick lived with implants the more worried he became about their impact on society. He had never had issues with addiction—to anything—and believed his impulse control to be very high. So the fact that he would choose to attend to the Web over the woman he loved was troubling.

Megan glanced up from the bikini racks and then back down without fully realizing it, still deep in thought. But in the brief instant she had looked out upon the spacious store, she had seen something that only registered on her subconscious, at the level of intuition. Without knowing why she had a sudden compulsion to survey her surroundings with greater care.

Nine women were shopping in the various departments, and four salespeople were either at cash registers or were helping customers. And two men were within eyesight as well.

While it wasn't noteworthy to see men in the women's departments, it was rare to see two of them without a wife or girlfriend.

The two men weren't moving in unison. Exactly. But Megan sensed that they were somehow together. Both were dressed casually, and both seemed to be trying hard not to look awkward or out of place. Which only made them look even *more* awkward and out of place.

They were both tall and trim and toned. And even dressed as they were, they couldn't help giving off a vibe that was distinctly . . . military.

The pair were making their way toward the department she was in, and as she stared at them she got the distinct impression they were going out of their way to look everywhere but in her direction. Their avoidance of the single viewing angle that intersected with her was just as telling as if they had stared straight at her, unblinking, and began to lick their chops.

She was their target!

While her rational mind warned her about paranoia and jumping to conclusions, her intuition screamed at her that she was in trouble. They were coming for *her*. And quickly.

Megan's heart began to race and she reached out to Nick Hall with all of her strength, but as she had known, at twelve miles she was too far to connect telepathically.

She walked briskly away from the two men, toward the sales clerk who had tried to help her minutes earlier. "I'm looking for a restroom," she said quickly as she approached.

The woman smiled pleasantly. "It's up the escalator to the third floor, and then straight ahead to the back wall."

"Thanks," grunted Megan as she accelerated by, glancing behind her and noticing that her pursuers were picking up speed as well.

She ran up the escalator and made it to her destination without seeing the men get on the moving stairway to follow. Maybe she *was* imagining things. Perhaps they were good friends buying gifts for their wives. But something in her remained certain that this was not the case.

She formulated a desperate plan as she left the escalator. She made a beeline for a sales clerk in the Babies and Toddlers Department, ten feet away. "I'm not feeling well," she practically shouted at the older woman, out of breath from running up the moving stairs. "Where is your bathroom?"

She already knew the answer, but asking the question was part of her plan.

The woman pointed toward the back wall and Megan rushed off in this direction. When she was out of sight of the woman she circled back and hid in the center of a circular rack of cotton robes, disappearing within as she had done when she was a little girl, to her mother's horror.

Megan held her breath and strained her hearing to its limits. "Did you see my wife come this way?" said a man's voice calmly, faint in the distance. "Black hair. Petite."

The sales clerk replied too softly for Megan to hear, but she had little doubt the woman would tell them where she had been heading, and this was confirmed seconds later when the two men strode purposefully toward the women's bathroom.

They stationed themselves just outside the door. They looked distinctly uncomfortable, each like a man who had been asked to hold his wife's purse, unsure of what to do with himself. Even so, it was clear they were prepared to wait as long as necessary for her to emerge.

Perfect.

She crept quickly back toward the escalators, keeping quiet and out of sight. "Text Nick," she whispered into her phone as she moved. "I'm in trouble. At Nordstrom in the Bella Terra Mall. Picked up a two-man tail."

She paused. "Send," she told her PDA, which immediately complied.

She reached the down escalator and practically launched herself onto it.

As she was rushing down the first few moving stairs, a third man appeared below her at the landing.

She stifled a gasp. His military bearing was all too familiar, and she had little doubt he was with the other men, completing the set.

She had thought she had been clever by freezing her pursuers at the bathroom and doubling back. But they had outsmarted her, after all.

The man was speaking rapidly into his phone, most likely inform-ing his partners who would arrive at the landing above her in seconds.

There was nowhere to run and no way to stop the escalator from depositing her on the second-floor landing, delivering her into the arms of the man waiting there.

But she still had one option open. Pandemonium.

She took a deep breath and prepared to scream like her life de-pended on it.

Because it probably did.

21

"Megan Emerson?" said the man below her on the landing, backing away five yards from the bottom of the escalator so as not to crowd her. Both his casual use of her name and his partial retreat surprised her, and she bit off her bloodcurdling scream just an instant before it began.

"I'm Boyd Solomon," continued the man rapidly as she stepped off the escalator. He glanced around to be certain no one was within earshot. "With the FBI." He held open his wallet in front of her.

Megan shot a glance up the escalator behind her. Sure enough, the man's partners were on their way down.

"IDs are easy to fake," she said bluntly.

"We were sent by General Justin Girdler," said Solomon. "Please come with us. You're in serious danger."

Megan wasn't sure what to expect, but this wasn't it. Would the general really give out her name?

The other two men joined them on the landing and held out their wallets. They introduced themselves as agents Dave Bergum and Dom Olinda. Megan took this chance to walk several steps to the right of the escalator to be closer to a cluster of customers who could sound an alarm if she screamed or appeared to be in distress. At least she hoped.

"You have the wrong person," she said under her breath. "I don't know any generals."

Solomon smiled. "The general told us you'd say that," he replied smoothly, also in hushed tones, his blue eyes a contrast to his swarthy features. "He apologizes for sending us, but said he had no choice. There are mercenaries after you, and they're closing in."

Megan couldn't help but glance around the store nervously as he said this.

"The general sent us to protect you. And to take you to a safe house forty miles east of here. He said a man would be waiting for you there. He wouldn't tell us the man's name, only that he had to be moved from Eos." Solomon shrugged. "Whatever that means."

Megan stared hard at each of the three men in turn, trying to bore into their souls, wishing *she* could read minds for once instead of only being able to block Nick from reading hers. Were they on the level?

"We have orders to be your bodyguards until we reach your . . . associate," added Solomon, meeting her intense stare with a relaxed confidence.

For the first time in minutes, Megan's pounding heart began to slow from the breakneck pace it had been maintaining. She glanced at her phone, still in her right hand, but Nick had not replied. Impossible. She had used her direct line *into his brain.* No way he would ignore her message. Not *this* one.

"Hold on," she said, quickly typing *U there?* into her phone and hitting send. "What does this general of yours do?" she asked.

"He's the head of Black Ops," replied Solomon immediately, while Bergum and Olinda continued to remain silent. Solomon smiled. "And these *are* fake IDs," he acknowledged. "We're not FBI. We're with Black Ops also."

For some reason this admission settled Megan down, convincing her that these men were on the level. "Is the man I'll be meeting okay? Is he in any danger?"

"He's perfectly fine," said Solomon. "The general got to him in time." He paused. "Not to make too fine a point of it, but we *are* exposed here. We need to get moving."

Megan nodded, and they began marching off at a casual pace, her three bodyguards forming a phalanx around her.

Minutes later they made it to the parking lot and a black SUV with tinted windows. Really? Megan was tempted to point out just how cliché this vehicle really was, but managed to suppress the temptation.

"Keep your head down," instructed Agent Solomon, sliding into the back seat beside her.

Megan glanced once again at her phone but Nick had still failed to respond. This was more troubling to her than she could say. No matter how distracted he became, he had never gone this long without responding, and this wasn't just a playful text but a full-on panicked one. Something was wrong.

"I've been texting Ni—my friend," said Megan, slumping down into her seat. "And he hasn't responded."

"I'm sure he ditched his phone so it couldn't be used to trace him," offered Solomon helpfully.

Megan knew he was wrong but remained expressionless. It would take a beheading for Nick Hall to get rid of his phone.

"Which reminds me," continued Solomon. "You'll have to ditch your phone also. Give it to me. I'll wipe it before I toss it."

Megan nodded reluctantly. She knew if the general were here, he would have her do the same. For the past four or five years, all phones automatically backed up their data and settings to the cloud for safekeeping, so she could restore it all when she bought a new phone. Still, the device was like an old friend.

She deleted all of her texts and then handed the phone to Solomon. "You're *sure* the man you're taking me to is unharmed?" she said. "And fully conscious?"

"*Yes*," said Solomon. "You'll be with him in less than an hour."

Agent Olinda pulled the SUV out of the parking lot and began driving. The ride was smooth and quiet, despite the fact that Olinda routinely exceeded the speed limit.

Megan turned toward Agent Solomon as the SUV hurtled up a freeway on-ramp. "Tell me more about the men after us," she said.

"You know as much as I do," he replied. "General Girdler told us where to find you and ordered us to protect you. With our lives, if necessary. He said a team of mercs were gunning for you and wouldn't be far behind. That's all I know."

"Where are we going?"

"The safe house is in Chino. The general will meet you and your friend there and give you a full briefing."

Megan considered. She had had so much free time on the *Eos* she had made it a point to study maps of Huntington Beach and surroundings online, looking for interesting places to visit. Chino was a center of agriculture and dairy farming. A small community that was the opposite of the dense, glamorous, high rent surroundings of Huntington Beach. Its sparse population would be a blessing for Nick. Hopefully, this emergency would convince the general to accelerate their time table for moving to New Zealand.

They drove in silence most of the way. Once they began heading north on the 57, Megan began asking Solomon the distance to their destination every ten minutes.

"How far away now?" she asked for a third time.

Solomon's face darkened, like a dad whose kids were driving him crazy, and Megan was surprised he didn't shout, "We'll get there when we get there." Instead, he visibly forced himself to relax and said, "About eight miles."

Megan brightened. "Call up the distance on your phone," she said. "I'd like to know exactly."

Solomon turned to her with the look of a man whose patience was more than wearing thin. "Why? Why does that matter?" he spat out.

"It's one of my quirks," said Megan with a shrug. "One of the things General Girdler loves about me," she added pointedly.

Solomon grunted but turned to his phone and began sliding his fingers over the screen. "Six point eight miles exactly. Satisfied?"

"Very," said Megan, who turned away from Solomon and began keeping careful track of their progress on the SUV's odometer. When they were exactly six miles from the safe house she reached out for Hall with all her strength but did not get a reply.

She continued this exercise every five blocks for the next two miles, with the same result.

They were now four miles out, which was well within their telepathic range. No response to texts or telepathic calls. Megan felt her heart begin to pound into her chest once again. "Have you had any communications from the safe house recently?" she asked Solomon. "Is my friend still waiting for me? Still okay?"

"*Yes!*" shouted Solomon emphatically, glaring at her as though he now understood why others would want to kill her. "I got a text from a colleague after we left the mall. Your friend has been told you're on the way and is eager to see you."

Megan nodded. This response cemented her certainty. She had no idea what was waiting for her at her destination. But she knew one thing for sure.

It was not Nick Hall.

22

Megan's mind raced as the SUV hurtled over the freeway. She was surrounded by three armed men in a moving vehicle. Not exactly an advantageous position.

She needed to change this. And quickly.

An image of Olinda and Bergum waiting uncomfortably outside of the women's bathroom popped into her head, giving her an idea. Men could be such babies at times.

"Aw, crap!" she barked suddenly, startling her three traveling companions. "We need to stop," she added with a mixture of frustration and dismay. "Take the next exit."

"What?" said Solomon. "Are you fucking *crazy?*"

"Look," said Megan. "I'm not happy about it either. But my period just restarted—with a vengeance. If I don't change this tampon immediately we're going to have a flood in here."

She had thought of faking a stomach issue, but since she hadn't complained up to this point, she decided against it. Diarrhea was something these men could relate to. They would know there was little likelihood of such an emergency out of the blue. So while the emergency she was making up now had never happened in her life, she was counting on them not to know this, and to be too uncomfortable about it to ask any questions.

All three men looked squeamish, turning into babies once again. For some reason, menstruation was a topic that even the most hardened of men would do almost anything to avoid. But she had to work fast. The next exit was approaching in a hurry.

"I know we're close to the safe house," said Megan. "But take the next exit! *Now!*" she insisted. "You're big, strapping men. I'm sure you can protect me for an extra five minutes. Or do you want me to change my tampon while we're driving?"

"Pull off!" ordered Solomon, making a face.

Olinda veered to the right, managing to change lanes just in time to catch the off ramp.

Megan forced herself to stay calm and think. Now what? Getting out of the SUV was her first priority, but it would take a minor miracle for her to manage an escape.

She frowned deeply as she scanned the area in front of the SUV. *Bad luck.* Freeway exits often led to a store, or at least a busy restaurant where she would have had additional options. This one led to nothing but a two-pump gas station, with a small convenience store attached.

They pulled into the station and up to one of the pumps. Solomon exited the vehicle and held the door open for Megan. "Make it quick," he said to her. "Agent Bergum will escort you," he added.

Megan searched the surroundings but there was nothing that seemed useful. No running car to race off in, and the station was completely deserted other than one attendant in the convenience store. She thought of calling out to him for help, but this would almost certainly fail and would probably get him killed.

Bergum walked her to the restroom door and stood beside it while she entered. The room consisted of a single stall and sink, and a window high up on the back wall. Megan stood on the toilet seat to look down through the window, but even if she managed to get through it in one piece, which would take some doing, Solomon and Olinda would be able to see her easily from where they were parked.

Shit! she thought. Her subterfuge had worked beautifully, allowing her to extricate herself from the SUV, but her luck was nearing its end.

Who were these men, anyway? The fact that they knew about Nick, the *Eos*, and the general was extremely alarming. Was Nick dead? Did this explain his lack of response to her texts?

Just contemplating this took her breath away, as though she had been hit in the gut. She shook her head vigorously, refusing to believe it. No one was more resourceful than Nick. He *had* to be alive. To think anything else was too debilitating.

And of course he was alive, she reasoned. Not only was he too resourceful to kill, but too valuable.

Which is why *she* was alive, she suddenly realized. To be used as leverage against Nick. After all, if they wanted her dead, they could have killed her in the SUV at any time.

Knowing they needed her alive gave her additional options. She could try to fight them without fear of losing her life.

She looked around the small room for a weapon, but found none. There was a bottle filled with liquid soap near the sink, fairly heavy, but not nearly heavy enough.

And then she considered the toilet, the shark of the design world. The one in the station was exactly like those found in homes. No matter how rapidly improvements were made in electronics and other technology, no matter how often every design, from the lowly soda can to the mightiest jet fighter, had continued to evolve through time, the basic toilet design had remained unchanged. Like the shark, it was perfectly evolved to fulfill its purpose.

Yes, many toilets now had sensors, and she had read of toilets in Japan that did everything but put on laser light shows, but the basic flush mechanism remained the same. A porcelain tank filled with water. And a bob that would shut off incoming water once the tank had been refilled after a flush.

And covering this tank, a rectangular ceramic slab.

A *heavy* ceramic slab. And one that was removable in case the bob failed to work properly.

Megan took a deep breath and decided this was her only hope. She carefully removed the white ceramic cover from the tank and carried it the few yards to the door. It was *really* heavy. Wow. Porcelain was like lead, and she only weighed a hundred and twenty pounds herself. But while it was heavier and more unwieldy than she would have liked, it was still a godsend.

She set the edge of the smooth white slab down carefully on the tiled floor, picked up the full bottle of liquid soap, and readied herself.

"Here goes nothing," she whispered, almost to distract herself from the insane attempt she was about to make. She threw the bottle of soap as hard as she could at the window a few yards away. As she had hoped, the plastic missile was heavy enough to crash through, making a shattered-glass sound that was unmistakable.

Even before the bottle had landed outside, Megan managed to hoist the porcelain slab to head-height, waiting.

She didn't have to wait long.

Reacting almost instantly to the sound of shattered glass, Bergum threw his shoulder into the door, breaking the flimsy lock and rushing inside to investigate.

Megan swung the unwieldy slab at Bergum's head with all of her might.

And missed!

The man's reflexes were extraordinary. He ducked the oncoming blow with athletic fluidity. Megan had positioned herself perfectly, out of his sight as he raced into the bathroom, but instead of connecting with his head the ceramic weight tore clumsily through the air into the now open door behind him. The force of the impact caused Megan to drop the heavy slab, and it slammed into the tile floor with a loud, echoing sound, breaking into a half-dozen jagged pieces.

Bergum recovered immediately and slammed her into a wall. He pulled a plastic zip-strip from his pants and zipped it around her wrists, which he forced together with a brutal efficiency. Then he spun her around and pressed a large, sweaty hand over her mouth, just as she was about to scream.

Bergum shoved her out of the bathroom roughly—the struggles of such a petite woman barely registering on him—but after a single step he found himself staring straight into the sights of a handgun, pointed at his head.

"Freeze!" shouted the attendant, his gun hand remaining steady.

Bergum stopped in his tracks and stared into the attendant's eyes, assessing the situation, calculating his odds of turning the tables. But after only a few seconds he remembered the role he was playing. "I'm with the FBI," he said with exaggerated calm. "If you let me reach into my back pocket, I can show you my ID."

Even as the attendant was considering this, Solomon and Olinda yanked open the outer door, their weapons trained on the man.

The attendant swallowed hard and lowered his gun. "You really Feds?" he asked warily.

Solomon took out his wallet and showed him his fake ID. "Yes. Sorry about the commotion. And don't let this little thing fool you," he added, gesturing toward Megan. "She's wanted in eight states. And she's a lot more deadly than she looks."

"You understand why I drew on your partner, right?" said the attendant. "She broke my window. And he broke through the door. Looked like he was assaulting her."

"Perfectly understandable," said Solomon soothingly. "Sorry again for the trouble. We'll get out of your hair now."

The attendant watched them carefully as they made their way to the SUV and then drove off.

Bergum, now sitting beside Megan instead of Solomon, finally released his hand from her mouth. She sucked in huge lungfuls of air hungrily.

Solomon shifted in the passenger's seat so he could face her. He frowned deeply, and shook his head. "Oh well," he said. "We did try to do this the easy way." A thoughtful look crossed his face. "We were so close to our destination. What tipped you off?"

"Who are you, and what do you want?" demanded Megan, ignoring the question.

Solomon smiled. "Don't worry. We'll have plenty of time to get to know each other," he assured her. "Plenty of time."

23

Nick Hall was on the edge of consciousness, in the dreamlike state between sleep and wakefulness. His thoughts drifted aimlessly from a movie he had recently seen, to the bloodshed at the Oscars, to a coral reef he had studied as a marine biologist, before finally settling onto Megan Emerson.

When he got to Megan he became fully awake, although he had yet to open his eyes and he was still quite groggy. Despite the lumbering slowness of his thoughts, he realized he had had the same recurring dream once again, even during this short nap. The dream that was his ultimate nightmare.

The one in which Megan announced she was leaving him.

Billions of people had loved before. Had thought they couldn't possibly live without the object of their affection. Love had provoked irrational and self-destructive actions long before this emotion had brought Romeo and Juliet to take their own lives.

But Hall believed his case was fairly unique in the annals of history. Not only was he madly in love with Megan but also totally dependent on her for his sanity. What would he do without her? How truly alone would he be? Shunned by anyone he could read, no matter how much they might otherwise care for him.

And how insidious was the Internet, that he found himself ignoring Megan to attend to it? Perhaps, he had to admit, no more insidious than alcohol to an alcoholic. How many alcoholics couldn't stop themselves from imbibing, even at the cost of everything they held dear?

Would he lose everything as well? The compulsion to splinter his focus was growing ever greater, and the trend was alarming. Eventually Megan would tire of being with a man who she couldn't be sure was really there for her. Tire of competing with a limitless network designed to distract and entice. He had to find a way to stay disciplined.

Hall decided he would apply himself like never before to battling this scourge. There had to be any number of writings on the best methods to help the ever-growing ranks of those who were addicted to the Internet, or rapidly becoming so.

He was acutely aware of the irony here. He would be searching the Web for articles about . . . how to stop searching the Web. But this is what he would do. And he wouldn't rest until he had found a way to get a handle on the situation.

The Megan-leaving-him nightmare was tormenting him much too frequently. And it had become much too real.

Hall shook his head in confusion. Where was the information he needed? He had become so used to whatever he wanted to know appearing in his visual field without him having to consciously call for it, its absence was a shock to his system.

His mind's eye was blank. He actively ordered the software in his implants to conduct a search, not sure why this was suddenly necessary.

Still nothing. Which was impossible.

His connection was down.

Hall gasped without realizing it. His Web connection had become one of his senses, as indispensable to him as smell, touch, or hearing, and its loss was just as scary.

He didn't even have any devices he could use to determine if this was an implant problem or if the network was down. The 6G network that had been around now for over a year was highly redundant and very powerful. This was the first time he had lost a connection since before he had faked his death.

But maybe this was a sign. He had wanted to reduce his dependence on the Web, and *boom*, just like that, the Web had crashed, right on cue. This would allow him to get a feel for the cold-turkey experience. Okay. *Good.*

He took a deep breath and walked to the large ornate mirror in the master cabin. His brown eyes seemed dead. His jet black hair

limp and without its usual vitality. He had a two-day growth of stubble, and his cheeks looked hollow.

In short, he looked like shit. And he felt like it too. He had been
battling feelings of depression, struggling to keep them from Megan.
He had been relieved when she had opted to get space the past few
days.

He was so tired of the cloak and dagger. So tired of the secrets and
the isolation and the mind reading. The *Eos* was truly magnificent,
but at the moment it was just a bigger, better appointed version of a
space capsule for all of his ability to escape its confines.

But even so, he was better than this. Better than wallowing in
self-pity. He needed to shave. To wear something crisp and present-
able. And when his connection returned, in addition to embarking
on whatever twelve-step program his search provided, he would also
look for romantic getaways in New Zealand.

And he would look for jewelers there also, he decided, with a conviction that surprised him.

He and Megan had both been wary of the institution of marriage
when they had met, not eager to rush into it the way Heather and
Alex were doing. But the truth was they were deeply in love, living
together, and joined at the hip. So what was the point of *not* being
engaged?

Two hours passed and the Internet was still not back. Two hours
that seemed like two weeks. He had shaved and showered and tidied
up the *Eos*, but he felt like he was losing his mind.

Okay, enough experimentation with cold turkey already. Hall decided it was time for the Web to return.

A thought stream rose above the ever-present white-noise in his
head. *Nick Hall,* it called out, in the same way Megan might have
contacted him telepathically. *My name is Kent Lombardo. And if you
ever want to see Megan Emerson alive again, you'll do exactly as I
tell you.*

There was a pause. *I have no way to tell if you're reading me or
not, but I've been told to assume you are. We're blocking the network
in your vicinity at considerable expense, so you can't do something*

stupid that you'll regret, like calling for help and getting Megan killed. I'm in a car and will be at the Eos *in about five minutes. I'm sure you'll have managed to read my mind before I arrive, so I won't waste any more time explaining the situation. See you soon.*

Hall staggered, and the *Eos* seemed to spin around him. How had someone gotten to Megan?

He reached out to the man who had broadcast this threat and tore through his mind like a threshing machine. The man's name was Kent Lombardo, as he had indicated. He had been special forces before joining a private military contractor named Blackwater, carrying out missions in Iraq, Syria, and Afghanistan. And very recently, he had been hired away by an ex-boss at Blackwater, a man who went by the name of Boyd Solomon.

Lombardo had no idea what any of this was about. He was simply following the instructions he had been given by Solomon. He didn't know anything about Hall other than he was still alive, despite the fact the public had been told otherwise, and could read minds. He didn't know who had hired Solomon, and he didn't know this person's plans for Hall.

Very smart. Knowing Hall would grind down Lombardo's brain until not even the tiniest speck of deception could hide, they had kept the mercenary in the dark. Lombardo had been instructed to treat Hall with great care as long as he was cooperative. To place a personal Internet dampening field on him. And to drive him to a location that would not be disclosed to Lombardo until they were on their way.

The merc had balked at first, insisting that if Hall really could read his mind he'd be a sitting duck when he approached the *Eos*. Hall could easily shoot him and go on the run. But Solomon had convinced him that Hall wouldn't be going anywhere. Assured him that Megan was his weakness and that he would do nothing but cooperate as long as her life hung in the balance.

Hall read that Lombardo had any number of vulnerabilities he could exploit. But he also read that if Lombardo didn't deliver Hall as instructed, regardless of the reason, Megan Emerson would suffer the consequences. Solomon had made this quite clear to the merce-nary just before the man had left, so it would be fresh in his mind for Hall to read.

Try as he might, Hall couldn't find any way out. Whoever was be-hind this was very smart, had somehow known he would do anything for Megan, and had orchestrated events with absolute perfection.

But how were they found? Who was the mastermind responsible? And how did he know so much?

Hall briefly considered hiding a weapon in his clothing, but real-ized this would be useless. What would be the point? The mercs car-rying out the op were sure to search him and would simply remove anything he managed to smuggle out.

And even if not, he wasn't about to try anything. Not when they had Megan. Kent Lombardo could press a gun into his own head, and Hall would struggle with all of his might to prevent the scumbag from pulling the trigger.

He had been complaining of boredom and confinement, but he should have been counting his blessings. He'd give anything to return to boredom once again. But the fates seemed to be choosing a differ-ent path.

Splashing cold water on his face, Hall set his jaw in determination, took a deep breath, and exited the *Eos* to surrender.

It was time to begin to learn why they wanted him. And what, exactly, he was up against.

24

Heather Zambrana rushed into her fiancé's office and gave him a quick peck on the lips. "What's going on?" she asked anxiously.

He had asked her to meet him in his office immediately but had not said why. And he should have been traveling to his meeting with the CEO and COO of Apple. The fact that he wasn't was a bad sign. "Did they cancel the meeting?"

Altschuler shook his head. "No. I did. The general texted me that he wanted to set up a call as soon as possible. Didn't say what it was about."

He checked the ever-present clock in his internal visual field. "He'll be calling in less than a minute."

He sat in one of the padded black leather chairs that encircled a round conference table in his office and motioned for her to sit next to him. They arranged the two chairs so both were facing the large 3-D monitor on the wall, and seconds later General Girdler and Colonel Campbell joined them virtually.

"I assume you want to wait for Nick and Megan," said Altschuler after their images had materialized.

Girdler blew out a long breath and looked as though he was in pain. "No. I'm afraid I have bad news. The two of them have disappeared."

"What do you mean, disappeared?" said Altschuler.

"I mean they're gone," said Girdler. "Your boat is empty. Neither one is responding to calls or texts."

Altschuler shook his head, refusing to believe it was true. "Maybe they went stir crazy," he suggested, desperate for an innocent explanation, "and snuck off. Maybe they're at a hotel somewhere having epic sex and don't want to answer any calls."

"They disappeared yesterday morning," said Girdler. "I didn't call this meeting until I was convinced they were gone and not just going on an unscheduled vacation."

Heather swallowed hard. "And you've searched the *Eos*?" she said.

"Yes. Very thoroughly."

"Any sign of, you know . . . foul play? Any blood?" she added, cringing as though afraid of the answer she might get.

Girdler shook his head. "Thankfully, no. Everything is in perfect order. No sign of a struggle of any kind."

"Doesn't make any sense," said Altschuler. "No one is more resourceful than Nick. And how do you capture a mind reader who can read you coming from miles away? One who can, literally, call in the Calvary in the form of Justin Girdler and Mike Campbell and the many thousands you two command. And Nick and I can communicate with our implants in a way that is indistinguishable from telepathy. At any distance. So at minimum, if he were in trouble, he would have contacted me."

Altschuler held up a hand. "Hold on a minute. I'll try to connect."

He reached out through his implants to his missing friend, but instead of sending a text he shouted Hall's name, a shout that would seem just as real as if Altschuler had been behind him, screaming into his ear.

No response. He tried several more times with the same result.

The other three meeting participants watched his face eagerly, but his darkening expression communicated the result louder than a bullhorn. He was failing to make contact with Hall as well.

"You did have eyes on them, right?" said Heather to the 3-D monitor, breaking the long silence. "Electronics, or bodyguards, or both, right? I mean, Alex and I are more heavily guarded than the president. So what about that?" she finished, unable to completely keep the rising panic from her voice.

This time Mike Campbell answered. "I'm afraid they weren't under observation. Too conspicuous. Since Nick, supposedly, disappeared from the Palm Springs facility, the military has pulled out all the stops to try to find him. The general and I have been monitoring their efforts. If we had put any eyes on them, this might have backfired, might have advertised that there was something at the Huntington Beach marina worth watching."

Heather shook her head in frustration and disappointment.

"In hindsight it was obviously a mistake," admitted the general. "But Mike and I have impeccable sources. And the military was getting nowhere. We thought there was a better chance of the *Eos* getting hit by a tsunami than Nick being found there. He assured me he was staying below deck at all times. And the military was truly looking in all the wrong places."

"Until they looked in the right one," said Altschuler.

"No," said Campbell. "We've worked our sources even harder since they disappeared. We don't know what happened, but our government or military had nothing to do with it."

A tear came to Heather's eye as she thought about the fate of her two friends. "Any chance they began to feel too vulnerable to trust anyone?" she asked. "*Including* us?" she added, her voice almost pleading for this to be true. "Maybe they decided to finally disappear for good—from *everyone*."

"At this point anything is possible," replied Girdler gently. "But we have to operate under the assumption they've been captured, or killed."

"So we have no idea who might be behind it?" said Altschuler. "Or what they're after?"

"None," said Girdler. "But as I've said, the list of countries and power players who might want to capture Nick is too long to even bother compiling."

"We have to find them!" said Heather, both of her eyes now glistening. "No matter what the cost."

"We're trying," said Girdler. "Believe me. One thing that makes this even more difficult is that our military has an active search on for them already, as you know. So now we have to run a hunt within a hunt. For instance, if we fix the facial recognition program we've sabotaged so it can now identify Nick once again, the others looking for him can use it as well."

"So what?" said Heather. "Whoever finds them from our side can't be as dangerous as whatever they're facing now."

Campbell gave her a respectful nod. "Good point," he said.

"We will find them," said Girdler, staring at Heather reassuringly. "I promise you. And soon."

Heather closed her eyes and took a deep breath, but chose not to respond.

"On a different subject," said Girdler, turning to face Altschuler. "Before we sign off, how'd it go with Congress, Alex? Any luck persuading them that delaying BrianWeb was the right course?"

Altschuler shook his head miserably. "None. They think my reticence is a smoke screen, a petty manipulation. To get them to indemnify Theia against possible future lawsuits if things go south. They basically told me to man up and just be damn sure the technology is water-tight. I'm supposed to be the best, so I need to quit whining and make sure BrainWeb is unbreachable."

"I'm not all that surprised," said Girdler with a frown. "But thanks for the effort."

Altschuler nodded. "Anything else?"

"No," said the general. "That's all for now."

"I assume you'll tell us the moment you know anything," said Heather. She gathered herself and added, "Good *or* bad."

"We will," said the general. "And let us know if either of you come up with anything that might help us."

Altschuler looked over at the woman he had come to love, who was still taking the disappearance of their friends hard, as well she should. Still, he felt compelled to do something to reassure her. "They'll find them, Heather," he said softly. "Really. And this is rock bottom. So it's only going to get better from here," he added confidently. "Right, General?"

"Yeah," said Girdler after a few second delay. "Sure. It's only going to get better from here," he repeated.

But the smile he wore on his face was forced, and he sounded anything but convinced.

25

Marc Fisher studied his prize in fascination on the monitor in front of him. About six feet in height, fairly handsome, black hair, brown eyes. Nothing about him that would suggest he possessed supernatural abilities. You could pass him in the street and have no idea you had passed the most uniquely talented man in the history of the world, unless you wanted to include Da Vinci, Newton, or Einstein, which Fisher didn't.

He was delighted at how well his plan had unfolded. But not surprised. After all, he was the top predator among a species that fancied itself the top predator. As usual, he had been brilliant, cunning, and decisive.

Through Solomon, he had ordered Lombardo to escort Hall to an RV he had purchased for the occasion. A very expensive RV. Spacious and comfortable. It wasn't the *Eos*, but it wasn't too far off. When you caught the goose that laid the golden eggs, you didn't manhandle it. You didn't throw it into the trunk of a car. You treated it like it was a delicate painting. He wanted Hall to understand just how much he valued him, and just how well treated he would be if he continued to cooperate.

Lombardo then had Hall lie down on a bed inside the camper and take a drug that would knock him out for a few days. Which actually made Hall the lucky one.

Lombardo, the poor bastard, had then completed the grueling drive from California to just outside of Washington DC in only thirty-seven hours, including brief stops for sleep along the way. Grueling, true, but why hire ex-special forces soldiers and pay them immense sums of money if they couldn't handle a little sleep deprivation?

Hall had awakened only a few minutes earlier, and the door to his room opened and a freshly showered Lombardo arrived with a cart, on top of which sat a linen napkin, utensils, ice water, a bottle of wine, a bowl of lobster bisque, and an elegant plate covered by filet mignon, caramelized potatoes, and mixed vegetables.

Judging from the speed and enthusiasm with which Hall consumed the meal just after Lombardo closed the door, he must have been starving. A few days in stasis would do that to a man, Fisher allowed, waiting patiently for him to finish.

Finally, his guest swallowed his last bite and pushed the plate away.

"Nick Hall," said Fisher, his voice broadcast through speakers in Hall's room, modified slightly so it couldn't be recognized. Not that it would be, unless Hall watched nothing but C-SPAN, but one could never be too careful.

While he could see Hall through any number of video cameras, Hall could not see him. He was impressed by how calmly Hall took the disembodied voice suddenly calling out his name.

"My name is Frank Earnest."

Hall digested this for a second or two and then shook his head in disdain. "Sure it is," he said.

"You seem certain it's an alias. Why?"

"Come on," said Hall. "Frank and Earnest? Two synonyms for *honest*? How stupid do you think I am? Was the name Integrity Doright already taken?"

Fisher laughed. "Very good, Nick. Very impressive. Didn't think you'd catch that so quickly. Yes, it is an alias. I don't feel entirely comfortable giving you my real name."

Wow. He liked this Hall already. The fact that he was so savvy would make his life easier. Fisher had once spoken with a woman who negotiated complex deals between pharmaceutical companies and biotechs. She had told him that she had always thought it would be an advantage to negotiate against a novice, someone who didn't really know what they were doing. But she soon found it to be just the opposite. The novice made *everything* difficult. A novice would fiercely negotiate terms that a veteran knew were accepted industry standards. A veteran, on the other hand, would quickly get to the heart of the negotiation, and even when not in agreement, would at least understand the nuances of a given position.

"I assume you've read where you are from Lombardo's mind."

"I assume you're the man behind all this," countered Hall.

"Yes."

"Okay," said Hall. "Since you answered my question, I'll answer yours. Yes. I did read my location from your puppet. I'm in a warehouse just outside of DC." He paused. "You do know there are warehouses in Huntington Beach, right?" he added wryly.

Fisher couldn't help but laugh.

"So why a warehouse?" continued Hall. "And why DC?"

Fisher wanted to taunt him. Wanted to reply that since Hall had been experimented on for months in a warehouse in California, he was simply trying to make him feel at home. He wanted to describe in intimate, graphic detail how he would torture and slowly butcher his girlfriend if he didn't cooperate. Removing one piece of her at a time.

But he restrained himself, determined to play the role of a good Samaritan. A reluctant participant. Determined that Hall believe he was in the hands of someone who did not wish him ill.

"The warehouse isn't near any residential areas," said Fisher pleasantly. "So no nosy neighbors. Which is important, since you'll be a . . . reluctant . . . guest of mine for a while. The shell of the warehouse is made of steel, so it's easy to lock up tight, and at night no one is within hearing distance." He paused. "Or mind-reading distance. This last was done for your benefit."

"Sure it was," said Hall dubiously.

Wow, thought Fisher. This guy was not going to be an easy mark.

"I'll want to see Megan Emerson, of course," added Hall.

"Of course. I'll see to it after our conversation."

"If she has so much as a bruise on her," said Hall matter-of-factly, "I will find you and kill you. Believe it."

"Oh I do, Nick. I can assure you of that. But as long as you help me in my purpose, I promise both of you will be treated like royalty. I trust you have no complaints about your room? Or your room service for that matter?"

Hall looked around. If he didn't know he was in a warehouse he would have thought he was in the master bedroom in a mansion, complete with a king-sized bed, oversized television, dressers, lamps, and a massive wrought-iron-framed mirror.

"Your kitchen is through the alcove on your left," said Fisher. "And your bathroom, with shower and hot tub, to the right. I spared no expense to make it as livable as possible. Anything else you want, you just have to ask. Massage chair. Treadmill, stair-stepper, or other exercise equipment. Books. A computer with a word program in case you like to write. A chess program. Whatever video games you might like, although you won't be able to connect them to the Internet. I'm sure you've noticed you aren't getting any signal."

"Where is Megan?" said Hall, back to the only subject he cared about.

"I'm afraid that's not something I'm ready to disclose."

"Why am I here?" said Hall. "What do you want?"

"First, I want to offer my sincere apologies for what I've been forced to do to get you here. If there were any other way to be sure I could acquire your services, I would gladly take it. Honestly, I feel terrible about this."

Hall smiled coolly. "I've found that when a person begins a sentence with *honestly*, what usually follows is the opposite of honest. Especially when the man says his name is Frank Earnest."

"Not in this case," lied Fisher. "But I understand how you might feel that way."

"So what do you want?"

"I'm a lot like you Nick. I can't tell you how I know so much about you, but I do. And while you haven't broken the law, per se, you've been an accomplice to Justin Girdler. Who has broken the military code, and also the law, given he financed you illegally. But you didn't do this because you're evil or a criminal. Or for personal gain. You did it for a higher purpose. You're willing to make sacrifices to prevent disasters from occurring in the future. You faced a thorny ethical problem, and you made the right decision."

Hall rolled his eyes. "Okay, *Frank*, I'll bite. So what's *your* higher purpose?"

"Our government is broken," said Fisher, ignoring Hall's venom. "Beyond all hope of repair. Given an increasingly dangerous world, in its current state of corruption and incompetence, the government is responsible for the suffering and misery of many millions. They've pushed the world's strongest economy to the breaking point while lining their own pockets. They've let world terrorism metastasize. A nuke will be set off in a major city in the next few years if something isn't done. Or worse. We have to change our ways or we'll be paying the price for generations." He paused. "I was convinced that there was nothing anyone could do about this. That we had to fiddle while Rome burned."

"But then you learned about me."

"That's right. And I realized that with your help, we could right the ship. We could root out the massive corruption in Washington."

"A city I happen to be at the outskirts of at this very moment," noted Hall. "Too bad there aren't more politicians in Huntington Beach," he added with the hint of a smile. "Would have saved you from having to move me so far."

"No. It's too bad there aren't *fewer* politicians in Washington," replied Fisher. "But with your help, there could be. And we could install a good man in the presidency instead of a politician. Be a nice change of pace, don't you think?"

"And I suppose you're that good man whom we'll want to install in the White House?"

"Not at all," said Fisher smoothly. "Like I said, I'm just a good citizen. Like you, doing something detestable to my own ethical sense, keeping you here against your will, for the greater good. When you've helped me get a handle on the corruption in this town, I'll introduce you to the man I have in mind. You'll be able to read him and see for yourself that there are no men more honorable or competent. No men better intentioned. No better leaders."

"I'll believe that when it happens," said Hall, and once again Fisher was impressed that despite his considerable charm and ability to lie convincingly, Hall wasn't fooled for a second. The man seemed skilled at reading people even without his ESP.

But even so, Fisher knew, if he repeated the lie long enough and treated Hall and his love interest with respect, seeing to their every comfort, even Hall might eventually begin to believe that he had noble intentions, despite being forced to use repugnant methods.

"It will happen," said Fisher, faking his most sincere voice. "You'll see. But for now all I want from you is to gather dirt. I'm not asking you to hurt good people. I'm asking you to take down corrupt politicians. If someone you read is pure evil, they deserve to be taken down. If they have no skeletons in their closet, and they've come to Washington simply to help their fellow man, they're fine, right? No one can touch them."

Hall remained silent.

"The good man I'm trying to install in the White House is a Democrat. So I'll want you to read a select group of power brokers and fund raisers for the party. I'll want to know their buttons. So I can persuade them to support my candidate over others in the primaries. And then I'll want you to read dirty politicians of both parties."

Hall shook his head in disgust, but remained silent.

"Look, I didn't kidnap you to stop a mass-murderer running amok through a city. Even though it could be argued that my actions could be justified if this were the case. But what I'm doing is much more important. A murderer can kill a handful of people. But a dirty politician, or a corrupt president, especially, can change the course of billions of lives."

Fisher paused to let this sink in.

"Even so," he continued in a softer tone, "I did a lot of thinking, soul searching, and praying, before finally deciding to take this step."

Hall was listening intently, but his expression remained unreadable.

"So will you help me, Nick? Help the country? Help us get on the right path? For the sake of the entire planet, and for generations to come."

"And if I don't?"

Fisher sighed deeply. "Then you'll leave me no choice. You'll force me to use the leverage I have on you. The very last thing I want to do. But I will. Suppose an innocent young girl was the sole victim of the most deadly and contagious virus known. And suppose she was breaking out of quarantine. Would you shoot her? An innocent girl? Or would you listen to your heart, take your finger off the trigger, and condemn millions to a grisly death?"

Fisher continued, not waiting for an answer. "The answer isn't pleasant. Or easy. But we both know what it is. As horrifying as it would be to shoot a child, you wouldn't have any choice."

"Yeah. I can tell you're a real saint."

"Not a saint. A flawed man trying to make the most ethically correct decision in trying times. But if you don't cooperate a hundred percent. If you try to escape, try to learn who I am, or try to learn where *Megan* is, you'll force my hand. No, I won't kill her. If I did this, I would no longer have any control over you. But I will hurt her. Badly. It will hurt me to my core to do so, but I will."

Hall's expression darkened, and if he had telekinetic powers, Fisher decided, every object in the entire room would have been spinning around in a hellish funnel cloud.

"But again," continued Fisher, as pleasantly and as reasonably as he could manage, "if you take down corrupt and evil politicians, if you do a noble and heroic public service, you and she will be treated like royalty."

"Until you get what you want and kill us both."

"No. When I have enough that I'm certain the great man I have in mind will win the White House, you and Megan can get on with your lives. I'll see to it that you're left in peace."

Hall shook his head in disgust. "I may have been born at night," he said. "But I wasn't born *last* night."

"I'm a man of my word," said Fisher. "You'll see." He paused. "But for now, I invite you to relax and enjoy my hospitality. The only thing I'll ask of you between mind-reading assignments is to grow a beard."

"A beard?"

"Yes. I know there's a manhunt on for you, and that you're immune to facial recognition. But you were also somewhat famous, and we don't want you to be recognized by some random man in the street. So grow a beard, I'll get you a hat, and we'll make sure to keep you in the shadows as much as possible when you're in public. Okay?"

Hall nodded.

"Now Congress won't be in session again for a few weeks. But in three days there is a meeting of party movers and shakers at the Hay-Adams hotel. My candidate will need their support, so this will be your first assignment. I'll get you a room at the Hay-Adams and give you a list of the people I most want to, um . . . mine, and you can have at it."

Fisher watched Hall's face carefully, and for some reason he had the sense that his mind was racing, even though Hall was better than most at keeping a poker face. But racing to what end? Fisher had made sure the mind reader had no option but to do as he . . . requested.

"I'm afraid it doesn't work like that," said Hall calmly after what had been a long pause.

"Doesn't work like what?"

"Your list. I can only read one person at a time, for about twenty minutes at a time."

"Come on, Nick. We both know that isn't true."

"Oh, really. I don't know where you've gotten your information, then, but it's wrong. I can only comfortably go deep on one person at a time. And after I do, I need a full day of rest before I can do it again."

"You really think I'm that stupid? You're just trying to stall. Drag this out for as long as possible hoping I'll make a mistake, and give you an opening. I have news for you. I don't make mistakes." His voice softened. "Besides, once we get started, you'll see that I'm right. That I'm doing this for the right reasons. And you'll *want* to help me."

"It doesn't matter if I want to or not, mind reading takes a huge mental toll on me. I can only do what I can do."

"Nice try, Nick. But I know all about the Oscars. You had to be in multiple heads, deep, for at least thirty minutes to pull this off."

"Yeah," said Hall without missing a beat, "which is why I passed out, as the entire world saw. But what only one man knows, a doctor, is that this exertion almost killed me. I was in a coma for two days."

Fisher studied Hall carefully. He still thought this was a bluff, but he had played it brilliantly. He *had* passed out. Fisher knew he was okay when he was a video presence in President Cochran's meetings four days after the Oscars, but that didn't mean he couldn't have been near death earlier in the week. And Fisher understood why he would want to keep this limitation secret. Why show any weakness or vulnerability unless you had to? Why not allow the world to think your power, and your endurance, were unlimited? It's what he would have done.

"Don't worry," said Hall. "The election is almost two years away. Plenty of time. And believe me, when you see what I can dig up in fifteen minutes when I'm properly rested, you're going to be doing back-flips."

Hall's features darkened into a scowl. "But I need to see Megan. Now. In person."

"You can see her," said Fisher. "But not in person. You're too impressive, so we're showing you the respect you deserve. If you see her in person, we run the risk that you'll escape and free her. We're keeping her a long way away from you. But you'll be able to see and talk to her by video every day. You can talk about anything you'd like, including her health and how she's being treated."

"With you listening in, right?"

Fisher's instincts were to lie reflexively, but he caught himself. Telling uncomfortable truths had a way of making one's other lies more believable. "Yes. I'll be listening. But I won't interfere."

"Set up a call with her right now," insisted Hall. He looked around meaningfully at his spacious prison. "I'll go ahead and wait right here."

26

A man who was known only as Victor stared through a two-story picture window in the lodge that was now his home and office. Endless empty land rolled on in every direction for as far as he could see.

Now that was an interesting conversation, he thought, reflecting on the video call he had just completed. And unexpected wasn't even the word for it. He was not a man who was often surprised, but in this case he certainly had been.

But was it a real opportunity? Or was it a trap?

He shrugged. It didn't matter. Either way, it was an opportunity too incredible not to explore further.

A Mexican of Spanish ancestry, Victor stroked his chin, which always sprouted a layer of razor-sharp stubble mere hours after he had shaved, a perpetual, jet-black, five-o'clock shadow that wouldn't reveal his growing number of white hairs until it had grown out for several days. Patiently, methodically, he thought through various possibilities. His deep-set black eyes sparkled with an intensity and a dazzling intelligence that those with whom he interacted tended to pick up on almost immediately.

Finally, satisfied with his initial analysis, he decided it was time to call in his most trusted lieutenant, Eduardo Alvarez. As brilliant as he was, a different perspective was always helpful.

"Maria," he said to his PDA in Spanish, "send the following text to Eduardo and read any response back to me. *Eduardo, drop whatever you're doing and join me in the main lodge*." He paused. "Send."

Only ten seconds later Alvarez responded, and Maria read the message dutifully. "I'm at the warehouse with Hayes, Volkov, and Eberhardt preparing the KN-100 Surveillance Disruptors for shipment to the Russian mob. Be there pronto, probably ten minutes."

Victor nodded, and stroked his chin in thought once again. He was only five foot ten, and his face was more round than angular, but his presence was commanding and intimidating, and no matter how many larger, more imposing men were in a room with him it was impossible to mistake who was in charge.

He sat down at his glass desk and surveyed the large room. The main lodge was no longer even recognizable as such. The heads of big game animals no longer covered every wall, and the facility had been so dramatically upgraded and modernized with furnishings and sophisticated cameras, electronics, computers, and 3-D monitors, that it now resembled an office suite for a Fortune 500 CEO more than a rustic structure that looked like it belonged to an earlier age.

And communications to and from the facility were untraceable. He had saved his most advanced technology to ensure this was the case. Anyone trying to learn his location, after considerable effort, would be misled into thinking the call had originated somewhere in Switzerland. And this would make sense.

What would *not* make sense, given that Victor was known for his mastery of ultra-advanced technology and his hatred of America and its people, was that he would ever choose to live on a throwback ranch in backwater, USA.

The Silver Lake Ranch was forty-seven hundred acres of grass, brush, creeks, lakes, woods, and hills in South Central Oregon. In 2016, Chuck Shulak, a proud Oregonian huntsman who had made a fortune on a national chain of funeral homes, decided he would turn the ranch into a retirement home for himself and a hunting destination for fellow sportsmen.

So he had large game brought in, built a runway, several large hunting lodges, each with accommodations, and a half-dozen other facilities, and changed the ranch's name to The Silver Lake Hunting Reserve. He spared no expense to make his reserve a place where hunters could channel their inner frontiersman as they trekked across miles of open country in pursuit of big game trophies, after which they could return to the lodge to share in the camaraderie of like-minded men.

Although Shulak made a valiant effort over the next several years to turn his reserve into the success he was certain it would be, it never did take off, and he lost money annually. The death of human beings had made him a fortune in the funeral business, but the death of big game animals wasn't going so well. Even so, Shulak loved the clientele who did come and the wide open country, and figured he could easily sustain losses for decades before his vast fortune ran out.

And then he promptly died. A sad event, yes, but one that at least provided him with the opportunity to get a perspective on his funeral home business from a corpse's point of view.

Shulak's heirs, who did not fancy themselves as reincarnations of Davy Crockett, couldn't put the property on the market fast enough.

Victor, using the alias Adam McClure and working through a real estate broker, had snapped up the ranch for the distressed price of seven million dollars and had turned it into his primary headquarters and residence, to go with a dozen other lesser facilities around the world. And it was proving perfect for his needs.

He was still deep in thought when his PDA notified him that his scheduled video-call with Nazim al-Hawrani, the leader of Islamic Jihad, was incoming on his most secure line.

"Hello, Nazim," he said in English, with just the slightest hint of an accent, to the man dressed in a white robe and headdress appearing on his monitor. "To what do I owe this honor, my friend?"

With Victor, adding the phrase, my friend, was a force of habit, but he knew that given the diseased and barbaric form of Islam practiced by al-Hawrani, no infidel like Victor could ever be a friend—or allowed to remain alive if al-Hawrani had the chance to kill him and he wasn't useful anymore.

"Hello, Victor," al-Hawrani replied, also in English, but in his case with a heavy and unmistakable accent. "How are things in Switzerland?"

"Neutral," he replied in a deadpan voice. "How else?"

Victor was about to ask al-Hawrani how he was doing but thought better of it. The terrorist and his organization were still reeling from their failure at the Academy Awards. While they had succeeded in killing almost a hundred people in spectacular fashion, the attack could have been one for the ages, but had been disrupted by means they still didn't understand.

"Let me tell you why I called," said the terrorist. "We've been getting hit lately by the Americans' new *Cloaked Justice* Drones. They're faster than the *FNP-100s*. And their mirroring technology is better. Meaning they are very difficult to spot, either visually or with radar." He paused, and his expression reflected that he had finally remembered to whom he was speaking. "As I'm sure you're aware."

"Go on."

"What do you have in the way of countermeasures? Anything?"

"It's at the very top of my list, my friend, I assure you. I have my team working on this problem night and day. My best guess is I'll have something for you in six months."

Victor maintained his own fleet of Drones, including the *Cloaked Justice,* so the challenge for his team wasn't just in coming up with effective countermeasures, but also then making sure that his own drones were immune. But this was not something he was about to share with al- Hawrani.

"If you can do it in four months," said the leader of Islamic Jihad, "I'll pay a million dollar bonus."

"Trust me, we are working as quickly as we possibly can. But if we are able to succeed early, I would never think of taking extra money from you, my friend." Victor smiled. "My only interest is making sure you remain a satisfied customer."

Victor had earned a reputation for under-promising and over-delivering, for being scrupulously fair, and for going the extra mile for customer service. He believed that this was vital in his line of work and was the only reason he was still alive. Well, that and his many missiles, drones, tanks, and other weaponry and his precise knowledge of where to strike anyone who tried to cross him.

"Thank you, Victor. I know you're doing your best. But I wouldn't have called if it wasn't important." There was a long pause. "Before I go, is there anything else you've been working on that you think might interest us?"

Eduardo Alvarez arrived and Victor waved him to a chair in front of his desk, out of sight of the cameras sending his image to al-Hawrani. "As a matter of fact, yes," replied Victor. "I have another team working on a way to remotely alter the programming of electronic bloodhounds. So they will fail to register an explosive of your choice."

Victor knew Islamic Jihad had had big plans for the undetectable explosive they had developed, and suspected they would jump at the chance to have one more bite at this apple.

"I can see how this would be useful," said al-Hawrani in measured tones, trying not to give away his eagerness.

"I will keep you posted on our progress, my friend. But I need to let you know that I will only sell this to a single customer. It will go to the highest bidder. Apologies for this, Nazim. As you know, this is not the way I prefer to operate."

"Then why are you?"

"My fear is that whoever has this will only get one, maybe two, uses before the Americans figure out what is going on and find ways to counter it. If I sold it to twenty buyers, and one of them used it first, the other nineteen might find they had paid for a technology that no longer worked." He paused. "I'm sure you can imagine that this would not win me any friends."

Al-Hawrani wasn't happy at the prospect of a bidding war, but understood the reason for it. A few minutes later the call ended.

The terror leader was a very bad piece of work, and Islamic Jihad was a blight on the face of the earth, but Victor didn't have to approve of someone to do business with them. As long as their actions would hurt the United States, he was all for them. In this case, since he wasn't a fan of the malignancy the jihadists represented, he was only too happy to facilitate both sides killing each other in an endless cycle that only created more havoc and disruption in America, and more business for him. And he didn't have to worry about any of this affecting his home country, since Mexico would be the last place a terrorist would ever strike.

The man known only as Victor had been born Juan Jose Perez in a tiny hovel in the resort town of Puerto Vallarta, the oldest of four siblings. He had been precocious. Brilliant. Street savvy *and* book savvy. He had taught himself algebra at the age of seven because he had found an old textbook and thought it was fun.

His mother had beautiful Spanish features and a fine figure and had worked as a maid for many years in a resort hotel. This was before Juan Jose's alcoholic father, when he was eight, had stolen every penny his sainted mother had ever saved, beaten her unconscious, and left her for dead.

For a single mother with four children who had been left in debt without any savings, a maid's salary wasn't enough. So she had turned to prostitution. Not that Juan Jose had figured this out until he was older.

But there was one thing he *had* figured out just after he was old enough to walk: he and his fellow Mexicans were second-class citizens—in their own country. American tourists looked down at them as scum, to be pitied or avoided or disdained. Many tourists saw them as *worse* than second-class, as somehow sub-human. This was rarely spoken, but it couldn't be more obvious.

Americans paraded into the resort city with their wealth, their fancy electronics, their expensive clothing, and most of all, their cloak of superiority. They never once recognized Juan Jose for his singular brilliance, but saw him as just another sub-human, a mangy stray lurking around the table hoping for scraps. Most of the Americans believed that any culture other than their own was backward and beneath contempt.

Everyone knew that America was the rich neighbor to the north, and Mexico its tenement neighbor to the south. The Americans tended to be rude, arrogant, and haughty, and most made little effort to speak Spanish. But why would they? The world spoke English. It had become the global language, which an alien race would be justified in renaming *Terran*. If fifteen educated people speaking fifteen different languages were in a room, they could still all converse, since it was almost certain that all fifteen would speak passable English.

Not only were his neighbors to the north smug and arrogant and obnoxious, they looked at his mother like she was a piece of meat.

He only learned later that this is precisely what she was to them.

By the time Juan Jose was twelve he had developed a thrilling hatred of Americans. And a disgust for his fellow Mexicans, who seemed to accept that they existed simply to be parasites on the backs of the tourists, dancing for pesos if this is what it took. Humiliating themselves in endless ways.

When he did come to understand how his mother managed to feed, clothe, and house her children, he became determined to protect her. He stole a gun and learned how to use it. He would stop by the hotel and check on her welfare as often as he could, but even so, she would sometimes return home bloodied or bruised and he would know she had been beaten. He would catch her weeping softly in her bedroom.

One night when he had come to check on her he heard a brief scream, one that was cut off in an alarming way. When he burst through the door of the room, his mother was on the floor, naked, her anus torn by an oversized bottle that a drunken patron had tried to sodomize her with. When she had screamed out in pain, the drunken American had hit her hard enough to break her neck.

The American was still apologizing and begging for mercy, in English of course, when Juan Jose shot him point blank in the face, and left Puerto Vallarta forever.

As he ran from the authorities, he vowed three things. One, he would never want for anything material again. Two, he would send enough money to the orphanage to ensure his siblings were well taken care of. No one he loved would ever have to demean themselves for money again. And three, he would find a way to punish America and the smug assholes who made up its population. Find a way to hurt as many of them as badly as he could, for as long as he could.

A week later he joined a drug cartel. The cartel's leader had been instantly impressed by his intensity and intelligence, and the story of the shooting at the hotel had reached far and wide.

The day he joined the cartels was the day he left Juan Jose Perez behind forever.

Like everything he did, he chose a new name for himself with great care and intelligence. He would be simply, Victor. The name meant *conqueror*, which was something he was determined to be as he bent the world to his will. Victor was one of the earliest names in Christendom, symbolizing Christ's triumph over death. It was also the first name of the fictional Dr. Frankenstein, who, like Christ before him, had managed to claim victory over humanity's most unconquerable enemy: mortality.

Victor's rise through the ranks was truly dazzling, and by the time he was twenty-seven he had gone into business on his own and quickly became one of the most powerful drug lords in Mexico, worth hundreds of millions of dollars and in charge of a personal army that many small countries would envy.

Given that Mexico was neighbor to the great and powerful superpower to the north, it was a natural staging and transshipment point for narcotics and contraband between Latin America and US markets. The money was so immense as to make war inevitable. And although it wasn't a war in the traditional sense, between rival countries, it was a series of wars: between the cartels and the American authorities, between rival drug lords for control of the best smuggling routes, and eventually between the Mexican military and the cartels. It was a business that created tens of billions of dollars of wealth in a poor country, and the total death toll from the cartel wars rivaled all but a few current, more traditional wars, numbering well over a hundred thousand.

But while Victor was delighted that his drugs and his cartel were inflicting pain on the despised United States, life as a drug lord was becoming too dangerous, even for him. The job was long on money and power, but short on life expectancy.

And there were better ways to gain power and inflict damage on America. Smarter ways. As head of a cartel, Victor had worked extensively with arms dealers, even purchasing a fully functioning submarine built by the ex-soviet union to help him smuggle drugs.

So he decided to become born again as an arms dealer. Let the cartel wars continue. He would simply disappear from off this stage, with all of his wealth, knowledge, and connections, and reappear on another. He would supply weapons to all takers, with his preference being any group who wanted to hurt America or her people, or take it down a peg: terror groups, the mob, the North Koreans, the Chinese, warlords, cartels, and so on.

Military grade weaponry was everywhere. One just had to be smart and connected enough to seize opportunities. The US had a habit of starting wars they never properly finished, discarding billions in armaments without a care along the way. And why should the Americans care? Their companies and politicians would get rich making more while their taxpayers picked up the tab. And the tax base in America was truly staggering, the result of a country that was raping the entire world to get its riches.

Victor took only one man with him on his new adventure. A man who had become almost a brother, Eduardo Alvarez. And he rebuilt an organization almost as large as the one he had abandoned, one with international reach. He earned a sterling reputation for being honest and fair in his dealings. He surprised everyone with the extra value he supplied.

And he had evolved the arms business, as dramatically in his own way as Jeff Bezos had evolved retailing. He was now the ultimate broker, trusted by everyone, even parties that would never trust each other, buyers and sellers alike, his reputation impeccable. And he was owed favors by everyone as well.

And recently he had undergone his last evolution, changing the emphasis of his business from heavy weapons to advanced, futuristic technology. To not only stealing technologies from militaries and corporations, but establishing teams of scientists to create his own.

Technology smuggling was even safer than traditional arms dealing, and he tended to work with a higher class of criminal, although he continued to serve his prior clientele, extensive as it was.

Technology was *everything* these days, and was becoming more critical every year. Profit was as high or higher than heavy weapons. And while the logistics and bribes required to smuggle twenty tanks to a buyer were immense, the requirements for smuggling twenty bubble memory prototypes, which could easily fit in the overhead compartment of a commercial plane, were laughably simple by comparison.

And Victor's ranch headquarters in Oregon was perfect for his needs. It was remote, and he had more than enough land to hide weapons, stolen technology, runways, personal aircraft, his own personal drones and countermeasures, and escape tunnels. And it was just a short flight to Silicon Valley in neighboring California, still the incubator of more high technology than anywhere else on earth.

* * *

"What's up?" said Eduardo Alvarez in Spanish after Victor's call with the leader of Islamic Jihad had ended.

Victor leaned back in his chair and locked his hands behind his head with a cat-that-ate-the-canary grin. "You won't believe who I just spoke with," he said. He went on to tell Alvarez how the communication had come about, and summarized what had been said and his knowledge of the caller.

Alvarez soaked in the information without a word, although he did raise his eyebrows on more than one occasion.

"What are your thoughts?" said Victor when he had finished.

"Well, the obvious one," replied Alvarez. "Can we trust anything you just told me? Especially considering the source."

"Impossible to be sure. But given everything I know, I tend to think this is legitimate."

"But isn't this falling into our laps a little too easily for comfort?" asked Alvarez.

"Yes. And this is suspicious. But another way to look at it is that when you have the biggest, most luxurious lap, things tend to fall into it. Either way, legitimate or a trap, I'd be the obvious choice."

"Okay," said Alvarez. "Assume for a moment we succeed. We have these magical BrainWeb implants and we learn exactly where to place them. What kind of demand would you expect from our customers? Is it a *have-to-have* item? Or just a *like-to-have* item?"

"Have-to-have," said Victor. "I haven't really thought about BrainWeb implants all that hard. Like everyone else, I was convinced they were at least a year or two away, and all the intel I gathered convinced me getting our hands on this technology before it came out was well beyond even our capabilities."

"Until now. At least in theory."

"Right. The more I think about this, the more I appreciate just how big it is. The advantage to our clients of having this technology in their heads long before it is available to anyone else is *immense*. And I'll be the first one to line up. Can you imagine? Internet access at the speed and convenience of thought."

"Knowledge is power, yes. But how much of an advantage will BrainWeb really provide?"

"Far more than you might think at first blush. Especially if you're the only one around you who has it. You'd be directly tied into limitless knowledge. Communication between two people who both had the implants would be effortless and undetectable. The stealth factor would be off the charts. Not just communication, but a user can be directing all kinds of resources without anyone knowing." Victor's face lit up in delight as he pondered the possibilities. "And all of this is just icing on the cake."

"What do you consider the cake?"

"I haven't paid all that much attention, but I have caught bits and pieces of some of the debates on the use of the technology. And the violation of privacy concern seems to be the most troubling to people."

"Meaning it will be the biggest advantage to our kind of people," said Alvarez.

"Yes. Perfect memory. And the ability to instantly convert whatever the user sees and hears into digital video and then save it. What will our clients give for that?"

Alvarez considered this for several long seconds. "I see why you classified this as have-to-have," he said finally.

"And I think we're only scratching the surface. I'm guessing it's much more useful than we can even imagine right now. For every advantage we can think of, I suspect we'll find three others we didn't fully appreciate until we have the technology in our heads. For the truly tech-savvy the speed and fluidity of interacting with computers in this way would be truly amazing."

"Okay, but the vast majority of our clients are Muslims," pointed out Alvarez.

Victor nodded slowly. It was an excellent observation. Most of their clients tended to be Islamists. Which made sense, since the vast majority of armed conflicts and hot spots in the world involved people of this faith, bastardized though their interpretation of the religion may have been.

The jihadists were not fans of modern technology, and largely wished to live as they had many hundreds of years before. But they would make use of technology to achieve their ends, as ISIS continued to demonstrate with a remarkably effective Facebook and Twitter campaign. Even technology that was directly contrary to their beliefs.

But Alvarez's point was still worth raising, since BrainWeb implants took technology to a new level of invasiveness, a new level of blasphemy.

"I've worked with these people for years," said Victor after he had thought this through. "As far as I can tell, jihadists are more than willing to stray from the confines of their religious doctrine to further their goal of caliphate. They can even ignore their religion completely to deceive others and they believe Allah will forgive them. As long as they're doing what they're doing in his service. Some won't be willing to go as far as to install BrainWeb, true. But I'm certain that most will."

Alvarez nodded. "Will it work in languages other than English?" he asked.

"Great question. I'll explore this further, but from what I understand, yes. This is a big step forward over the prototypes, courtesy of the genius of Alex Altschuler. He programmed in an AI unit that makes use of translation programs, using English as a base, of course. Even so, a user would have to teach it his or her language. Look at a door and think *door*. That sort of thing. But the program learns very fast, and the expectation is after a week or two, or about fifty hours of training, it will catch on, getting better and better every day. It learns fast. You just have to correct it when it makes an error."

Victor tilted his head in thought. He already knew how he was going to proceed, but he was giving his friend more and more responsibility and was interested to see if he would come to the same conclusions. "So what are your recommendations going forward, Eduardo?" he asked.

Alvarez met his eyes with a thoughtful expression but was in no hurry to respond. They had worked together for many years now and he was well aware that Victor hated answers that were not well thought out and logical. He preferred a *good* answer to a quick one.

"We can't afford *not* to pursue this," he said after almost a minute had passed. "But we still can't be sure it isn't a trap. So we need to send in the third string. So removed from us that if they spilled everything they know it wouldn't cause a single problem for us. Expendables. If this is on the level, we get what we want. If not, *they* fall into the trap and we walk away."

Victor's grin spread across his entire face. "Outstanding," he said. "That's just what we'll do. Let's plan and implement this as soon as we can."

27

Megan lay on her bed, which was annoyingly comfortable, and closed her eyes, running through possibilities for at least the tenth time since she had arrived a week earlier. She didn't expect to come up with any answers she had missed the first nine times, but what did she have to lose? She had thought being marooned on the *Eos* had been boring, but her current situation took boring to an entirely new level. Now there were no trips to tourist or shopping locations, and most importantly, no Nick.

Megan had first been taken to a house in Chino, as she had been told, but this had simply been a staging area. Once inside they had received further instructions, changed vehicles, and forced her to eat several tranquilizers that had knocked her out cold for an indeterminate length of time.

She had awakened in a large two-story house, four or five thousand square feet by her estimation, in the middle of a desert. The house had smooth stucco siding, arches around the entryway and windows, and a roof made from solar panels incorporating a recent breakthrough that allowed the home to be entirely self-sufficient, without need of hooking up to an electric company. Given the massive power requirements of the two large air-conditioning units that kept the inhabitants from roasting alive, this was the only way the house could be this secluded, since power lines were nowhere to be seen. A wide gravel road that cut through the desert and its sporadic covering of sagebrush and cactus connected the house to civilization somewhere past the horizon.

For perhaps the fourth time she replayed the conversation she had had upon first awakening with the man who had abducted her, Boyd Solomon. While this was his actual name, he had obviously lied about working with Justin Girdler. He had first brought her to the kitchen where he had prepared orange juice, bottled water, and a four-egg, three-cheese omelet, knowing that she would awaken with an appetite.

She had taken a forkful of the omelet and decided she was starving, and that whatever one might say about the man, he was a competent chef.

"Are you going to tell me what this is all about now?" she asked.

"I would think it would be obvious."

"You're using me to get control of . . . my friend."

"Yes. Nick Hall. The mind reader. I lied earlier when I said I didn't know who he was."

"And you have him?"

"We do. Once we had you, he was as tame as a lamb. You obviously mean a great deal to him."

"Where is he, and what are you having him do?"

"Right now he's unconscious in an RV, heading to his destination. I won't tell you what he'll be doing."

"Who do you work for?"

"I'm afraid I won't be telling you his name, either. I'm the only one who knows who he is. When you're dealing with a mind reader you need to limit information. Since Hall will never be within a thousand miles of here, I don't have to worry about him finding out."

She took a few more bites of omelet and washed it down with the last of her orange juice as she considered what he had said. "And where are we?" she said, gesturing to a window with closed blinds, blocking the relentless sun.

"Once you get a peek outside you'll see that we're in a desert. We're the only structure within three miles of here."

Megan took this in but didn't respond.

"Olinda and Bergum are here as well. And a man named Angel Sanchez. We're being extremely well paid to act as babysitters, possibly for months or even years. Escape is impossible. The doors are locked from the inside and can only be opened after entering the proper code into a touchpad. The windows are unbreakable."

Megan rolled her eyes. "Really? Don't you think this is overkill? Four of you? Against a hundred-and-twenty-pound girl?"

"My boss is very careful. And you're the key. You're a lot more secure than your boyfriend. Hell, we could leave him unwatched and he wouldn't try to escape. Not when we have you. But if *you* escaped, my boss is convinced he'd stop cooperating and find a way to escape no matter what we did."

"So I'm basically a prisoner with an indefinite sentence."

"Not a prisoner. A guest. I'm a very hard man, not above the harshest of tortures. But I've been instructed to treat you like a Disney princess. If a pea under your mattress is interfering with your beauty sleep, I'll see it's removed. I'll provide any food or entertainment you would like, except a phone or Internet. We have an exercise room, and we can escort you outside a few times a day, or better yet, night, when it's cooler, to get some fresh air."

He paused. "And just so you know, by the way, if you somehow managed to escape during one of these outings, you wouldn't get far. As I said, there is nothing around for miles. Nowhere to run. No place to hide. So save your effort and we'll all be better off."

"And I assume you'll want me to talk to Nick periodically and tell him how well I'm being treated?"

"Yes." Solomon managed an insincere smile. "More orange juice?"

Megan nodded. As bad as it was, it could have been worse. If you had to be a prisoner, being treated like a queen was better than the alternatives.

"The man who built this house twenty years ago was very wealthy," said Solomon, "and very private. It used to be hooked up to both electric and phone lines, but only the phone lines survived. But since we have a land-line we can make the connection very secure. So no need to worry about any eavesdroppers when you tell Nick how well you're doing. And how unharmed you are."

"Thanks. That's very comforting," said Megan wryly.

She finished the omelet and stared intently at Solomon. "But you never answered my initial question. Where are we?"

"We're in a desert in the Southwestern United States."

"Wow, that really narrows it down. To about a *billion* square miles. Most of California, Arizona, Utah, and Nevada is desert. I mean where are we, *exactly*?"

"That's something we've been instructed not to say."

"Why not?" demanded Megan in disbelief. "Why would this matter? I'm not asking for the mailing address. Just curious what city we're near."

"Personally, I don't think it *would* matter. But my boss feels differently. As I said, he's a very careful man."

"Is he worried that I'll tell Nick during one of our calls?"

Solomon didn't respond.

"Because *so what?* Say I tell him I'm in the Nevada desert near Reno. He's thousands of miles away under guard. And even if he escaped, the Reno area is large enough that he'd never find us."

Solomon shrugged. "My boss thinks this Nick is some kind of wizard. He can't see how this information could possibly help him, but he'd rather err on the side of caution."

"That's ridiculous," said Megan.

"If it's so ridiculous, why are you so eager to find out?"

"If I'm going to be prisoner for months or years, I should at least know where I am."

"I'm afraid you're going to have to get used to disappointment."

* * *

Megan finished focusing on her remembered first conversation with Solomon and replayed other conversations she had had with each of her four jailors during the past week. She then considered everything she had managed to learn about the security setup and possible strategies for defeating it.

This took painfully little time. Because she had nothing.

There had to be a way out of this. But for the life of her she couldn't see it. She had considered a number of possibilities but had ruled them all out. Faking a sickness. Lying during her calls with Nick and saying she was being mistreated. Threatening Solomon that she would say he had raped her, getting him in trouble with his boss, unless he helped her. Telling them she was allergic and had to be moved. Sure, allergic to what? Sand?

The despair and the boredom were crushing. And while Nick sounded okay during their calls, and was obviously being as well treated as she was—as long as he danced to their music—she was already beginning to lose hope.

She had to find a way to escape. It was the only way to free Nick up to turn the tables.

But she also had to face the fact that there might come a time, after all hope was truly gone, when she might have to take her own life, removing this weight from around Nick's neck.

Megan Emerson choked back tears, shut her eyes even tighter, and began imagining ways to escape once again, no matter how unlikely.

28

Alex Altschuler soaked in the four-person Jacuzzi in his master bathroom and moved to the left so a powerful jet would hit the small of his back.

"Ahhhh," he purred. "That's the ticket," he continued aloud to no one but himself, turning off his brain for the first time all day.

This lasted less than a minute. Other than during sex, he found that his mind had a mind of its own, and refused to holster its world-class firepower. His mind would not be quieted, even if his thoughts weren't on lofty mathematics or science, but only on reflections of where he was in his life.

So much had changed in so little time.

He was now living with a woman he loved, and while they had yet to formally tie the knot, they made decisions and shared their lives as though they were already married.

The bathroom he was in was larger than his *bedroom* had been less than a year before. And he had lived in an affluent neighborhood even then.

But he continued to feel like an imposter. Super wealth didn't quite seem to fit him. He had heard stories about the founder of Walmart driving a pickup truck, even after he was worth billions. Some took this as a sign that he was the stingiest man on earth, but Altschuler admired him for it. The man had not let wealth make him something he was not, and Altschuler was determined to follow suit. And Heather felt exactly the same way.

The best thing about the mansion was that it was just outside of Fresno, and closer to Theia's offices, which were undergoing a dramatic expansion, than his old house had been. Still, he had only purchased the estate, and he and Heather had only relocated there, at General Girdler's insistence, for security purposes. A high-tech touch-sensitive and motion-sensitive fence walled in the extensive grounds, on which numerous bodyguards could be stationed without interfering too much with their privacy, and which served as a buffer zone that any crazed attacker would have to get through to reach the house.

But their home was *too* majestic, inside and out. Beautiful, but lacking warmth and approachability.

A house should look and feel like it was built to be *lived* in, not just admired. It was the difference between a thousand-dollar silk tie that constricted your neck or a loose fitting T-shirt that was the essence of comfort.

Altschuler sighed and repositioned himself yet again so that several jets would hit his shoulder blades.

And he had never wanted to be a CEO, either. He was a geek, not a charismatic leader. He felt much more comfortable around a computer, or doing leading edge science, than around people.

It was true that he had come an enormous distance in only six months. From a shy genius nerd with little self-confidence in social settings to someone who felt comfortable, and who was fairly articulate, when interviewed almost weekly by the likes of ABC, 60 Minutes, or cable business channels.

Even so, the job of a CEO tended to involve too much publicity and too much politicking. He was the face of Theia Labs, responsible to the shareholders for enhancing Theia's image and making it the darling of Wall Street. He had to make sure all the super-inflated egos on the board were stroked and that each member felt needed and involved.

He had to admit he enjoyed his newfound fame and status at the start. But getting recognized on the street or at a restaurant, while great in the beginning, was getting out of hand. He was someone who had chosen the shadows to the spotlight his entire life, and who valued his privacy.

To his credit, once he had figured out that he didn't enjoy being CEO and wasn't the best man for the job, he had acted rapidly to bring in a world-class management team, which had been easy, since

Theia had become the hottest company in history. He had chosen Hank Cohen, the number two man at Intel, and promised that if he joined Theia as president, Altschuler would trade titles with him within a year, although this had never been made public.

Steve Jobs had done the same in his early days at Apple. Recognizing he was out of his depth and with pressure from the board, he had hired the president of PepsiCo, John Scully, to become CEO, winning him over with words that had become forever enshrined in the cherished lore of nerd-dom. "Do you want to sell sugar water for the rest of your life?" Jobs had said. "Or do you want to come with me and change the world?"

Altschuler couldn't wait to begin doing science again. Solving problems, as only he could. Given the double-edged sword that he was helping to release, the fate of civilization could well rest on his ability to help push quantum encryption over the finish line. But as it stood now, he was too busy to even keep up with the state-of-the-art, let alone extend it.

But that would change before too long. Hank Cohen would be at the helm and Altschuler would be the executive in charge of special projects, which meant having nearly unlimited toys and the resources to play in the sandbox however he chose. Nirvana. Now this would truly be paradise. No need of money, a woman he loved, and the freedom to pursue his intellectual passions.

As he thought of Heather he consulted the clock in his head. She would probably be out another hour or so.

She was with a girlfriend scouting wedding venues, although they were leaning more and more toward getting married out of the public eye. To not announcing it until it was over. They could afford a royal wedding. The Taj Mahal could be their venue, and they could make their entrance in a golden chariot pulled by Clydesdales. But despite the pressure from the public who wanted to see a spectacle, they were all but certain to have a small wedding, attended by only their immediate families and a few close friends.

And the big question was, would Nick and Megan be among them? Were they even alive? And if they were found, would Nick be able to attend, even wearing a disguise? And how could they invite a mind reader? How ethical was it to expose friends and family to a man who could lay bare their souls without any warning?

Altschuler gasped.

The Internet was down. He hadn't been aware he was even using it, but it's absence made itself felt like a blow to the head.

It couldn't be. He knew too much about the workings of the network. There was so much redundancy built into the system, especially in Northern California, that nothing short of an EMP blast could have killed it.

Or a dampening field.

And this wasn't something one could just buy at the local electronics store. Which meant he was in trouble.

Altschuler rose up and threw a robe around his dripping frame. He continued dripping as he walked into his bedroom. "Rory," he said to the house PDA, "are we getting a network signal in the house?"

"None at all."

He picked up a landline phone on his end table and couldn't get a dial tone.

"Initiate total lockdown!" he shouted. "Contact Ladarious on the in-house com system and tell him cells and landlines are both down, which can't be accidental, and to be on the lookout for a possible breach."

"Done," said the PDA seconds later.

"Tile the views from all surveillance cameras evenly across the television in the master bedroom."

The 90-inch monitor designed to blend in perfectly with his wall came to life, showing numerous views of both his home's perimeter and a number of locations inside.

Altschuler blew out a sigh of relief. Everything looked normal. It was a false alarm.

But even so, something made him uncomfortable, something in the movements of the guards. He had a genius for many things, including a pattern-recognition ability to rival a chess grandmaster, and something wasn't right. He couldn't put his finger on what, but it didn't matter.

"Rory, emergency reboot of surveillance system," he ordered.

The images on his screen blinked out and the monitor remained blank for almost thirty second before the tiles returned.

But this time they told a very different tale.

The bodies of four bodyguards were spread out on the grounds in various poses, hit before they had the chance to take a shot or shout a warning.

Eight black-clad men wearing ski masks were approaching doors on each side of the home's perimeter, while inside the two remaining bodyguards were checking locations within the house that didn't show up on cameras. They must have checked the monitors before his reboot and been fooled into thinking there was no threat outside.

Things were scary, but there was nothing to worry about. Altschuler had initiated lockdown mode, so these eight intruders, professional and imposing as they were, would be no more successful getting through the doors than a wolf trying to blow down a little piggy's brick house.

Altschuler's heart leaped into his throat as the monitors showed the exact opposite. The men were entering effortlessly, from all four sides at once. Impossible!

His mind accelerated to yet another gear. He knew the two bodyguards remaining would try to be heroes and hold the fort, but they were outmanned and outgunned. He couldn't let them sacrifice their lives for nothing. And Girdler had agreed to let Altschuler override any orders given to the security detail in case of an emergency.

Altschuler was about to contact his head bodyguard, Ladarious Thomas, through the intercom system, when Thomas beat him to the punch. "Sir, you were right," he began, with military formality. "We have a breach at four locations. I don't know where they came from. All outside monitors and sensors were negative."

"Meet me at the panic room!" barked Altschuler. He reflexively tried to get his implants to call up the proper military language for what he wanted to communicate, and he was jarred once again by the absence of the Web. He shook this off and managed to drag the right words from his memory instead. "Do not engage. I repeat, do not engage."

"Sir, I think we can—"

"Panic room!" interrupted Altschuler. "Now!"

"Roger that," said Thomas. "Adams and I are on our way."

Altschuler paused for just a moment to check the monitors. The assault force was closing in on the two remaining bodyguards, but they were already moving toward a stairway and should be able to make it to the second floor without a problem.

Altschuler, still in his robe, although finally not leaving puddles behind him, rushed through several wide hallways until he came to his destination. "Rory, open the panic room door," he ordered. "Authorization code: *my ass must really be in trouble.*"

Access still showed red, and he didn't hear the telltale sound of locks being released.

"Rory, I repeat," he said in strained tones, "authorization code: *my ass must really be in trouble.*"

Several seconds passed. "Why isn't the door unlocking?" he demanded, as Thomas and Adams finally joined him.

"I'm not sure," replied his PDA. "Running a diagnostic now."

But it was far too late for that. Altschuler knew it, even before he saw the canisters rolling toward the three of them, undoubtedly releasing a cloud of invisible gas as they did.

"Rory, tell Heather I love her more than she can imag—"

But his last word remained unspoken as the gas took effect and he, along with his two remaining bodyguards, crashed to the ground, inches from the doorway to a panic room that was supposed to have been their salvation.

PART 4
Duplicity

"A man without ethics is a wild beast loosed upon this world.

—Albert Camus

29

"Today's your big day, Nick," said the disembodied voice of the man calling himself Frank Earnest. "How are you feeling?"

"Bored," said Hall, "but mentally and physically well-rested. I can promise my abilities will be strong and precise for fifteen to twenty minutes. More than enough time."

"Good," said Marc Fisher. "I got you a room at the Hay-Adams hotel. Kent Lombardo and a man named Gary Hogan will be escorting you. He and Hogan will become permanent fixtures in your life."

"Why two?" asked Hall. "You know I won't try anything while you have Megan."

He had spoken with her every day, as his captor had promised, and she confirmed she was being treated well. So he had decided to appear as cooperative as possible, and to gradually even pretend to be coming around to Frank Earnest's point of view.

The more belligerent Hall was, the more he seemed to resist, the more Earnest's guard would be up. But the more he cooperated, the more likely Earnest would make a mistake. At least this was his hope.

And he had to admit that if everything Earnest said was true, his point of view did have some merit. Hall hadn't followed politics for many years, but there was a time that he had. Closely. And after doing so for only a year the amount of corruption and double-dealing became sickening. By both parties. By politicians who could look into the camera and say things they knew to be absolute lies with charm and conviction, even when there was video evidence of them saying precisely the opposite only months earlier.

What was startling to Hall was how easily they got away with it. Over and over again. It was one thing to lie when there was no record. Another to lie with total ease, not only knowing you were lying but that a record existed.

So he had stopped paying attention. What was the point? A pox on both their houses. He hadn't checked recently, but he was pretty sure the approval rating of Congress was below the approval rating of the Ebola virus.

"Nick, you've got this all wrong. Don't think of your two escorts as men whose job is to prevent you from escaping. I *know* you won't try to escape. Think of them more as bodyguards. There to protect you. Like you're a delicate crystal vase."

"Now how about the truth."

"That is part of the truth," said Fisher. "The rest of the truth is that I'm very careful. And one never knows. And by using two men, I can ensure there are eyes on you at all times—even if one of them needs to use the bathroom. And just so you won't be surprised, Mr. Lombardo will also be bringing two bracelets for you to wear, designed just for you, one on each wrist."

"How thoughtful," said Hall wryly. "But he doesn't need to buy me jewelry to get me to go to the hotel with him. A nice dinner and flowers would be plenty."

"Very amusing."

"Okay. I'll bite. What horrible thing do the bracelets do?"

"Not horrible. They have sophisticated electronics built in. Each creating a wireless-free zone around your body. One would do, but I'm careful, so they are redundant."

"I've already told you. You don't need to restrict the Internet. I won't use my connection to escape or get help. Not while you have Megan. You know that."

"Your arguments didn't sway me before, so why do you think they will now?"

Hall remained silent.

"Each bracelet has a tiny light indicating it's working. No way you could break both of them without Lombardo or Hogan noticing what you were trying to do. But even so, if one stops working, it will sound an alarm. And since your two . . . escorts, will always be within range of you, they've been ordered to shoot you with a tranquilizer dart the instant they hear this."

"Good to know," said Hall, unconcerned. "Next question. You're aware I can only do this for fifteen minutes—not the entire day. So why the hotel room? Parking a car nearby would work."

"I appreciate that you're trying to save me money. The Hay-Adams *is* a pricey hotel," he said, and although Hall couldn't see him, he said it in such a way that Hall knew he was smiling. "But I want you to be as comfortable as possible. I'll make sure you have a full-sized keyboard along with a laptop. You'll be much more productive typing in a record of the dirt you dredge up at a hotel desk rather than inside a car."

Hall nodded. Voice recognition had become nearly perfect and future generations would grow up becoming comfortable dictating their writings to a computer. But Hall still preferred to compose with a keyboard. He could touch-type very fast, and for some reason he was better able to organize his thoughts this way. He had been doing some writing to ease the long stretches of boredom and they must have observed how quickly his fingers flew over the keys.

If Earnest would let him use the Internet, he could record everything he learned instantly in the cloud, which would be a hundred times more efficient than typing notes. But the man was smart. If Hall was able to use his implants, he would send all the information he had to General Girdler, who could activate enormous resources to find and free Megan no matter how long it took.

His cold turkey withdrawal from the Internet had been nearly unbearable for days, but like anyone who had had one of his senses impaired, he was learning to adjust to the new reality. He still subconsciously tried to call up information several times an hour, and it was always jarring when this request returned nothing, but he was coping with this better each day.

"Since you can only read one person at a time," continued Fisher, "the man you'll be searching for, or feeling for—or whatever it is you do—is named Guy Shaw. Have you heard of him?"

Hall shook his head.

"No reason you should have. He's the president of the labor union SEIU, which stands for Service Employees International Union. He's arguably the biggest fish there is in Democratic Party politics. SEIU is sometimes referred to as the 'purple ocean' at political events, because members all wear lavender shirts. Anyway, this union represents more than two million workers in over a hundred jobs, mostly focusing on health care, government, and property services."

"Property services?"

"Janitors, security officers, food service workers, that sort of thing." He paused. "The Democratic Party is composed of very defined constituencies, representing large and important blocs of voters. Blacks, labor, women, gays, Hispanics, and so on. Labor is one of the most important of these, and SEIU is arguably the most important union. In fact, this organization was instrumental in helping to get both Barack Obama and Timothy Cochran elected, donating and spending more than any other organization during their campaigns. Their support for a candidate doesn't *ensure* he becomes the Democratic Party nominee, but let's just say it goes a long way."

Fisher paused for a moment to let Hall consider what he had said. "So find me dirt and vulnerabilities I can use. And remember, I need dirt that you can find evidence for outside of Guy Shaw's mind. Knowing there once was a body doesn't help much. I need to actually be able to *find* the body. Understand?"

"Yes," said Hall simply.

"Good. The faster we get my candidate set up for success, the faster you and Megan can get on with your lives."

Hall resisted an overwhelming urge to shake his head and frown. But he had to maintain a poker face. To try to lull Earnest to sleep.

While Hall's strategy was to stall for time, he had a feeling this wasn't really necessary. Earnest would be a fool to kill him too early, even after Hall had supplied him with enough compromising information to ensure his candidate's nomination. He would wait until the Republican nominee was coronated and let Hall continue to work his magic. Then, just weeks before the election, when it was too late to do any damage control, he would come out with a devastating blow aimed at the Republican, culled from the results of Hall's probing.

Earnest's candidate would sail into the White House in a landslide.

"But let me caution you," said Fisher. "Guy Shaw didn't get to the top of SEIU by being a Boy Scout. So you'd better not play any games with me and pretend you couldn't find anything useful. And what you find had better check out. I know we both want Megan Emerson to continue to get VIP treatment."

Hall's eyes burned with white-hot rage but he managed to keep this from his voice. "You'll be very satisfied with my results," he replied. "You can count on it."

30

Hall's stay at the Hay-Adams lasted a little more than an hour. He made sure his two guards knew that most of this time was necessary for him to type up the information before he forgot.

By now Hall was used to the underbelly of humanity. Everyone hid ugly secrets and he had been exposed to them all.

But most in this group of power brokers took the concept of ugly secrets to another level entirely. They had the usual sexual perversions and idiosyncrasies that all humans had, but the corruption was off the scale. This wasn't surprising to Hall. Some who rose to positions of power did so because they were supremely gifted, but many climbed the ladder because they were ruthless and possessed very loose ethics.

And there was also the age-old problem of who watched the watchers. Guy Shaw, head of possibly the most powerful labor union in the country, had very few checks on his power. He was the fox guarding the henhouse. So corruption became irresistible, because there was little chance of getting caught. And it was easy for those in power to find crimes they could convince themselves didn't really hurt anyone.

Beating a man to death was one thing. This was something most people would never do, even knowing they couldn't be caught.

But what about insider trading? Buying shares you knew were going to rise on a big announcement. Who was this hurting? Those selling the shares prior to the announcement were glad you bought them. If you had not, someone else would have. After the news was out and the stock rose, those who bought your shares wanted to buy them, and would have bought them from someone else if not from you. So who was hurt?

This was the type of crime that only a veritable saint, the most ethical of men, could resist if they were sure they wouldn't be caught.

It was also true that a few of these power brokers were compassionate and well-meaning. Even among the most powerful, Hall continued to find good, talented people, who rose to the top but still maintained the strictest of ethical standards. People who restored Hall's faith in humanity, or at least ensured he didn't lose it entirely.

But Guy Shaw wasn't one of these. In fact, he was about as far from this characterization as it was possible to get.

* * *

Marc Fisher was positively giddy when Hall returned from the Hay-Adams hotel. Just securing the complete support of Guy Shaw, alone, would make him the odds-on favorite to win the primary. And he never doubted for a moment that Hall would return with more than enough leverage for him to put Shaw in his pocket a dozen times over.

"What did you find, Nick?" asked Fisher when Hall was back in his room.

"I've taken lots of notes and I'll write these up into a full report. But I can give you the gist of it now. And I can lead you to the bodies in every case. I know where his secret computer files are hidden and the passwords to get into them, so you can get all the evidence you need."

"I was right, wasn't I?" said Fisher, putting the proper mixture of sadness and frustration into his tone. "These people are very corrupt. Don't you see why it is so important to get a good man into the White House?" He rolled his eyes, certain that he was more ruthless and corrupt than Shaw could ever be. But also a better actor.

"Yes," said Hall. "This was my first assignment, but I wouldn't be surprised if you were entirely right."

"So what did you find?" asked Fisher in almost bored tones, masking his eagerness.

"He's made gains from insider trading a number of times. He's embezzled millions of dollars from the pension funds of low-wage employees. He's paid his wife and members of his family hundreds of thousands of dollars in fake consulting fees. He's evaded taxes each year for over a decade, hiding income in offshore accounts—which I have the numbers for—and not disclosing property. He's taken bribes any number of times. He's expensed five-figure business trips that he didn't even really take." Hall paused. "That's all I can remember for now, but my report will be very thorough."

"I'll look forward to reading it."

"Just remember how helpful I'm being," said Hall. "And how helpful I'll continue to be. But this changes instantly the moment Megan Emerson has so much as a bruise on her. Or even if she stops getting VIP treatment."

"You have nothing to worry about, Nick," said Fisher. "But back to Shaw. Anything on the sexual front?"

"A lot. But no definitive proof. So it would be a *he said, she said* situation."

"Tell me anyway," said Fisher. "You never know what I might find useful."

Actually, he did know this would be useful, despite what he had told Hall about proof. The more of Shaw's sexual habits and indiscretions he knew of, even if he couldn't prove them, the better he would be able to intimidate the shit out of the man.

By demonstrating not only that he knew of Shaw's illegal activities but also had intimate knowledge of his bedroom behavior, he would prove just how deep in Shaw's head he really was. The SEIU leader would go mad trying to figure out how Fisher could possibly know what he knew. He would fear him and wonder what other dirt he might have, beyond even what he chose to disclose.

Fisher would assure Shaw that he only wanted his support, and that if this was given, his past would not come back to haunt him, and his future would be blindingly bright.

But he couldn't tell this to Hall. He still needed to come across as a good Samaritan, a crusader for justice, and these calculations didn't fit this image.

"He's had several extra-marital affairs," replied Hall. "I'll be sure to include names and details in the report. He also uses prostitutes frequently."

"Why? Seems like he could get all the sex he wants for free."

Hall sighed. "He gets off on peeing on women before he has sex with them. He knows his wife and mistresses don't share this particular . . . interest. So he spends some of the fortune he's been accumulating illegally on women who are more than happy to become human urinals for the right price."

Fisher grinned broadly in delight. This was working out even better than he had hoped. He was all but guaranteed the White House. And they had only just begun.

***

Marc Fisher finished reading Hall's formal report and couldn't stop smiling. He tried a few of Shaw's accounts, using the login information Hall so kindly provided, and slipped right in like a dream.

Hall had more than earned his hot tub and exercise equipment. Hell, Fisher would give the man full body massages *himself* if he would continue providing information as useful as this.

He prepared himself a Manhattan, his cocktail of choice, and looked through his twenty-ninth story window at the streets below. By tomorrow at this time, he would be back in his primary residence in La Jolla, California, looking out over the Pacific Ocean and fantasizing about being the leader of the free world.

As a warmth from the Manhattan suffused his body, he instructed his PDA to get Guy Shaw on a video connection. After Shaw accepted the call, and the briefest of preliminaries, Fisher got right to the point. "Guy, let me tell you why I called," he said, relishing the moment. "I know it's a bit early, but between you and me, I'm planning to declare for the presidency. And I want to know that I'll have your full support."

Shaw eyed him in disbelief. "Marc, you're a good politician," he said. "And being Chair of the House Intelligence Committee is a great credential. So don't worry," he added with an insincere smile. "I'll give you plenty of chances to win me over. But I'll have to consider all the candidates who declare."

"Yeah. About that. I'll want you to *pretend* you're considering others. But I really need you to commit to me right now that I'll be the one who gets your full support."

Shaw's face darkened. "Marc, have you lost your fucking mind? You know I can't do that."

"Really?" said Fisher, his eyes now gleaming with a feral intensity and his lips curled back into a predatory smile. "Because I'm betting you can. In fact, you're about to find out just how persuasive I can be."

31

Colonel Mike Campbell answered the secure call from Justin Girdler and the general's 3-D image appeared on the screen on his desk. Girdler looked ashen. "There was an assault on Alex's home less than an hour ago. He's been abducted, but there is every reason to believe he's still alive."

Campbell's mouth dropped to the floor, and so many questions crossed his mind at the same time that for a moment he was unable to speak, like an old-fashioned typewriter whose keys had all been pressed at the same time, causing a hopeless jam. He managed to prioritize the questions and spit out the one that was most important.

"Heather?" he asked anxiously.

"She was out. Doesn't know about it yet."

Campbell blew out a breath. That was lucky. At least one of them was safe. Nick, Megan, and now Alex. *What the hell was going on?* Their group of six was being picked off one by one, like actors in a bad horror movie.

"How?" asked Campbell simply.

Girdler had been put in sole charge of security, for Alex and for Theia's pilot manufacturing facility. He had pulled strings and had not taken no for an answer, insisting that he was in a better position than anyone to understand the importance of security in both of these cases, and only a handful of men in the US had as much experience. Campbell had offered to help, but the general had told him this wasn't necessary.

Girdler sighed. "I have no idea how. But they were able to control the security system from the inside. They knew the door codes, our procedures, and altered the monitors somehow. I just learned of the attack a few minutes ago and have scrambled teams to try to find them. If they call in, I'll have to take the call, of course."

"Of course."

Girdler shook his head in confusion. "I triggered satellite proto-cols right away also. Somehow, the satellites haven't been able to find them either. I have no idea who's behind this, or how they managed any of it. But the dragnet I've triggered is massive, and I can't believe they'll slip through no matter how good they are."

"Would you ever have believed they could get this far?" asked Campbell pointedly.

"No. But they can't be supernatural. We'll get Alex back."

"How are you sure he's even alive?"

"That's just it. *Everyone* is alive."

"What do you mean, *everyone*? All your people on site?"

"Yes. Thank God. These were all good men. The hostiles used tranquilizer darts and gas. None of the men had more than a bruise or a scratch. No sign of blood or a struggle. Has to be the cleanest op I've ever seen, in every way possible, especially considering what the hostiles were up against."

"Wait a minute," said Campbell in excitement. "No matter how good the people who did this are, they can't possibly know about Alex's *implants*. They'll strip him of any electronics, but they have no idea he can communicate with us from inside his head. So he must still be unconscious. The moment he awakens, he can tell you exactly where he is and who took him."

"Provided *he* knows."

"Yes," said Campbell, "provided he knows." He paused. "Any idea at all who's behind this? Who do you know who's good enough to manage an op like this?"

"No one. And no group. What they did is impossible."

"Whoever they are, the fact that they didn't use lethal force makes this even more mysterious. I'm thrilled your men are okay, but it makes no sense. Are they a crack assault unit or grade school kids at a paintball outing? Since when are our enemies so gentle? How many times have you seen an attack on a heavily guarded and forti-fied position where the hostiles took so much care and effort not to hurt anyone?"

"Never," said Girdler. He shook his head. "You're right. It doesn't add up. Can't just be charity or a happy accident. Too well planned. And their instincts would be to kill, leaving no possible witnesses or possibility of miscalculation. They must have done this to confuse us. Throw us off the trail, since this isn't the MO of any group we know."

Campbell winced, almost imperceptibly. It was time to address the elephant in the room. "I know you've only had a few minutes to digest this, Justin, but . . ." He hesitated, his reluctance to continue evident. "Well, have you considered how this looks?"

Girdler's face crinkled up in confusion. "How this looks?"

"Come on, Justin. I spoke with Drew Russell yesterday. I know you've been having him use his voodoo to assess your situation. And his assessment matches ours, as I know he told you. The horse is out of the barn. A court martial is now all but certain. Probably beginning in just a few days."

"I know," said Girdler in resignation. "But I'm not going to let this affect me. Until they pry this office from my cold, dead hand, I'm going to continue carrying out my responsibilities."

"I get that," said Campbell. "I really do. But you see how this looks, right? Someone just pulled off an impossible attack. And *you* were in charge of security. They seemed to have access to codes and information they couldn't have had. Information that only *you* know."

Girdler frowned. "I am being slow, aren't I?" he said in disgust. "You're absolutely right. There is a primary suspect after all. Me."

"I'm afraid so."

Campbell stared at his boss, mentor, and long-time friend. They had been through so much together. He would trust his life to the general without an instant of hesitation. This man could not be behind this abduction. It was absurd. Preposterous. He would believe hamsters could perform brain surgery before he would believe *this*.

But it was the only possibility. This couldn't even be an attempt at framing the general, since no one could possibly have the information needed to do this. And why try to frame him? The winds had turned against Girdler, decisively, and he was going down anyway.

The success of the raid was impossible. And Girdler's involvement was impossible. So what was left?

"All fingers really do point my way," said Girdler. "With no other explanation possible. I really am the only one who could have done this." He paused. "I'm guessing they'll be sending a team to apprehend me as soon as they figure this out. Probably by tomorrow night at the latest."

There was a long silence as both men were left with their thoughts. Campbell was sure they were missing something. They had to be. But the walls were closing in, and unless they could think of even a remote, crazy way this could have happened, they would continue to do so.

"Nick could have done this," said Campbell, as the thought suddenly occurred to him. "He's the only other person alive who could have. By reading whatever information he needed from you or someone else."

"I can't believe that," said Girdler. "He would never sell us out. No matter what."

"Even if Megan's life was on the line?"

Girdler opened his mouth to speak, but then closed it again.

Campbell considered. What *would* Nick do if he had to choose between helping these hostiles capture Alex, or watching Megan be tortured and killed? How would he make the most soul-destroying ethical choice any man could make? It could have been Nick. Under duress.

"This doesn't make sense, either," said Girdler. "Think about it. If Nick were behind this, he wouldn't need an assault team. He's Alex's trusted friend. He could have said he escaped and asked Alex to meet him somewhere private. Drawn him out. Why leave him in his fort and make it so complicated?"

"I don't know. I don't know anything. Except everything is going to shit. Unraveling. And we're being outplayed. Badly." The colonel paused. "When Alex regains consciousness and can contact us, we'll learn more. But I'm afraid at this point, nothing's going to stop a team from coming to arrest you sometime in the next twenty-four hours."

"That's okay," said Girdler with a forced smile. "They'll have to try me before they hang me. So we have some time. But I need you to come out here as soon as you can. I want you to take the lead on the investigation when you arrive."

"I'll scramble a jet and be there tonight."

"Thanks, Mike. And when we get off the phone, I have an unpleasant assignment I'd like you to take."

"What?"

"Call Heather and deliver the news. I was going to, but under the circumstances, as the only suspect, I'm not sure this is a good idea."

Campbell nodded. "I'll call her right away."

"And meet up with her immediately when you land. She'll need a strong shoulder to lean on. And you'll want to talk to her and inspect the grounds as part of the investigation anyway."

"Will she be secure at home, or should we move her to a safe house?"

"She'll be fine. I'll have Drew Russell reset the security system, looking for bugs left behind, worms, and so on, and change out passwords. Won't take a guy like him long. As long as he blesses it, she should be safe. But you should stay with her in a guest room, just to give her added comfort."

"Roger that," said Campbell. He gave his friend a reassuring nod. "And, Justin, hang in there."

"I will. But watch your back, Mike. These guys seem supernatural. They've kidnapped three of our cabal. And by kidnapping Alex the way they have, they're a day away from seeing to it that I'm rendered impotent, as well, when the military takes me into custody."

"I'll be careful," said Campbell. "But they've disrupted the four members of our group who are most important. I'm not sure anyone will think Heather and I are worth the effort."

"I hope you're right. But assume you're not. At the risk of depressing the shit out of you, this may only be the beginning."

"Even so," said Campbell, "we'll figure this out. And you've done too much for this country for me to just stand by while you're being railroaded. I promise you, Justin, I'm not going to let this stand."

32

Alex Altschuler forced his eyes open as the events at his home came rushing back to him, and the full horror of his situation.

But at least he was still alive, he thought, fighting back panic. Or at least he *thought* he was. He was seated in a steel chair that had been affixed to the floor, his hands and feet strapped flush to the chair by sturdy plastic strips, ratcheted to the proper tightness and then locked there.

A little less inviting than he had imagined Heaven to be, and a little more air-conditioned than Hell. So he decided to stick with his initial, *alive*, verdict.

He took a deep breath and noted that his lungs didn't seem to feel any after-effects from the gas that had been used in the attack.

The assault team must have been able to hack the security at his home. It was the only way they could have altered the camera feed the way they had, and entered the way they had. It was the only explanation for his PDA not responding to his command to open the panic room door. Someone had managed to change the password.

But he wouldn't have thought this possible, even for someone with his skills.

He was in a small room with a bed, dresser, lamps, and even art on the wall, looking for all the world like a lovingly assembled room for favored relatives or guests rather than a prison. But given his state of immobility, it was a prison nonetheless.

And he was still unable to access the Web, he realized suddenly. The implants and their capabilities had become an integral part of his thought processes, even more so than they were for Nick Hall. The severing of his connection to the Internet was a lobotomy, its absence crippling.

But why was it still gone? The attack was over. There was absolutely no reason for those behind the attack to take this precaution. He was immobilized and had no phone or other electronic devices.

So the continued presence of a dampening field could only mean one thing: they knew he was equipped with BrainWeb implants.

And this could not be. Because only five people in the world knew this to be true.

* * *

Victor had just returned from a trip when Eduardo Alvarez entered his office eagerly.

"Congratulations, my friend," said Victor warmly in Spanish, embracing his subordinate. "I understand the third string came through."

"Yes. With flying colors. The intel we got was perfect. I'll be damned. Part of me still thinks there is something we're missing. Some trap."

"Caution is never a bad thing," noted Victor. He had gotten to where he was by being smart, fair, and cautious, after all. Alvarez's instincts were good. Victor felt just as uneasy as he did, despite the brilliant success of phase one. "Speaking of which, I assume you're certain you weren't followed."

"Certain. I picked Altschuler up myself, as we discussed. I had the team take him a few hundred miles into the desert and leave him. I didn't retrieve him until they were long out of sight. So there is still no way this attack can be traced to us, even if they're later caught. I used tried and true methods to ensure I wasn't being followed, from space or the ground, and then I assumed I was being followed anyway, and used additional countermeasures. Then I ran Altschuler through the ringer. No hidden bugs. No tracking technology of any kind."

"Good work," said Victor.

"While I was doing this, the men completed reinforcing the room he's now in. Mary can now electrify the walls if this ever becomes necessary," he added, referring to the PDA that controlled the lodge. "She's been programmed to alarm and give our guest enough voltage to drive him unconscious if she were to see him attempt to break out."

Victor nodded. "Is he awake?"

"Yes. Just five minutes ago."

"Mary," said Victor to his PDA, "display video of our guest."

In seconds the scrawny genius appeared on the monitor. Both men studied him carefully.

"Given your enhancements to the room, why the need to strap him to a chair?" asked Victor.

"If he awoke with full freedom of movement, I thought he might try to escape, since I wouldn't have had the chance yet to explain why this was impossible. I didn't want him to try it and get hit with electricity. It's non-lethal, but I'd prefer not to take any risk with his mind until we've had the chance to milk it."

Victor raised his eyebrows and nodded his approval. "Smart," he said simply.

"Do you want to interrogate him now?"

"Not yet. Let him stew for a few more hours. To allow ample time for his imagination to torture him about what might be going on, and what might happen to him. An unknown threat lurking in the shadows can wear a man down faster than a known one."

"Given the success of phase one, can I assume phase two is a go for tonight?"

"Yes," said Victor. They had decided to be paranoid to the very end, so even though phase one had been everything it was promised to be, they still wouldn't be drawn in as participants to phase two. They would use the same men who had carried out the raid on Altschuler's home. "But tell the men involved we've decided to pay them double for their excellent work so far."

Under-promise and over-deliver. Reward loyalty and good work. Enhance loyalty and customer satisfaction by being surprisingly easy to work with and generous, rather than surprisingly stingy. These were the principles that had gotten him to where he was. His success, and his life, depended on being liked and trusted by all his employees and customers, even if they mistrusted and despised each other.

"And offer them three times the going rate for a successful completion of the op tonight," added Victor. He paused. "But before you do, let's review our plan one last time. Just to be sure we haven't missed anything."

Alvarez smiled. "You can never be too careful," he said.

33

Altschuler's agile mind had run through dozens of possibilities, had imagined endless nightmare scenarios. He had no idea which one of these, if any, were the truth, but they were all bad.

Was Heather okay? Had they captured her as well? Two bodyguards protected her when she left the residence, but compared to the security around him this was nothing. If she had been killed, he didn't know what he would do. His entire world would collapse.

Finally, after a few hours of escalating muscle soreness from being pinned to a chair for too long, agonized thoughts, and an agonized bladder as well, two men came into the room. Both had short black hair and features that made him think they were Hispanic.

"Dr. Altschuler," said the first man, nodding. He was slightly shorter than his colleague and projected an aura of total command. "Welcome. Can I call you Alex?"

The man's voice was elegant and pleasing to the ear, and his English smooth and almost perfect, with just the slightest hint of an accent. He appeared calm and unthreatening, although Altschuler was well aware that this could change in a hurry.

Altschuler decided he wasn't in the best position to dictate what he was called. "Alex is fine," he replied.

"Good. I'm Victor, and this is my associate Eduardo."

Altschuler nodded at the two men. "Forgive me for not shaking your hand," he said, moving his right arm a few inches before the plastic restraint refused to give additional ground.

Victor cut him loose, escorted him to a bathroom, and then gave him a bottle of cold water. Five minutes later he was seated in a more comfortable chair in another part of an elegant home that appeared to have been originally built as a hotel of some kind, with his two captors facing him. They made sure he knew what he was up against if he tried to escape and then Victor began. "You're probably wondering what you're doing here?" he said.

"Yes. And also how you could have captured me in the first place. I would have bet my life you couldn't have done what you did."

Victor smiled graciously. "Thank you for the compliment, Alex. But I'm glad you didn't bet your life. We need you alive and well."

"How did you do it?"

"I'm very, very good," replied Victor slowly, and while his partner was alert, taking everything in, it was becoming clear Eduardo would remain a silent observer throughout. "But let me tell you why you are here. We want the precise positioning coordinates in the brain for your four implants. We know you've either memorized them, or can call them up from the cloud. Under our close supervision, of course."

Altschuler's face wrinkled up in confusion. This made no sense. These coordinates were useless without actually having the implants. And when the implants were available, the coordinates would be known by a large number of physicians involved in the clinical trials. They'd be practically in the public domain, and Victor could obtain them with ease.

"Anything else?" said Altschuler cautiously.

Victor spread his hands as though he were the most reasonable man in the world. "That's all," he said.

"But how does this information help you? Without the implants themselves, positioning information is useless. And implants won't be available for at least another year or so," he lied.

Altschuler tried not to show his nerves. The ten thousand sets that had recently been completed at the pilot manufacturing facility were top secret. But so were the security codes to his home. So maybe they knew of the clinical batch, although the factory and implants were even better protected than he had been.

"Yes, we are well aware your implants are unavailable," said Victor. "We are following news about your company very closely. But let's just say we have our own technology. Our own hardware."

Altschuler fought off the urge to sigh in relief. They didn't know about the pilot factory. And there was no way implants lacking

Theia's hardware or algorithms could work. Not without the data Kelvin Gray had generated by butchering dozens of innocents and the algorithms that Altschuler had developed.

"So if I tell you the positioning coordinates, you'll let me go?"

Victor spread his hands magnanimously once again. "Yes. It's as simple as that. If you do this for me, we'll remain friends. I'll hook you up to a polygraph, of course. If you give me accurate coordinates, this is over. If you decide to lie, I'm afraid our friendship will end, and it won't go well for you, your family, or your fiancée."

"What have you done with Heather?" demanded Altschuler as a geyser of panic exploded within him.

"Relax," said Victor. "We don't have her. We purposely planned the raid for when she was out. Again, so we could make this as friendly as possible. But I assure you, if you cross me, it won't matter that she isn't currently in our possession. I trust we understand each other."

"Don't worry," said Altschuler. "I'll tell you what you want to know." He hesitated. "But I'm having trouble believing you would just let me go. After all, I've seen your faces, and you've given me your names."

Victor shook his head in amusement. "Thanks for reminding me of the risk of letting you go," he said. "Do you *want* me to kill you?"

"Your intelligence and competence comes through in your every word, your every expression. So I know I couldn't possibly remind you of anything you haven't already thought of."

Victor studied him with interest. "It's safe to let you go," he said, "because your government, and others, already know my name, and already have an artist's sketch of my face. But for facial recognition programs, they would need a photograph. With all due modesty, I'm quite famous in certain circles. And they've been hunting me for years."

Altschuler stared into his eyes, looking for deceit, but found none.

But nothing about this made sense. Had they really accomplished the miraculous feat of capturing him just for positioning coordinates? For information he would have gladly given them with very little provocation.

And it seemed as though the only way they could have succeeded was if he was betrayed by someone in his inner circle. But anyone in his inner circle would know he would put up very little fight to protect this particular information, and that they wouldn't need to go to this trouble. This realization almost came as a relief, since he couldn't bring himself to believe any of his friends would have betrayed him.

But there was still the matter of the dampening field. If they knew he had active implants, a betrayal by one of his friends was the only answer. But he couldn't just ask Victor why the Internet was down, because they had stripped him of all electronics, so how could he even know this? But then he hit on a solution. "I think I remember the coordinates exactly," he said, "but it might be best to look them up on the Web. Just to be sure."

Victor frowned. "I'm afraid we're in an Internet dead zone," he said. "So if you really think this is important, we'd have to change locations."

Altschuler considered this response. Could it be true? It seemed unlikely. Unless they were at the bottom of the ocean or inside a mountain, Internet coverage was awfully comprehensive these days. But a dead zone was much easier to believe than a betrayal.

"On second thought," said Altschuler. "This won't be necessary. I'm sure I remember them." He paused and forced a slight smile. "Bring on the polygraph," he added.

34

Heather gave Mike Campbell a warm hug as he entered the house she shared with Alex Altschuler, and tears began streaming down her face. Campbell was acutely aware that he wasn't supposed to have a relationship with her, and that the two bodyguards who had been in the room with her must be scratching their heads at this greeting, but he wasn't about to pull away.

"I am so sorry," he whispered in her ear before separating.

"Gentlemen," he said, facing Heather's two bodyguards. "Please patrol outside. The security system has been sanitized and reset, so I'll take responsibility for Ms. Zambrana's safety inside the mansion."

The colonel had made it to Fresno in excellent time. The previous guards, who had been rendered unconscious, had been taken to a nearby hospital and were just beginning to regain their senses.

Heather wiped away tears and offered the colonel a bottle of water, which he gladly accepted, and they sat across from each other on two couches in her palatial family room.

"Thank you so much for coming," she said. "Has there been any news? I've called the general, but I wasn't able to reach him."

"I haven't gotten any updates since I left the East Coast. But I'm sure if he learned anything important, we would be the first to know."

"Alex is alive, right?" she said, her voice breaking. "I mean, why spare everyone else and just, you know . . . not spare him?"

"Anything is possible," said Campbell, "but I can't imagine he's not. Like you said, they seemed to want to spare life. He's brilliant, famous, and a billionaire. If you can capture someone like this, why kill him? He's too valuable alive."

"Then why hasn't he contacted me yet?" she whispered.

Campbell sighed. "He's probably still unconscious. Or the people who took him know about his implants."

"That's not possible."

"The people we're up against seem to know a lot of things they couldn't know."

"How could this have happened?" demanded Heather, raging against an unfair cosmos. "You know Alex. He is a great man. But more than that, he is a good man. You've heard Nick sing his praises. And no one knows his true mind better, or has had more opportunity to compare it to the average."

"I know, Heather. I know. But Alex is out there. We can't be sure, but I can feel it."

"But you're not expecting any ransom calls, are you?"

"No. I don't think this is a kidnapping for ransom. It smells different. But I spoke with Drew Russell, our computer genius, on the way here, and he's programmed your PDA to record all incoming calls. And also, if your PDA doesn't recognize an incoming caller, it will divert the call to me and the general, no matter where we are, in case it's the kidnapper."

Heather nodded. "I'm surprised the general hasn't called me," she said. "I know he's busy searching for Alex, but it isn't like him not to contact me at all."

"I think he was worried you wouldn't want to see or hear from him after what happened."

"Why would he think that?" said Heather in confusion.

"Well, he *was* in charge of security."

"And it was incredible. Not his fault if someone planned an even better attack. I know how much he cares about Alex and me, and I would never hold him responsible."

Campbell gritted his teeth. "Well, about that. The way this op was handled, it pretty much points to him. Their knowledge of the security was just too complete and too perfect. He and I spoke about it, and he's well aware of how it looks."

Heather shook her head. "But it's a frame, right? It has to be."

"I agree it has to be. The problem is that no one could know enough about the security here to frame him."

Heather looked uncertain. "Come on, Colonel. We're talking about the general here."

"I know. I've worked with him for over a decade. He's been a friend and mentor. The man I know would never betray Alex. He thinks the world of him, like you said. And of you. But just for full disclosure, he *is* facing a court martial soon. And it's going very badly. The noose is tightening around his neck, and he's probably looking at jail time. This after he's devoted his entire life to service to this country. He's sacrificed his marriage and private life to a large degree. And he's been a hero. And this is the thanks he gets."

"This is truly horrible. He deserves far better. But what could this possibly have to do with Alex?"

"It's a stretch. And I don't believe it. But everything points to him, so it makes sense to at least consider that it might be true, as much as we'd rather not."

Campbell lowered his eyes. "It isn't just that the walls have been closing in, it's that mental illness runs in his family. Paranoid Schizophrenia, which has a genetic component. That's one of the reasons he chose psychology and ended up in PsyOps. To better understand the workings of the human mind and human behavior. Maybe to better understand himself, if he were to someday inherit this condition."

"So you think he might have lost his mind?"

"It's the only way he could be behind this. A lot of people really are out to get him. So maybe this triggered the paranoid condition. If so, there is no telling what he might do. If you're having delusions or hearing voices in your head, or if you think the people you love are out to get you, anything is possible. I gave this a lot of thought on the way here."

"Have you seen any signs? Has he been acting irrationally?"

"Not at all. He's taken the pressure better than anyone I know could have. He's never become emotional or angry. Just the opposite. He was calm and rational when I spoke with him earlier today, just after Alex was abducted."

"So it's possible, but unlikely."

"Yes. But even the delusional can fool you. And I wanted you to at least be aware of this possibility."

"First Nick and Megan, and now Alex. How is this happening?"

"Something very big is going on here," said Campbell. "Somebody has an end game. We just can't see it yet." He paused and decided to change the subject. "Are you okay spending the night here? Or would you prefer a safe house?"

"I'd prefer to stay here. If you think the security has been restored."

"I do," said Campbell. "But along with a new team manning the premises, I'd like to stay in the guest room next to yours. Just so you have a friend nearby."

She stared into his eyes gratefully. "Thanks, Colonel."

He was about to respond when his phone rang. He glanced at the screen. "It's Girdler's commanding officer," he told her, obviously surprised.

"Campbell here," he said into the phone.

"Mike, It's Nelson Sobol. Have you seen or spoken with Justin?" he asked with urgency in his voice.

"Not recently."

"Are you alone and secure?"

Campbell glanced at Heather and put a finger to his lips, motioning her to remain silent. She was part of his inner circle and the man she loved had just been kidnapped. She deserved to be in the loop.

"Yes. Hold on," he said. "I'm going to throw you up on a bigger screen."

Campbell instructed his phone to send the call to the closest monitor and seconds later Sobol's face loomed large above him. And the man could not have looked any grimmer.

"Where are you?" asked Sobol.

"I'm in Alex Altschuler's family room. His fiancée and her bodyguards are outside on the grounds, and this is a secure line."

"What are you doing *there*?"

"Justin sent me. He wanted me to help comfort Dr. Altschuler's fiancée and help in the investigation."

"What the fuck are you talking about!" snapped Sobol. "What investigation?"

Campbell felt a knot in his stomach. "The investigation of Altschuler's kidnapping."

"Altschuler has been kidnapped?" bellowed Sobol, the veins popping on the side of his neck.

Campbell shot a glance at Heather, who couldn't have looked more confused. He quickly filled Sobol in on the op that had resulted in Altschuler being taken. "Justin must have been too busy setting up the dragnet to contact you," he added, suspecting that Girdler knew this was his last day in power and hadn't cared about a gross dereliction of protocol.

"I'll call you back in five," said Sobol, ending the connection. Not exactly the response Campbell had expected.

Eight minutes later he was back on the screen. "Colonel, you've been lied to. Other than you and the bodyguards who have just regained consciousness, no one knows about the kidnapping." His expression had now hardened to the point he could use his face to break diamonds. "There is no dragnet of any kind. No investigation. Girdler hasn't made any attempt to find Altschuler. And no one has seen Girdler, or been able to reach him, in hours. He's disappeared."

"Maybe he's just in transit somewhere," said Campbell, but he didn't believe it himself.

"He was about to be informed of a court martial. Since his hours as head of Black Ops were numbered, we kept close tabs on him, in case he was a flight risk. So he's not just out of touch. He disappeared on purpose."

The knot in Campbell's stomach grew to the size of a cantaloupe and he had to fight to take a breath. If Girdler hadn't done anything to find Alex, then he had to be in on it, after all. They had stretched the benefit of the doubt as far as it would go. Girdler's guilt was now certain.

"When did you speak with him last?" asked Sobol.

"About three or four hours ago," replied the colonel. "Just before I left Bragg." He paused. "Can I ask why you called me in the first place? You didn't know about Altschuler. So why were you so eager to reach the general?"

To his credit, Sobol didn't hesitate. "Theia's pilot manufacturing plant was just hit. The one whose security Girdler is also in charge of.

The one whose very existence was supposed to have been as classified as the plans for our missile defense system. The one protected by state-of-the-art security and enough manpower to win a war."

Campbell just stared at the screen with his mouth open, unable to respond.

"They got all ten thousand sets of implants," continued Sobol. "All of them."

The implants were tiny, all four able to fit in a case the size of a quarter, although the final product packaging would make their footprint quite a bit larger. But all ten thousand sets made for the clinical trial could fit nicely into two large suitcases.

"The raid was immaculate," said Sobol. "Just like the one on Altschuler. They had perfect inside knowledge. Codes. Guard movements and shift changes. They knew where to find the hidden safe in which the finished implants were stored. I could go on. But it was an inside job, through and through."

Heather looked ill, but managed to remain silent and out of sight.

"Any leads at all?" asked Campbell.

"None. A private jet landed on a secluded stretch of road nearby and took off with the men responsible, and the implants. The jet was stealth enabled. As advanced as anything in our own arsenal. And the satellites covering the area went down." He paused. "Just to rub salt in the wound, as soon as these fuckers were airborne they triggered explosives that turned the pilot manufacturing plant into slag."

"How many casualties?"

"None," said Sobol, shaking his head as if not even believing this himself. "Just like you described when they were collecting Altschuler. They took everyone out with gas or darts. Then they took five minutes extra, in the middle of a hit-and-run operation, to stack all the sleeping bodies into the back of a truck and move them far enough from the blast zone so no one was hurt."

Sobol frowned deeply. "You probably know I haven't been a big fan of Girdler for a while now," he said. "But I never thought he had it in him to do something like this. So now he has Theia's human brain trust and ten thousand sets of implants. The combination is worth a fortune. When I catch that bastard, I'm going to kill him myself."

Campbell had distanced himself from Girdler publicly, at the general's own insistence, for some time now, so Sobol thought he had grown estranged from Girdler just as Sobol had. Which is the only thing that kept him off the hot seat now.

"I'll issue a warrant for Girdler's arrest as soon as I end this call," continued Sobol. "And set up a manhunt. We'll find him. And when we do, we'll find the implants." Sobol paused. "Why do you think you were the only one he told about the kidnapping?"

"I have no idea," replied Campbell. "But I'm going to find out."

"Good. You take point on finding Altschuler and keeping his fiancée safe. I'll let you know if I need anything else."

"Roger that," said Campbell as the call ended.

* * *

Heather stumbled closer to Campbell like she was one of the living dead. "Girdler orchestrated everything," she whispered, horrified. "Maybe he has gone crazy. But it's hard to believe someone who is delusional could execute a plan like this so well."

Campbell considered. The fact that the assault teams had made sure there were zero casualties at either attack sounded like the doings of the man he knew. But would a man suffering from paranoid delusions go to this much trouble to spare lives? Think this clearly?

"If he isn't delusional," said Campbell finally, "then he had to have done this for the money. Which I find even harder to believe. In all the time I've known him, wealth has never been a motivation."

"People change," said Heather.

They both fell silent and continued to ponder the inexplicable.

Heather's eyes widened. "Wait a minute. With Alex and the implants both gone, and the factory destroyed, it's game over for BrainWeb. With Alex out of the picture, only Girdler can access the required specs. The copy Alex gave to the board of directors is garbage. So Girdler not only controls Alex and the clinical trial supply of implants, he is now the only person alive with access to the knowledge of what makes BrainWeb work. Do you think he's doing this so he can prevent the technology from ever being used?"

"An interesting thought," said Campbell. If this were true, the audacity of the plan was astonishing, even for Girdler. But his genius at devising this sort of strategy was unparalleled. Only he was skilled enough, and bold enough, to attempt a plan so daring and complex.

Girdler *had* been the most vocal against the technology. So was this his way of accomplishing by force what they had failed to accomplish by fiat? By destroying the implants, the pilot factory, and taking Alex out of commission, the BrainWeb technology wouldn't reemerge for decades. Theia Labs could still restore sight and hearing to the impaired, but mind-controlled Web surfing would go the way of the albatross.

So was this his end game? Had he become the front man of an anti-technology group that would stop at nothing to make sure BrainWeb never saw the light of day?

Heather took a deep breath and stared into Campbell's eyes. "And then there were two," she whispered.

He forced a weary smile. Apparently, being in their exclusive six-member group wasn't the best way to ensure a long and dull life.

"Don't worry," he said. "The erosion of the group stops now. And I don't plan on letting you out of my sight."

Heather nodded, but even he knew this wasn't comforting given what had gone before. And she was a lot less worried about her own safety than she was about getting Alex back.

As head of PsyOps, Campbell had considerable resources at his disposal. But Justin Girdler was a brilliant strategist who knew very well how to counter his every move.

Campbell was confident of his own abilities, but under the circumstances, it was hard to like his chances.

35

Nick Hall counted the minutes until his daily call with Megan. It was the only thing keeping him going.

Nothing like forcibly being kept separated for an extended period of time to put everything into perspective. He had been feeling sorry for himself on the *Eos*. Sure. Too much time with the woman he loved. Too much sex.

He had been an *idiot*.

He would give anything to be able to hold her again. To joke with her. To see her incandescent smile and hear her unselfconscious laughter, which brightened a room like a starburst.

At least he had gotten through the worst of his Internet withdrawal, which had been brutal. But he vowed that once he got back together with Megan—he wouldn't allow himself to consider a scenario in which this didn't happen—he would get a dampening bracelet of his own, with an indicator light. So when they were together he could turn off wireless coverage around him and she would know he was paying attention. That he was there for her. When he wanted to use the Web, he could switch off the bracelet—but she would *know* that he had, just as a woman in a normal situation would know that a man was sneaking a look at a cell phone.

Frank Earnest was allowing them a single five-minute video call a day, with no restrictions on what they could say, although they did know their captor was eavesdropping, so any discussions of escape, if Hall could ever come up with a plan, would have to be very creative. Megan continued to be treated well, as promised. She had mentioned she was in the desert in the Southwest, beyond sight of other homes or civilization, but that is all she knew.

For his part, Hall had relayed to her what he had been doing and why. She had listened but hadn't commented much, knowing the walls had ears.

He had read the minds of several other politicians and Democratic Party power players during the past week and had never failed to come away disgusted. While Frank Earnest had never failed to come away delighted.

But his mood had reached its lowest point. His captor hadn't made the slightest mistake, and he showed no signs he was about to.

And although he continued to claim he would let both his prisoners go when he had what he needed, Hall couldn't imagine him taking this risk. Not a man as careful as Earnest.

No, a man this careful would make sure he and Megan became the kind of skeletons that only a future mind reader could ever find.

36

Altschuler stared deeply into Victor's eyes and recited the placement coordinates for the implants slowly and carefully, trying to stay calm so the polygraph wouldn't pick up on his stress. He knew this was irrational, because the system accounted for the stress of being tested and he was telling the truth. But it would have been a nightmare if the polygraph glitched and indicated he was lying.

He held his breath while Victor and Eduardo studied the results. After a few minutes, Victor nodded. "Thank you, Alex. This has been helpful." He paused. "As I'm sure you're aware, two new surgical robots have come out over the past few months. Which were you planning to use for your clinical trials?"

Altschuler couldn't help but be impressed by the extent of Victor's knowledge. About a year earlier, when Gray was performing experiments on Hall and others, he had used a programmable robotic surgery device, since the implants were very small and needed to be placed with inhuman precision. At this time, a human surgeon was required to make the initial incision and guide the procedure, which Heather had done for him, but newer robots had since come out that had eliminated even this requirement. They were perfect for Theia's needs.

"The AutoSurge Four," said Altschuler. "The one made by Hayashi Incorporated. It's the most expensive, but its brain scans are the highest resolution and most precise. We don't think we'll need as much precision as it can give, but we plan to be as conservative as possible until we're certain."

"Thank you. This was my thinking also, but I wanted to be sure I hadn't missed anything."

Altschuler considered warning him that these coordinates would never work for different hardware and software, and that he was certain whatever attempts at designing implants Victor's scientific friends were making were doomed to failure, but decided against it. Why give the man any reason to hold him longer?

"Okay," said Altschuler. "I've given you what you want. So please release me as you promised."

Victor frowned. "Well, I did tell you I'd release you, but it wasn't so much a promise. And I'm afraid I was misleading you. But only a little. We need to keep you a little longer, just to be certain everything works right."

Altschuler's heart raced. He had known this was too good to be true. Too easy. His face reflected bitterness and disgust at Victor's betrayal. "*What* works right?" he asked angrily.

"Theia's implants. We need to get an AutoSurge Four. And then we need to perform the surgery on a few volunteers." Victor smiled. "Just to be sure everything is working as advertised. If everything checks out with our volunteers, then I'll undergo the procedure myself. Once I'm satisfied BrainWeb is working in my own head, we'll let you go. Won't be longer than another week or two, at most."

"If you're planning to use our implants," said Altschuler, "it will be a hell of a lot longer than that. As we've already discussed, none will be available for at least another year."

Victor raised his eyebrows. "That's funny," he said. "Because I acquired ten thousand sets just last night."

An icy chill raced up Altschuler's spine. Victor couldn't possibly have known these implants had just been manufactured, let along managed to steal them, but Altschuler didn't doubt it for a moment. The number ten thousand was too specific, and too accurate, and the smug look on the arms dealer's face too genuine.

Altschuler had been played for a fool. He should have known Victor was too smart to go to this much trouble for information that would be useless to him.

So now his captor had everything he needed to get BrainWeb working perfectly.

What, exactly, was going on? And what in the world was he up against?

37

Nick Hall paced in his room like a caged lion. A few more weeks of this and he would lose his mind. It was a wonder he hadn't already.

It wasn't just the confinement and boredom. It was the stress as well. The worry. For himself and Megan.

And things had gotten worse than ever. When he had been escorted a day earlier to Virginia to read the mind of Senator Bob Sirrine—known to have his sights on the White House and considered by many to be the Democratic Party's frontrunner—he had read devastating news in the minds of dozens of people he passed.

Alex Altschuler was missing. It was an International story. His whereabouts were unknown. The identities of the kidnappers were unknown. And whether Theia's CEO was alive or dead was unknown.

The cable channels were running it constantly, hosting experts who conjectured as to why someone might take him. Many blamed anti-technology groups. But Hall knew better. Unless the Luddites had upped their game considerably—unlikely due to their disdain for technology—Altschuler could only have been captured by a group that was exceptionally sophisticated.

Hall still had twenty minutes before his daily call with Megan and was desperate to take his mind off of their current situation. He decided he had plenty of time to read Lombardo and Hogan, which he did twice a day. Just in case. He knew as much about these men now as they knew about themselves, but he religiously scanned them in case a conversation with Earnest, each other, or some outside interaction revealed a mistake. Something he could work with.

So far it had been fruitless. Neither had been told where Megan was being kept, or anything else that would have helped Hall. The man calling himself Frank Earnest was too careful.

Still, Hall would keep at it. If he could find just the tiniest loose thread to hold onto, he could unravel the entire sweater. He knew exactly how formidable he could be.

As he was reading Lombardo his eyes widened in shock. There it was! Just when he was at his very lowest, a ray of light had found its way through a crack in his cave.

And he suddenly had a lot of thinking and planning to do.

38

"How are you today, Nick?" said Marc Fisher, three hours after Hall's call with Megan. "Ready for tomorrow?"

"Yeah," said Hall. "About that." He hesitated. "After I read Bob Sirrine yesterday, I've been doing a lot of thinking. The more I do this, the more I've come around to your point of view."

Fisher beamed. He had hoped this would be the case. Why wouldn't it? Hall was a reasonably ethical man, who could only read so much corruption in the minds of politicians before he would become utterly sickened. It was the weakness of those cursed with a conscience.

Not that it mattered if Hall came around. He had him by the balls anyway. And Hall's information always checked out, and was never anything short of spectacular.

"That's great," said Fisher, faking enthusiasm. "I had a feeling you might."

"You did say you'd let me and Megan get on with our lives once you have enough to ensure your guy gets in, right?"

"Absolutely," said Fisher. "I'll never trouble the two of you again."

The truth was that when he had what he needed, Nick Hall and Megan Emerson would each be rewarded with a bullet to the brain, but he needed to continue the facade so Hall would continue to cooperate.

"Great," said Hall, but a guilty expression crept over his face. "So now that I'm sort of a convert, I'm going to level with you." He paused for a long moment, as if reluctant to continue. Finally he blew out a long breath and added, "I'm afraid I've been . . . misleading you."

"About what, Nick?" growled Fisher with a sudden intensity.

"I really don't need any rest after reading a mind for fifteen minutes. Or a day in between."

Fisher shook his head, relieved that Hall's revelation hadn't been worse. He had always suspected as much. He hadn't pressed it because he had all the time in the world and things were going beautifully.

"Go on," said Fisher.

"I was trying to stall. I didn't believe you would let us go. So I was trying to slow-play your project. But now that I've come to agree with you, and trust you, I want to get back to my life. As soon as possible. So I'm coming clean. Congress is in session. Get a hotel room within a few miles of the Capitol Building and give me a list. I can go for an entire day, getting what you want on ten to fifteen politicians. A lot more if you'd let me use my implants to record what I learn instead of having to type it in. "

"Fantastic, Nick. I'm not happy you lied to me, but I can't say I blame you. What I've done to you and Megan is indefensible. But I'm glad you finally decided to be honest with me. The country, and the world, will be far better off with an ethical man in the White House." He paused. "I'll book a room for tomorrow and put a list together as soon as we're done talking."

"Great," said Hall. "But since I'll be gone for an extended time, I'll want to move my daily call with Megan to the morning."

"Of course, Nick. I'll have my men let her know."

* * *

An hour after Hall's call with Earnest, Kent Lombardo brought him dinner as usual. Shrimp bisque flambé, spinach salad with pine nuts and dried cranberries, crab-stuffed salmon, and turtle cheesecake for dessert. He had never eaten better, and the story of Hansel and Gretel entered his mind, not for the first time. Beware of captors fattening you up for the slaughter.

Hall stopped Lombardo before he could leave. "There is something I want you to get for me," he said.

Lombardo shook his head, annoyed as usual at having to cater to a prisoner, bringing him food and movies, downloading books to his Kindle, and picking up meals at the best restaurants in the area. "I can't wait to find out what," he said sarcastically.

He knew intellectually that Hall could read his thoughts and he didn't need to speak, but Hall had purposely never displayed this ability, figuring that if Lombardo and Hogan let their guard down there was more chance they would make a mistake.

"Careful," said Hall. "You don't want me to report that you aren't treating me well."

Lombardo just glared at him but didn't respond.

"I need a telephone book of the DC area."

"What? Where the fuck would I get a phone book? I'm not even sure they make those anymore."

"They do. They may not print them, but you can get a PDF file of the directory. That's what I want. I'd do it, but as always," he said, holding out his arms and showing his dual bracelets, "I'm Internet blocked."

"What use is a DC phone book to you? Who you gonna call? You don't have phone privileges."

"I'm not calling anyone. I've been bored out of my mind. So I've decided to work on my memory. See how far I can get memorizing a phone book. You know those savant guys can memorize the whole thing."

"That is the stupidest idea I've ever heard. Memorize one of your science fiction novels."

Hall's face hardened. "Memorizing a phone book is like the gold standard of memory tasks. Just random names and numbers. And this is what I want." He sat down in front of his dinner and placed the linen napkin on his lap. "I know your orders, Kent," he finished. "And this simple request is well within them."

Hall read his mind as he thought it through. He hated being the gopher, but he was being paid extremely well for easy duty. And he had detected an extra glint in Hall's eye that indicated he would not let this go easily. And the last thing he needed was Hall reporting that he wasn't being cooperative.

"Okay, Nick. If you want to try to memorize the fucking phone book, be my guest."

39

The instant Hall appeared on the monitor, the earliest he had ever called, Megan sensed there was something different about him. There was an excitement in his eyes she hadn't seen for too long. An energy and alertness.

Was it actually *hope*, or was she imagining things?

Since his captor was watching also, he was giving off just enough for the woman he loved to pick up, but not enough for Earnest to catch. At least she hoped that's what was happening.

"How are things?" he began. "You know, wherever you are."

"Same old, same old," she said in bored tones, but she watched him with greater intensity than ever, straining to catch the slightest change in his body language.

"I love you," he said unselfconsciously, usually one of the first phrases one or the other of them uttered during a call.

"I love you, too, Nick," she said softly. "Why did you schedule such an early call?"

It was early for him on the East Coast, but for her it was well before the crack of dawn.

He quickly explained that he wouldn't be able to call her at the usual time since he had come clean with Earnest, and would be spending eight to ten hours near the Capitol Building. "But this will speed things up," he said excitedly. "We may be able to get our freedom in weeks rather than months or years."

Megan's eyes narrowed. Why had he chosen to take this step? She had known he was stringing Earnest on. Buying time. But why change gears now? Nick wasn't stupid enough to believe Earnest would really let them go.

"That's great news!" she said, faking as much enthusiasm as she could.

"Yeah. I'm excited." He paused. "But on another topic," he said, giving her the quickest of winks, "before we run out of time, there is something I've been meaning to ask since we were first . . . separated. Have you been sleeping okay? I know what stress does to you. I've hesitated to bring it up, worried that if I got you thinking of insomnia I might actually cause it. But you've been looking tired, and I'm worried about you."

He had shaken his head just the slightest amount when he had asked if she was sleeping okay, and this was all the guidance she needed. "You're right," she said with a sigh. "I have had trouble sleeping. But I didn't want to bother you with it."

"I was worried about that," he said. He paused as though reluctant to continue. "Still hearing voices in your head?" he added softly, his tone one of understanding and compassion. "Is that still the issue?"

Megan paused. *Voices in her head?*

What was he trying to communicate?

Hall's chin bobbed up and down almost imperceptibly, encouraging her to work out the puzzle.

"Because if you are," he continued, "remember what the doctors said. They said if this happens, don't even try to sleep. Read a book or do something else. Stay alert. Ignoring the voices doesn't help. Really focusing on them is the only thing that can make them go away."

This time the message was unmistakable. *Stay alert.*

Someone was coming for her. Something was about to change. And she shouldn't risk sleeping until it had.

And it was Nick, himself, who was coming, she realized a moment later. His was the only voice she had ever heard in her head. He needed her to be alert for a telepathic call.

"Thanks for the reminder, Nick," she said, giving him just a hint of a telling nod herself. "I'll give that a shot."

40

Kent Lombardo entered the luxurious hotel room with Hall and Hogan right behind him.

The Mayflower Renaissance hotel was built in 1925 and had a rich history. It had hosted any number of presidents and presidential inaugural balls. FDR had penned his famous, "We have nothing to fear but fear itself," speech within its walls. An iconic photo of Bill Clinton greeting Monica Lewinsky in a crowd at a 1996 campaign event had been taken at this hotel. And in 2008, room 871 at the Mayflower had hosted New York Governor Elliot Spitzer and a high-end prostitute, leading to a scandal that had ended in Spitzer's resignation.

But in all of its storied years of existence, the Mayflower had never hosted someone capable of reading minds.

Until now.

Hall sat on an elegant wood-framed upholstered chair, in front of a desk that was nicer and more substantial than the usual fare, obviously built for businessmen, and in this town, lobbyists. He unpacked his laptop and full-sized keyboard and prepared to get to work, while his two escorts took a seat on opposite ends of a couch nearby and braced themselves for a very long day.

Hall read that they were dreading this assignment. Not that they had any fear he would try to escape. But while the usual outing was an hour or two at most, they would be stuck here for more than eight hours. Basically doing nothing. Watching a man type into a computer for an entire day was exactly as interesting as watching paint dry. Their instructions were to stay as long as possible, but to return to the warehouse by six, when their nameless boss planned to contact Hall for a report.

"You can turn on the TV if you want," said Hall. "It won't bother me. I'm going to be a while."

Hall could read that both men were debating if they should. Both came to the conclusion, independently, that watching TV wouldn't pose any security risks, since they could still keep tabs on him.

Lombardo picked up the remote and glanced at his partner. "Maybe we will," he said, turning the TV on and hitting the menu button to make a selection.

Minutes later they were watching the last remake of Godzilla, which neither man had seen for years, becoming more engrossed in the movie, and less in him, by the second.

Hall groaned. "Sorry to interrupt," he said, gesturing to his open laptop, "but the battery is low, and I left the charger in the car."

Both men were annoyed, and had some uncomplimentary thoughts for him, but this was especially true of Gary Hogan, who was low man on the totem pole and knew what was coming. Sure enough, Lombardo pulled keys from his pocket and handed them to him. "Go down and get the damn cord," he instructed.

Hogan grabbed the keys, took one last look at the television, and then left the room.

Within seconds, Lombardo was once again engrossed in the movie.

Hall gathered his courage and resolve and mentally braced himself for what was to come. He waited another minute, until he knew he could wait no longer. Then, as quickly and quietly as he could, he rose from the desk and flung his closed laptop at Lombardo ten feet away on the couch, like a Frisbee. Lombardo caught sight of the approaching missile at the last instant from the corner of his eye and managed to dodge, but the laptop still glanced off his side painfully.

Lombardo stood to get his bearings, reaching for his dart gun, when he caught a face full of desk chair, spinning him toward the TV and onto the floor. His nose was broken and he had a gash in his cheek that was leaking blood.

"Toss me the tranq gun, barrel first!" barked Hall.

Lombardo was absolutely stunned by this development. A cuddly puppy had turned into a rabid wolf before his eyes. He ignored the blinding pain coming from his broken nose and prepared to attack. The dart gun had landed just behind him, but he had other options.

"Really?" said Hall, holding the heavy chair over his head, poised to strike again. Two of its legs had broken off, but it had a heavy base and its remaining two legs would be all that he needed. "*I can read minds, Kent.* Your hand gets any closer to that knife strapped to your leg and you'll be wearing this chair again."

Lombardo considered. He was now injured and in great pain, and Hall could get in at least one more lick with his bludgeon. But he was a professional, trained in hand-to-hand, and Hall was not. He would beat the shit out of this little pecker.

"Yeah, you're a trained pro," said Hall. "And I'm a little pecker. And you *could* beat the shit out of me if it was a fair fight. But it's not. Ever fight someone who knows your next move before *you* do?"

This gave Lombardo additional pause.

"The tranq gun!" demanded Hall again. "Now! Toss it here or I'm going to turn your face into *hamburger*."

Hall shook his head in disgust. "Are you kidding? Shooting me while trying to *pretend* you're giving me the gun won't work either. How stupid *are* you? I can read your fucking mind! Nothing you think of trying will work, *dumbshit*! Now grip the barrel with two fingers and toss it toward me."

Lombardo stared deeply into Hall's eyes and resignation came over him. He reached behind him for the gun and tossed it toward Hall as he had been instructed.

Hall picked up the weapon and shot Lombardo in the chest. The man was already on the ground, but was angled toward Hall, and fell the rest of the way to the carpet.

Hall quickly moved the unconscious mercenary a few feet farther behind the couch so he couldn't be seen by the returning Gary Hogan, who Hall read was rising in the elevator, charger in hand. He picked up the laptop and tossed broken wooden legs and splinters out of sight behind the couch.

Hogan was approaching the door. Hall could see through the man's eyes as he slid the keycard against the sensor. He pulled the door open and stepped inside, his only concern getting back to the movie before he missed something important.

He *had* missed something important. Nick Hall hiding behind the opening door.

Hall squeezed the trigger and Hogan fell to the ground, unconscious before he even knew what hit him.

Hall rushed into the bathroom and raised his wrists, one by one, a few inches above the marble sink and slammed his bracelets into the hard surface. Close enough that he wouldn't injure himself, but still forcefully enough to break the internal components.

The Internet came surging into his head.

He was back!

At the same instant, an alarm tone sounded on the phones of both men collapsed to the floor, alerting them that he had freed himself from his personal dampening field. He recovered both offending phones and smashed them on the bathroom floor. He then took Lombardo's knife and managed, with great difficulty, to remove both bracelets.

Hall checked the time. He now had about eight hours before Frank Earnest would know anything was out of the ordinary.

A day earlier Frank Earnest had finally made a mistake. He had been too busy to chaperone Hall's daily call with Megan, so he had given Lombardo the responsibility to set it up and listen in.

And he had given Lombardo the phone number where Megan was being kept, informing him it was a land-line for heightened security. This was all that Hall had needed. It was a 520 area code. The phone book PDF Lombardo had downloaded for him, even though it was only for Washington, had a table with all area codes across the country.

And 520 was for Tucson, Arizona.

Bingo. He had known Megan was in the desert in the Southwest somewhere, but he needed to narrow this down by a thousand-fold, which this area code did nicely.

Now that his implants were working he confirmed that 520 was Tucson and he was able to call up a map of the precise geography covered by this area code.

He had rehearsed his every step the night before. He didn't even want to think about what would happen if he wasn't able to get to Megan before his escape was discovered. And the most important part of this was ensuring that Lombardo and Hogan didn't regain consciousness until long after this time. Earnest had never once called them to check on things when he was reading minds, always assuming they had the situation well under control.

Hall was convinced Earnest was a politician himself, and the good man he was working to help was no one but himself. Why else did he take such care to ensure Hall never saw his face, or heard his actual voice?

Hall studied the make and model of the tranq gun in his hand while his implants magically called up the specs. One dart should be good for four hours of sleep. Three darts would put a hundred and fifty pound man out for ten hours, although this wasn't recommended.

Hall unloaded an additional three darts into each unconscious man, making four in total. If this didn't kill them, it would put them out for twelve or more hours.

He felt for a pulse and found one in both men, slow and weak, but there. Good enough.

Hall stayed for an additional ten minutes, reading key members of congress and effortlessly transmitting details of scandals and transgressions and dirty laundry to the cloud for later retrieval. This time he wasn't doing it for Earnest, but for himself.

He liked to think he had fairly rigorous ethical standards. But the school of hard knocks had taught him that he couldn't be naive any longer. It was time to store some leverage for a rainy day. One never knew when it might come in handy.

This accomplished, he stripped Lombardo and Hogan of their identification and cash, checked himself in the mirror, and left the room, carefully placing a do-not-disturb sign on his door as he did so.

41

Mike Campbell had set up several command centers from which he could direct the dozens of underlings he had working around the clock to find Altschuler, but progress had been all but nonexistent. And his wasn't the only group searching for the diminutive genius. Altschuler was considered a national treasure and the public pressure to get him back was immense.

Heather, who was known to be his fiancée, had been forced to barricade herself inside her home and had hired a publicist to field endless interview requests, making it clear that she would not be making herself available to the media under any circumstances.

Hank Cohen, the executive Altschuler had recruited from Intel, had taken over as Theia's interim CEO until such time as Altschuler was found or confirmed dead, and Heather at least had peace of mind that the company was in good hands.

Campbell visited Heather and filled her in on the latest reports. There was no sign of Girdler and no sign of the implants. And although he stopped short of telling her this, they were running out of hope. The more time that passed, the colder the trail became. Despite beefed up security at harbors and airports, the implants were ridiculously easy to hide and could be anywhere in the world by now.

And so could Alex Altschuler.

They began brainstorming once again, as they had endless times, searching for additional angles of attack. Heather had no experience with manhunts and knew nothing about military capabilities, but she climbed a learning curve like a hot-rodder on steroids, and her fresh perspective, her very ignorance of how things were typically done, had actually been helpful.

Their discussion was interrupted by a call coming in on Campbell's personal line. He answered the phone absentmindedly.

And heard the voice of Nick Hall.

Campbell almost fell out of his chair.

"*Nick?* Thank God you're alive," he said as a burst of adrenaline shot through him. "I have Heather with me. I'm putting you on speaker now."

"Nick!" said Heather excitedly. "Where have you been? What's going on?"

Hall summarized his situation in less than a minute, ending with his escape from Lombardo and Hogan at the Mayflower hotel.

"Any idea who this Frank Earnest might be?" said Campbell when he had finished.

"My guess is a high-ranking politician. But I don't have much time to talk. I need you to get me to Tucson. Now!" he added, panic beginning to show in his voice. "We have to get to Megan before they move her, or hurt her."

"We will," said the colonel. "Hang tight while I work out the logistics."

He lowered his head for half a minute, deep in thought. "Okay, Nick," he continued finally, "here's what you need to do. Take a cab from the Mayflower to Andrews Air Force Base. This should only take about thirty-five minutes. I could send someone to pick you up, but this would take longer. I'll have the Navy scramble an F-14 Tomcat and bring it to Andrews since it's one of the few remaining fighters with two cockpits. I'll make sure it's there and fueled up as soon as possible. The pilot can fly you to Davis-Monthan Air Force Base, which is only about ten to twenty miles from downtown Tucson. I'll meet you on the runway with a helo and an assault team."

"Sounds perfect!" said Hall in relief.

"What's the air distance from DC to Arizona?" asked Campbell, counting on Hall to use his implants to call up the answer instantly.

"Nineteen hundred and ten miles."

After a pause Campbell said, "The Tomcat can get you there in two hours and change. Any faster and you'd need a mid-air refuel, which I want to avoid."

"Two hours is outstanding," said Hall. "Heather," he added, changing gears now that his travel arrangements had been worked out, "I am so sorry to learn about Alex. I'm going to help find him just as soon as I can."

"Thanks, Nick. You're the one man who might really make the difference."

"Where's the general?" asked Hall. "He didn't answer his private line. And I made sure my implants broadcast that the call was coming from me."

Campbell shook his head and frowned. "He's turned, Nick. Maybe mental illness. But he was behind Alex's capture. Did you know the ten thousand implant sets for the trials were stolen as well?"

"*What?* What the hell is going on?"

"It's Girdler. He's behind both. And he's nowhere to be found. He's the subject of a massive manhunt and there's a warrant out for his arrest. But with his brains and expertise he can stay hidden forever."

"There must be some mistake," said Hall. "I've been in Girdler's mind. He isn't capable of this kind of betrayal, and money doesn't drive him. There must be another explanation."

"He was in charge of security for both Alex and the implants. He was the only one who could have succeeded. Only him."

"I don't believe it. Maybe there's another mind reader in the game. Maybe someone figured out the secret."

"Then what would they need with the implants and Alex?" said Campbell. "I wish this were true, but it has to be the general. And he did skip town."

"He knew he was framed and had no chance. You and I would have done the same, even if we were innocent."

"I thought of that. But if this were true, why didn't he contact me to let me know?"

"He didn't want you involved. He's insisted you distance yourself from him ever since he knew he had turned poison. He doesn't want to risk taking you down with him. From what I know, he's selfless like that."

Campbell sighed. "There's a history of mental illness in his family. I assume he's become delusional. Once that happens all bets are off. It's the only way I can square what I know of him with the reality."

"I'm about to get into a cab," said Hall.

"Hold up, Nick," said the colonel. "You're going to need at least a cursory disguise. I assume there are stores nearby. At minimum, get a hat, glasses, and bulky clothing—so you look bigger. You know the drill. And don't worry, you won't lose time, because if you left now for Andrews you'd probably have to wait a half-hour for the F-14."

"Got it," said Hall. "I've grown a beard, and no one has recognized me yet. But this is a good added precaution."

"A beard?"

"Long story. So what else?"

"Have the cab take you to the main gate at Andrews. I'll have someone waiting for you. Tell him your name is Clay King and that I sent you. He won't ask for identification."

"Thanks, Colonel."

"I'm just thrilled you and Megan are okay," said Campbell. "I'll see you in Tucson in three hours or so."

"Roger that," replied Hall.

42

Hall wore a baseball cap and thick black-rimmed glasses, but didn't take the time to buy additional clothing to bulk himself up. His face was well known, but he was also thought to be dead, so it would take monumentally bad luck for him to be recognized.

He instructed a cabbie to take him to the main gate of Andrews but to first complete a circle around the White House from about two miles out. The cabbie raised his eyebrows at this but didn't question it further. He had taken any number of fares near the White House, but what was the point of being two miles away? And why a full circle, or square as the case may be, before heading on to Andrews?

While Hall was in a store purchasing his makeshift disguise, he had continued to read members of congress, who were still within his range, and record key findings to his storage site in the cloud. He had learned many times over that the president was working out of the Oval Office today, which he decided was too great of an opportunity to pass up.

As the cab circumnavigated the White House, Hall had more than fifteen minutes to read President Cochran and found more than enough to have his balls in a vise, although he had to admit the president was on the whole a very good man. Having read too many minds in Congress to count, Hall decided the country had made a great choice. Cochran had done a few things that would bring down his presidency if they got out, but he had done them for noble rather than selfish purposes, unlike many of his fellow politicians.

Hall knew full well what it was like to have to make hard choices. Not only did he have blood on his hands, but he had broken the law for what he became convinced was the good of civilization, and he had put Justin Girdler in an untenable position. Like the president,

Girdler had secrets that couldn't survive close scrutiny, but was also a very good man.

Or at least he *had* been.

As they drove to the base, Hall fantasized about what it would be like to see Megan once again. To hold her. And his eagerness, his anticipation, mixed with the fear he would be too late or something would go wrong, was numbing. His emotions reeled like the patterns in a spinning kaleidoscope, complex and ever-changing.

He arrived at the main gate and introduced himself as Clay King. A Captain McBride immediately exited the gatehouse to meet him. Hall told him that Colonel Mike Campbell had sent him and this was more than enough for the man, who didn't recognize him as the famous, but long-dead, Nick Hall.

What happened next was a blur, since Hall couldn't quite believe it was real. He was introduced to a pilot and given a crash course on how to be a civilian passenger in an F-14, which apparently was about as common as a total eclipse of the sun.

And then, minutes later, he was behind the pilot in his own private cockpit, being fitted for a helmet. A dragonfly-shaped tinted visor covered the upper half of his face and an oxygen mask covered the lower, with a thick hose extending down from his chin.

The pilot had promised he would be as gentle as possible with the acceleration, limiting it to two Gs, and then they were off. As the pilot fired up the engines, which issued an intimidating roar and vibration like nothing Hall had ever heard or felt, Hall removed the baseball cap from his head and clutched it in his hand like it was a lifeline. As he looked down at it, a humorous quote he had read danced across his mind. *It is impossible to travel faster than the speed of light, and certainly not desirable, as one's hat keeps blowing off.*

Given that the jaws-of-life couldn't have pried the hat from his hand, he felt he was in no danger of losing it. Wetting his pants, maybe, but not losing his hat.

The F-14 roared down the runway on its way to a thunderous take-off, pinning Hall back against his seat, and he decided the thumping of his heart was actually louder than the jet.

What followed was two hours of total exhilaration, and total terror. The fighter jet reached a speed of almost a thousand miles an hour, well below its top speed, but being in such a tiny cockpit with nothing between him and the great beyond but a transparent shell, he felt as if he were traveling several times this speed.

A little more than two hours after takeoff the jet set down smoothly on the runaway at Davis-Monthan Air Force Base.

Hall was a bit wobbly as he stood once again on the runway, but he replaced the cap on his head, adjusted his unnecessary glasses, and thanked the pilot profusely. It had been the ride of his life, but more importantly, it had gotten him where he needed to be with as much time as possible to find Megan before his escape was discovered.

Twenty yards away, two figures were closing fast.

Colonel Campbell, in full uniform, and Heather Zambrana. He embraced the colonel warmly and gave Heather an extended bear-hug. "I was wondering if I'd ever see the two of you again," he said.

"We were wondering the same," said Campbell. He opened his mouth to make a request of Hall, but the mind reader beat him to the punch.

"I understand your discomfort at being this close to me, Colonel. I know you're privy to secrets even I shouldn't know. I promise to only read your strongest surface thoughts, the ones I can't avoid. Really."

"Thanks, Nick."

"Don't thank me. Everyone deserves the privacy of their own thoughts. Thanks to you for putting up with it. And for being there for me when I need you the most."

Campbell smiled. "Nah. I'm sure you have plenty of friends with access to F-14s," he said dryly.

"Not as many as you might think," said Hall, returning the smile. He turned to Heather. "I wasn't expecting *you* to be here to greet me. A very happy surprise."

"I told her there were possible dangers," said the colonel, "but she wouldn't take *no* for an answer. You know the way she feels about you and Megan."

"Besides," said Heather with a twinkle in her eye, "Mike has made me an honorary member of PsyOps while we try to find Alex."

They began walking toward an imposing military helicopter parked ahead on the runway, which the colonel explained was a Pave Hawk. Sister to the Black Hawk, it had the same elongated, dragonfly body, and room for a crew of four or five, including a pilot, co-pilot, and gunner, and could carry eight to ten troops as well.

"A hell of a lot more chopper than we need," said Campbell. "But this will do nicely." He handed each of them a sophisticated set of padded black headphones, with a speaker arm they could position under their mouths. "An assault team is standing by in another Pave Hawk for my orders."

"Who's going to pilot this thing?" said Hall.

"I am," said the colonel.

"You can pilot a Pave Hawk?" said Hall in dismay.

"Haven't for over a decade. But I wasn't always in PsyOps. Long story. I'll tell you someday." He shrugged. "But it's probably like riding a bicycle. I'm sure it'll come right back to me. Right?"

Hall grinned. "And I thought the F-14 was terrifying."

"Don't worry. For routine flying like we'll be doing, these helos can almost fly themselves nowadays."

They lifted high above the runway and then banked sharply to the South. "I've programmed in the geography covered by the 520 area code, ignoring all population centers. The software turns this area into a grid and then calculates the optimal search and rescue pattern to take. I've programmed it to assume we can spot our quarry at five miles out."

"Perfect," said Hall appreciatively.

The Pave Hawk flew relatively low to the ground, following a complex pattern whose mathematics only Altschuler would truly appreciate. Hall called out telepathically to Megan as forcefully as he could every fifteen seconds, while Campbell continued to plan. Heather remained silent, looking out of the window at the desolate desert below and trying not to distract either man.

Hall knew he might have been able to locate Megan using his ESP ability alone, but given she was a needle in a haystack telepathy upped his chances considerably. And he knew she had understood the message he had tried to convey during their call: stay alert and ready.

After twenty minutes without a response Hall began to worry. Had they moved her? Had he miscalculated somehow?

"Megan, honey, I love you," he broadcast with all of his might. *"Please be out there somewhere."*

"Nick, thank God!" came a faint response, gushing into his mind. *"You're really nearby. Incredible!"*

Absolute euphoria coursed through Hall like a drug. He threw his head back and drew in a deep breath, closing his eyes in relief. *"Hold on, Megan,"* he broadcast, and then hurriedly told the colonel he had made contact and to maintain their position.

"How did you do it, Nick? You were in Washington this morning. I wouldn't have thought you could even fly this far west by now, let alone find me."

"Yeah, well, you'd be surprised. I'll tell you about it later. I'm with Mike and Heather in a military helicopter, by the way, and you're in Tucson, Arizona. But I need you to go to the window that gives you a view of as many geographic features as possible. Rock or cactus formations, hills, mountains, that sort of thing."

"Moving to a window now," she replied.

"Broadcast the image you're seeing to me," he requested, and seconds later it arrived. His implants picked it up as if he was seeing it himself and he relayed this to the Pave Hawk's onboard computer. The computer compared it to detailed satellite imagery of the geography in a five-mile radius around them and spit out precise GPS coordinates less than a minute later.

"We have you located," he informed Megan. *"But I'm signing off for a few minutes. I need to read the minds of your captors and consult with Mike and Heather. I'll be in touch soon."*

Hall turned to his two companions. "There are four men with her," he said, and both heard him clearly through their headsets despite the noisy whipping of the chopper blades through the air as they hovered in place. "Named Angel Sanchez, Dave Bergum, Dom Olinda, and Boyd Solomon. Solomon is in charge, and the only one who knows what's going on."

Hall paused for several seconds, his head tilted up, as though listening. "The man behind this is named Marc Fisher. Ring any bells, Colonel?"

"Son of a bitch!" growled Campbell. "Yes. He's the Chairman of the House Intelligence Committee. I've had dealings with him on a number of occasions. And I'm not entirely surprised. He's one of the few with knowledge of the events at the Oscars. And he's wealthy, power hungry, and well connected. A real snake. He can be charming and friendly if he needs you. But rumors are that he's pure evil underneath and that anyone who gets in his way lives to regret it."

"I can't wait to meet him," said Hall with a bitter edge to his voice. "But for now, what are your thoughts on freeing Megan?"

"The assault team can get here in minutes," said the colonel. "They can easily take out these four men. The house is out in the open and isolated. The wrinkle is we need to get Megan out of there first, or this gets a lot more difficult, and a lot riskier. This part will be up to you, Nick."

Hall nodded. "I understand. Go on."

"We also need to make sure they don't warn their boss—warn Fisher. So the team will suppress cellular coverage to the house before the attack. In preparation, I've already had them contact the local phone company that runs the landline, and they have someone standing by to cut that service also, as soon as we tell them. We'll hang back until they're cut off."

He paused. "As long as Megan isn't in the line of fire or a possible hostage this couldn't be easier. As soon as you tell me she's a few hundred yards away from the structure we'll go in strong."

"The doors are locked from the inside," said Hall. "But I've read the code from Solomon's mind. Megan can enter this into a touchpad and escape. The trick is for her not to be seen doing it."

"I assume you can text them as Fisher, correct?" said Campbell.

"Yes. But unlike at the Oscars where I had technical help standing by, I won't be able to make it look like the text came from Fisher's phone."

"Will it say it's coming from Nick Hall?" asked Heather.

"No. I can choose any name I like. I could choose Marc Fisher. But they would know from the number it isn't him, and it wouldn't arrive as part of an earlier conversational thread the two had established."

"Just text that you had to borrow a phone," said Heather. "Long story."

Hall nodded, deep in thought. "Yeah. That should work, depending on my message."

"As Fisher, tell them to gather in the room with the biggest monitor to await a call from you," suggested Campbell. "While they're waiting, Megan can get the hell out of there."

"Won't work," said Hall. "Only Solomon knows Fisher's identity and contact is always in private."

"Then order them to gather to watch CNN," said Heather. "As Fisher, tell them you're in a crisis mode and had to borrow a phone. That there's a critical news story they need to see. It will be on during the fifteen minute segment, but you aren't sure when. But they'll know it when they see it."

Hall considered. "Nice," he said in admiration. "I like it. Colonel?"

Campbell nodded. "There are no guarantees. But it should work. If it doesn't, you'll know it and can think of something else."

"Okay, then," said Hall, taking a deep breath. "Get the other Pave Hawk in the air. I'll tell Megan what's going on."

43

Dom Olinda was in the kitchen waiting for a frozen lasagna to cook in the microwave when Solomon rushed into the room. "Gather up Sanchez and Bergum," he said. "Just got an urgent message from headquarters. Meet me in the living room."

Olinda found the other two men and joined Solomon as instructed. CNN was on the monitor in the room and Solomon was staring at it intently, waiting for a commercial to end. He motioned the three of them over. "We've been instructed to watch this channel. Didn't tell me what we were looking for, but that we'd know it when we saw it. And it's important."

The TV cut back from commercials and a moderator explained enthusiastically that they were back to an hour-long special on the successes of charter schools.

"What the fuck?" said Bergum. "*Charter* schools?"

"Yeah. No shit," said Solomon. "This doesn't pass the smell test. Especially since the boss said he was using someone else's phone to send the message. Let me re-read it."

As he glanced down at his phone he noticed it was no longer getting any reception.

"Check your phones!" he barked. "Any signal?"

His companions quickly confirmed that reception was out for all of them.

"Fuck!" spat Solomon. "We're about to be attacked. It's the only explanation. And we're sitting ducks in here." He paused. "Bergum and I will gather up laptops and other shit we can't leave behind. Olinda and Sanchez, find Megan and meet us in the garage. We'll take the SUV into town where we can hole up separately and assess the situation."

Olinda was impressed. Solomon could have chosen to dig in here. The attackers' options would be limited for fear of hitting the girl. But long-term it was likely to be a losing strategy. And while they'd be exposed in the SUV, they could cover the three miles to town in just a few minutes, after which they could fade into the woodwork.

Olinda and Sanchez exited the living room to gather Megan. "Last I saw of her she was in her bedroom," said Olinda as they made for the back stairs.

As he was nearing the staircase he passed a window and caught motion outside. He stopped in disbelief.

It was a Megan Emerson, forty yards away from the house and moving fast.

She couldn't be outside alone. Their PDA set the inside locks automatically, so they couldn't be left open by accident.

And yet she had somehow escaped.

Sanchez nearly collided into his partner, having not expected Olinda to put on the brakes so abruptly. "She escaped!" said Olinda, nodding toward the window. "I'm going after her! Tell Solomon."

Without waiting for a response he rushed to the door, hastily entered the proper code, and raced outside. Megan was now barely visible in the distance.

He began sprinting after her at five-minute-mile pace. Since the ground was baked dirt, hard and smooth rather than sandy, this was a pace he could sustain for ten or fifteen minutes. He had been a track athlete in college and his special forces training had been rigorous in this regard as well, and he gained ground on her with every step.

In little more than a minute he was almost a quarter of a mile from the house and would overtake his winded quarry in seconds.

That was when he heard the roar of helicopters, flying low and moving in fast.

44

Hall explained the deteriorating situation to Campbell as the second Pave Hawk passed them low to the ground, eating desert at two-hundred and fifty miles per hour on its way to the target, which would become visible in less than a minute.

"Olinda has caught up with Megan," said Hall, his stomach tightening. "The rest are just pulling out of the garage in an SUV."

Campbell thought for a moment and then transmitted orders to the assault team in the second helicopter. "They're exiting in an SUV. No hostages or friendlies in the vicinity. Shoot out their tires and try to capture them alive, but lethal force is authorized if necessary."

"Roger that," came the reply through the headphones.

"We'll go after the hostage to the north," continued Campbell. "When the hostiles have been captured, stay on the ground and sit tight for further orders."

With that the colonel banked the Pave Hawk violently.

"Olinda's heard us coming," said Hall, ignoring the chopper's stomach-churning drop. "He plans to hold a gun at Megan's head and negotiate with us."

Hall cursed under his breath. Couldn't CNN have been showing something that might be relevant? Anything. Politics. Terrorism. But charter schools? Hadn't the fates been cruel enough already?

"How good of a shot are you, Colonel?" asked Hall.

"Very good, but not great."

"He's going to ask us to disarm. But I could lodge a gun in my pants, in the small of my back. You could stand just a little behind me. What if you pulled the gun at the same instant I told Megan telepathically to lurch down as hard as possible? Could you hit him in the head if you only had one chance at it?"

"Four out of five times," said Campbell. "I wish I could give you a guarantee, but I can't."

Hall considered. "I'll hide the gun," he said. "We may not have another choice." He paused. "We need a trigger word. Something it would be normal for me to say."

"How about, *be reasonable?*" suggested Heather.

"Good choice," said Campbell. "Nick, tell Megan to duck the instant she hears this."

Hall broadcast the plan to Megan as she and Olinda came into view in the distance, two insects that were growing into people rapidly as the Pave Hawk stormed over the cracked brown terrain.

Campbell reduced speed and landed fifteen yards away from them. The three passengers exited the Pave Hawk and approached Megan, who was in Olinda's iron grip with a gun pressed against her head.

In the distance machine guns fired, followed by the boom of tires blowing out and being shredded as the other helicopter took out the fleeing SUV.

"Drop your weapons!" demanded Olinda. "Now!"

The colonel was about to comply when Hall held up a restraining hand. "Wait a minute, Colonel," he said as he rooted through Olinda's mind. The man was a soldier for hire, yes, but until he had followed Solomon to his current assignment he had performed this job with honor, with stints in Iran and Turkey.

Hall faced the man and stared deeply into his eyes. "You know if you shoot her, my friend here is going to kill you, right?"

"Maybe. But you aren't going to make that sacrifice," shouted Olinda with certainty. "So don't act like you don't give a shit about her. Drop your weapons!" he bellowed. "Or you'll be wearing her brains. Now! I won't ask again."

"Keep your weapon, Colonel," said Hall calmly.

"*What are you doing?*" broadcast an understandably panicked Megan Emerson.

"*Trust me,*" replied Hall, and then turned his entire focus on Olinda.

"So let's suppose we call your bluff," he said out loud to the mercenary. "You're telling me you'll shoot her rather than surrendering. Knowing we'll kill you if you do?"

"Absolutely!" thundered Olinda. "Let's see who blinks first." He moved his gun so it was now pressed into her cheek. "Say goodbye to your girlfriend. You have five seconds. Five. Four —"

"I'm a mind reader, Dom Olinda," interrupted Hall unhurriedly, knowing that only Solomon had been made aware of this. "Let me demonstrate. Your ATM password is *Adam Wulff*, after a fallen comrade. You had two dogs in high school named Dash and Myla." He shook his head. "See? So no matter how scary a performance you put on, you can't bluff me."

Olinda's eyes widened at the accuracy of these proclamations.

"And you aren't going to shoot this woman," continued Hall. "I know this for an absolute fact. I've seen it in your mind. So surrender, and we'll take your cooperation into account."

"I'm not buying it," said the mercenary. "What foreign language did I take in high school? And what are the last four digits of my social security number?"

"Chinese. And five one two eight."

Olinda looked at Hall as though he were an outer space alien, but he knew that he was beaten. He dropped his arm and his gun slid from his fingers and onto the hard, parched ground.

While Campbell affixed plastic handcuffs around Olinda's wrists, Megan rushed over to Hall and threw herself into him, and both blinked back tears of joy.

They kissed, but only briefly, continuing to hold each other tightly, soaking in the warmth and feel of body against body.

The colonel escorted the prisoner to the Pave Hawk, and he and Heather waited for their two friends to finish their passionate reunion. When they finally separated an eternity later, Heather and the colonel hugged the newly freed prisoner as well.

"Thanks for the rescue," said Megan happily.

"Glad to help," said the colonel. "But I have to say, I feel like *I'm* the lucky one."

"What do you mean?"

"You and Nick were using telepathy just now, right?"

"Right," said Megan in confusion.

"You were expressing your love for each other, weren't you? In sickening, syrupy detail, right?"

She grinned. "Right again."

"So I'm the lucky one," he finished with a twinkle in his eye. "If I'd have been forced to actually hear this, I'm pretty sure I would have had to kill myself."

45

The small helicopter lifted from a helipad at Marine Corps Air Station Miramar in San Diego and headed southwest, with Campbell piloting and Hall the sole passenger.

Marc Fisher had homes in Des Moines, Iowa, Washington DC, and La Jolla, California. But they had learned that he was currently at the home he considered his primary residence, the La Jolla beach house, hosting meetings of the party faithful until eight p.m. It was probably not a coincidence that this was five o'clock in Washington, about an hour before he expected Hall to be back in his warehouse prison and ready to report his findings.

Campbell had left Heather and Megan in capable hands at Miramar. The group had flown the four hundred miles between Tucson and San Diego in a military jet considerably less flashy than the F14. But while the jet they had chosen was only capable of commercial airline speed, they made it to Miramar in just over an hour, and the two men were back in the air within minutes of landing.

Hall checked the time in his mind's eye. He had escaped a little more than six hours earlier from the hotel.

Could it really have only been six hours? He felt like a supersonic pinball that had been bounced around at incredible speed from DC to Tucson to here, but he still had an hour before Fisher's last guest was scheduled to leave, and two hours before Fisher was planning to call him in DC for his report.

La Jolla was a mere thirteen miles southwest of Miramar and they made it to Fisher's house in minutes, flying over it once to make it easier for Hall to locate Fisher in the highly populated area. Once he had, Campbell took them a mile out over the Pacific and hovered while Hall probed Fisher's mind at length.

While the colonel had no idea what Hall was reading, his body language said it all. The mind reader was in revulsion, a man with thousands of roaches crawling over his body. A man who had been thrown in a septic tank filled with feces and rotting bodies. Hall's face was contorted with horror and disgust and he looked physically ill.

Hall wasn't aware of his own body language, but he did know that he had to work hard to keep the gorge from rising in his throat. If Campbell hadn't been keeping the helicopter perfectly steady he would have vomited.

Being inside Marc Fisher's head was agony. The man had the outside appearance of a human being, but he was not. It was like taking a bite of a perfect, shiny apple to find nothing but squirming maggots inside. Hall couldn't have said if people had souls, or located one if they did, but he *was* sure of one thing: Marc Fisher had been born without one.

Fisher was a relentless, ruthless, compassionless machine, covered in a friendly, polished veneer. He had memories of two rapes and three murders, and had never felt the slightest remorse over these actions.

There was nothing he wouldn't do if he could get away with it. For power, or even just for the thrill of showing his superiority and basking in the freedom he knew his complete lack of conscience provided. He was an absolute psychopath, at the most severe end of the spectrum.

Not only was he fully aware of this, he couldn't be prouder of it.

He had used people all of his life. Seduced a number of women to fall in love with him, used them financially and sexually, and then spit them out without a care. Stabbed countless others in the back. Betrayed people who thought they were his friends. Taken credit for others' work, and poisoned their careers and reputations if it afforded him the slightest gain.

Hall didn't even need to dig. Fisher's mind was a seething, disease-ridden cesspool, made even more disgusting by its cold, analytical nature, by its clear intelligence. Hall had now read thousands of minds, and many of these had been despicable, but none could match this one.

Marc Fisher was an abomination to the species.

Hall relayed some of what he learned to Campbell, including Fisher's intention of killing him and Megan when he had what he needed.

"Any unimpeachable evidence of the murders or rapes?" asked the colonel when he had finished. Both men were once again wearing headphones so they could communicate without having to make their voices hoarse from shouting over the steady roar of the blades.

Hall shook his head. "You said he was rumored to be pure evil, and that's an understatement. But he's also very smart. And careful. Not the kind to leave much evidence behind. I've found overwhelming circumstantial links to certain crimes, but he's left no smoking guns."

"You said that one of the mercs knew he was working for Fisher. When we interrogate him, maybe we can get him to turn on this son of a bitch."

"And what if he won't?" asked Hall.

"That's complicated. Mind reading is inadmissible, so just because you know what he did, this isn't enough. And even if this mercenary does take his boss down with him, this is still problematic, since we all agree your survival depends on you staying off the grid. Even when only a handful of people knew about you, it led to your capture. So would you charge him with kidnapping? If you did, you'd have to show up in open court. Your abilities would come out. Your cover would be blown."

Hall chewed his lower lip, deep in thought. "We'd have to get him on something else. And while there isn't any perfect, direct evidence of his crimes, like I said, in some cases there is a mountain of compelling circumstantial evidence. I'm sure he'd still go down in flames."

"I'm not," said Campbell. "I think it's less than fifty-fifty. He has a huge amount of power. And members of Congress have an uncanny knack for keeping their jobs after doing things that would get civilians thrown in jail."

Hall frowned deeply. "Unfortunately, this is a good point. Worse, I read that he's made great use of the information I've been feeding him. He's been as ruthless and effective as ever, and has some real power players in his pocket. If he threatened to release what he has on them, they'll move mountains to help him slip any noose." He shook his head in disgust. "And if he does, with the leverage I've given him, I still think the odds are good he makes it to the White House, even without any more help from me."

Hall shuddered at the thought of a President Marc Fisher. After being in the man's mind for just a few minutes he doubted he would ever feel clean again.

He paused in thought for an extended period, oblivious to the breathtaking beauty of the mighty Pacific around him, an endless canvas of deep blue broken up only by the occasional yacht or sailboat.

"Colonel," he said finally. "Let me read him for a few more hours. Maybe if I dig even deeper I'll find something that will nail him. But I'd feel better if you were back watching Megan and Heather. I know they're at a military base, but even so . . ."

"I understand."

"Is there anywhere nearby you can set me down?"

"Yes. There's a helipad a few miles from Fisher's house."

"Great. Set me down, and I'll take a cab back to the base when I'm finished. Tell Megan I'll be with her before she knows it."

"Are you sure this is wise? No one has recognized you yet, but you need to lie as low as possible until we can regroup."

"I agree," said Hall. "But I'm willing to take the chance I won't be discovered for the next few hours. I really need to take care of this."

Campbell nodded. "I'll have you on the ground in five minutes."

46

Nick Hall sat quietly in Marc Fisher's family room, sipping from a bottle of water he had taken from the refrigerator.

The politician must have hired an expensive interior decorator, and it showed, although there was nothing avant-garde in his furnishings, oil paintings, and knickknacks, just simple, understated elegance. The color white predominated, which Hall suspected wasn't an accident. The color of cleanliness and virginity. Of purity and piety. The man's attempt at projecting the opposite of his true nature.

Fisher was taking a long shower, relishing the prospect of mixing himself a Manhattan and learning what bodies his mind-reading puppet had managed to dig up this time.

And given that Hall finally admitted he could read mind after mind without pause, and the target-rich environment he was in, this would truly be the mother lode.

Fisher finally finished showering and strode into the room in which Hall waited, his hair still wet. He stopped short upon seeing his visitor sitting calmly on the couch.

"Hello, Frank Earnest," said Hall evenly. "Or should I just call you, *Marc?*"

Hall was struck by how quickly Fisher assimilated the situation. The man truly had ice-water in his veins, because the new reality barely threw him. He was outwardly the picture of calm as he weighed options and made calculations at dizzying speed.

"*Nick Hall,*" he said warmly. "I'll be damned. Welcome to my home. But a report over the phone would have been fine," he added with a predatory smile. "You really didn't need to go to the trouble of meeting with me in person."

"Yeah, Marc. I did. I really, really did."

"I paid big for a computerized state-of-the-art security system. But I guess it wasn't made to keep out someone capable of reading how to deactivate it from the owner's mind."

"I guess not."

"I assume you've managed to free Megan, or you wouldn't have come here?"

Hall nodded. "That's right."

Fisher knew his mind was being read, but he couldn't stop his thoughts from coming as they normally would. In a flash, Fisher reasoned that Hall had to have had help. Even *with* his abilities, escaping his guards in DC, freeing Megan in Tucson, and coming here, all within eight hours, took considerable resources. Resources that only the military could provide. And it couldn't have been his benefactor, Justin Girdler, because Girdler was on the run.

If Fisher had to guess, he would guess Mike Campbell had helped him, something he intended to investigate as soon as Hall left. If this was the case, he would see to it that Campbell was roasted like a pig on a spit.

Hall was impressed by the speed and accuracy of Fisher's assessments. Evil. But not stupid.

The politician continued to weigh options, which included finding a way to reach the gun he had hidden on the premises. But just after he had this idea he smiled and thought, *You read that, Nick, didn't you?*

"Yes," said Hall. "You can't surprise me, as *you* know better than anyone. And I can't help but be offended that you, a good Samaritan looking out for the country like you are, would consider killing me."

Fisher ignored this. "Congratulations on your escape," he said. "So what was my mistake?"

Hall told him.

"Nicely played," said Fisher, genuinely impressed, after Hall explained about the 520 area code. "You know, I kept Megan's location a secret just to err on the side of caution. But I really never imagined you'd be able to free her, even if you knew exactly where she was. Or that you'd even have the balls to try."

He leaned in toward Hall intently. "But why are you here?" he continued. "I don't see any cops. So I take it you're not pressing charges," he added smugly. "Actually, I might just call the cops myself and have you arrested for breaking and entering." Fisher's lips slid back into a cruel smile, quite pleased with himself.

"You aren't worried about what I've read in that sick mind of yours?"

Fisher shrugged. "I'll remain at large no matter what you try to throw at me. Count on it. The man I hired won't turn on me. And *you* won't press kidnapping charges. You have no proof, and you aren't about to let yourself become a back-from-the-dead celebrity. As for the rest of what you have on me, you can slow me down. Depending on what you bring, you can cause me considerable trouble. And it's true your escape has reduced the *certainty* that I'll be the next president." He flashed his soulless smile once again. "But I still like my chances. A lot."

"I could kill you," said Hall evenly.

Fisher laughed. "You probably could, Nick. But you won't. You're not wired like me. You're bound by a conscience that prevents you from doing sensible things. That's why I'll always win. Because I don't let society or wiring tie one hand behind my back."

He shrugged. "And if I were to tragically pass away," he added, "all the dirt you gathered on our beloved political class will be automatically released at once. Throw the entire country into a tailspin. And you wouldn't want that."

"It won't be released automatically. Lying is like breathing for you, isn't it? Even knowing I can read minds, you can't help yourself. You didn't create a failsafe data dump in case you were killed. You told those whom you're blackmailing that you did. But you were bluffing. You knew they'd believe you and wouldn't dare lay a finger on you." He shook his head. "Did you really think I'd believe anything you said without checking?"

"I was hoping, yes. But my little test didn't work out. No matter." Fisher paused. "So let me ask again, what are you doing here? Because we both know you won't kill me."

"I wouldn't be so sure about that," said Hall. "You're forgetting I've been in your head. I know exactly what you've done, and what you are. You're an abomination. I know that you were planning to kill me and Megan the moment you were certain of victory. So the way I see it, the classic moral dilemma discussed in philosophy and ethics classes comes into play. If you could kill Hitler when he was a boy, knowing what he would become, would you?"

"I'm hardly Adolf Hitler," said Fisher smoothly. "He killed many millions. Me, just a few."

"Only because the circumstances are different. We both know if you had been in Germany and had the chance to do everything Hitler did, except this time come out victorious, you wouldn't hesitate."

Hall could read that Fisher was eager for this visit to be over. He would make himself the Manhattan he had long been imagining, sit down, and begin planning, making sure any loose ends he had left were tidied up before Hall could bring any investigations. If Hall would even go to the trouble, knowing Fisher would just worm his way out of them.

"This has been really nice," said Fisher. "And thanks for the philosophical discussion. But I have a lot to do. So let me see you to the door."

Hall rose and walked to the door himself. He opened it and then turned to face Fisher. "You've lost, Marc. You're going down. And I'm going to take you there."

Fisher's lips curled into a humorless smile. "I'm afraid not, Nick. You're weak. And I'm strong. And I've already won."

Hall took a long look at the most vile man he had ever met and sighed. "Others have underestimated me before," he said. "And I have no doubt you'll do the same." A weary smile came to his face. "Goodbye, Marc. Enjoy your sense of triumph while you can."

47

Hall exited Fisher's home and shut the door behind him.

He strolled to the ocean, standing at the intersection of surf and sand, and watched the last of the sun vanish beneath the Western horizon, letting the beauty wash over him.

He was at peace with the world. Fisher could do untold damage as president. And while he wasn't Adolph Hitler, he was close enough. Hall had seen the mark of the beast on this man.

No matter how Hall had analyzed the famous moral dilemma, he had come to the same conclusion. He *would* kill Hitler when the genocidal maniac was a boy. He wouldn't want to. He would fully expect to go to hell for doing so. But he would.

And he would kill Marc Fisher as well.

It was the only way. He had come to this conclusion in the helicopter, but had seen no reason to drag Mike Campbell into it with him.

As he watched the waves coming in he continued to monitor Fisher. So smug. So sure he would recover. So certain he knew what Hall would and wouldn't do.

The man wasted little time before mixing himself the Manhattan he so desperately longed for. It never occurred to him to check the small vial of botulism toxin he kept hidden at this residence so it would be available if he ever needed it again. It never occurred to him that Hall would dig through his mind to find this piece of circumstantial evidence tying him to the most heinous of his crimes.

Hall watched the cocktail glass come to Fisher's lips, seeing it through the man's own eyes. Fisher took a sip, sighed in contentment, and set the glass back down on his table.

Fifteen seconds later, as he was rolling on the floor, struggling to take a next breath that refused to come no matter how great his efforts, he finally understood. Hall read in his mind that with his last thought, he realized that he had, indeed, underestimated his former prisoner.

And that this would be the last mistake he would ever make.

Hall waited five minutes and then reentered the house. He filled Fisher's oversized bathtub to the brim, pulled the plug, and then with extraordinary care, emptied the remaining cocktail and open bottle of bourbon into the water. The toxin in the tiny unmarked vial had already been diluted millions-fold, and the further dilution of the single drop he had used to poison the bourbon into a hundred and twenty gallon tub was more than enough to render it harmless.

His research also indicated that the toxin was heat sensitive, so he carefully placed the vial on top of a fake gas log in Fisher's fireplace and turned it on, letting the remaining toxin roast in the thousand-degree heat for thirty minutes, many times the temperature and length of time required for inactivation. He then recovered the tiny unmarked vial with an oven mitt and threw it in the trash.

Hall spent a few more minutes making sure he had left no fingerprints behind. Finally, satisfied, he exited the premises for the last time, disposed of Fisher's trash in a nearby dumpster, and called a cab to take him back to the military base at Miramar and the woman he loved.

PART 5
Victor

"A man does what he must—in spite of personal consequences, in spite of obstacles and dangers and pressures—and that is the basis of all human morality."

—Winston Churchill

48

Mike Campbell worked his magic securing military transportation and before midnight he, Heather, Megan, and Hall were back in Altschuler's mansion. They all took much-needed showers, and Campbell asked Hall not to shave off the beard he had grown while in DC. The colonel was expert at applying hair dye, fake tattoos, and makeup, and with Hall's beard in place promised to transform him into someone not even his closest friends would recognize.

Hall made love to Megan and they spent almost an hour comparing notes on their captivity. They discussed what they had been thinking and feeling. How they had managed to cope, to survive the boredom, and to combat their growing fears that they would eventually die as prisoners.

Megan was impressed with Hall's ingenious and daring rescue, but not surprised, although she was pretty sure he had set a record for having flown in a wider variety of military aircraft in a single day than any civilian in history. Both had found that being forced apart, unsure if they would ever be reunited, had further intensified their feelings for each other. Finally, after one of the longest days either had ever experienced, they could not hang on to consciousness any longer and fell into a blissful slumber.

When they awoke in the late morning they made love once again, and Hall explained his plan to put a metaphorical cow bell on his implants when he was with her so she would know when he was using the Web.

He explained that while he was in DC, cut off from the Internet and cut off from her, it had become abundantly clear to him which one of these he could live without, if necessary, and which one he absolutely could not.

As they lay naked in each other's arms Hall said, "I did a lot of thinking on the *Eos* just before we were captured. *A lot*. Thinking about our future together. I never raised the subject of marriage since we haven't know each other all that long, and I know you aren't a big fan of this institution." He kissed her gently on the cheek. "But screw it," he said with a defiant tone. "I'm done worrying about that. Done second-guessing myself. I've decided you *have to* marry me." He grinned. "And I'm not giving you a choice."

"Please tell me that's not your actual proposal," said Megan, rolling her eyes.

Hall gazed at her soft, expressive features, and swallowed hard. "No. *Of course not*," he lied. "How lame do you think I am?"

"Good to know. Because proposing while we're both naked is pretty pathetic. Bad form."

"Really?" said Hall. "Who made up that rule?"

"I don't know. It just seems like it should be a rule. You never see a guy propose to a girl when their naked bodies are wrapped around each other in the movies."

"Of course not. Because you'd have to be watching a *porn* movie. And that genre isn't really big on romance—or monogamy." He grinned. "Don't worry, I plan to get a ring and be clothed when I finally make the official romantic gesture."

"And I don't have any say in this?"

"None," said Hall playfully.

"Okay then," said Megan, a wry smile on her face. "I guess that will make my decision easier." She pulled away from him and stood, preparing to dress. "But for now, we really should go downstairs and get to work finding Alex."

Hall nodded his agreement.

"And out of deference to Heather, since her fiancé is missing and possibly dead, let's avoid any displays of affection."

Hall laughed. "Out of deference to *Heather*? I have the feeling it's the colonel we'll have to worry about. I think he'd probably shoot us if we started getting too affectionate."

They spent the bulk of the day with Heather and the colonel, sharing details of their ordeal and being brought up to speed on the hunt for Altschuler, which had so far been fruitless.

The group took a break for dinner while Mike Campbell left to attend to some duties. He rejoined them later that evening. "I heard something interesting on the news," he said when they had reconvened, locking his eyes on Hall as if he were studying him under a microscope. "You'll never guess what."

The two female members of the group appeared eager to hear what it was, but Hall's interest was far more subdued.

"Turns out they found Marc Fisher dead this morning in his home in La Jolla."

Heather and Megan reacted with shock and dismay, while Nick Hall's expression remained unreadable.

"The authorities aren't sure what happened," continued Campbell. "But for now they believe he died of natural causes." He eyed Hall with a suspicion bordering on certainty. "What do you think about that, Nick?"

"Interesting," grunted Hall. "What are the odds?" he added woodenly, unable to put his heart into faking surprise despite the content of his words. "But I have to say," he continued with a sudden intensity, his expression a mixture of contempt and disgust, "the world is lucky to be rid of this asshole. Like Hitler, Stalin, Saddam Hussein, and other monsters before him."

"Funny coincidence," said Campbell. "You were near his home last night right about when it happened. I'm guessing you weren't around when he passed on, or you would have read the distress in his mind."

"Must have just missed it," said Hall unconvincingly. "Must have been cabbing it back to Miramar at the time."

Campbell raised his eyebrows, clearly not believing this for a single instant. He studied Hall for several seconds. "Well, that's good enough for me," he said finally. He shook his head and just the hint of a smile crossed his face, an unspoken, *I don't know how you did it, but remind me to stay on your good side.*

"Nick?" broadcast Megan telepathically. *"What happened?"*

Hall had told her all about the soulless, psychopathic Marc Fisher, about his disease-ridden mind, his many crimes, and his plans to become leader of the free world. But Hall hadn't told her that he had decided to end the man, taking the law into his own hands.

"We can talk more about Fisher tonight," he responded telepathically, letting out a heavy sigh. *"We had too much catching up to do last night. And today, I wanted to, um . . . you know, discuss marriage with you."*

"What? You didn't think, 'I murdered a man yesterday, will you marry me?' made a great proposal? And I thought proposing while naked was bad form."

"Could you still love me if you knew I did it?" broadcast Hall, his expression grim.

There was a brief pause. *"Given what you've told me about him . . . probably. But I want to know everything."*

"You will."

Hall vaguely heard his name being called several times by the colonel, but he had been too engrossed in his telepathic conversation to hear. "Sorry, Colonel," he said. "I must have checked out for a moment. Could you repeat that?"

"I was saying that I had done a lot of thinking after I dropped you off and returned to the base. And I had come to the conclusion that unless Fisher, you know, mysteriously died, he could do considerable damage to the country and world. So I've decided this really is for the best. I'm not a spiritual man. But maybe this is karma. Or maybe God does exist, and decided Marc Fisher really needed to go."

"You never know," said Hall, and hatred and disgust flashed across his face at just the thought of the man.

"They say the Lord works in mysterious ways," said the colonel. He nodded very slowly at his mind-reading friend. "Maybe this time I got to witness one of these mysterious ways in action."

49

"How did it go?" said Victor when Eduardo Alvarez appeared on his 3-D monitor. Victor needed to know for certain that Altschuler's implant coordinates were accurate and that their placement within the brain could be done automatically, without need of a surgeon. Or even need of another human being in the room for that matter.

Some of the people to whom this technology would be sold would have a colleague they trusted implicitly, but many others would be unwilling to trust *anyone*, even within their own organizations. And many would prefer that no one else knew they were harboring implants so they could use them with maximum effectiveness.

"Could not have gone better," reported Alvarez. "The AutoSurge Four is very user friendly—and very precise, as advertised."

Victor had sent his second to Switzerland to perform the test on two mercenaries who were paid more than enough to compensate them for the small risk they were taking.

"Did you get the footage I sent over?" asked Alvarez.

"Just got it," responded Victor. "Maria," he added, addressing his PDA, "send the video file I just received to the top right quarter of the monitor so Eduardo and I can both view it."

"Who am I looking at?" said Victor when the video began.

"Our second volunteer, named Craig Rymer. The native English speaker. I assisted the other volunteer, so Rymer is the first man to ever successfully self-install the BrainWeb implants."

As Alvarez was responding to Victor's question, the video continued, showing Rymer standing next to the AutoSurge, a stainless steel unit about the size of a refrigerator, with a large touch screen monitor, an elongated steel bench, and a half dozen robot hands, each capable of millionth-of-an-inch precision. The camera zoomed in on Rymer's hands as he programmed in the precise physical dimensions of the

implants, their required orientation, and their positioning coordinates, checking them twice against the printout Alvarez had supplied.

Then Rymer laid on his back on the steel bench and slid his head
into an oversized helmet, open at the top to expose his skull. A liquid gel was pumped into a flexible bladder inside the helmet, which
contoured precisely to the sides of his head, ears, jaw, and neck. Then
a mild electric current was sent through the gel, hardening it, so that
Rymer couldn't have moved his head to save his life. The gel would
stay hardened for an hour, far longer than was necessary to place the
implants.

"You can't see what's happening inside the helmet very well,"
noted Victor.

"In the instructional video we'll dub in an animation from the
company showing exactly what's going on."

"Good."

The procedure took approximately twenty minutes after Rymer
had been immobilized, the majority of this time devoted to the completion of a detailed brain scan. Once the robot had the data it needed, four of its arms each picked up a tool that resembled a steel bottle
cap. Each of these was pressed down onto four precise, dime-sized
regions of Rymer's exposed head, and then another tool within—a
sharp one—remove all hair trapped within the circular region. Still
another tool was brought to bear to shave these dime-sized spots further until they were perfectly smooth. Finally, antiseptic was applied
to these newly created bald spots on Rymer's head. All of this was
done at superhuman speed, the way an ink jet printer could precisely
deposit up to two hundred thousand ink droplets in a single second.

The device then located the BrainWeb implants that had been set
on a tray near its arms, gripped them, placed them in the proper orientation, drilled through Rymer's skull, positioned them in his brain,
and then retreated, all in mere seconds. Alvarez had spliced in a slow-
motion version of these events after the real-time version was completed so each step could be seen more clearly.

After the requisite hour the hard gel immobilizing Rymer's head
became liquid once again and was pumped out of the bladder.

Rymer removed his head from the helmet, stood up, and was filmed doing several fine motor tasks that had been prearranged, as well as brain games to demonstrate that the procedure had not required anesthesia, and that recovery of physical and mental acuity was immediate.

"Well done, Eduardo," said Victor appreciatively. "This video will win over the most nervous of customers."

They then discussed how their two guinea pigs had fared using the implants to access the Web. The results were even better than Victor had hoped. Imagines they were seeing were converted into visual data and piped into their visual cortices, but they had also confirmed that, as expected, this same data could be used to digitally transmit all that they were seeing to a computer, as if their eyes were video cameras.

"What about the non-English speaker?" asked Victor.

"I chose a man whose first language is Arabic, since the vast majority of our customers will be speaking this language."

"Excellent choice."

Alvarez nodded to acknowledge the compliment. "After four hours of training," he continued, "this subject can already use the implants, although imperfectly. Still, he was raving about them. Our computer experts say the language training program embedded in the implants is outstanding, and that the great Alex Altschuler has truly outdone himself."

A triumphant glint appeared in Victor's eye. "I've heard enough, my friend," he said with an easy smile. "Pack it in. Have the AutoSurge reverse the process and pay these men for their troubles. Then join me here as soon as you can. In the meanwhile, I'm going to have my own set of implants installed."

"You'll find it interesting to note that both men offered to give up their fee if they could keep the implants. I told them this was impossible, of course. They knew going in that we were going to reverse it."

"That is interesting," said Victor. "Very promising. It shows just how quickly they came to appreciate the value of the technology, and the advantages it provides. After I have BrainWeb up and running we'll make sure you're fitted for a set as well, Eduardo. This will make us an even more effective team. Both of us can give personal demonstrations to customers if need be. And your footage of Rymer will make the perfect instructional video. I'll begin letting it be known that we are in possession of these implants, and that we're open for business."

Victor paused. "On another note," he said, "we need to hand Altschuler off to our temporary partner, as promised."

"You think he'll kill him?"

"I do. I'm not sure what he has against Altschuler, but I don't care. I agreed to deliver Altschuler and I will. After that it will out of my hands."

"I can set up the transfer. Where do you want to make the handoff?"

"At the ranch. At the northeast runway."

"You would let him get that close to headquarters?"

"Yes. He'll just assume I have any number of runways in the middle of nowhere to use as transfer points. If he's tried to trace my calls, he'll think I've been calling from Switzerland, like everyone else. It will never occur to him that I would be bold enough to bring him this close to me. Believe me, after he's gone, Oregon will be the *last* place he'll ever look for me."

"I'll make the arrangements when I get back," said Alvarez.

"Have a good trip, my friend," said Victor warmly. "And excellent work."

50

Several days passed, during which Campbell had come and gone, unable to completely abandon his extensive responsibilities as head of PsyOps, and they had turned the mansion's library into a war room, adding extra communication equipment, monitors, and computers so the colonel could orchestrate the extensive hunt for Altschuler from this location. The fact that Altschuler's home actually *had* a book-shelf-lined room called a library, larger than the largest rooms even in affluent homes, spoke volumes as to the opulence of the estate.

Hall had told Megan the truth about Marc Fisher's demise, and why he had concluded this was something that had to be done. After almost an hour of further discussion, she had come to agree that his actions had been necessary, and they decided never to speak of it again.

On their fourth night in the mansion, Hall was making chicken-and-cheese quesadillas for himself, Megan, and Heather when Campbell returned to the premises and rushed into the kitchen.

"Welcome, Colonel," said Hall in greeting, standing at one of two large cooking islands in the oversized room. He gestured to the large pan on the burner in front of him, where melted cheese was filling the kitchen with a mouthwatering aroma. "Quesadilla?"

"Sure," said Campbell, although the look on his face made it clear that food wasn't the foremost subject on his mind.

The colonel pulled out a quaint, yellow-and-white wooden chair and joined Heather and Megan around the country-style table in the center of the kitchen. Both women were sipping glass goblets of red wine, which they had decided, tongue in cheek, was the perfect choice to accompany a homemade chicken quesadilla.

"We've had a breakthrough," said the colonel without preamble. "We know who Girdler is working with."

The blood drained from Heather's face. This could be the information that could lead to Alex's return. Or it could be the information indicating he would *never* return. She visibly braced herself for what might come next.

"He's a Mexican-born arms dealer named Victor."

"Victor?" said Hall. "Victor who?"

"He only uses one name. His past is murky, and we don't know his birth name, but this is what he calls himself."

"And Alex?" whispered Heather.

The colonel hesitated and then said, "I'll tell you a little more about this in a moment. But the bottom line is that we don't know anything more about Alex than we did before."

Heather chewed on her lower lip and nodded.

"How do you know that this Victor is involved?" asked Megan

"Because he's putting word out around the globe that he has thousands of sets of BrainWeb implants, along with the exact, easy-bake-oven recipe for self-installation."

Hall slid a finished quesadilla onto a plate and sprayed the pan with a non-stick coating before starting another. "So he's just announcing he's ready to take orders?" he said. "Just like that?"

"Just like that. At one million dollars per set."

Hall whistled. This seemed too steep, but after only a few seconds of thought he realized the man would have any number of takers at this price. Other than Altschuler, also an active BrainWeb user, no one understood the power of this technology better than Hall, or the advantages it would give someone, especially if they had access to this technology and others did not.

"If he's advertising like this," said Heather hopefully, "shouldn't he be easy to find?"

"Unfortunately, no," said the colonel. "Justin—General Girdler," he amended, deciding that after his former mentor's incomprehensible betrayal, a first name was no longer appropriate, "has been after him for years. I've been involved on occasion also. And we've never even come close. Victor is the best there is. He has the most advanced technology available, and he knows how to use it to keep us off his scent. His people have made modifications and improvements that I'm not sure even *we* have."

"Which explains the sleight-of-hand that allowed him to get away with the implants so easily," noted Hall. "How he could conceal his plane from satellites."

"Yes. But even he couldn't have found and taken them in the first place if not for *Girdler*," spat the colonel bitterly. "Even so, when word began to come in today that Victor had the implants, it all made perfect sense."

The colonel's face hardened. "And it gets worse. Because Victor's motivation is more than just money. He has a real bug up his ass about the US. He's the worst guy in the world to get access to this technology. He *loathes* America. I'm not sure why, but this hatred is so well known it's almost his calling card."

"But he isn't a jihadist," said Heather, "correct?"

"No. His hatred isn't based on religious ideology. But whatever it's based on, he's the most prolific and dangerous arms dealer there is. No one else comes close. I worried that the implants had fallen into the hands of a dangerous terror group. But Victor is the very worst-case scenario. He sells to *all* dangerous groups, terrorist or otherwise. He's been slowly morphing into a technology dealer rather than a traditional arms dealer, making him even harder to catch, since tech is a lot easier to move and hide. He is connected to every miscreant on the planet. He doesn't discriminate. Anyone in any kind of conflict, including various mafia groups, can acquire his weapons and services. Especially those who target the US."

"Perfect," said Megan sarcastically.

"Girdler has delivered BrainWeb to the one enemy he most wanted to track down, the one enemy capable of putting this technology into the hands of every bad actor on the planet, of inflicting the greatest possible damage to the country he devoted his life to protecting. The general's betrayal is even worse and more unforgivable than if he had done this for money alone."

"If this Victor has withstood Girdler's every effort to find him for so many years," said Hall, cooking up the last of the quesadillas, "how did he find him to propose a partnership?"

"Victor's contact information is well known," said Campbell with a deep frown. "At least to those who run in the circles who need to know it. But it's untraceable. He reroutes communications in such a complex way that not even our best man, Drew Russell, can unravel it. If you want to reach Victor, you call a number and leave a message. If he likes the message, he calls you back."

"So didn't the general take advantage of this when he was hunting for this guy?" said Megan, staring deeply into her wine glass. "No one has his genius for deception and planning. Couldn't he just pretend to be a terrorist or other customer, call Victor, and set a trap?"

"He tried. Believe me, he tried. But Victor investigates the hell out of anyone attempting to forge a relationship with him. And I suspect he's even more clever than Girdler. Every attempt failed, and some of these were remarkably well crafted, as you would expect."

Campbell turned to Heather and couldn't help but wince. "Heather, let me come back to Alex for a moment. When I learned Victor was behind this, about four hours ago, I immediately left a message on his line. I told him we knew he had Alex and were prepared to pay a substantial ransom for him." He pursed his lips. "I haven't heard back."

Knowing how Heather might take this he quickly added, "But this means nothing. Victor probably hasn't even gotten the message yet. And even if he has, we've said from the beginning this wasn't likely to be a ransom play. I'm almost sure he has Alex, but I'd be very surprised if my call is returned. If he really can get a million dollars a pop for the implants, times ten thousand sets, we're looking at ten *billion* dollars. But I'll remind you again, you don't kill someone with a mind like Alex's. He's too valuable."

Heather took a deep breath, her eyes moistening, but she didn't reply.

"We have to retrieve Alex," said the colonel. "And we have to retrieve the implants. *Before* Victor disperses them around the world." He shook his head. "Because we sure as hell aren't going to contain

them. Nothing could be easier to move. He could send them to customers by sticking them in a standard envelope or photo mailer, and
no one would be the wiser."

"But you've gone to great lengths to explain how slippery this
guy is," said Hall, as he began transferring four plates, each holding
a tortilla packed with melted cheese and chicken, over to the table.
"And the general himself couldn't get close after years of effort. So
what are the chances that you can find him now?"

"Actually—a lot better than you would think."

"Why is that?" asked Megan.

"It's true our efforts were a total failure," said the colonel, reaching for a plate. "But we never had a mind reader helping us before,
either," he added with just the hint of a smile.

51

Colonel Mike Campbell landed the helo on the deck of the USS *Boxer* sailing in international waters, a hundred miles off the coast of San Diego, and cut the power to the rotor. His visit was expected, but no one was there to greet him at his request, since Nick Hall was with him. While Hall had now been the subject of Campbell's masterful makeup, hair dye, and tattooing artistry, there was no reason for him to take yet another chance that he would be recognized.

The *Boxer* was one of the Navy's Wasp-class amphibious assault ships, almost three football fields in length, with a human-carrying capacity of thousands. Seen from above it was a flat seagoing platform of immense square footage, a landing field for as many as forty-two aircraft—mostly bulky V-22 Osprey and CH-53 Sea Stallion helicopters—set atop a boxy multi-storied hull.

For a period of time the *Boxer* had served as the flagship for the international anti-piracy task force off the coast of Somalia, and it was the ship to which Captain Richard Phillips, famously held captive by pirates, was transported for medical treatment and rest after his ordeal in 2009.

Now, in addition to its officially assigned duties, it served as an interrogation facility for high-value terrorist prisoners held by the US government. Until 2011, high-value prisoners of this type had been sent to Guantanamo Bay or secret CIA Black sites for interrogation, but the Obama administration, having promised to end the Bush administration's detention policies, instituted a program of questioning terrorists aboard US warships in international waters. This program used legal sleight-of-hand to justify holding prisoners for as long as necessary while still leaving open the option for prosecution in civilian court.

For the past six weeks, the *Boxer* had been home to Abu al-Ansari, a high-ranking member of the terror group ISIS, still one of the more dangerous of the seemingly never-ending parade of such groups.

Campbell had identified fourteen prisoners who were sure bets to have had previous dealings with Victor, but al-Ansari was the closest to their base of operations in Fresno, so the decision to pay him a visit had been obvious.

Campbell escorted Hall to a small stateroom three levels below the vast upper platform, eighty yards from where al-Ansari was being held, set up at the colonel's orders with advanced communication equipment that ensured no calls could be traced.

Both men sat at a steel table in the very stark room, decorated by nothing but dull gray paint and cold steel. After several minutes, Hall was able to locate al-Ansari's mind, and soon thereafter he was able to verify that the terrorist had interacted many times with the enigmatic arms dealer known only as Victor, as they had surmised.

Hall displayed the script he and Campbell had written in his mind's eye and cleared his throat while the colonel dialed Victor's number. The call was answered only by a tone, indicating it was ready to receive a message.

Hall took a deep breath and concentrated on delivering the scripted words in such a way that they wouldn't seem read or pre-rehearsed.

"Victor, hello. I'm an American-born jihadist who works closely with Abu al-Ansari. I'd rather stay anonymous, so you can call me John Smith. As you may know, al-Ansari was captured six weeks ago and has been imprisoned on the USS *Boxer* off the coast of California. But we have a sleeper planted on the ship, and he can relay short communications back and forth between al-Ansari and me. Al-Ansari is scheduled to be taken ashore sometime within the next two months, and we believe we will be able to free him then. I have made him aware you are taking orders for BrainWeb implants, and he would like me to secure a hundred sets as soon as possible for key members of ISIS, regardless of whether his escape is successful."

Hall took a deep breath and then completed the message, asking the arms dealer to return the call and giving him the number to use.

After this there was nothing to do but wait. The colonel pulled several thick dossiers from a briefcase and began to work, while Hall used his implants to project a movie into his visual cortex such that he perceived it to be larger, and clearer, than if he had been in a theater.

Almost four hours later the untraceable phone in the stateroom rang and both men sprang to attention. Hall let it ring a second time and then snatched it from the receiver. "Smith here," he said.

"Mr. Smith," came the reply, a silky smooth voice with the barest hint of a Mexican accent. They had set the incoming volume high enough for the colonel to hear both sides of the conversation, provided he kept his head within a few feet of the receiver. "This is Victor. So you claim to be an associate of my friend Abu al-Ansari. Why should I believe you?"

"Why shouldn't you?" responded Hall calmly. "And why does it even matter, as long as I'm prepared to give you ninety million dollars?"

"You asked for a hundred sets, correct? I think you should check your math."

"Come now, Victor, my boss has been a great customer of yours for many years. You and I both know ninety million for one hundred sets isn't all that much of a quantity discount."

Victor paused. "I must admit, my friend," he said, "you make some good points. Your boss has been a valued customer. And such a discount for this kind of quantity is not uncommon. So ninety million is acceptable. And you are also correct, I don't care who you are, or if you are truly affiliated with al-Ansari. As long as you transfer the full ninety million into my Swiss bank account, you can just tell me where you would like the implants delivered, and we can conclude our business."

"I need to see a demonstration first."

"I am happy to send you a video."

"I need a demonstration in person," insisted Hall. "Al-Ansari's orders, I'm afraid. He tells me no one has a better reputation for trustworthiness than you. But this is *ninety million dollars*. And he has come to rely on my judgment. So when I get a personal demonstration, I will also be making sure the technology is impressive enough to warrant this amount, as he and I currently believe to be the case."

"Then I'm afraid we are at an impasse, my friend. Because your request for a personal meeting forces me back to my original question. How do I know you are telling the truth? How do I know this isn't a feeble attempt at a trap?"

"I am prepared to wire two million into your account now, as a gesture of good faith. Obviously, if I decide the implants aren't worth it, I will expect this to be refunded."

"Obviously," said Victor dryly. "But while this is a nice good-faith gesture, it will take more than this for me to be comfortable arranging a face-to-face."

"Again, my boss impressed upon me that I can trust you with my life. So I am prepared to have you do whatever it takes to convince yourself this isn't a trap. I can meet your people wherever you want, and I will come alone and unarmed. I can wear a blindfold during key travel transitions so I won't know where we're going. Al-Ansari assures me that if you handle the logistics, there is no way anyone can follow me to your destination."

"Interesting proposal," said Victor non-committally. "And you are able to communicate with al-Ansari?"

"I am," said Hall. "As I said, we have a man on the *Boxer* who facilities such communication."

"Give me some time to consider this," said Victor, and then silence ensued for almost a full minute.

"Here is what I am willing to do, John Smith," he said at last. "I will give you the banking information you will need to wire in the two million good-faith money you spoke of. After you have done this, I will have you brought to me, in the manner you suggested. But first I need for you to prove you are truly an envoy of al-Ansari."

"How?"

"You will need to get the answer to two questions from him," replied Victor. "I know al-Ansari won't tell his interrogators anything other than his name. But if you truly are an associate of his, he should be happy to answer them. Question one," he said, "he and I met for dinner in Turkey three years ago. What was the name of the restaurant we were in? Question two: what did he ask me to acquire for him during this meeting?"

"What if he can't remember?" said Hall.

"He will, I assure you."

"Then you'll have your answers," said Hall confidently. "But I'm not sure how long it will take before our man inside can pose these questions, and report the answers. When I have them, I will leave another message for you."

"That is acceptable," said Victor, who then ended the call without another word.

Hall threw himself back in his chair in relief, letting the tension out of his body. "That couldn't have gone better," he said to the colonel. "I think we can really do this."

"We're not there yet," said Campbell. "But this was a good start. I wouldn't be surprised if someone as clever as Victor throws us a few curve-balls before this is over. But with you in the mix, we should be able to handle whatever he throws at us." He paused. "I assume you're confident you can fish out the answers to Victor's questions from al-Ansari's mind?"

Hall nodded, closed his eyes, and tilted his head in concentration. Two minutes later he opened his eyes and faced the colonel, a satisfied grin spreading slowly over his face. "They met at a restaurant named Beyaz Izgara in Istanbul. Victor was sure al-Ansari would remember this because al-Ansari told him it was the most secure restaurant in the city, and also his favorite. During the meal, al-Ansari requested several high-speed 3-D printers capable of printing plastic guns."

"And to think," said the colonel, shaking his head in wonder, "Girdler and I have been trying to infiltrate Victor's organization for years, but without a mind reader. What were we *thinking*?"

"Don't beat yourself up," said Hall in amusement. "It's a common mistake."

"Are you *positive* you still want to do this? Victor is very dangerous, even for a mind reader."

"I'm positive. Getting Alex back and keeping our enemies from upping their game using the implants is well worth the risk." He paused. "How long should I wait before I call Victor back?"

"Let's give it another three hours."

Hall nodded. "Okay. Let me wire him the two million I promised from the account Alex set up for me. And then we can call Megan and Heather with the good news."

52

A still-disguised Nick Hall arrived at the designated clearing in the Olympic National Forest in Washington State and parked his motorbike, as instructed, grateful that it wasn't raining—at least not yet. He walked twenty yards away from the motorized vehicle, also as instructed, and waited, searching any mind he came across in the area for intel.

While one side of the park abutted the Pacific Coast, Hall was on the opposite side, in a section of lush rainforest that was drenched by almost a hundred and fifty inches of rain each year, making it the wettest place in the continental United States, with only certain rainforests in Hawaii being slightly wetter.

Unlike tropical rainforests those of the Pacific Northwest were dominated by coniferous trees, mostly the Sitka Spruce, Western Hemlock, and Coast Douglas-fir. But what made this forest unlike any Hall had ever seen was the wide variety of lush green mosses that covered the bark of most of the trees, and even extended from many branches as moist, plush tendrils.

But as much as Hall would have liked to admire this furry green fairytale forest that filled his nostrils with crisp, clean, potpourri-scented air, he didn't have this luxury. He wasn't here as a tourist.

The crew Victor had sent to collect him had been careful, as expected, and one of them had called Hall several times to direct him to his final destination after he had entered the park on his newly acquired motorbike. Hall had been sure to bring a physical cell phone with him in this case, since they would be looking for a phone to confiscate once they searched him.

Hall had directed Megan and the colonel as he traveled, ensuring they stayed within five miles of him. While they had no reason to believe Victor's people would bring an Internet dampener with them, since they would be stripping him of all electronics and would never suspect he already had implants, they decided to keep Megan within telepathic range as a precaution.

Hall located the minds of the three men who were coming for him without much trouble. They were two miles away and closing in, driving a van. They planned to park on a road just a quarter mile away through the trees, and then come the rest of the way on foot.

He scanned their thoughts one after another and cursed under his breath. Campbell had warned him this wasn't going to be easy.

"Colonel," thought Hall, turning his implants into a thought-to-speech cell phone. "I've scanned the men coming for me. None of them know where Victor is headquartered. You were right, this guy doesn't take any chances, even when he has the upper hand."

"We'll get him," replied the colonel confidently.

"They'll be here any minute," continued Hall. "As expected, they'll do everything but give me a rectal exam to be sure I have no hidden weapons, electronics, phone, or transmitters. But here's the rub. Even after they've convinced themselves I've come alone and can't communicate with anyone, they plan to knock me out."

"What?" said Campbell in genuine surprise. "Knock you out, how?"

Hall was surprised as well, but perhaps he shouldn't have been. Fisher had done the same for his journey to DC, so maybe this had become the popular strategy. "I'm a customer, so they'll be civilized. They'll give me pills to take. I can always refuse, but they've been told that if I do, the meeting is off."

"What are their instructions after you're unconscious?" said Campbell, frustration evident in his voice.

"They'll switch cars, activate sophisticated technology to interfere with anyone trying to track them, even with satellites, and eventually get in a helicopter. But no need for you to kill yourself trying to keep up since I know their final destination."

"Which is?"

"They'll be flying me south into Oregon. The pilot has been given coordinates to a runway there. I just texted them to you," he added after a brief pause. "As far as these men know, this runway is in the middle of hundreds of miles of untouched nature. Don't know what it's doing there, but it's just a transfer point. They'll hand me over, collect their fee, and go."

"Very smart," said Campbell. "Victor probably has hidden runways in any number of locations. And I know he has more than a few private jets. We think he even bought an old Russian submarine that was scheduled to be decommissioned."

"No kidding?" said Hall. "Who'd have guessed *that*? He doesn't have a secret lair hidden in a dormant volcano, does he?"

Campbell ignored his feeble attempt at humor. "If they were taking anyone but you, their measures to ensure they couldn't be followed would work beautifully. After you reach Oregon, they'll take you the rest of the way to their headquarters. And knowing Victor, he'll probably still assume you were followed, as unlikely as this is, and try additional evasive maneuvers."

"Like what?"

"Our best guess is that he works out of Switzerland. So he'll probably have you flown from this runway to somewhere like London, Paris, or Germany. Then, when you're completing the trip on the ground, he'll have his men run some switches to lose any possible followers."

Hall noted that the men who were coming for him had stopped the car a quarter mile away, and two of the three had begun making their way through the woods to his location. "I only have another few minutes before I have company," said Hall. "But we might have a big problem here. What if they put me on a plane in Oregon while I'm still out cold? I won't be able to read where they're taking me."

Their plan had assumed he would remain conscious at all times and could call Campbell the moment he reached someone with knowledge of their final destination. This way, Campbell could send in an overwhelming force that would arrive before Hall did, since the men bringing him would be wasting time trying to lose a possible tail.

"That *could* be a problem," agreed Campbell. After a moment of thought, he added, "Have you read yet if they've brought an Internet dampener?"

"They haven't."

"Good. If you aren't awake until you're in Victor's presence, you'll just have to read where you are and tell me then. Along with the locations of Alex and the stolen implants. Pretend to stay unconscious as long as possible so you minimize the time you have to hold your bluff until we arrive. I'll have a team ready to go in Switzerland so they can get to you as soon as possible after you call me with the location."

"Okay," said Hall. "Not ideal, but it should work. They're arriving now, so I need to focus. I'll contact you the second my Sleeping Beauty stint is over."

"Don't worry, Nick," said the colonel. "I've got your back. No matter what happens, with your mind reading and implants, and my resources, we'll get through this."

53

Megan and the colonel returned to Heather and their makeshift war room in Fresno, making it back before Hall landed in Oregon as they had expected. Oregon was closer, but losing possible followers was time consuming and required the use of a circuitous route.

Campbell had already made sure a satellite was pointing at the runway in question, and he called up this feed on the monitor while Heather retrieved a jar of peanuts and bottles of water for each of them from the kitchen.

The airfield was not only as isolated as advertised, but was painted a mottled brown-and- green so it would be difficult to spot from above, even though this airspace was well outside the path of any commercial or military flights.

"That is the wildest thing I've ever seen," said Heather. "A pristine runway in the middle of nothing but brush and trees and dirt."

"You'd be surprised," said Campbell, swallowing the small handful of peanuts he had thrown into his mouth. "The US is truly vast, and has far larger stretches of untouched nature than most people could possibly guess. And the criminal element knows how to take advantage of this wilderness. Mexican cartels have any number of marijuana and opium poppy fields in America, complete with runways and helipads, in places so isolated they hadn't seen humans in centuries before the cartels arrived."

"But this particular runway isn't quite so isolated, right Colonel?" said Megan.

"Not quite." He chased the peanuts with a long swig of water from the plastic bottle. "I had one of my men research the area while Megan and I were in transit," he explained to Heather. "You're looking at the outermost border of a place called the Silver Lake Ranch. It was a failed hunting preserve, and someone named Adam McClure bought it a few years back in a fire sale. Probably just prospecting. This McClure doesn't list it as his primary residence, and I'd be surprised if he visits more than once a year. Just holding on hoping land prices go up. The ranch is over four thousand acres, so he'd have no idea this was even on his property."

"Interesting," said Heather.

"I'll show you both something even more interesting," he said, motioning Heather and Megan closer to the monitor. "See how the top of the shot, the northernmost end of the runway, has the tiniest bit of shimmer to it?"

They studied the feed carefully and both nodded.

"It's subtle, but there's actually a plane parked there. Fantastic, isn't it? Victor has access to stuff that's barely made it out of the lab. There are several ways to achieve near invisibility. Electromagnetic fields that actually shunt light away from an object. Or in this case, a coating of thin, flexible display panels, tied into feeds from multiple cameras on the plane. A computer calculates what an observer above would see if the plane wasn't there, and renders this on the displays."

The discussion continued for a few minutes until a helicopter finally came into view, landing on the runway very near the phantom plane. An SUV materialized moments later, most likely having been hidden behind the plane, and four men emerged. Three of the men carried the still-unconscious Nick Hall into the plane, and the invisibility technology made it seem as though they had been swallowed up by nothingness. The fourth man returned to the helicopter and spent five minutes speaking with the men who had brought Hall, probably confirming they hadn't been followed and making arrangements to wire final payments.

"If I had to guess," said the colonel, pointing to the man by the helicopter, "I would say this is Victor's fabled right-hand man, Eduardo Alvarez." He finished his bottle of water and shrugged. "But I don't know this for certain."

The glimmer remained at the top of the screen for ten minutes and then traveled down the length of the runway until it was gone. The plane had taken off.

"Can you track it?" asked Heather.

"Yes. The panels on this one confound line-of-sight, but not radar, and I've scrambled a jet that can hang out of range, but close enough to track it. Victor has the technology to foil this as well, but he's not using it. I'm guessing he's convinced no one could follow Hall to Oregon. And as I told Nick, he'll have them make additional evasive maneuvers when they're on the ground in Europe anyway."

Heather took a deep breath. "Hang in there, Alex," she whispered under her breath. "We're coming for you."

54

Nick Hall regained consciousness and his faculties gradually returned. He kept his eyes shut and remained still, determined to play possum for as long as he could.

There were over a dozen minds within reading range, although he didn't bother to count. One of these was the man who called himself Victor.

And another was Alex Altschuler! And he was in perfect health.

Fantastic. A surge of adrenaline was released into Hall's bloodstream, and if he weren't intent on pretending to be unconscious he would have pumped his fists in triumph, like a running back who had just scored the game-winning touchdown.

Hall continued to read Altschuler's mind to get a better idea of what he had been through, noting that his friend couldn't get any Internet reception in the room in which he was being held, which explained a lot. Altschuler was bored out of his mind and going through BrainWeb withdrawal, but was otherwise in perfect shape.

He left Altschuler's mind and turned to Victor's. He read immediately that he was in the same room with the man. Victor was keeping busy while waiting for him to awaken. Hall had been laid on his back on the arms dealer's black leather couch, which he had to admit was surprisingly comfortable.

As he continued to access Victor's thoughts, he understood why Girdler and Campbell had never managed to track this man down. He was brilliant, with a mind that was as tight as a drum. Careful, organized, inventive, and disciplined.

But what Hall read next so surprised him he barely managed to continue faking unconsciousness.

He was still in Oregon!

He was in the main lodge on a ranch that served as Victor's headquarters. The arms dealer had as many tricks up his sleeve as Campbell had thought. Victor was nearly certain Hall—in the guise of the American jihadist calling himself John Smith—could not have been followed to the landing strip. But even so, just in case, he had carried off an ingenious deception.

There was a compartment in the belly of the plane he had been carried into that lined up with a trap-door-opening in the runway just below it, completely hidden using high-tech display panels to make it invisible from the air.

As soon as Hall was taken inside the plane, he had been lowered through both openings and into one of a series of tunnels Victor had carved at various locations on the property. Then the plane had taken off, a red herring that would lead anyone following on a wild goose chase, never suspecting that Victor's guest, and his headquarters, remained behind, deep in the heart of Oregon.

It was simple, yet brilliant.

And the security and tunnels and other surprises at the ranch were off-the-charts impressive as well. Victor had spared no effort or expense. The land surrounding the main lodge had been mined with explosives, and he could activate these mines on demand. The arms dealer monitored the area on a continual basis using state-of-the-art drones indistinguishable from birds and bats, which transmitted their feeds to a sophisticated computer.

Hall used his implants in cell phone mode and contacted the colonel.

"Nick?" said Campbell in delight. "Thank God you're awake."

"Awake and playing dead as we discussed," thought Hall at his implants.

"We're tracking the jet you're on now," Campbell assured him. "Does the pilot know your destination?" he asked eagerly.

"Yeah, about that," said Hall. "I'm not in the jet you're tracking."

He quickly explained Victor's deception, and that he had never left Oregon.

"Incredible," said the colonel, unable to hide his admiration. "He's even more impressive than I thought."

"I have great news, though," said Hall. "Alex is here and in perfect health!"

Campbell closed his eyes and blew out a relieved breath. "Outstanding!" he said. "Heather and Megan are downstairs in the kitchen having coffee. We didn't expect anything to happen for a while. But I'll let Heather know the great news as soon as we're done." He paused. "What about the implants?"

"All ten thousand sets are here," said Hall. "Although one set is inside Victor's head."

"And he's gotten them to work?"

"Yes. Perfectly. At the moment, he's busy training the implants to respond properly to his thoughts in Spanish while he waits for me to awaken. But he's brilliant, and by thinking in English he can already use them nearly as effectively as I can."

"Okay. Let's get what we're after and get you the hell out of there," said Campbell. "Oregon is close enough to Fresno that I'll come to run the op myself. Hold on."

Less than a minute later the colonel returned. "I have a helo on its way here so I can get to you as soon as possible. So what security are we looking at?"

"It's truly mind-boggling," replied Hall. "The property has several runways, hidden helicopters and weapons caches, and tunnels. Not just the ones under the runway. Victor usually works and lives out of the main lodge, but he planted mines throughout the entire property."

"Mines? *Landmines?*" said Campbell in disbelief.

"Yes. But he controls them through his PDA, and they're only activated when the site is in lockdown mode. Even if this were to happen, I have all the passwords needed to log on to the PDA and deactivate them. And I have the passwords I need to modify the drones Victor has flying around so they won't sound any alarms."

"What else?" said Campbell.

"He has invisible laser alarms crisscrossing the premises in a circle fifty yards out from the main lodge."

"How does he prevent false alarms?"

"A computer monitors the feeds and can calculate the size and shape of whatever crosses. If it's an animal, it doesn't alarm."

"Can I presume you can disable this system, also?"

"Yes. But there is one system I can't disable. He has high-energy anti-missile and anti-aircraft lasers planted on site. He has sensors that tell him when any aircraft comes within thirty miles of the property. Given where he's located, the only aircraft that come within this perimeter are ones he already knows about. Any others and he'll assume he's under attack. He can then trigger his lasers and other anti-aircraft measures and escape in one of his stealth helicopters or planes in minutes."

"Why can't this system be disabled?"

"The sensors that alert him to incoming aircraft don't have a password. This is one system he purposely set up without an off switch."

Campbell cursed under his breath. "Understood," he said. "It looks like we'll have to come in on the ground. Good thing, because we wouldn't want this op to be too easy," he added sarcastically. "Is that everything?"

"Everything but human security. In addition to Victor and his second-in-command, Eduardo Alvarez, there are sixteen men who live here. Their jobs are to help prepare weapons shipments and basically do whatever Victor tells them, but mostly they patrol the area and keep their eyes open. But with surprise, and me guiding the attack, you should be able to get through them and to the main lodge to capture Victor, Alex, and the implants."

"With an asset like you on the ground, and given what you've told me, it sounds like a relatively small strike force would be optimal."

"I agree. If one of you are seen and the alarm is sounded, with tunnels under the main house and hostage possibilities, not to mention armaments and defenses most armies would envy, the op would be blown."

"How about a team consisting of me and five others? Does this seem about right?"

"Yes," replied Hall after a few seconds of thought. "I'll do my best to direct all of you. And to make sure you surprise *them* and not the other way around. But I'm only one man, so I can't monitor everything at once. You and your team will still have to look sharp."

"Understood. I'll try to round up five of the twelve men who were with you on the Oscar raid. These soldiers are as good as it gets and they've worked with you before and know about your special skills. They'll be willing to take orders from you without question."

"Perfect. But given you have to get here and stage the assault, and you can't fly too close, how long do you think it will take?"

"I'll try to be ready to pull the trigger within three hours."

"Shit!" said Hall.

"I know. It isn't ideal. Your best bet is to play possum for as long as you can. Even though you can read his mind, Victor is very clever. Without al-Ansari in proximity for you to draw answers from, he could trip you up pretty fast."

"I guess I'm about to find out how patient Victor is willing to be with a guest crashing on his couch."

"If he somehow discovers you're awake," said Campbell, "stall. Pretend to be wildly disoriented. Tell him you think you're having some weird reaction to the drug they gave you. Ask for a shower and some time to recuperate. Anything to buy time."

"Got it. I'll try not to blow my cover before you and the team are in place," said Hall. "But *hurry!*"

55

Mike Campbell burst into the kitchen like a man on fire. "Victor played the shell game with us," he announced to the two women on his team. "Turns out Nick remained where he was in Oregon, despite appearances to the contrary. This ranch in the middle of nowhere is actually Victor's *headquarters*."

"Is Nick all right?" asked Megan anxiously.

"He's fine," said the colonel. He turned to Heather. "And so is Alex. He's a prisoner there, but in perfect health."

Both women began speaking excitedly at once, peppering him with questions. But before he could untangle them and respond the unmistakable drone of a helicopter reached their ears.

"That's my ride," said Campbell. "Follow me," he added as he exited the kitchen on his way to the front door and the helicopter that was slowly lowering itself onto an open section of lawn, twenty yards away from the mansion. "I'm heading up the assault team," he explained as they walked, "and I need to get it organized and staged as soon as I can."

As they exited the house the clamor from the helo intensified. "I'll call you from the air and give you more details," shouted the colonel.

Heather and Megan exchanged glances, and while they didn't share telepathy, Campbell would never have known it. "We're coming with you," shouted Heather, while Megan nodded vigorously beside her.

"There is no way I'm—"

"We aren't asking to be in on the assault," interrupted Heather. "But we want to be nearby. So we can see Alex and Nick right after they're rescued."

The three reached the helicopter and Campbell pursed his lips in thought. Finally he nodded. "We'll be taking a jet to Kingsley

Field, an Air National Guard Base in Oregon, about fifty miles from Victor's ranch. But when we land you're on your own. Get a cab or rental car and find a motel as near the ranch as you can. I'll bring Nick and Alex to you before we head back to the base for our return trip to Fresno."

"Thanks, Colonel," said Heather, more invigorated than she had been since Alex's disappearance. "This means a lot."

Campbell gestured at the open door to the helicopter. "After you," he shouted.

56

Hall continued to sift through Victor's mind, absorbing his tragic childhood and his start in the Mexican drug cartels before he transformed himself into the ultimate arms dealer.

And that was when he came upon Victor's initial conversation with General Justin Girdler.

Girdler was working with him, after all!

Hall had never allowed himself to fully believe it. After having been in Girdler's mind, he had been unable to imagine the general could be behind a betrayal so vast, so despicable. But he had only been fooling himself. In this case, the only explanation that had ever made sense for the effortless capture of Altschuler and the ten thousand implant sets was the correct one.

The general had sold out his closest friends and everything he had believed in.

Hall isolated Victor's memory of this first conversation and replayed it word for word, needing to know exactly what had been said. Not only could he see and hear this encounter as clearly as if he were watching it on television, he could also read what Victor had been thinking while the discussion was taking place.

It had begun when the general had left a voicemail message on Victor's private line . . .

* * *

Victor stared at the phone in disbelief. A message from General Justin Girdler. Incredible. The man who had done more to hunt him down than any other. Girdler had been closer to finding him than he knew on several occasions, and the American had a mind almost as strategic and devious as his own. Almost.

And now, if this message was to be believed, Girdler wanted to propose an alliance. One that would be extremely worthwhile to them both.

Was it a trap?

Of course it was, decided Victor. And not the general's first such attempt, either, although all others had been made while he was still a lowly colonel. But never had he made it so obvious. Usually, Girdler had others pose as up-and-coming players, interested in doing business with him.

But Girdler knew that Victor wasn't an idiot. Knew he couldn't be fooled by a ploy this transparent.

So what was the point of this? Did he just want to hear Victor's voice? Did he think he had new technology that would allow him to trace the call? If this were the case, he still would have had someone pretend to be a possible customer, so Victor would remain on the line for a longer period of time.

The arms dealer hadn't had his curiosity piqued this much in a long time. He spent the next day mining his tremendous network for intelligence on the recently minted general. What he learned was shocking. Girdler was in hot water. Boiling hot water. Victor's sources were convinced he was about to lose his job and even his freedom in a court martial, but none could tell him precisely what charges were about to be levied.

So perhaps Girdler wasn't the upstanding, square-jawed American hero type Victor had always assumed. Perhaps he had some dark motivations of his own. It was definitely worth a return call to find out.

Moments later he had Girdler on the phone, staring at his 3-D image, although his own image was not transmitted. "General Girdler," he said in a friendly tone. "How nice of you to call. I don't know whether to be honored that I'm still in your thoughts, or insulted that you really believed you could bait me."

"Hello, Victor," said the general. "Don't be honored, *or* insulted. Be intrigued. Intrigued by a proposal I'm prepared to make. One that will increase your wealth and power. One that will benefit both of us."

"Okay. I'll play along. Consider me intrigued. What do you have in mind?"

"I assume you've heard of Alex Altschuler? Theia Labs? BrainWeb technology?"

Victor rolled his eyes. "I may be hidden," he said. "But I do still live on this planet."

"Good. Only a few people know this, but Theia has a secret manufacturing facility and has just finished a production run of ten thousand implant sets. Altschuler knows the exact specifications for positioning them properly in the brain." He leaned forward intently. "And I can get you these implants and Alex Altschuler both. Not to mention a monopoly on the technology."

Victor coughed. "You've lost your mind, General. You really need to get some help."

"I'm in charge of security for both Altschuler and the implants. I can give you codes, operating procedures, shift changes, locations, everything. Follow my instructions and you can't fail."

Victor digested this. The general actually seemed serious. "You used the word, *monopoly*. This has a very specific meaning. Even if I have the ten thousand sets, *and* Altschuler, that still doesn't give me a monopoly."

"Yes it does. Only Altschuler knows the software and algorithms behind the implants. He gave his board of directors a copy of this data, but it's flawed. Believe me on this. All you have to do is blow the factory after you've taken the implants and you have the only supply the world will probably see in twenty years. Think about the advantages BrainWeb could give your customers."

"So just like that, you help me steal the implants and kidnap Theia's CEO?"

"Yes, but in the opposite order. You have to kidnap Altschuler first and pretend not to know about the pilot factory. That way he'll give up the placement information without a struggle, certain that this won't matter since you'll never be able to acquire the implants anyway."

"And what do you get out of this?"

"Twenty million dollars wired into an account I specify."

"That's all you want? Twenty million dollars? You know that ten thousand sets, if you really can deliver, are worth considerably more."

"I'm a man of modest needs," said Girdler.

"No one knows better than you do how much I loathe the US. You know I'll sell the implants to your worst enemies. You've spent your entire life fighting for your country. So I'm not buying it. This has to be a trap."

"Fuck my country!" spat Girdler bitterly. "I've given it *everything*! And I'm about to be repaid by being thrown in a military prison somewhere. After all I've done!" he screamed, spittle flying from his mouth and hatred and raw emotion turning his face red.

"So, what are you saying, that you want to work with me *despite* the fact that I hate your country? Or *because* of it?"

"I'm saying neither. I don't give a shit either way. I've come to you because you have a reputation for being honorable. So if we do enter this arrangement, I'll make sure a number of your key customers know about it. So word *will* get out if you double cross me on this. No one knows you better than I do, Victor. I've studied your methods. You've worked too hard to build your reputation to risk that. So you're the only one I feel safe dealing with. The only one I can be sure will honor my conditions."

Victor considered. The general made a very good point. If he were Girdler, he would reason the same way. This is why he worked so hard to achieve the reputation he had. So people would deal with him instead of others. "So what conditions do you have, other than the money?"

"First, no one gets hurt. I deliver the implants and Altschuler to you on a silver platter, and you carry out the ops. But zero deaths. And zero injuries. This has to be guaranteed. Dart guns and stun guns only. And you have to make sure the men guarding the factory are out of the blast zone before you blow it."

"So you're committing the ultimate treason—for money—and you don't want to break any eggs? You do realize my customers will use the implants to help them break plenty of eggs, right?"

"Of course. But I know the men in question here. I chose them, and I've led them. In some cases I know their wives and kids. I need your absolute guarantee they won't be harmed. Or the deal is off."

Victor considered. "If I decide to work with you, and depending on the quality of your plan, this might be acceptable. But go on. What is your other condition?"

"I get Altschuler when you're done with him. In pristine condition." Girdler smiled icily. "Not that he'll remain that way for long. But I want any damage done to him to be my doing, not yours. I'll get personal satisfaction from it."

"What is your beef with Altschuler?"

"It's personal. And private."

Victor nodded. He hadn't expected Girdler to tell him, but it was worth a try. He wondered if Altschuler was somehow behind the trouble the general was now in.

"Okay," said the arms dealer. "Again, if this continues to pass all of my tests and I decide it's legitimate, you can have Altschuler. But only when I'm finished with him. Only after I've confirmed his data and have implants in my own head, working as advertised. This might take a week or two after I capture him."

"That's fine," said Girdler. "After you take him, I'll be the obvious suspect. So I'll have to go to ground just prior to your attack on the factory. The manhunt for me will be extensive. To say the least. So I'll need some time to lie low, alter my appearance, set some things up. So I probably won't be in a position to take him off your hands until a few weeks after the op anyway. But I will need half of the money deposited into my account just after you capture him. The military will be as hot as a kicked hornet's nest after the implants are stolen, and eluding the dragnet won't come cheap."

"Let me do more research, and more thinking, and get back to you."

"You know how to reach me," said Girdler.

* * *

Hall extricated himself from Victor's mind feeling sick to his stomach. There were few people he had respected as much as Justin Girdler. How had the man turned like this? And what did he have against Alex?

There was no way for Hall to know. Girdler hadn't come within mind-reading range of him for a long time now. For good reason.

Hall reentered Victor's mind to learn when he would be handing Alex off to the general.

He stifled a gasp.

Girdler was on his way *now*.

Victor hadn't told him this was his headquarters, simply that it was a secluded hand off location away from prying eyes.

But if Girdler arrived before Campbell and his team, Alex would be lost for a second time, and Hall's cover could well be blown.

The colonel's attack on the compound had been urgent before. But now it was even more so.

57

"Do we have any smelling salts, my friend?" said Victor.

Eduardo Alvarez frowned. "I'm afraid not," he replied. He shook Hall vigorously, still sprawled out on Victor's couch, and it was all Hall could do not to grunt or call out.

"How much of that tranquilizer did you give him?" asked Victor. "He should have awakened a long time ago."

"We gave him a proper dose," insisted Alvarez. "I guess some people are just more susceptible to it than others." He shrugged. "I'm not a doctor. But he is still breathing."

"Let's keep it that way," said Victor. "The last thing we need is for him to die on us. Not great for our reputation, as Al-Ansari would not be a happy customer."

"He'll be up," insisted Alvarez, glancing in Hall's direction in annoyance. "Soon."

"I was hoping to demonstrate the implants for an hour or so and get him on his way. Before Girdler arrived. Now it looks like this won't be possible."

Hall read that Alvarez was wondering why this mattered. Girdler would be arriving at the outermost landing field, miles from the lodge. One of Victor's men, named Roman, would escort a blindfolded Altschuler to the runway and hand him off to Girdler, who would immediately take off again. So Alvarez was at a loss to understand why Victor would care if this John Smith character was still on the premises or not.

What Alvarez didn't know, but Hall did, was that Victor had been flirting with the idea of taking Altschuler to the runway himself. He and the general had been on opposite sides of a chessboard for many years and he had a healthy respect, even admiration for the man. So part of him was eager to meet Girdler in person. But given Smith's continued state of unconsciousness, this decision was being taken out of his hands. He needed to remain here.

Just as well, Victor decided finally. He didn't need to take an unnecessary risk just to assuage his curiosity.

"Tell Roman to round up Altschuler and take him to the runway now," said the arms dealer. "Girdler will be here sometime within the next forty-five minutes, and we don't want him to have any idle time on the ground."

"Understood," said Alvarez.

"And give Roman a tranq gun," said Victor. "I promised Girdler he'd get Altschuler in mint condition. I doubt he'll try to escape while he's being taken to the runway, but just in case, I'd rather deliver him unconscious than with holes in him."

He paused, glanced at the still form of Hall on the couch, and rolled his eyes. "And have Roman use the shortest duration darts you have. If he does need to use them, we want Altschuler to wake up sometime in this century."

58

Campbell had never traveled so efficiently in his life. Seven of the twelve commandos from the Oscar raid had been available on short notice, and the five of these he had chosen had also raced to Oregon from their California bases of operations.

The colonel and all five men wore earpieces so they could receive the expected communications from Hall, as he had done during the Oscar op, and all were dressed in faded green-and-brown camouflage and carried stun grenades, high-powered binoculars, knives, and automatic pistols with silencers attached.

Hall had briefed the colonel about Victor's agreement with Girdler, and that the general would be arriving today to collect Altschuler, which ratcheted up the urgency even more. Campbell had thought his original three-hour estimate had been on the optimistic side, but he and the team were nearly in position twenty minutes earlier than expected.

"How soon until you're ready to go?" asked Hall, as usual thinking these words into his implants, which were then converted to speech and sent to Campbell's earpiece. Campbell was aware that Hall could have tried to fish this information from his mind, but in cases like this it was easier for him just to ask, and made interactions less awkward for others.

"Almost in place," replied the colonel, a response that the small microphone attached to his lapel transmitted back to Hall's implants. "Five minutes."

"Girdler is due to land within the hour," said Hall. "They're having a guy named Roman move Alex right now. To the same runaway I landed on. Which really complicates our lives."

"True," said Campbell. "But with even a little luck we should be able to finish up here and free Alex before Girdler lands."

"And if we don't? What if Girdler takes off with Alex before we can stop him?"

"I'll alert the NSA now to be sure the eyes in the sky are on anything leaving that runway. Girdler won't have the stealth and anti-satellite-detection technology Victor has." He paused. "Don't worry, worst case, even if Girdler leaves, we aren't going to lose him. I promise you we'll retrieve Alex. And I also promise to stop the general." Campbell's tone became bitter. "At this point it's become more than a little personal."

"Can Girdler pilot a plane?"

"No. But he knows where to find a pilot for hire. And with the twenty million dollars you say Victor wired him, he isn't exactly short on funds."

Campbell had instructed the other five commandos to fan out and take cover at sixty-degree intervals, forming a rough circle of men, with the lodge at its center a hundred yards from each of them. The area they would need to traverse and clear encompassed several storage depots, sheds, and three other lesser lodges that surrounded the main building.

Finally, the colonel got word that the last man was in position at the exact opposite side of the main structure from where he was stationed, two football fields distant.

"Okay, Nick, we're all in place," said Campbell. "Confirm you've disabled the laser sensors, mines, and drones. And that no human eyes will see us begin to move in."

There was a brief pause. "All confirmed," replied Hall from his command center, a black leather couch, still thinking words at his implants and pretending to be unconscious.

"Okay. Everyone move in slowly and cautiously. Nick will direct you whenever he can. We need to clear this area of all men, but we also can't be discovered by even one. Nick tells me that they all have electronic alarm devices in their pockets, which they can activate by sliding a small plastic switch with their thumbs. So before you strike, be sure you won't miss. And be sure your target isn't in sight of others who can sound the alarm."

The ranch had varied terrain, so the opportunities for conceal-ment also varied between the six attackers. The land was flat in some places and had slopes and hillocks in others, contoured enough to crouch behind. On the east side, a fifteen-foot-wide creek wandered lazily past the property. In addition to structures and worn-down wooden fences that looked as though they had been built during the Revolutionary War, the vegetation was random, from willow, black cottonwood, and alder trees, to meadows of brown and green wild grasses, growing out of control.

Campbell crept forward cautiously, wondering if he should have left the commando business to men who were younger and more ca-pable than he was. He had been behind a desk for too long and was suddenly worried he might be the weak link in this chain.

"Andrews!" called out Hall. "Two men are seconds away from exiting the building to your left. No others inside. Neither knows you're there."

Several seconds passed. "Both men are down," reported Andrews.

Hall continued to shout out warnings and directions to the com-mandos, enabling them to avoid being seen and to take down Victor's people one by one.

Campbell approached a small lodge with four bedrooms. "Colonel," said Hall, "the door is unlocked and no one is watching the main en-trance. Two men are inside. One in the kitchen, and one in the large bedroom on the southeast side."

"Roger that," whispered Campbell as he slowly opened the door, wincing as it made creaking and groaning sounds loud enough to be the envy of even the most flamboyant of ghosts.

He crouched low and held his automatic pistol in front of him, keeping the gun in line with his eyes as they darted to every corner of the room. He heard Hall barking orders to other soldiers and knew he was on his own for a while.

He entered the kitchen as a towering man with Greek features was putting a pizza in an oven. But even as Campbell turned his gun to face him, the man moved with unbelievable speed, having seen Campbell's reflection in the dark glass of the oven. The pizza crashed to the ground and the man wheeled around with his gun now drawn. Campbell depressed his own trigger and sent a brief burst of silenced rounds into the man's chest, just moments before he would have sent his own volley in Campbell's direction.

The crash of the pizza had been loud. Too loud.

The colonel waited beside the doorway to the kitchen for the other resident of the house to investigate, but after more than a minute had passed, Campbell concluded the ruckus had not disturbed him, after all. With doors closed in both the kitchen and bedroom, the sound hadn't carried, or else the man hadn't felt the need to investigate a clumsy colleague.

He opened the door cautiously and turned toward the southeast bedroom, determined to rid the structure of its last resident so he could sound the all-clear. He was halfway to his destination when he heard Hall's panicked scream in his ear. "*Colonel, behind you!*"

Campbell dived to his right as a bullet came whistling by his face, drawing a groove of blood across his cheek. He hit the dusty wood floor with bone-jarring force and rolled, as the shooter closed the few yards distance between them and prepared to fire again.

Campbell's long-forgotten training in hand-to-hand combat instantly returned, and he came out of his roll launching a desperation kick. His heavy boot caught the side of the attacker's knee, tearing his meniscus and causing the shooter to change his aim and miss the colonel once again.

The man screamed in agony and fell to the floor, dropping his gun, which Campbell sent skating across the floor to the other end of the room. But just before Campbell could fire his own gun, his injured adversary seized his arm with one hand and kept the weapon from pointing in his direction.

"*He's going for a knife in his ankle holster!*" screamed Hall.

Campbell had been hypnotically focused on the struggle for control of his arm, and Hall's warning came just in time. He kicked out at his adversary's other hand, just as the knife was coming into play.

The man cursed in surprise and pain as the knife was ejected from his grip, having thought Campbell had been unaware of this move.

The colonel was battling a younger, stronger opponent, and despite the damage to his adversary's knee, the man was beginning to bend Campbell's arm around so the gun pointed back at him, after which he would find a way to force the trigger down. With the last of his strength, Campbell flicked his wrist as hard as he could and flung the gun ten feet away.

The younger man went after it immediately, like a dog chasing a thrown ball, and Campbell yanked his legs out from under him, causing him to crash once again to the floor. But the man's reaction to this was almost supernaturally swift, as he rolled onto his back and slammed the side of his right fist like a heavy brick into Campbell's left ear, temporarily dazing him and obliterating his earpiece.

Given Campbell's glassy-eyed look, the man crawled several feet away and chanced reaching into his pocket to root for a silver-dollar-sized electronic alarm, pulling it from his pocket. But before he could feel for the plastic switch he needed to slide to the left to activate the device, Campbell recovered his senses—just enough. He couldn't reach the alarm, so he dived toward the younger man and pounded at his injured knee with a fist, eliciting another howl of anguish. Before the man could fully recover, Campbell pressed his brief advantage, pulling a combat knife from his belt and plunging it into his opponent's chest. Despite the red bloom that spread across the man's shirt, Campbell stabbed him repeatedly, unable to stop until long after all vestiges of life had drained from his face.

Campbell remained on the floor for several minutes, panting from exertion and waiting to fully recover his senses, strength, and equilibrium. The blow to his ear had dazed him badly, and only an adrenaline-fueled miracle had allowed him to find the last burst of energy and clarity that had saved his life.

Finally, the colonel gathered himself, rose, and stumbled out of the door. From everything he had heard before he lost communications, almost all of Victor's people had been taken out, and no alarm had sounded.

And he *had* been the weak link, after all. As far as he could tell no others had had any difficulty with the mission, especially given Hall's assistance.

"Nick," he said into his microphone, hoping that Hall was also reading his mind. "I've lost audio. Send our nearest man to meet up with me here, so I can communicate through him."

The colonel waited, searching the area with his high-powered binoculars. After five minutes, no one appeared to be coming his way. He was about to take his chances and assume the rest of the team had made it to the main lodge when he noticed something alarming through the binoculars.

The other five members of the team were now all retreating. *Retreating?*

But why? Had one of them tripped a silent alarm? Were the mines about to be re-armed? From everything he had heard and could view through the binoculars, the mission could not be going any better.

They wouldn't just retreat like this on their own. The order must have come from Hall. Campbell would have given anything to know what had prompted the civilian mind reader to issue these orders.

Then another thought came to him from left field. What if Hall had sent them to rescue Alex Altschuler? Maybe he had read something alarming that caused him to think Altschuler was about to be killed. He cursed under his breath at the bad luck of losing his earpiece, although a part of him realized just how lucky he really was, since by rights he should have lost the hand-to-hand skirmish along with his life.

So what should he do? Should he retreat also? Hall wouldn't have called a retreat unless the situation was all but hopeless.

But so what? They couldn't let the implants leave here with Victor under any circumstances. If they lost this opportunity they would never get another. And even if his chances were one in a hundred, he had to try. He couldn't live with himself if he did anything less.

He took a deep breath and slowly moved forward toward his goal, the main lodge, one careful step at a time, keeping to the tall grass and other cover whenever he could find it.

Finally, after several more minutes, he reached the main lodge. He paused for just a moment and prepared to open the door, this time without Nick Hall to tell him if anyone was behind it.

He took a deep breath, knowing it could well be his last, and entered.

No one was in sight.

Relieved, he listened carefully and heard speaking coming from a room down the hall to his right. And it was Spanish. Almost certainly Victor himself.

He crept through the open door to the room as quietly as he could. Victor and Eduardo Alvarez were deep in conversation, and both were turned away from him. Their posture and lack of interest in who might be coming through the door made it clear that they had not been alerted. So why had Hall, who looked to be asleep on a black leather couch, called off the attack?

"Freeze!" shouted Campbell, his gun extended, and both Victor and his second-in-command jumped like cats hit with a squirt gun. Victor recovered quickly, reaching under his desk for either an alarm or weapon, but Campbell sent a short burst of gunfire in this direction, discouraging him from moving his hand another inch.

A rush of triumph flooded through the colonel's veins. They had done it. It was over.

And then he felt the muzzle of a gun pressed hard into the back of his neck.

"Drop your weapon!" shouted a familiar voice.

It was the voice of General Justin Girdler, a man who had been a friend and mentor for many years. A man who had been almost a father to him.

"Drop it or you're dead!" shouted Girdler, and his tone left no doubt that he would carry out this threat without hesitation.

59

Campbell's shoulders slumped in defeat and surrender and the gun slipped from his fingers and to the floor with a steel clang. Agonized thoughts stabbed at him like ice picks. How had this happened? They had been on the verge of total victory.

And why hadn't Hall told him Girdler was coming from behind? Why was he still faking unconsciousness?

Or had he somehow been rendered unconscious for real?

This was the only explanation. With Hall awake, Girdler could not have snuck up on them, could not have even gotten to within miles of them, without him knowing it. After Campbell got the drop on Victor and Alvarez, Hall could have shouted a warning to Campbell from the couch.

Nothing made sense. Hall had called off the team and had failed to warn him.

"This is my protégé," Girdler told Victor. "Colonel Mike Campbell. As I am sure you're aware."

"I am," said Victor.

"How did he find you?" asked Girdler, shaking his head in irritation. "I'm better than he is, and I tried for years."

"I don't know," said Victor suspiciously. "But it seems too unlikely a coincidence that he found me right when I invited you to this location for the first time. Perhaps you set a trap for me after all, General."

"Perhaps you aren't as bright as I've always thought," snapped Girdler. "If this were a trap, why would I *stop* this man? I'd be *helping* him. He had you dead to rights."

Victor considered, and while he must have known this was true, he still appeared troubled by what he clearly felt was an improbable coincidence.

Girdler raised an eyebrow. "So," he said, suddenly looking amused, "who's the guy on your couch?" He gestured toward Hall with his head while he continued to hold a gun on the colonel.

"A prospective customer," said the arms dealer.

Girdler laughed. "*Now* I get what's going on," he said. "I didn't cross you, Victor. You've been duped. A customer is the *last* thing this guy is. I know him well. He's working with Campbell."

Victor's eyes widened. "You're positive?"

"Never more," said the general. He shrugged. "Looks like Campbell finally managed to do what I failed to do. Fool you." He shook his head. "Well, this location is blown to hell. I'm sure he reported back that you were here."

"I have other secure locations I can get to."

"You were very lucky I was here and recognized something fishy was going on."

"Where is Alex Altschuler?" asked Victor.

"Campbell's men began shooting and Altschuler tried to run for it. Your guy shot Altschuler and then he, himself, was hit by one of your uninvited guests."

Victor shook his head. "And that's all it took for you to recognize that something fishy was going on?" he said wryly. "Very perceptive."

Girdler smiled. "I concede it didn't take much of a detective to figure out. But you were the beneficiary. So I'll tell you what. How about if I stay behind and take care of Campbell and his slumbering friend, since others are sure to be arriving any minute. You leave in peace to whatever new location you choose. But I'm sure you'll agree that you owe me something for this service, and saving your ass in the first place. And you know I gave you the deal of the century on the implants."

"What do you want?"

"Another five million?" said Girdler with a smile.

"Done," said Victor.

Campbell was feeling ill and barely able to think, let along speak, but he finally found his voice. "Justin, what are you doing?" he said, his tone tortured. "Betraying your country? Betraying *me*? How can you do this?"

"Fuck my country!" shouted Girdler. "Fuck you! We're all dead and gone to dust soon anyway. Heaven is nothing but a fable. So fuck this world! I've sacrificed long enough. Time to look out for number one."

Campbell opened his mouth to respond when Girdler pulled the trigger, and the colonel dropped to the floor, his world instantly turning black.

60

Campbell's eyes fluttered open and his first thought was euphoric: there *was* an afterlife after all.

But when he spied Nick Hall beside him in the SUV his thinking changed. On the other side of Hall, Alex Altschuler was also present, strapped into a seatbelt like Campbell but with his eyes still closed.

"Nick?" he muttered, half addled, still trying to fathom how he could possibly be alive.

"Colonel!" said Hall excitedly. "You're awake. Welcome back."

"How long was I . . . out?" he asked.

"Just a few hours. You were hit with a tranquilizer gun."

"What's going on?" mumbled the colonel, glancing at the front seat where Justin Girdler was at the wheel.

"We're only a few minutes away from Heather and Megan. They're at a motel. How about you finish recovering your senses and we'll bring everyone up to speed at the same time when we reach them."

Campbell nodded and closed his eyes again. He hadn't fully recovered from whatever was in the tranquilizer, but he felt great. Drowsy, yes, but also in a drug-induced, and thrilled-to-be-alive induced, euphoria.

"Where is the rest of the assault team?" he whispered.

"I aborted the mission," replied Hall. "I sent them back to Kingsley Field and home. They're all in perfect health."

"And Alex?" said the colonel, managing to gesture feebly in his direction.

"Out cold. But he should be waking up any minute. He should have come to before you did." Hall shrugged. "But I guess he doesn't weigh much, so it makes sense."

Altschuler mumbled something unintelligible right on cue, and he lifted eyelids that, judging from the effort this required, weighed at least a hundred pounds.

"Welcome back, Alex," said Hall. "Glad you could join us."

"Nick?" he whispered weakly. "Barely recognize you. Hate the beard."

Hall laughed. "Yeah, I don't love it either, I'm afraid."

Hall held off all questions until they arrived at the motel. When they did, the small low-rent room became an emotional maelstrom. Heather had feared her fiancé was dead for some time, and their relief at being reunited after such a long separation was understandably intense. And while Megan had been reunited with Hall previously, his safe return from a perilous mission also brought forth a passionate outpouring of emotion.

And through it all, everyone on the team except Hall managed to glare at Girdler with unbridled hostility, and pose bitter questions about his presence, creating a stew of conflicting sentiment. Absolute love and absolute hatred battled for supremacy, creating an emotional electricity in the room that was almost palpable.

While the two couples greeted, Campbell realized that his automatic pistol had been magically returned to him and he pointed it steadily at his former mentor. After the greetings had concluded the two women and Alex Altschuler were clearly in approval of Campbell's actions, and if glares could kill, the general would have been dead many times over.

"Put the gun down, Colonel, and hear him out," said Hall. "You realize he didn't have to give you your weapon back, right? He knew how you were likely to react."

The colonel stared back at Hall in disgust. "Are you suddenly his guardian angel?" he spat. "Why didn't you warn me at the ranch? We could have stopped Victor!" His upper lip curled into a snarl. "So were you working with Girdler this entire time?"

"You're still at little addled from the tranquilizer," said Hall calmly. "Or you would know better than to even ask that. You know the lengths I was willing to go to stop Victor. Yes, I could have warned you. And yes, I did choose to side with the general. But that didn't happen until a few minutes after you lost communications with me. I would have tried to explain, but you no longer had an earpiece."

"And what would you have explained?"

"I'd rather let the general field that, since this was all his doing. But put down the gun. There is a rational explanation for all that happened. You may not agree with it, and that is fine. But are you really going to shoot him before you learn what it is?"

Campbell knew Hall was right and reluctantly lowered his weapon, still glaring at his former mentor. He looked around the cramped motel room and everyone but Hall shared his confusion and uncertainty.

The colonel found it ironic that this was a group that had met on luxury yachts and in multimillion dollar mansions. But now here they were, in a cheap motel in the middle of nowhere. How the mighty had fallen.

Or was this room somehow a better representation of the collective nature of the group than the previous luxury settings? Perhaps they were less like prize poodles, preening in a cosmic show, and more like cockroaches, living hidden under the floorboards in a seedy motel, but always finding a way to survive despite the presence of so many angry boots above them.

And Campbell knew enough psychology to realize that his hatred of Girdler now was inversely proportional to how much he had loved, admired, and respected him before. Being hurt by an enemy was one thing. But being betrayed by someone you loved and trusted was the ultimate pain.

"Go on," said Campbell, nodding at Girdler. "Have your say. Let's get this over with."

61

Heather and Megan sat at the front ends of each of two queen-sized beds, spaced a few feet apart, on ugly floral bedspreads. Altschuler lowered himself onto the desk chair on the right side of the room and Hall sat on the desk nearby, pushing a phone and pad of paper to the side to make room. Campbell took a seat on top of a long dresser positioned in the center of the room, just under a television affixed to the wall.

All eyes were on Girdler, the lone inhabitant of the left side of the room, standing with his back against the wall, both literally and figuratively.

"I know I've put everyone here through hell, and I'm truly sorry about that," began Girdler. "If I thought there was another way, I would have taken it. I can understand the hostility you're feeling. And I don't blame you for it. But I'm asking you to throttle back while I explain. To not waste all of your energy on a constant out-pouring of hatred in my direction. I get it. You feel betrayed and you despise me. But I need us to have a calm, reasoned discussion, and this won't help."

The expressions and body language around the room softened, but not by much.

"I don't care what you say," spat Campbell. "There can be no justification for putting ten thousand sets of implants into the hands of someone like Victor. A man in a better position than any other to ensure this technology is used by our worst enemies."

"That's what I thought, also," said Hall. "Until I read the general's mind at the ranch. I'm still not entirely in agreement with him, but what I read did cause me to change course a hundred and eighty degrees."

Campbell frowned deeply but nodded at the general to continue.

"I don't have to review my concerns about widespread adoption of the BrainWeb technology," said Girdler. "They're concerns we all have, and concerns we've discussed at length. But these worsened after Nick was outed. We all agreed when this happened that the cat was out of the bag, never to be fully returned. Too many people knew, not only that Nick was still alive, but about his ESP. And secrets this good have a way of leaking."

"Okay," said Altschuler. "So you became even more worried that dangerous players would mount initiatives to perfect mind reading. So what?"

"I'm just getting started," replied Girdler. "The BrainWeb implants were the catalyst behind Nick's ability, and are likely to be a critical ingredient, an absolute requirement. So it occurred to me that no matter how many groups were hunting for the secret to mind reading, they couldn't succeed without the implants being available. Conversely, once the implants become *widely* available, cracking the ESP code becomes a near certainty."

"Why is that?" asked Heather.

"Implants won't become as common as cell phones, but I guarantee they'll number in the hundreds of millions. And when they do, when the secret of the Oscar raid has leaked to every corner of the world as it is certain to do, every major global player, and every power-mad psychopath, will be looking to recreate the path through the brain that triggered Nick's abilities. They'll be going through subjects, voluntary or otherwise, like so much cordwood. Hell, I wouldn't be surprised to find high schoolers experimenting on their friends. The prospect of perfect ESP is too alluring, and no government can afford to lose this arms race."

Girdler paused. "Nick told me about Marc Fisher on the drive here. With implants on every street corner, to what extremes will the Fishers of the world be willing to go to solve this? Knowing a solution would quickly gain them unlimited power. And after Nick went missing, this increased my concern even more, since some group might be in position to do a thorough study of him, in addition to eventually having access to any number of implant sets."

"You still haven't told us anything new," said Megan. "These were always your fears. So now you're just telling us your fears grew even greater. As Alex has already said, so what?"

"Exactly," said Altschuler. "I could see you making these arguments to try to justify your actions if you had put the implants out of commission. Not that any of us would find them persuasive. But putting the implants out of commission isn't what you did. You gave them to our greatest enemies."

"So is that everything?" said Campbell. "You were worried, and then you became *very, very* worried? You're going to need to do a hell of a lot better than that to even begin to justify your actions."

Girdler sighed. "I really was getting there. I just was hoping to build the case, brick by brick, even if you're familiar with some of the early bricks. But I can see I need to cut to the chase. My job is to think things through from every possible angle, leaving no stone unturned. As I did this with respect to BrainWeb, I came to concerns that I've never voiced to anyone. Not even to the people in this room. We all know the privacy argument. The implants can convert video to vision and vision to video. Same with hearing and audio. So anything you hear or see can be recorded and stored in the cloud. So humor me, what's the biggest fear about this scenario?"

Megan rolled her eyes. "That an implant recipient can abuse this," she recited in bored tones. "Can invade the privacy of those he or she is near. Post videos and information about others to the Web, without their consent."

"That's the common wisdom," said Girdler. "And this was my view until recently as well. But then I realized that this misses the point entirely. We've been worried about someone hacking the implants," he continued. "But what if someone hacked the cloud? After all, given Alex's security, this is a hell of a lot easier than hacking the implants. The cloud in this context is just massive storage in the Web. A locker you buy or someone gives you that you can beam data into. The cloud doesn't belong to one source or one company. It's just capacity, data storage, be it from Dropbox, or Carbonite, or Amazon, or hundreds of other providers."

There were nods around the room, but no one was yet able to see where this was leading.

"So say you're an implant recipient and you upload what you see and hear to the cloud," continued Girdler. "Say a video of your last sexual encounter with your girlfriend, for example. And you have no intention of violating her privacy. You just upload it for your own use." Girdler paused. "And then someone hacks into your cloud account and steals it."

Campbell looked unimpressed. "I'll admit this hadn't occurred to me," he said. He glanced around the room and could tell no one else had considered it either. "But I don't see this as being that big of a deal. It could happen. But most people aren't going to be uploading all that much to the cloud, despite the much-touted privacy concerns. Before BrainWeb, some people chose to upload naked photos to their computers. Most didn't. And granted, some who did, especially celebrities, got hacked, and their photos got out. But this wasn't the end of the world."

Girdler shook his head. "True," he said. "But now imagine the *government* is doing the hacking. The NSA. Rooting around in people's online storage lockers, looking for whatever they want. This is a little more troubling now, isn't it?"

Altschuler rubbed his chin in thought, and it was obvious this had suddenly become a more intriguing discussion to him. "No doubt," he replied. "But this still isn't so bad. In practice, like the colonel said, most people will stream very little of their daily lives to the Web. And terrorists and other bad actors will adjust. They'll learn not to use the cloud to store incriminating information, or plans for future attacks. Similar to how it is now. If you're a terrorist, you keep your nefarious plans on a laptop, you don't send them through cyberspace in an e-mail that could be intercepted by the NSA." He raised his eyebrows. "I do have to admit that the thought of the NSA having a new data trove to spy on hadn't occurred to me. But I agree with Colonel Campbell. It's a worry, but not an enormous one."

"Right," said Girdler. "Because, like you said, most people won't stream much to the cloud anyway."

"Exactly," said Altschuler.

Girdler's expression took on a new intensity. "Now let's take this to the next level. What if you didn't have a choice?" he said meaningfully. "What if *everything* you saw and heard, *every second of the day*, was transmitted to the cloud—*without your knowledge?* Wouldn't that give the NSA a bit more data to sift through?"

Altschuler's mouth dropped open. "Holy shit!" he said. "That *would* change things. And you could modify the software in the implants prior to manufacture to do just that."

All eyes were on Altschuler as his agile mind raced. "And it wouldn't be very difficult, either," he continued. "You could store the data stream of all sights and sounds in a large buffer. Whenever a user accessed the Internet, which would be almost non-stop for most users, you could squirt the data in the opposite direction, to the cloud. You could mask it completely, so no one could possibly know or detect that your life's experiences were being uploaded without your knowledge." He rubbed his chin. "But we could make sure this was never done."

"Really?" said Girdler. "Are you positive? This has never come up before in any meeting I've had with the government. I purposely haven't brought it up. I don't want to give anyone any ideas. But you'd better believe I'm not the only one who will come to these conclusions. I'm just the one who has been most immersed in the BrainWeb technology. But I'd bet my last dollar the NSA is well aware of this possibility already. And they have a way of pressuring companies to cooperate with them. And even if you don't implement the software at the factory, Alex, if they find a hack—and what group has better resources to find any chink in your security armor than the NSA—they can download the software to do this remotely."

Megan turned to Altschuler. "Is that true, Alex?" she asked anxiously.

He nodded, his face looking numb. "Yes. It's absolutely true. The NSA could, theoretically—and without that much difficulty—funnel everything each of us sees and hears into their computers. Everything."

"And everything we *think* also, correct?" said Girdler.

Altschuler looked sick. "Yes," he said, barely able to get this syllable out of his mouth. "And everything a user thinks."

"Wait a minute," protested Heather. "Slow down. Why would that be?"

"The BrainWeb implants respond to thoughts, right?" said Altschuler. "You think, *tell me the weather in New York* and the weather is retrieved from the Web. After a few days you're so in tune with the implants you aren't even aware of the need to think at them. But you are. The system's software is extraordinarily complex, and while it is trained to ignore all thoughts that aren't directed at the implants, it is constantly monitoring *all* thoughts, waiting for a command."

Campbell's eyes widened. "So BrainWeb itself is a mind reader?" he said, now so fascinated and alarmed that he forget to be angry at Girdler. "So each of us can be turned into a Nick Hall."

"No," said Girdler. "The implants can only read the thoughts of the brain they're in, not those of other people. And they only read a user's surface thoughts, those you think in the form of words. The implants can't dig through a user's mind like Nick can. Can't fish out your social security number unless you're mentally reciting it. Can't tell you the name of the girl you took to the prom."

"But still," said Megan. "The NSA could have a record of everything you see, hear, and actively think. This does bring invasion of privacy to a new level."

"But this would require the NSA to break the law," said Heather. "To be despicably intrusive. The country wouldn't stand for it."

"This is true," said Girdler. "But power expands to fill a vacuum. And knowledge is the ultimate power. I'd love to think this would never happen. But you don't have to be a conspiracy theorist to acknowledge that it isn't impossible. It's easy to imagine someone at the NSA getting overzealous, hacking the implants, modifying their software, and stealing all of our lives. With no one the wiser."

"He's right," said Campbell. "The government and NSA have a history of overreach. Girdler and I know of programs we can't disclose, but two of these are well-known, even to the public. One, called PRISM, gave the NSA unlimited access to the servers of major technology companies, including Facebook, Apple, Google, YouTube, and many others, and the tremendous wealth of data stored within these servers. Another that began in 2007 wasn't exposed until 2014. It was a program that used spy planes to carry devices called *dirtboxes* over populations of interest. The devices mimicked cell phone towers, in effect fooling all phones in the area into broadcasting to them. In this way, they could suck up data from thousands and thousands of phones without the owners knowing."

There was a long, stunned silence in the room as everyone sorted through the implications of what was being said.

"And like the colonel mentioned, there are other examples that have never come to light," said Girdler. "But even so, I'm not saying it's inevitable that the NSA will subvert the BrainWeb implants in this way. But I am saying *it could happen*. Does anyone disagree with that?"

Campbell looked around the dingy room and could tell that no one did. And suddenly everything clicked into place, and he understood exactly what the general had done.

And he didn't know whether to congratulate the man, or vomit. Or both.

"So this gave me even more reason to want to delay the launch of the implants," continued the general. "Because I don't really trust my own government. And for good reason. I'm part of it. As head of Black Ops, I know of programs that most people would be appalled by, would consider horrific abuses of power. No one is in a better position than I am to understand the shortcuts the government is willing to take, or has more reason not to be trusting."

Altschuler nodded. "So added to concerns you already had, this was the straw that broke the camel's back."

"Absolutely. And I didn't have this epiphany until fairly recently. But after I did, I decided BrainWeb couldn't be allowed to go forward until quantum encryption was perfected. Until we could be certain these devices could not be turned into the ultimate spies—inside each of our heads."

"You argued before Congress to delay the launch for security reasons," said Megan. "But if you raised *this* issue, I'm sure everyone would get it. I know everyone in this room is *horrified* by the possibilities."

"This might have worked," said Girdler. "This might have been enough to get buy-in to delay the launch for years." He frowned. "But it might not have. It might have just given certain people ideas they didn't have before."

"And then you remembered the fictional Trojan Horse," whispered Campbell knowingly. "Which you love to point out as being one of the greatest examples of a PsyOps success story in history."

The corners of Girdler's mouth turned up into a humorless smile. "That's right. I needed to be certain the implants were stopped. At least for a few years. And I wondered if I could kill two birds with one stone. Sabotage the launch to give Alex more time to solve security. And at the same time, deliver a devastating blow to our enemies."

Altschuler gasped, finally reaching the conclusion that Campbell had arrived at minutes earlier. "You modified the implants at the pilot factory," he said. "Didn't you? Exactly the way we've been discussing. You turned BrainWeb into the ultimate bug, the perfect spy device. And then you partnered with Victor to ensure these electronic spies would be installed in the brains of ten thousand of our worst enemies."

"Exactly," said Girdler. "The fact that I was being court-martialed made it all believable to Victor. And I sold it in other ways also. And when I went to ground, he knew the almost unprecedented dragnet our government had out for me could not have been faked. So my being a fugitive actually played into my hands. Because of this, I knew he wouldn't suspect I had never changed allegiances, and was just using him to deliver my ten thousand Trojan Horses. Never suspect that he was doing the absolute *opposite* of hurting the US."

Hall blew out a breath and entered the conversation for the first time. Facing Campbell he said, "That's why I decided I couldn't let you stop Victor, Colonel. We needed him to sabotage our enemies."

"Mike, I am so sorry I had to threaten you," said Girdler. "And so sorry for what I said. But I had to play my role in front of Victor all the way until the end."

Campbell wasn't sure what to think. He needed more time to think things through. "I was sure I was dead," he replied. "So I can't complain too much about how this ended."

"The general got within mind-reading range just toward the end of our op," said Hall. "I read about his Trojan Horse plan, and the reason for it. I read the agony he was going though as well. He threw his career away and willingly made himself a fugitive. Knowing that the people he cared about the most—in your case, Colonel, someone he loved like a son—would think he had orchestrated the ultimate betrayal, although he hoped to set the record straight once Victor had sold the implants."

Campbell blinked rapidly as he considered the enormity of what Girdler had done. The audacity. This was exceptionally devious, even for Girdler.

"How did you manage the software change?" said Altschuler. "Without my help?"

"As head of security I had total access to the factory. You gave me the software coding for BrainWeb as a fail-safe. And there is a man named Drew Russell who is almost as good as you are in the programming realm. I explained everything to him, and he was able to complete the required modification, and de-bug it, before the implants rolled off the line."

"So he de-*bugged* the bugs?" said Megan in amusement. "Sounds counterproductive."

Girdler allowed the briefest of smiles to cross his face. "So when these modified implants are installed," he continued, "they will beam all sights, sounds, and thoughts of their users to a storage center Drew Russell set up for the purpose. Data storage capacity has soared over the past few years, and prices have plummeted, but even so, the amount of storage required is daunting. But Drew assured me he has set aside enough for the task."

Altschuler stared off into space, zombie-like, as he pondered all the implications of what Girdler had done. "I'll need some time to wrap my brain around this, General," he said. "But I doubt I'll end up approving of what you've done." His face turned bitter. "But forgetting this for a moment, why did you let Victor capture me? This wasn't necessary. The implant positioning data was in the information you already had. So you risked the life of someone who considered you a friend, just for theatrics?"

"I'm sorry, Alex," said Girdler softly. "But remember, I wasn't just implanting spy devices in the heads of enemies, I also needed to take BrainWeb offline for a few years. Your disappearance does that. With you out of the picture, and the data you gave to the board crap, the implants are dead on arrival. Until we say otherwise."

"You could have come to me. Told me."

"I could have. But I felt the stakes were too high, and I didn't want to take any chances. I'm sorry. But rest assured that you were never in any physical danger. Victor values his reputation above all else, and he agreed to hand you over to me unharmed. I knew he would honor this."

"I was inside Victor's head," said Hall. "And the general is understating the case. General Girdler insisted that no one get hurt during your capture and the theft of the implants. And he insisted that you be delivered to him in pristine condition. Or the deal was off."

"Speaking of delivering Alex to the general," said Campbell, "what really happened during the hand off at the ranch?"

"Some goon brought Alex to me, right on schedule," replied Girdler. "And then my phone rang. It was Nick. I had an unlisted number and a new, untraceable phone, so I knew he had to be in mind-reading range. Sure enough, he said he had read my plan. He told me you were here with an assault team while he played possum, but that he had called off the team after he came to understand what I was attempting to achieve. He also told me that he couldn't reach you, and that you were intent on stopping Victor no matter what the risk. Something I could not admire more, by the way," he added earnestly. "But anyway, Nick said he needed me to hurry to the lodge to stop you."

Campbell nodded in fascination. Everything that had been so blurry had now been brought into perfect focus.

"I didn't have much time to act," continued Girdler. "So I shot Alex's escort and took the tranq gun Nick told me he was carrying." He winced and gave Altschuler an apologetic look. "I didn't have time to explain everything to Alex, so I decided to, ah . . . give him some much-needed sleep. As a friend."

Altschuler ignored this attempt at humor—or reconciliation, whichever it had been. "Let's get back to the ethics of what you've done," he said. "I know these are our enemies. But we still don't have the right to invade their privacy so absolutely. You're spying on these people without any warrants."

Girdler sighed. "I'm well aware of that. But consider that this is spying technology that *can't* be used on innocent civilians. Only those who break the law will ever receive these implants. They have to engage in an illegal transaction with Victor, for stolen technology. So this is a bit karmic. They get what they deserve. And I admire your standards, Alex, I really do. But we're already spying on these people. On their computers and communications. But on the whole, we're doing it poorly. But even so, these efforts have prevented the deaths of millions. This just isn't advertised."

Altschuler wore a thoughtful expression, but still wasn't entirely convinced.

"This is our last, best chance," continued Girdler. "You saw what happened at the Oscars. What they tried to do. Terrorism is growing, not shrinking. And as weapons of mass destruction become more commonplace, as technology improves, they will have more ways to commit atrocities, to tear down civilization. I've seen the computer simulations." He gestured to Campbell. "Mike, tell him."

Campbell drew in a sharp breath. "He's right, Alex. The war on terror isn't going well. Saying that Islamic terrorism is the ultimate cancer doesn't even begin to describe it. We're going to be swallowed by the barbarian hordes, so to speak. It's only a matter of time."

"I'm sure you aren't a big fan of the ends justify the means arguments, Alex," said Girdler. "But this is our one chance to turn the tide.

Not all of the implants will go to terrorist leaders, but many will. And we'll hear their conversations with other leaders. For the first time, be able to match names and faces. We'll know their every plan. We can unravel every network of sleepers. In six months we'll have more than enough intel to cripple most terrorist networks, although we'll have to plan this carefully, so they never suspect what is happening before it's too late. But the intel will be amazing! We may be able to set them back beyond any real possibility of recovery."

Altschuler tilted his head in thought, and Campbell guessed that he was coming around. And why not? Girdler's arguments were frighteningly compelling.

"It's good to have you back, Justin," said the colonel. "Well done." He shook his head. "Although I have to admit, I didn't think I'd be saying this when you were shoving a gun into me and telling me to go fuck myself."

Girdler winced. "Good acting, though, right?"

Campbell extended an arm and shook his mentor's hand warmly. "I know I've said this before, but remind me never to play chess with you."

The expressions on Heather's and Megan's faces made it clear they were ready to welcome Girdler back also. Finally, even Altschuler capitulated. "I still don't love this plan," he said, facing the general. "But I appreciate that you don't either. That this really is a necessity, for all the reasons you've given. And that it's easy to stand here moralizing while the terrorists burn the world down around us." He followed Campbell's lead and shook Girdler's hand, and Megan and Heather soon followed suit.

"I'll still never be able to fully forgive you for the emotional agony you put me through," said Heather as she released Girdler's hand. "Even if Alex does."

"I understand. Again, I can't blame you."

"So what now?" said Altschuler.

"My hope was to convince you to stay missing once I got you back from Victor. Restoring sight and hearing to the blind and deaf could still go forward, but BrianWeb could not. Not without you.

Your disappearance would remain a mystery until we decide it's time for you to reemerge."

"Let me guess," said Altschuler. "You were also hoping I would set up a skunk works research effort to perfect encryption, right? Change my appearance some, like Nick has, and operate under the radar."

"Good guess," said Girdler. "In my dream scenario, Heather would join you, and see to it that a healthy percentage of your billions was transferred into a Swiss bank account for your use. Even if none of this had happened, I honestly believe that it would have been a good time for you to lie low. You were too attractive of a target. BrainWeb too much of a flashpoint technology, stirring up too much greed and too much passion."

"Anything else?" asked Heather.

"Only for Nick and Megan. My hope was that if they resurfaced, they could stay off the grid and continue their work trying to find an antidote to ESP."

Altschuler stared into the eyes of his fiancée and an unspoken communication flowed between them. "We'll have to give it more thought and discussion," said Altschuler, "but given the stakes, I suspect we'll agree to this. To be honest, we aren't mansion people anyway. And I'm the type of nerd who enjoys working on an impossible problem like quantum encryption more than being a high-profile CEO."

"Outstanding," said Girdler happily. "Truly outstanding."

"What about you, General?" asked Megan.

"My plan had been to take my twenty million and live out the rest of my life avoiding the dragnet. Oh yeah," he added, remembering. "I guess it's *twenty-five* million now." He looked at Hall. "Or is my confidence in Victor's trustworthiness too high? I'm betting he wires the extra five million, as promised."

"He will," said Hall with a smile. "Say what you want about him, but he has a clean, clear mind, and he fully intends to honor this commitment."

"You did save his life," said Campbell. "Just because you were doing it so he could sabotage our enemies is beside the point."

Altschuler stared thoughtfully at Girdler. "You said your plan *had* been to disappear into anonymity," he said. "Past tense. So has this plan changed?"

The general grinned. "As a matter of fact, yes. While you and the colonel were catching up on your beauty sleep, I had a very interesting conversation with Nick here. Very interesting. And while the guts of my plan remain, I think we might just be able to make some key improvements to it. Improvements that should even benefit me," he finished happily.

62

President Timothy Cochran eyed his private cell phone warily. For the first time in his recollection it had failed to identify a caller. Which was worrisome, because this number was only known to his family and a few close advisors.

He was lounging on the spacious bed in the presidential bedroom with his head propped up against the headboard, watching the news, while his wife was taking in a romantic movie he had no interest in seeing in the White House theater. He threw his feet over the edge of the bed, rose to a sitting position, and answered the call. "Who is this?" he asked warily.

"It's Nick Hall, Mr. President," said the image on his screen. "The mind reader," added Hall, as if Cochran could possibly forget who he was. "I've changed my look, which is why you don't recognize me."

Cochran didn't reply for several seconds, digesting this bombshell of a surprise. "Hello, Nick. How is it that you have this number?" he asked suspiciously.

"About that," began Hall, glancing down with a guilty expression on his face. "Turns out I was within mind-reading range of you a short while ago. And I stored certain information of interest in the cloud for later retrieval. Like your private cell phone number. And other . . . items."

"And other *items*? What's that supposed to mean?"

"I'd rather not specify if I can help it. Why raise topics you would find . . . troubling?"

"If this is a thinly-veiled attempt at blackmail, it isn't all that thinly-veiled."

"My purpose for this call is not blackmail, Mr. President," said Hall. "Far from it. But it is true that I read enough in your mind to ruin your marriage and bring down your presidency. And muddy the water on your legacy. But my intent is for this information to never see the light of day. To never be disclosed to even a single person. The truth is, while I'm not a big fan of either Republicans or Democrats, I have become a fan of *you*."

Cochran's eyes narrowed as he tried to figure out how much of what Hall was saying was the truth.

"All things considered," continued Hall, "I think you're a good man. Everything I know tells me you'll agree to do what I ask because you honestly believe it's the right thing to do. But just in case, I thought it made sense to disclose that I had read your mind."

"What do you want?"

"That gets a bit complicated. I'm going to bring some other people in on this call. I just need you to hear us out and not call the Secret Service or any other group at your disposal. I need you to be alone and private for an hour or so. If this is a bad time, I can call at a time of your choosing."

"No," said Cochran. "I'm alone. Now is as good a time as any."

"Great," said Hall. He moved his phone so it now took in the face of General Justin Girdler.

Cochran's jaw dropped, but he recovered quickly. "So you're working with an enemy of the state?" he said in disgust. "You just said you thought I'd be willing to help you, even without your threat. So I guess that was just total bullshit?"

"The general isn't an enemy of the state," said Hall firmly, "no matter what you might think. Hear him out, and he'll convince you of that." He paused. "But before he does, there are others here listening to this call. I'll introduce them."

Hall first introduced Mike Campbell, whom the president knew of in his role as head of PsyOps. He then introduced Megan Emerson as an important player in his search for an ESP antidote, for reasons he would go into later. Megan said hello, and Hall knew that she relished the chance to be part of a phone conversation with an actual president of the United States.

He also introduced Heather Zambrana, but she needed no introduction, as her romantic entanglement with the CEO of Theia Labs had made her famous in her own right.

And finally, Hall introduced Alex Altschuler.

The president was as shocked by this as he had been when Girdler's presence had been revealed, and he strung together a rapid-fire series of incredulous questions, which Hall assured him would all be answered in due course. And then Hall turned the floor over to the general.

Girdler walked Cochran through his misgivings about BrainWeb, its potential to be transformed into the ultimate spy device, and all that had transpired since he first contacted the arms dealer named Victor.

The president asked pointed questions, but it seemed to Hall he was quickly coming around to Girdler's point of view. And why not? The potential for misuse of the technology was staggering, and appalling.

Based on his knowledge of Cochran's thoughts and memories, Hall had believed the chances were good he would help them, but his blackmail threat served as the perfect insurance policy.

As Girdler continued to present his case, the president was astonished by the complexity and success of his Trojan Horse plan, and eventually agreed that he had done the right thing. The ability of the NSA to spy on citizens was too tempting, and the potential for criminal misuse of the data by unscrupulous politicians and other power players too great. Not to mention that the treasure trove of intel they would be generating on America's worst enemies was a game changer, a once-in-a-lifetime opportunity too golden to pass up.

"Brilliantly done," said Cochran when Girdler had finished. Hall thought he was being sincere in his praise, but he was still a politician, so there was no guarantee.

"So why did you decide to tell me about this?" continued the president. "And how would you recommend we proceed?"

"I'm telling you because Nick thinks the country is lucky to have you. And I know you were in my corner during the recent court martial maneuverings. Also, Nick has enough leverage on you to make it worth the risk of reading you in on this."

Cochran nodded, but didn't respond.

Girdler sighed. "As to how I would like to proceed," he said, "I thought you'd never ask. First, call off the manhunt for Nick Hall."

"I'll see to it. It wasn't getting anywhere anyway. But Nick has a face that is well known, so even without a manhunt, I'd recommend he still avoid public places." Cochran paused. "What else?"

"I want a pardon from you so my record is clean. But not just yet. And I want you to call off the manhunt for me. But again, not just yet."

"Why the delay?" asked Cochran with genuine curiosity.

"Because Victor is very smart. If he learns through his sources that I've been pardoned, or that the manhunt has been called off, he'll get suspicious. Nobody wants that."

"Agreed," said the president.

"So I'd like you to put out the word that I'm to be captured alive at all costs. That way, if I do slip up and get caught, I'll survive long enough for you to arrange a catch-and-release. After a year or so, you can call of the manhunt entirely. And just before you leave office, you can grant a full pardon."

"Go on."

"I want you to personally see that funds are diverted to a special Black project, with me in charge, using an alias we'll come up with. The project's goals will be as follows. One, perfect quantum encryption so no one can turn BrainWeb into Brain-*Spy*, like I just did. Two, set up an organization to manage and strategize around the massive intel we'll be receiving from this Trojan Horse program. And three, find a way to counteract ESP if this is ever developed."

"This last is the project Nick was working on before the events at the Oscars, correct?" said Cochran.

"Exactly. But I want to combine all three of these projects under one organizational, and possibly physical, roof. And it would be the blackest of Black projects, with all the secrecy and security this affords. But you will be the only one with full knowledge. I'll be in overall charge of the project as I said. Alex Altschuler will run the security initiative. Nick Hall the ESP initiative. And Mike Campbell the intelligence initiative."

"So far I'm more than willing to support this," said Cochran. "And not because of any dirt Nick has on me," he added pointedly.

"I know that, Mr. President," said Girdler. "We just couldn't take any chances. Sorry we had to even bring it up."

"What else?"

"I want Drew Russell on the team as well, as head of software."

"I'm unfamiliar with this person," said Cochran, "but I don't see why this would be a problem. But as I'm sure you're aware, the intel end of this will be a massive undertaking. It will require ten times the security of Fort Knox, and ten times the secrecy of Area 51."

"Well put," said the general with a smile. "I couldn't agree more. My thought is we would limit the raw data to as few people as possible. They would be heavily screened, with comprehensive background checks that would be more invasive than a proctology exam. And then we keep their testicles in a jar. Because if word ever leaks out about what we're doing, we blow the best chance we'll ever have to stop this terrorist blight. We can feed intel to other agencies without them knowing where it's coming from or how we got it. Mike and I can make sure we're careful so we maximize this advantage and don't spook any of the bad guys. Until it's time to roll them all up."

"General, I'm on board a hundred and ten percent. And given your expertise and what you've just accomplished, I truly can't think of a better man to run this show."

"Thank you, Mr. President," said Girdler. He paused, and looked decidedly uncomfortable. "But as much as I believe you really do support what we'd be doing, there is enough at stake that I'm afraid I'll have to sick our human lie detector on you. Just to be sure."

Cochran thought about this for a few seconds and then laughed. "What the hell," he said. "I'll arrange a secret meeting with Nick. I should have given him my personal thanks for his heroism at the Oscars long ago, anyway."

"I'm surprised you're taking the prospect of being near a mind reader so well," said Girdler.

Cochran shrugged. "He already knows all of my secrets. And I really do see what you've done as an incredible coup, General, as Nick will verify. Finally, I know he can read me from a distance whenever he wants, like he did the first time. So I appreciate your honesty in even telling me that this was your intent." He smiled. "So bring on the great and powerful Nick Hall. I welcome the meeting."

"Thank you, sir," said Hall. "It will be an honor to finally meet you in person."

* * *

The call ended minutes later. "That went well," said Girdler happily. "Against all odds, it looks like we've managed to get the entire band back together. And we've even added two new members, Drew Russell, and the president of the United States."

"I have to admit," said Campbell, "I didn't see that last one coming."

"I say we celebrate," said Girdler. "I've already made reservations tomorrow night at the nicest French restaurant in town. Dinner is on me."

Megan laughed. "Nothing like thinking you'll be considered a disgraced traitor, forever on the lam, and ending up in charge of the most important Black Op since the Manhattan Project to bring out your generosity, huh General?"

"I'm ecstatic about how things turned out, don't get me wrong. But that had nothing to do with me springing for dinner. Turns out I recently came into twenty-five million dollars."

"So dinner is really on Victor," said Hall in amusement.

"Yes. He truly is the gift that keeps on giving. Speaking of which," added Girdler, "I've decided to spread the wealth. I'm giving six million each to Nick, Megan, and Mike, and keeping seven for myself."

"That's very generous, General," said Campbell. "But entirely unnecessary."

"Are you kidding? It's the least I can do after the hell I put all of you through. And seven million for me is more than enough."

"I don't know," said Hall. "Marc Fisher was responsible for the hell Megan and I went through, not you."

"Yes," said Girdler. "I'm well aware I put Alex and Heather through the worst of it. And I'll never be able to make up for that. I just wish they weren't billionaires so a gesture of a few million dollars might be meaningful. But if they ever lose their money, I'm splitting my share with them."

"Good to know," said Altschuler wryly. "So let me understand. We don't get any of Victor's money. You had me kidnapped by a deadly arms dealer. Because of you I'm no longer the highest profile CEO in the world. And you stopped BrainWeb, probably costing me a hundred billion dollars. Is that about right?"

"Wow," said Girdler in amusement. "When you put it *that* way, I get why a sincere apology might not be enough. You did hear the part about me buying you dinner tomorrow night, right? And I'm prepared to go even further. How about this? Feel free to get an appetizer and dessert. *Now* who's going the extra mile?"

The entire group laughed.

"Speaking of dinner," said Campbell. "The president probably won't have called off the dragnet for Nick by then. Are we really going to risk celebrating in public with two men who are both the subjects of manhunts that rival the one we conducted to find bin Laden?"

"Yes," said the general. "What the hell. We deserve a celebration. And judging from the brilliant makeover you gave Nick, I think you missed your calling. You should have been a Hollywood makeup artist. I can't wait to see what kind of magic you can perform on me."

"Even I can't turn a lump of clay into a diamond," said Campbell, shaking his head.

Girdler laughed. "I'm not saying you have to make me handsome. I'm looking for a disguise, not a miracle."

"Not to spoil the fun," said Megan, "but let me ask a serious question, General. You mentioned the possibility of housing us all under one Black Ops roof. Would that include Nick? Is everyone suddenly comfortable working around a mind reader?"

"Good question," said Hall. "How about it, everyone. And be honest. I know that I'm a pariah, so don't pull any punches."

"Can't you just read the answer to this question in each of our minds, Nick?" asked the general.

"No. I've promised not to read the thoughts of this group unless I can't help it."

Girdler grinned. "Then there's your answer. This promise is good enough for me."

The three other parties in question nodded their agreement.

"Besides," continued Girdler, "if the president is willing to submit to full rectal probing, who am I to be squeamish about you reading the occasional extraneous thought. But I will make sure you have a retreat close to wherever we put our headquarters. So you can get some solitude from the thoughts of others when they become too much to handle."

"Sounds perfect, General. Thanks."

"You deserve this and much more," replied Girdler.

He turned his head and surveyed the entire group. "But for now, I say let's take the rest of tonight and tomorrow off. But after this, I'm afraid there's a daunting amount of work to be done."

No truer words had ever been spoken, thought Hall. The responsibilities of their small cabal had grown exponentially. Now, all they had to do was take down global terrorism, cure ESP, and solve quantum encryption so they could make the world safe for the most revolutionary technology in history.

No problem, he thought wryly. He was just surprised Girdler hadn't also tasked the group with curing cancer and inventing an anti-gravity machine, just for good measure.

But despite the enormity of what they needed to accomplish, having full knowledge of the extraordinary talents of this group of people, and how well these talents, and their personalities, meshed together, he would be the last person to ever bet against them.

"Daunting, yes," said Hall, looking as content as he had ever been. "But nothing this group can't handle." He glanced around the room, and each of his friends were responding to his confident declaration in the same way, with expressions of resolve and eyes that gleamed with unbridled enthusiasm. "And I know I speak for everyone here when I say, I can't wait to get started."

FROM THE AUTHOR:

Thanks for reading *Brain Web*. I hope that you enjoyed it!

As always, I'd be grateful if you could post however many stars you feel the novel deserves on its Amazon page.

Also, please feel free to Friend me on Facebook at *Douglas E. Richards Author*, and to write to me at doug@san.rr.com.

BRAINWEB: WHAT'S REAL, AND WHAT ISN'T:

As you may know, I conduct fairly extensive research for all of my novels. In addition to trying to tell the most compelling stories I possibly can, I strive to introduce concepts and accurate information that I hope will prove fascinating, thought-provoking, and even controversial.

Although *Brain Web* is a work of fiction and contains considerable speculation, some of it does reflect reality. Naturally, within the context of a thriller, it is impossible for me to go into the depth each topic deserves, nor present the topic from all possible angles. I encourage interested readers to read further to get a more thorough and nuanced look at each topic, and weigh any conflicting data, opinions, and interpretations. By so doing, you can decide for yourself what is accurate and arrive at your own view of the subject matter.

THE ATTACK ON THE OSCARS: The plastic explosive described in the novel is purely fictional as are the electronic bloodhound devices. This being said, a number of devices designed to detect chemical signatures of explosives and narcotics are currently in use, and more are being developed, although none are as sophisticated as the device depicted in the book.

The Cosmopolitan Theater is fictional, although information about the Dolby Theater, which does host the actual Academy Awards, is accurate, including the number of speakers inside the venue and the fact that the orchestra really was stationed a mile away from the theater in 2013.

As most people know, Hugh Jackman has hosted the Academy Awards (and will again, five or ten years from now when this book takes place :)). Finally, while star popularity is subjective, the group of actresses the fictional terrorists planned to kill appear on a number of published lists of the most popular stars, at least in 2015.

THOUGHT-CONTROLLED WEB SURFING: Artificial limbs and video games are being developed that can be controlled by thoughts, although these don't even approach a fraction of the sophistication of the fictional BrainWeb implants. This being said, thought-controlled Web surfing *is* being worked on. Below are excerpts from a November 20, 2009, article in *ComputerworldUS*, which is also excerpted in my novel, *Mind's Eye*.

Scientists at Intel's research lab in Pittsburgh are working to find ways to read and harness human brain waves so they can be used to operate computers, television sets, and cell phones. The brain waves would be harnessed with Intel-developed sensors implanted in people's brains.

The scientists say the plan is not a scene from a sci-fi movie. . . . Researchers expect that consumers will want the freedom they will gain by using the implant.

"I think human beings are remarkably adaptive," said Andrew Chien, vice president of research and director of future technologies research at Intel Labs. "If you told people twenty years ago that they would be carrying computers all the time, they would have said, 'I don't want that. I don't need that.' Now you can't get them to stop. There are a lot of things that have to be done first, but I think [implanting chips into human brains] is well within the scope of possibility."

Intel research scientist Dean Pomerleau said that users will soon tire of depending on a computer interface, and having to fish a device out of their pocket or bag to access it. He also predicted that users will tire of having to manipulate an interface with their fingers.

Instead, they'll simply manipulate their various devices with their brains.

"We're trying to prove you can do interesting things with brain waves," said Pomerleau. "Eventually people may be willing to be more committed . . . to brain implants. Imagine being able to surf the Web with the power of your thoughts."

With respect to digitizing incoming data and tying this directly to the visual centers of the brain, this is being actively worked on, most notably by Dr. Sheila Nirenberg at Cornell. I've excerpted a few paragraphs of an article from *National Geographic* below (Oct 1, 2013), entitled, "MacArthur Genius Working to Bring Sight to the Blind."

Nirenberg thought if she could just rewire the eye's output cells so that they started translating images into electrical signals, those signals could be sent to the brain and vision would be restored.

The idea? Creating a coding and translator device that would take the images being processed, encode them into electrical pulses, and then send them to the brain.

The patient would have to undergo a brief gene-therapy session in order to redirect the output cells in their eye—normally used to transmit image signals to the brain—into also accepting signals from a camera.

"We shoot a compound into the eye that will get expressed in the output cells," Nirenberg said. "The person will wear a sort of camera that has an encoder device that takes the information from the camera and translates that into the retina's code."

A tiny processor—about the size of the one in a cell phone—helps in the process.

And voila: a person who previously had cloudy vision at best would suddenly not just be able to discern between light and dark, but could actually see again.

Finally, the following paragraph is part of a description of Nirenberg's work on the MacArthur Foundation website:

In another line of research, Nirenberg is adapting and applying her discoveries in neural coding to machine vision algorithms with the goal of advancing the state of the art in robotic "vision" and brain-machine interfaces.

MIND READING: Dozens of books have been written about a variety of ESP abilities and I won't comment on these here. Some studies purport to show that some subjects are able to read the identity of a card from another's mind, for example, at an accuracy above that which would be expected from guesswork alone. I have read research papers that use huge sample sizes and complex statistics, but there is too much data and I am not a good enough mathematician to feel comfortable making a determination if this is a real phenomenon or not.

What I can say is that perfect mind reading like that depicted in the novel is almost certainly not real. If someone truly could read minds like Nick Hall, you wouldn't need thousands of trials and complex statistics to make a case, you could show this in seconds.

Could this type of mind reading be done in theory? I don't see why not. We've already shown we can get computers to decipher thoughts based on the electrical activity of the brain. While these signals seem far too weak to me to make it through two skulls (from the brain of the person being read to the brain of the mind reader), one could imagine thoughts producing other signatures: electromagnetic, quantum, or something as yet undiscovered.

For a hypothetical mind reader to be able to pick up these brain-waves, so to speak, and interpret them seems absolutely impossible to me. But then again, in a fraction of a second, my cell phone can convert my voice into a digital signal and beam this signal to a friend thousands of miles away, where it is then converted back into my voice. This seems impossible to me also, and yet my cell phone seems to work perfectly, despite my extreme skepticism.

POLITICIANS: The novel is a little hard on politicians of both major parties, but then again it *is* fiction, and it *is* a thriller (and thrillers are much less fun if everyone is a saint).

I'm sure many politicians are good people who are in this profession for the right reasons. But it is also true that most of us can be easily fooled by unscrupulous people, and the more of a conscience *we* have, the less we are able to believe the charming person on our television is the opposite of what he or she seems.

The unscrupulous often don't come across as monsters at all. Quite the opposite. Bill Cosby is a perfect example. While at the time of this writing, his guilt or innocence has not been determined, if he did even half of what he is accused of, this would be stunning, since

Cosby was seen by huge swaths of the population as one of the most kindly, beloved grandfather types in American history.

I think few would argue that some politicians are quite well meaning, while some are in it only for themselves. Differences of opinion chiefly arise as to the percentage of politicians in each of these camps. I admit to only reading one book on this subject, leaving me with an unbalanced view, so I encourage anyone interested to do a more thorough study than I did. I also should admit that I only read this book because I happened to catch one of its authors being interviewed by Stephen Colbert.

The book, *The Dictator's Handbook*, written by Bruce Bueno de Mesquita, a Senior Fellow at the Hoover Institute at Stanford University, and Alastair Smith, a Professor of Politics at NYU, provides arguments and research indicating that, in general, politicians, even in democracies, will do what it takes to achieve and maintain their own power, even at the expense of doing what is right for their constituencies and country. Here is an excerpt from a review by R. James Woolsey, Undersecretary of the Navy under President Carter, and Director of the CIA under President Clinton.

"In this fascinating book Bueno de Mesquita and Smith spin out their view of governance: that all successful leaders, in dictatorships and democracies, can best be understood as almost entirely driven by their own political survival—a view they characterize as 'cynical, but we fear accurate.' Yet as we follow the authors through their brilliant historical assessments of leaders' choices—from Caesar to Tammany Hall and the Green Bay Packers—we gradually realize that their brand of cynicism yields extremely realistic guidance."

And last, an excerpt from a review in the *Wall Street Journal*:

"To political scientists Bruce Bueno de Mesquita and Alastair Smith, the authors of 'The Dictator's Handbook'—a lucidly written, shrewdly argued meditation on how dictators, and politicians in democracies, preserve political authority—it's not only unsurprising that politicians craft legislation with an eye toward re-election but also deeply rational. All leaders, whether of democracies or autocracies, dictatorships or monarchies, desire the same goals. 'Why do

leaders do what they do? To come to power, to stay in power and, to the extent that they can, to keep control over money.'

In a style reminiscent of 'Freakonomics,' Messrs. Bueno de Mesquita and Smith present dozens of clever examples of how researchers identify and compare graft in autocracies and democracies. Messrs. Bueno de Mesquita and Smith are polymathic, drawing on economics, history, and political science to make their points.

The reader will be hard-pressed to find a single government that doesn't largely operate according to Messrs. Bueno de Mesquita and Smith's model. So the next time a hand-wringing politician, Democrat or Republican, claims to be taking a position for the 'good of his country,' remember to replace the word 'country' with 'career.'"

PSYCHOPATHS: Everything in the book about the behavior characteristics of psychopaths and the prevalence of this condition is accurate. For those interested, *Without Conscience: The Disturbing World of the Psychopaths Among us,* By Dr. Robert D. Hare, is the definitive work on this topic for the layman.

While one percent of the general population can be classified as psychopathic (based on something called the Hare Psychopathy Checklist, Revised), studies have shown that three percent of business executives fall into this category. And while no studies have been done on our political class, given that psychopaths are deceitful, narcissistic backstabbers who never take blame and don't get embarrassed, even when caught in a bald-faced lie, it wouldn't be terribly surprising if they were enriched among politicians as well.

INTERNET ADDICTION: Much of the material discussed in the fake ABC news show, between made up guests Sandra Finkel, Jacob Resnick, and the host, Blake Shaw, is accurate, with the exception of those parts pertaining exclusively to the fictional BrainWeb implants.

The Carr book that is quoted, *The Shallows: What the Internet is Doing to Our Brains,* is real, the Boston Consulting Group study is real (many people really would be willing to give up sex before the Internet), and so on.

Web surfing really does have a physical impact on our brains, and addiction is becoming a real problem.

As far as I know, the story about the experts in 1880 predicting New York City would ultimately find itself drowning in horse manure is real, also. As someone interested in technology and future trends, I love this story, because it does a beautiful job of highlighting the dangers of extrapolating the future from what we know now, since we aren't capable of foreseeing game-changing technologies that often appear.

BOTULISM TOXIN: The information in the novel about this toxin is accurate. This is the most deadly substance known to science. As an interesting aside, I got to know the man responsible for the development of Botox, Les Kaplan, President of R&D at Allergan, when I was a biotechnology executive and he was on our board of directors.

MISCELLANEOUS: The two programs attributed to the NSA, *PRISM* and *Dirtbox*, are real, although *Dirtbox* was conducted under the auspices of the Justice Department. The information about the USS *Boxer* is accurate, as is the policy of interrogating terrorists on warships (although I have no idea if the *Boxer* has ever been used for this duty).

Descriptions of the Mayflower Hotel, the Olympic National Forest in Washington State, and the locations of military bases and relative distances are accurate. The Oregon hunting lodge used by Victor as his headquarters is entirely fictional, although the trees described are accurate for this part of the country, and there are many ranches in Oregon that are similar to this one.

Finally, today's PDAs, beginning with Siri and now including numerous others, aren't nearly as sophisticated and integrated into our lives as the one's depicted in BrainWeb, but it is clear to me we are heading in this direction.

ABOUT THE AUTHOR

Douglas E. Richards is the *New York Times* and *USA Today* best-selling author of six technothrillers, including *Wired, Amped, Mind's Eye, BrainWeb, Quantum Lens*, and *The Cure*. He has also written six middle grade/young adult novels widely acclaimed for their appeal to boys, girls, and adults alike. Douglas has a master's degree in molecular biology (aka "genetic engineering"), was a biotechnology executive for many years, and has authored a wide variety of popular science pieces for *National Geographic*, the *BBC*, the *Australian Broadcasting Corporation, Earth and Sky, Today's Parent*, and many others. Douglas has a wife, two children, and two dogs, and currently lives in San Diego, California.

Made in the USA
Columbia, SC
04 February 2024

31466268R00191